THE BLACK
AND THE WHITE

D0885439

Alis Hawkins

SAPERE
BOOKS

THE BLACK
AND THE WHITE

Published by Sapere Books.

20 Windermere Drive, Leeds, England, LS17 7UZ,
United Kingdom

saperebooks.com

ISBN: 978-1-913518-37-0

This book is dedicated, with great fondness, to the memory of Peter Ralph — gentleman, charcoal burner and friend.

CHAPTER 1

February 1349

I wake to dimness and silence, blinking bleariness from my eyes. In the dim light, I can just make out the turf dome of our collyers' hut above me.

Something is not right but I cannot think what. Cannot think at all. My eyes close and I fall back into sleep.

Coughing wakes me again. The pain of it is like a blade, its edges chipped and jagged, cleaving my chest, tearing up through my gullet. And the very sound — the hack of it — takes me home. Back to our house in Lysington, back to my sweat-soaked bed and my father's hand holding a cup of water. The memory rips a greater pain through me, the pain of pestilence, deaths, burials.

My father's hand held the cup because my mother is dead. They are all dead. My family. All dead.

A cold terror raises the flesh on my scalp. *I was dead, too.*

Master William leant over me, I remember him doing it — he anointed my head and my hands and my feet with holy oil, prepared me for death.

Hoc est corpus meum — this is my body.

The dryness of the host on my hot tongue. The sting of the wine in my throat.

I closed my eyes and died in our house at Lysington. Is this not our hut, then? Is it a chamber of Purgatory?

I lie still, my heart skittering in my chest, my fists clenched, barely able to breathe. Do the dead breathe? Do the hearts of the dead beat still? And then the truth sweeps through me like an inrushing tide of relief. *I dreamed it all.* The devil sent lifelike visions of death and grief into my dreams but I have not moved from the hut, from the forest. I have been here all along. Nobody is dead. They are all still there, waiting for us. My mother might, even now, be birthing the child who kept her from the forest.

The candle gutters, a low stub in a pool of wax and I realise that this is what troubled me when I first woke — the candle. Why has it been burning while I slept? And no workaday tallow candle, either. It is sturdy wax and, even burned to a nub, I know that I would need both hands to compass it around. A church candle. *But how can that be?*

I try to raise myself and something tumbles to the floor. As I lean on one elbow to see what it is, my wits spin in my head. I close my eyes until everything comes to rest. Sitting up has caused my heart to thud heavily in my chest and, with each beat, I repeat a litany of relief. 'Nobody's dead. Nobody's dead. It was a dream. Nobody's dead.'

The spinning finally ceases and I lean over a second time to see what has fallen to the floor. There, lying on the strewn bracken, is my father's little wooden statue: his patron saint — Saint Cynryth — the White Maiden.

Something cold chills my skin. In my dream, I grasped that same little image in my hands as I sank towards death. The dream-shade of Master William took the saint from my fingers and handed her to my father. Such a dream…

What is it that makes me glance across at the hut's other bed, the better, roundwood- framed one that my mother sleeps in when she comes with us? Why am I not content to close my eyes and sleep again, comforted that all is well, that my mother is safe at home? What draws my eyes, I cannot say but, when I look, there he is. My father.

No, that cannot be right. If I am in the hut, he should be outside. Always, one of us is on the hearth, minding the coaling pit lest the stack shift and turn bonfire. What is he doing in here with me, sleeping the time away?

I half-rise, half-roll from the pallet and kneel on the floor, weak and trembling. Though something in me wants to turn away, I make myself look at my father. Against his usual tight-curled habit, he is on his back, nose pointing up. His mouth is open a finger-width but no air whistles in and out. I touch trembling fingers to his forehead. He is cold.

Dead, then.

I put my hands over my ears, but the demon-voice is inside my head.

Happy now? Wished him dead often enough, didn't you?

No! I shake my head. My wits are muddled. He cannot be dead. No one is dead. It was a dream. If he is cold, it is just the winter air.

Look, then, the voice goads, *look and see if he isn't dead — quick-like, in his sleep, like you always saw him in your mind.*

'No! No, *no!*'

No one knows those thoughts. I have always pushed them down. Deep down. How can any demon know them?

I stare at my father's face. Is he truly dead?

My hand unsteady, I reach towards his chin and pull the blanket back.

'*Mother of God!*'

Beneath the pale wool, my father has sewn himself into his shroud. Or rather, half-sewn. The needle he used is thrust through the shroud at the point where he stopped. The shroud is a half-sheet's width, its edges doubled into a fold and closed with clumsy stitches. My eyes trace the lumpy seam he has made from toes to breastbone.

That half-sheet tells me that I dreamed no dream, that everything I remembered when I woke is true. For I watched him wrap the other half about the bodies of my mother and my newborn sister.

The pestilence came and killed our village. My mother and her child are dead. My brother and his wife and children are dead. All dead. Along with more than half the people I have ever known.

I fall back on my pallet and find that there are no tears left in me. When the pestilence came, I knew it would decide things between us. If I was pest-struck, then my fate was death and my father would be proved right. If I watched him die, it would mean that I had not been sinful in defying him.

After my mother died, I fell into a cough-racked fever and all seemed settled. My father tended me and, when Master William gave me the last rites, I repented of my rebelliousness and made my peace with God.

But, now, I am alive and my father is dead.

I push myself to my feet and breathe awhile, hands gripping my trembling thighs. When my breath calms, I steady myself with one hand on the roundwood door-frame and pull aside the wadded sacking that hangs there. The light squints my eyes and I raise a forearm to ward off the glare.

White. The world is white with snow.

I turn back for a blanket and my head spins with the sudden movement. How long is it since I ate anything but the sacrament? I was fevered and coughing blood a whole day and a night before Master William came to give me the last eucharist; how long did I lie in that death-like sleep? Long enough for my father to bring me here before he sickened and died. Or did he come, already sick, knowing he would die, wanting to die here?

Yes, that would be like him.

In the chill silence that snow always brings, I make my way on shaking shanks across the charcoal hearth, stopping after a few steps to slow the sudden galloping of my heart and pull the slipping blanket more closely about me. I hang my head and breathe deep and, as I do so, I see that the russet of my tunic is spattered with a darker brown. I pick at the spots with a fingernail and recall a day of racking coughs, the taste of blood in my mouth, the anointing. Only Master William came to give me the death rites, no white-robed boys, no neighbours with prayers to speed my soul. The pestilence has made strangers of us all.

I look about me. Nothing stirs. I might be the only living thing in a barren, white world. The trees are still, their branches stiff with snow. Not a solitary bird calls in the frozen air. A shiver of terror goes through me. Never in my life have I been all alone. Not here. Not in the village. Always, there have been folk about me.

On the other side of the clearing is our cart. The sight of it almost brings me to my knees with relief. I was almost ready to believe that my father and I had come here on the wings of angels or dragged by demons. But no, it seems that my father brought us here in the usual way.

And, now that he is dead, I may go back to Lysington, back the village, to our manor. My father might have preferred to live and die here, but the forest is not my heart's home as it was his. He might have preferred to turn his back on our land and make our family's living here in the King's Dene Forest, charring wood for coal, but I was always dragged here unwillingly.

But, if I am to go home, I need our mare for I am in no state to walk so far. I turn and look around the hearth but there is neither hide nor hair of her to be seen, not so much as a hoofprint in the snow. Did my father just unhitch her and let her go after bringing me here? The cart does not look abandoned, the shafts are propped to keep it level and the canvas is tied down. What else did my father think fit to haul into the forest along with his dying son? I shuffle around to the back of the cart and untie the canvas. Then, a corner clasped in both trembling hands, I peel the snowy pelt towards the shafts, until the whole freight is revealed.

I stand and stare without understanding. Lying beneath the canvas, is every moveable thing from our house in the village. Trestles and board, flour chest, clothes press, our familiar copper pans and earthen pots, my mother's bread trough, the small indoor water butt, a bench and three stools. A space in the middle shows where the wool-stuffed pallet lay, with me on top.

What was in my father's head that he would bring everything here? Were his wits addled by the pestilence? Or does this mean there is no village to go back to — that every soul in Lysington is dead?

I stand there, trying to master the fear that threatens to overwhelm me.

No. They cannot all be dead, surely? Elsewhere, the pestilence has always left folk, there are always some who survive. And yet, the silence that surrounds me is empty of life. Even the flat grey sky seems immovable, as if it has been decreed that the sun will never be seen again, nor any blue of the heavens.

I lean against the cart and grip the wicker-work of its side. Like all charcoal carts it is long and light, built for the sacks of charcoal we haul — four feet high and almost as much in girth but light enough for a woman to lift. The solidity of the whip-weave, its familiar feel, calms me. Something in the world is still as it was.

As my heart slows, I feel a gnawing in my belly. Without the mare I must walk home, but I cannot do that yet, starved as I am. I must eat.

Inside the flour chest I find a few bushels of oats, along with bags of beans and peas. Making a pottage is surely not beyond me — I have seen my mother do it often enough. Trembling from weakness and cold, I clear away the snow and lay a fire. I am glad of the candle still flickering at wick-end in the hut, for the ember-basket holds nothing but cold, black coals.

With a few pulls of dead grass from the hut's turf-thatch and a frond of dry bracken from the floor, the fire is easily started. While it catches and begins to flame around the kindling, I fetch logs from the stacks of cordwood at the edge of the clearing. My father always had the makings of the next coaling pit to hand and I am grateful for that now. I will not have to go searching for firewood while I recover my strength.

But I will have to fetch water for my pottage. The water butt on the cart is empty. Will my legs carry me to the well? But if they will not, now, then they may never — I must feed myself. And yet, I do not want to leave the hearth, the hut. Not alone.

I look about me, open my mouth to shout into the forest, then shut it again. I am alone, with all my worldly goods. Who knows who might come? The pestilence has made some men desperate.

I cross myself, take the bucket from the cart and set off for the well.

I shuffle along, bucket in hand, like an old man, keeping to the upside of the path, afraid that, weak as I am, I might miss my footing and slither down the bank to fetch up against a tree.

My breathing is loud in the stillness and I walk through a cloud of my own misted breath. Droplets form on the edge of my hood and on my eyelashes, making my eyes feel wet. One hand frozen to the bucket's rope handle, I put the fingers of my other hand in my arm-pit to keep them warm.

Less than halfway to the well, I stop to catch my breath and still the trembling in my legs. Leaning against a tree, I look up, searching the treetops for the smoke that will tell me another collyer is tending a pit nearby. Sometimes, as we make our way back to the charcoal hearth from Lysington, with the hills of the Dene spread out in front of us, it seems that the whole forest is smouldering — the smoke from a thousand coaling-pits rising above the trees. Coaling is the life of the forest and the smoke of the craft is its out-breath. The King knows that, and so do his ministers. The Dene is the forge for the King's war. Without our coal there would be no smelting of the forest's iron, and without iron there would be no armour, no horseshoes, no swords, no arrow-heads for our archers, no cartwheel rims for the long roads of France.

Carefully, I turn a full circle on the snow-blanketed path but there is not a single wisp of smoke in the clear, cold air above the trees. Are there no pits burning in the forest now — has every collyer gone home or fallen to the pestilence?

The thought that I might be alone, at the mercy of the Dene's fairies, sends a cold terror through my veins. My skin crawls and I can almost feel the Fair Folk watching me from their secret hiding places in the trees. How will I defend myself, alone as I am? I do not even possess a bow.

Suddenly, I realise that I have left my fire untended. It could be put out in a heartbeat with an armful of snow. I switch the bucket from cold hand to warm and set off again, ignoring the pain in my toes from the snow. After the jut of hillside that separates our hearth from the well, the path broadens out and I am in less danger of going arse-over-tip down the hillside. I quicken my pace and lift my eyes from to my feet to the well, wondering whether I will have to break thick ice to fill the bucket.

But, when I see what is there, my feet stop walking.

CHAPTER 2

At the right hand side of the well's wide cistern, in a broad cleft in the snow-hung rock, stands a woman. She seems almost to be made of snow for she is dressed in a white kirtle and a long, white cloak. A greeting rises to my lips but, as soon as I draw breath, I know better than to give it voice. This woman is not mortal.

I set the bucket down on the snow and move towards her. If she stood on the ground instead of in the rock-fold, she would scarcely reach above the buckle of my belt; only my plague-befuddled wits could ever have taken her — even for an instant — for a living woman.

I stop a pace or two in front of her. She is beautiful; far more beautiful than the blue-clad Mother of God who stands in our church. But this carved woman is not serene like the Virgin; she seems more full of passion and one hand reaches out to me as if she is saying, 'Wait, I'm coming'. Or, perhaps, 'No, don't go'.

And, though she is no more than an image made of wood, I know her. She is far more lovely and more lifelike than the clumsy little figure which lay on my chest as I slept in the hut but, still, this is the same woman. This is my father's beloved saint — Cynryth, the White Maiden.

I move forward until I am no more than an arm's length away from her. Now, I can see the smallest details of her beauty. Her hair, not quite covered by her head cloth, is the colour of a newly-opened chestnut, her lips cherry-red. The braiding around the neck of her white gown is picked out in yellow, like the little daffodils that grow on the slopes of the Dene in spring, and her eyes are the blue of speedwells.

Leaning towards the rock, I put my cold hand to her outstretched fingers.

They are warm to the touch

My father's devotion to Saint Cynryth began just after Easter in my ninth year when a peddler, drawn off his customary track by some wandering inclination, found himself at our hearth.

Like most of his kind, he was a quick judge of men and, offered a stool and a bite of bread and cheese, he was soon telling my father tales of the ancient greenwood of England. And the sweetest, saddest tale of all was of the White Maiden of the well, Saint Cynryth. It was the tale of a headstrong girl who, deceived in love and almost taken to the Otherworld by a wandering fairy, resolved to take no man as a husband but to wed herself to Christ and live a solitary life in the forest.

As the peddler told his story, I believe the White Maiden stole my father's heart, right there on our hearth. I know it did not matter a jot to him that our parson, Master William, had no knowledge of a saint called Cynryth.

'Salster is distant from here,' he would point out whenever the parson tried to dissuade him from his devotion to such an uncertain figure. 'Even you, Master William, who have studied at Oxford, you have never been to Salster so you have not seen her shrine.'

According to the peddler, Saint Cynryth's name amongst the common people — the White Maiden of the Well — had been given to her long after her death.

'In later times,' he told us, 'when her name no longer came readily to people's minds and tongues, a barren woman had a vision at the well the saint had drunk from — a vision of a maiden, all in white, carrying a newborn child. And, that very night, the woman conceived a son.

'Ever thereafter, Saint Cynryth was known as the White Maiden and her well as the White Maiden's Well. It lies in woods on a hill outside the city of Salster and there are miracles done there to this very day.'

My father had said nothing when the peddler fell silent and the man had soon been gone. But, it seemed, he had been storing up the tale of the White Maiden and her well in his heart and thinking on it — perhaps he had already begun offering prayers to Saint Cynryth — for, not many days later, he had a vision of the saint one moonlit night.

'Saw her at the well, I did,' he told me. 'She was there, standing in the rock beneath the moonlight when I went there last night. Shinin' white like the stars. Spoke to me, she did. Said this was her place. That the well was hers to care for.'

Back in Lysington, my father had told nobody but Master William of Saint Cynryth's appearance to him, nor would he allow my mother and me to tell anyone.

'Folks'd come traipsing through the woods to see where she come to me,' he said. 'Come pawing at the well, they would, touching it. I won't have it.'

He wished to keep the saint to himself. And his care for the well where she had appeared to him could not have been greater had Cynryth been a living woman, dependent upon the sweetness of its water.

On the very day of his vision, he began to create a shrine at the side of the well, pulling aside ferns and moss from a shallow niche in the rock, scraping it clean of soil and roots, scrubbing the little alcove until the stone was as clean as the altar in church. Then, being a competent, whittling kind of woodcarver, he made a small statue of the White Maiden, to match the one that the peddler had tried to sell him from his pack. He even took it to an image-carver in Gloucester to paint at his direction.

'I'll have you make a proper figure of her one day,' he told the carver in Gloucester when he took his little whittled image to be painted. 'One day, when I have the means, I will *commission* you.' He spoke the word as another man might have produced a rare find. *Commission*.

From that day on, her whittled little image watched over the well, a candle burning at her side on Sundays and offerings of flowers or green leaves laid on the shrine every other day. And that same little figure came to Lysington with us, that last time. It lay on my plague-ridden chest as I sank towards death.

But now, in its place by the well, stands an image so life-like that it seems almost to breathe; a wood-carved woman who is warm to the touch.

Sitting on the side of the cistern, with the topstones numbing my arse, I stare at the saint as she reaches towards me. My father's reason for bringing us to the forest is clear to me, now. Without a word to my mother or me, he must have given the image maker his commission when word of the pestilence in France had come to us. He trusted the saint to keep us safe and the outlay of a tidy sum would have showed her his devotion.

The carrier surely came to our house two days ago. A Gloucester man would be glad of any excuse to leave his plague-struck city, especially to deliver the likeness of a saint who looks fit to bless anybody who lays eyes on her.

If the saint's image arrived while I lay dying, my father would surely have seen it as a clear command from her. *Come to my holy place, come into my care and protection.*

Later, when I have eaten my burned pottage, I stand at my father's bedside, studying his self-sewn shroud to see how I may finish the task he started. The shroud's seam — competent enough around his legs, the stitches large and uneven but firm — stops, unfinished, just below his breastbone. Here, the stitches are looser, as if strength or will failed him, and the rest of the sheet lies, ungathered, beneath his head and shoulders.

As he leaned back that last time, drained by the unaccustomed demands of women's work, did he look across and see me breathing still? Did he see the crude little Saint Cynryth — for so she seems, now that I have seen the beauty of the other — rising and falling on my chest with each breath?

For the first time, I consider the fact that the little statue lay on my chest, not on his. He was devoted to the saint, yet he lay down in his shroud and left her with me. And he is dead, while I am alive.

His death has left me free from collyering, free from his disapproval. Free to go with Master William to Gloucester, let him intercede with the bishop to allow me to study and become a priest.

If there are any left alive in Gloucester.

I turn my mind away from such a dreadful thought and cast my eyes around the hut at the last things my father saw. It is little enough for a lonely deathbed: the pallet bed where I lay, two stools, that church candle.

In all our years of coaling in the forest, there has never been a candle of any kind in the hut — rushlights always answered our needs. But a rushlight will not burn above half an hour. It seems that, at the end, my father wanted light about him. And not just light but something consecrated. Did he know he would die here, unshriven, with no priest in sight?

Perhaps, my angel whispers, *the candle was not for him but for you. To speed you on your way if you should die, or, if you should live, so that you should not wake to utter darkness and be afraid.*

Is that how it was? Did my father recall the times when I woke in the night as a tiny boy, screaming and terrified, though of what I could never say; times when only a candle's light would calm me?

His clothes lie, folded small, on the hut's second stool. And, on top, to keep them from vermin, he has put his good boots, his knife and his money-bag. My mother would have been surprised at this unwonted orderliness. Every night she used to pick up his overtunic and his boots, smoothing the wool flat, hanging his boots on a beam out of the way. His tools he always kept tidy but never his clothes.

After hooking the doorway's sacking back to let the light in, I cross myself and reach beneath his dead fingers for the still-threaded needle. I take a deep breath, grasp the two sides of the sheet, marry the torn edge to my mother's delicate hem-stitching, and fold the shroud over his face.

Before I can falter, I quickly pierce fold with needle and begin to sew. My stitches are as large and clumsy as his own but they are the best I can manage. The last stitch knotted, I bend to bite the thread, only to jerk away as my cheekbone bumps the top of his head.

My heart suddenly thudding, I sit back on my haunches and gaze at the shrouded shape of him. If I walk to Lysington, tomorrow, and come back with the mare the day after, he will have been dead and above ground three days at least. And, all the while, his soul has been in danger for he died unconfessed.

Another two days if I am to take him back and bury him. And, even then, he would not be buried in the churchyard.

Nobody is buried in the churchyard any more. Not since the pestilence.

With a stab of pain to my belly, I recall the moment when the funeral cart bearing my mother and little Elinor trundled past the lychgate.

'Where are we going?' I shouted at Master William. 'Where are you taking them?'

'Martin, I'm sorry. But you've seen the churchyard — old graves are falling into the new! We've opened another burial ground in Newman's Field.' He put a hand on my shoulder and shook it a little. 'Be thankful, Martin, that your mother and sister will lie in consecrated ground. There are tales from Bristol of folk laid in pits, covered in lime and buried without rites!' He crossed himself.

Newman's Field. How can folk lie easy in a field which, last year, grew beans and corn, where crows pecked after gleaning, where sheep dropped their shit all over the stubble?

I look down at my father's shroud. What are the words Master William always used at a vigil? I strain my wits but the words will not come. Perhaps the pestilence has sucked them from my mind as it has sucked the strength from my limbs.

Desperate for some godly words to say, I stammer my way into the night canticle. But, even as I speak the words, I am afraid for my father. For, in coming to the forest, he has preferred Saint Cynryth, the White Maiden, to Our Lord.

He has not made a good death and I am in terror for his soul.

CHAPTER 3

The day after I put my father in the ground, the mare turns up. And with her, my brother, Richard. It is a mark of my loneliness that I am almost glad to see him.

'Martin! Is it you? Or a ghost?'

Half-falling off my stool, half-rising, I sway to my feet and face my brother as he comes towards me across the clearing.

'Mare wandered home,' he says. 'Now snow's melted, I reckoned I better come and see what was what.' He looks me up and down. 'So. Alive, then.'

I lift my chin. I have never been a favourite with either of my older half-brothers but I have always had more trouble from Richard than Adam. 'Yes. Alive and well. Thanks to Saint Cynryth.'

Richard snorts and wipes the snot which came down his nose on the back of his hand. 'What — Dadda's little saint no priest ever heard of? Reckon she saved you?'

'Alive, aren't I, like you said?'

He looks at me as if I were a hog and he was judging how many days to wait till he slaughtered me. 'Most likely weren't taken with plague in the first place,' he says. 'Be like you, Martin, to reckon you was sick just so's people'd take notice.'

Everybody says that Richard and Adam take after their mother. Plainly, the woman was big and knuckle-boned with little laughter in her.

'Well, I'm grateful to you for returning the mare,' I tell him, risking a cuff for what he will think 'priest talk', 'and for coming to see that all is well but I expect you'll be wanting to get back —'

'Hold hard! What about the old man?'

'Dadda?' I wait a moment or two to vex him then drop back into our village speech. 'Dead. Died afore I woke up.'

'That so?' It is not a question that requires an answer. 'Where is he, then?'

'Buried.'

'Buried!' He glares at me. 'Where?'

'Over by the well.'

'What? Buried him like a dog? Dug a hole and put him in?'

'No —' I stop myself. I know what will happen if I tell him that I made our father as safe as I could, that I said as much of the funeral mass as I could remember when I put him in the earth. Richard will start complaining that I think myself better than everybody else, good enough for a priest. Weak as I am from the pestilence and from half a day's grave digging, I cannot stomach a fight.

'No what?' he wants to know.

'Didn't bury him like a dog. Buried him in front of the shrine with his saint.'

He shakes his head. 'Should'a brought him home. Buried him proper, not yere.'

'Buried him afore the saint's shrine,' I tell him a second time. 'Like he'd've wanted.'

Richard half-turns his head away, as if my words disgust him. 'Don't be foolish, Martin. Not simple, are you? You know 's well as me no parson never dedicated that well to no saint. *If* Dadda's little Maiden even *were* a saint.'

He is working up to something. Richard never lets slip a chance to advance his own cause.

'What d'you say?' he wants to know. 'Believe the wilful maid in Dadda's story to be a true saint, do you?'

Whatever I might have believed before, the beautiful White Maiden stands at the well, now. And I can feel her reaching towards me.

'Don't see no reason to doubt her.'

'No? Thought parson William would've talked more sense into you.' Richard hooks his thumbs in his belt. 'Where's the spot where they honour her, then? Her true shrine? For, as sure as shit runs out of a cow in spring, that over there —' he jerks his head in the direction of the well — 'isn' it.'

'Salster,' I tell him. 'White Well's near to Salster.'

'Salster? That's a rare long way. How're you going to make your way there, then?'

My heart suddenly thuds with fear. This was a trap, for sure. 'Who says I'm going there?'

'What? You think you're goin' to bide here after burying our father in unholy earth? Beneath a saint of unproved power?'

A trickle of chill disquiet runs down the nape of my neck. 'She's not *unproved!*'

Richard takes a step towards me. I back away.

'That's so, is it? Master William gave the church's nod to Dadda's shrine, did he?' His eyes, not brown like my father's and Adam's but rat-grey, are sharp on me. 'Didn't, did he? Master William never heard of Saint White Maiden Cynryth.'

I swallow. 'Doesn't know every saint in the world, does he? Only the Pope knows every one.'

Richard sneers and sucks his teeth. 'Well, saint or not, you've buried him out of sight as you saw fit.' His eyes are cold. 'And him being dead serves your purpose nicely, I'll say that.'

'Serves my purpose? How?'

'Wanted to go studying in Gloucester, di'n't you?' Before I can reply, he shakes his head. 'Folks in Lysington won't like it when I tell 'em he's dead and buried out yere.' He stares at me, eyes narrow. Then, for no good reason that I can see, he seems to tire of the subject. 'Where's he lie then? Show me.'

We walk without speaking, the forest silent about us but for the rooks rasping to each other in the naked trees.

As we come around the hill and the narrow path widens out in front of the spring, fear stabs my gut. How will I explain the new statue to him? Somehow, I know, Richard will find a way of making the saint's image my fault. He will make out that I encouraged our father in his devotion, encouraged this waste of good money.

I keep my gaze away from the fold in the rock and gesture to the mound of red forest earth on the right side of the well. 'There.'

Then, while Richard's eyes are on the grave, I glance up at Saint Cynryth.

She is not there.

My eyes dart around the well. Has she fallen? Has somebody moved her?

Richard sees me looking about. 'What you afraid of, Martin? Reckon he's fit to haunt you?'

I turn to face him. Could he have taken the saint and hidden her? No, his way to the hearth would not have brought him past the well.

I thrust my chin at him. 'Not afraid of anything. Done my duty by Dadda, haven't I? Came here to be near his saint, he did, whether living or dying, and I've done as he wished.'

'Done what suited yourself, you have, Martin. As ever.' He looks at me without blinking. 'Why d'you live and not him, then? If you was both plagued, why'd his little maiden let you live and see him die?'

I asked myself the same question during my vigil over my father's body and the only answer I could find was that my father had spent all the power of his years of devotion on me. All the prayers he made, daily, at the little saint's shrine had saved my life.

'Gave me the shrine statue,' I tell Richard. 'Put it in my hands when I was dying, back 'ome. Woke up in the hut still holding her. Healed me, she did.'

His eyes narrow once more. 'Where's it now, then? Such a thing has power.'

I swallow. 'Buried it with him.'

He shakes his head, eyes cold. 'Should've kept it by you, Martin. To protect you on your way to Salster.' Then, without another word, he starts back along the path.

When I catch him up, on the hearth, Richard gestures at the cart. 'Whatever Dadda wanted, he brought every stick and stitch he possessed yere with you. Must've meant you to have his chattels so they're yours. And Hillfield's mine. The house, too.' He stares at me, then — long and hard — as if I might be out of his sight for a long time and he wants to know me when he claps eyes on me again.

He is banishing me. Denying me a home in Lysington.

Why does a lump grow in my throat at the thought? Of all my dreams, all my dearest visions of the future, none have ever included our village. And yet, here I am, fighting tears like a whipped brat.

'I must see Master William,' I tell Richard, 'seek his advice.'

He looks at me without a shred of pity. 'Parson's dead. Died yesterday.'

Master William, dead? Good as he was, I was sure that God would spare him.

'Richard, you got no right to send me away! Lysington's my manor, same as it is yours —'

He steps forward, stabs a finger at my chest. 'And he was *my father*, same as he was yours. But he's dead and buried out yere and nobody the wiser. And you're hale and well. Aren't you?' He glares at me. 'You better set your face for Salster and any shrine his little saint's s'posed to have. Pray that she makes peace for him. Sees his soul safe.' He takes a step towards me. 'And if you don't find no white well and no saint, then you better get to Dernstan of Salster's shrine and wear out your knees for our mistaken father's soul.'

CHAPTER 4

Two days later, I stand, mare and cart beside me, before the Foreign Bridge outside Gloucester. For minutes, now, I have been rooted to this spot, staring at the river, unable to put foot to the bridge. I have never travelled further than this. I have never seen Bristol, nor even Monmouth, which lies to the west of the forest, on the banks of Dene's other river, the Wye. Gloucester, with its great abbey of Saint Peter, has always been our city, an easy half-day's walk from home.

I glance at the city walls, away to my left. Within, the pestilence moves from house to house, street to street; but here all is quiet. The tide is on the ebb and the silty Severn mud lies flat and waterlogged beneath the heavy sky.

The wind pushes and buffets at me, flattening my hood against the back of my head. It is like a mighty hand pushing me on but I will not be bullied.

What lies between here and Salster? I do not know and my mind is full of fears. I fear cities peopled only by the dead, where unquiet souls quit their hasty graves to walk the streets. Manors overrun by weeds and the animals of the wood come to scavenge the unburied dead. Roads made perilous by those who have fled their homes in fear of their lives and now must prey on others to live.

I have no weapons save my knife and nobody to keep watch with me. I am alone.

I long to speak with poor, dead William Orford. To ask him what I should do, to hear his advice. But, most of all, I want him to give me absolution.

I have sinned and wished my father dead for my own advantage.

His countenance would turn solemn, I know, for he told me, oftentimes, that the sins of the spirit are more condemnable than the sins of the flesh.

You must do penance, Martin. A heartfelt and costly penance.

I know I must go to Salster, that it is what Master William would have approved, that it is what my father would have wanted. A heartfelt and costly penance that would mend my soul and save his from the fires of hell.

For my father's sake and my own, I devoutly hope that I shall find his little saint's shrine in the woods outside the city of Salster, just as the peddler said. For I must prostrate myself before that shrine and pray that, as she healed me, so she will save my father's soul.

My thoughts turn, for the ten dozenth time, to the beautiful statue of the saint that appeared at our well and then disappeared as suddenly as it had come. I went back to the shrine again and again before I left the forest, only to find it empty each time.

The wind shoves at me impatiently, a shoulder in the back, pushing me forward.

I glance at the cart. It is a good deal lighter than when my father left the village with me, all but dead, in the bed of it. All that I will not need on my pilgrimage, I have left in our hut but I am still worried that the load will prove too much for the light-built cart and for the poor mare who must pull it all the way across England.

I look into her docile eye. 'Come on, then.' And I cluck her forward on to the bridge.

As the nail-studded wheels rattle on the cobbles I wonder whether they are in a fit state to take me all the way to Salster. They were not made for such a journey and, for their preservation, as for so much else, I am relying on the protection and blessing of Saint Cynryth.

Once, when I was a small boy, just coming to understand that the world did not begin and end with our village fields, I boldly asked a visiting carrier how he had known the way to Lysington. The man — newly arrived with a half-empty cart and a package of spices from Widow Gage's adventuring son — looked at me, man to man, his lower lip jutting in thought. 'It's journey and ask, son, journey and ask.' But his advice was given when England was well and full of folk who would speak to strangers.

Just after Gloucester, a Severn boatman tells me the way I must go but either his directions are at fault or my following of them is for, by nightfall, I have not reached the village he directed me to.

As dusk gathers me in with its shadows, I feel my old fear of the dark growing inside me once more. If I am lost so soon, how will I ever reach Salster?

That night the demons come for me. Every time I close my eyes to sleep, they creep over me, sliding up the nape of my neck and into my hair on cold dread like a slug on its own slime. They whisper profanities and I push my fingers into my ears. They slither round my fingertips, over my nails, hissing threats and maledictions.

Your father is in Hell.

We will lead you into a marsh and drown you.

We will kill you in the night, while you sleep.

We will pluck your soul as you die.

You will be eaten by foxes and badgers and nothing shall remain for the angel to gather on the Last Day.

You will scream in Hell for ever.

Driven almost to madness by my fear, I throw the blankets off and scrabble out from under the cart, my stomach hollow with terror, my scalp prickling as if each hair has been pulled by its own demon, a taste like the memory of blood in my mouth. I stare around me in desperation at the familiar things of this world — the turf-banked fire with my little stool next to it, the mare, hobbled and head-hung in sleep. I put a hand on the cart's wicker side, feeling the solid knit of the hazel-whip weave.

The canvas flaps in a small, chill breeze. The back ties must be loose. Was I careless, or has something untied them?

My blood freezes and I stare into the dark where the end of the cart is, my eyes straining. Is there something — somebody — under the canvas? Though I look till my eyes burn, I see no movement under the heavy covering. But I cannot not turn my back on it and sit down again at the fire.

Taking my knife from its sheath and mustering my courage, I pull the side ties free and fling back the canvas. In the dim light of the cloud-scattered moon, everything in the cart seems just as I left it. On one side, the flour-chest, on the other, the press. Cordwood stacked on top of the trestle-board between them. At the back of the cart is the space where I will stack the pallet and blankets in the morning, along with the cooking pot, stool and ember-basket.

I put my knife back on my belt and take hold of the canvas to pull it over the cart once more but my eyes are drawn back to the press. The lid is not quite shut.

My heart bumping in my chest, I stand on the cart's wheel and peer over the side. My legs almost give way.

Fingers. I see fingers thrust into the dark gap between lid and press.

'Mother of God —' I jerk back, fall from the wheel on to my arse, scramble backwards on palms and heels.

Fingers. A hand.

The ground is cold and damp beneath me and I stand, gasping for breath as terror presses in on me.

Dear God, who is in there?

Slowly, I rein my terror in and master it. The press is not large enough for anybody but a small child to hide in.

A small child or a shape-shifting fairy.

I swallow. No. A fairy would have sat by the banked-down fire, watching and waiting for me to wake. He would have spoken to me, lured me, led me away. Fairies do not hide, they appear in plain sight to charm and deceive you.

I force myself to go back to the cart. My knife in my teeth, I pull myself up on to the wheel and look down.

The hand is not curled around the side of the press as if to pull its owner out, it is thrust, stiff and straight, into the air. As if its owner is already dead.

I think of the village children I saw, wrapped and stitched, on the funeral cart in Lysington, and of my father, wrapping my tiny sister with my mother, binding them heart to heart in cold linen.

My knife in my right hand, I reach over with my left and fling open the press.

Of all the horrors in the world, none, I think, could surprise me as much as what I see. As great as my dread was, so great is my astonishment now. Inside the press, her hand reaching up under its lid as if begging to be rescued, is the statue of Saint Cynryth.

I lean forward, take the saint by the elbows and raise her until she is eye to eye with me. Her appearance, here, in the middle of nowhere is a miracle. A miracle even more powerful than her healing of me.

Holding her to me, I jump down from the wheel and lay her down, gently, on my pallet under the cart.

The saint has come to me. I might be all alone, I might have missed my way, the demons of the Devil might beset me, but she has come to me and saved me a second time. As she appeared to my father in a vision and claimed our well for her own, so now she has come to me to lay claim to my pilgrimage. My father gave his store of prayers to the saint, garnered over years, for me, for my life. And she has come to ensure that I repay him in kind.

CHAPTER 5

I do not know whether the saint has protected me from harm in keeping me from my fellow men or whether the demons that beset me have guided my feet into false ways but, for four days now, I have travelled through high and windy sheep country without seeing another soul on my path.

By day, loneliness has oppressed me and, by night, the terrors of the devil's flitting demons have made the dark hours long and full of horror. I have given up lying beneath the cart. Now, I sit with my back to the cartwheel, the saint half-wrapped in a blanket at my side and the unbanked flames of the fire keeping ill-willing spirits at bay.

And, as I keep the watches of the night, I pray at every one that my father's soul will be safe in his saint's keeping until we reach Salster. Once we reach the woods to the north of the city where the peddler's tale said her shrine is to be found, I will make a present of the miraculous statue to whoever tends it and ask for masses to be said for my father. Surely, his soul will be safe then?

But neither prayer nor plans can wholly calm the fear that I am taking too long about my journey, that — saint or no saint — my father's soul is in danger every day I am upon the road and I must make better speed if he is not to be damned for all eternity.

Nights of fitful, head-jerking sleep start to tell upon me. As we tramp along, I begin to fall asleep on my feet at the mare's side. My head fills with fancies and, more than once, it seems to me that my father is walking beside me. But, each time I blink and turn my head, he is gone.

On the fourth day, I finally see the shape of houses on the road ahead and, hailing a boy with a slingshot dangling from his hand, I learn that the pestilence had not yet come to his village.

'Will they give me water for my mare?'

'Are you sick?'

'No.' I do not tell him that a miracle healed me; I do not think he would believe me.

'Most likely they will then.'

And they do, though not with overmuch civility.

What news of elsewhere?, they want to know.

What news of elsewhere? We asked the same question of every visitor to Lysington in the days before the Death came upon us. But, knowing how close it was did not make us wise. We should have run away. If my mother had not been with child, we would have stayed in the forest, safe. With the White Maiden.

I swallow down bitter regret and tell the villagers what I know, but it is not the news they have braved my fearful company to hear. They want to hear that the pestilence stays close to the southern shore, that it is ebbing, that those who fall sick do not always die. They want to hear that it is over, that they will be spared, that all will be well.

My water-butt filled, I ask what town I must head for next on my journey east.

There is another village on this same path, soon, they tell me. After that, I will be on the right road for the next town. Cricklade.

At dusk, I make camp in low spirits. Leaving the village was hard; being amongst the living dispelled the demon voices and made me ache for Lysington and for those I have left behind.

But these are no times for dallying with strangers and the villagers saw me to my road as quickly as charity allowed.

The weather has beaten me further down — it has been blustery all day, the wind poking at the smallest gap in my clothes, chilling me through every threadbare patch. Bundled in my own tunic and my father's, his overtunic and mine, still I shivered and bound blankets about me.

As I lay a fire, huffing at the kindling and feeding the tiny flame with splinters and strips of bark, I try to push aside the demon-fingers that tap at my shoulder, the whispers telling me that there is something out there in the darkening dusk, watching me.

It does no good to tell myself that I have heard nothing, seen no living soul since leaving the village earlier. As darkness closes in, the notion grows in me that somebody, or something, is squatting out there in the fading light, waiting.

I water the mare and lead her a little way off from the fire to graze. Her teeth crop at the hollow turf with a muffled, hollow sound, as if there might be something beneath waiting to burst out. I shake my head, trying to dislodge such foolish notions but they refuse to budge and my hands are clammy on the mare's rein. My hackles prickling, I narrow my eyes into the gloom, trying to make out a figure, a shadow. Better to see what is stalking me and to know it for what it us than to fear a monster. But there is nothing to be seen, only winter grass fading to grey in the dusk, and the distant rise of the land showing dark against the lighter sky.

By the time I have warmed yesterday's pottage through, I am all a-jitter, my hungry stomach in knots. The pottage is flavoured with a piece of old bacon I was given in the village and I should be savouring it but, after two mouthfuls, my jaw clamps shut.

It is not a movement in the shadows that fills me with fear but a sudden doubt: Lent. Are we in Lent? *Am I eating forbidden flesh?* A pilgrimage is marred if the church's fasts are broken and I have extra care to take as my pilgrimage is not for my own soul but for my father's.

Quickly, I calculate. My new sister was less than a day old when we got back to Lysington on Candlemas eve — the first day of February. Three days later, she and my mother were dead. We stayed in the village for their week-mind. I was ready for a fight with my father but, when I told him that we should not think of returning to the forest before their memorial mass, he nodded like a cowed wife. By the sixth day I was fevered and coughing.

Two weeks have passed since then. Straining my wits to recall anything from before the pestilence, I am almost sure that Master William had told me Lent would begin on the last Wednesday of February.

The bacon is not a sin. I have a day's grace and tomorrow is Ash Wednesday.

Later, when it is fully dark, I sit at the fire, feeding the leaping flames with cordwood to keep the darkness away. I hear my father's voice in my head, chiding me for such waste.

Bank the fire and go to sleep, boy! That's good wood you're frittering away.

I how that I should not be using the wood on the cart — every ell I spend on the fire is time I must pay back in finding firewood — but I cannot bear the dark and the terrors that come with it. Besides, I am my own man now, making my own decisions. My father cannot tell me what to do any more. Cannot stop me burning wood and cannot stop me using his money to buy my way into a college when I get to Salster. He can no longer stop me becoming a priest.

No, he can't stop you. But that's because he's dead. You buried him in the forest. Alone. There he lies, unconfessed, unabsolved.

Abruptly, my head snaps round. I heard a sound. A movement, somewhere in the dark.

His soul is unquiet, a demon's voice whispers, *he is following you.*

Fear stabs my guts and I strain my eyes into the darkness.

Nothing.

I press fervent thumb-crosses to forehead, lips and heart. *Christ, keep me safe!*

A log shifts in the fire, falls in a shower of sparks. Startled, I fling out a hand and cry aloud when it touches something soft and warm.

The mare throws her head up, shying at the unexpected cuff.

'Sweet Mary —'

You left the forest, left him there. And now he follows you.

No! The saint keeps him safe! His body is quiet in his grave and his soul is being purged!

And yet ... perhaps he is not in Purgatory.

A terrible vision gathers in the dark around me — my father rising from his grave as one of the walking dead, lumbering after me, limbs plucked and goaded on by demons. I feel cold hands about my neck, the cold breath of a dead man on my face, and terror drives me to my feet.

Snatching a log from the pile next to the fire, I stare out into the darkness. A chill breeze raises gooseflesh on me. Terror almost stops my voice but I force myself to challenge the dark. 'Are you there?'

Silence consumes my shout.

Terror overcomes me and I fall to my knees before the saint. 'Save me, Lady! Save me. Save me. Save me!'

CHAPTER 6

The next day, I do not hide the saint. Instead, I prop her at the front of the cart, like Our Lady in a festival procession. Her speedwell eyes fasten on the far horizon and her hand seems to reach out to pull me all the way to Salster.

All morning, my mind picks at fears of what will happen when I reach Cricklade. If the pestilence is there, there will be no succour. I might not even be let in through the gates, just pointed onwards.

The thought makes my spirits sink further for I am in sore need of human companionship and tears come to my eyes at the mere thought of a night out of the wind, away from the constant fear of being followed. But soon, my thoughts turn from comfort to the weather. The wind, blustery the last few days, has been dropping all morning. Now, it has stilled, the air silent as snow gathers in the clouds overhead.

I do not want to stop. Not if I might reach Cricklade before the snowfall begins. Before night and the demons come. I cluck the mare into a faster walk.

Ha ha, ha ha, ha ha.

The cry is like a blow from behind.

Magpies.

I turn my head and there they are. A straggle of them, their black and white livery as vivid as a slap against the dun ground.

Quickly, I count them and the rhyme beats like blood in my ears.

One for sorrow, two for mirth
Three for a wedding, four for a birth
Five for heaven, six for hell

Seven —

There are seven. Seven for the devil.

They stare at me, heads cocked, hard little eyes clever and pitiless. Seven. The Devil himself is near.

I begin to run, dragging the mare into a trot, desperate to leave them behind.

Most do not even turn their heads to watch us go but two follow, hopping and flapping after us, rising into the air. Watching them climb the air, I slow my pace, thinking they are done with me. But no. They come to rest, once more, on the ground ahead and stand there, heads turning this way and that, waiting.

Two of them. Two for mirth. But there is nothing of joy in these birds. As I get closer their hoarse chatter-laugh comes, mocking me.

Ha-ha ha-ha, ha-ha ha-ha.

Look at him. Lost-alone. Lost-alone.

I pretend they are not there, stride on, the mare's bridle clutched in cold fingers, forcing her to walk faster than she wants to.

The magpies keep pace, hopping along on those three-toed feet of theirs. Three-pronged, like the devil's fork. I look away, fix my eyes on the track. But I know they are there. They stay in the corner of my eye. Do the demons bring them? Or do Old Nick's minions just know to come when they hear that rattling laugh?

Ha-ha-ha-ha, ha-ha-ha-ha.

I long for a wind to blow the magpies and their laughter away. Far away. But there is no wind. The air is stilled to a muffled hush, as if the land is holding its breath, waiting. Waiting for the snow.

I look up at the sky's goose-grey evenness. Will it be a light fall or will it set in and leave us calf-deep by nightfall? Even an inch could hide the track and send me awry. I pull the mare up and look back the way I have come. As hard as I strain my eyes, narrowing them until my whole face feels folded into their sockets, I can see nothing. But something is out there watching me, following me. I know it. I feel it. The magpies know it, too. That is why they laugh at me.

Whatever it is that dogs my steps, if the weather forces me to stop, I will be at its mercy.

On the northern side of the track, a line of trees marks the beginning of wooded land. Woods. Shelter.

The mare shakes her head, snorts. She dislikes my indecision. But is it better to stop here, shelter in the woods and face whatever pursues me, or to keep on and hope to reach the town by nightfall? Pestilence or not, at Cricklade somebody will tell me which way to go, where to point my nose next.

The first flakes start to fall. My decision is made for me.

The wood is not coppiced and neither ditch nor wall hampers our passage. But the cart still makes slow progress — the ground is negligently kept, with thick underbrush on either side of the track. Does nobody have rights here? Certainly there has been no clearing of fallen limbs for many months past.

Still, the state of the wood suits me; I scarcely have to walk a hundred paces to gather enough firewood for a day and a night's burning. With that and the cordwood still on the cart, if I have to wait out the weather I will neither freeze nor starve.

The air is thick with snow by the time I have built my fire and soft, furred flakes fall into the new flames.

Within an hour, a hand's breadth lies on the ground and the blanket I have draped over me is weighted with it. The mare stands, head low, the snow on her shaggy back making a pied creature of her.

I build up the fire and prepare for dark but the daylight lingers unexpectedly as the emptied clouds thin and the rays of the sinking sun set the snow aglitter. The hissing and shifting of the fire is the only sound in the snowy silence and I gaze about me at a world of gold and black and frozen white.

The mare mumbles the snow with her soft lips and I remember that she has had no water since this morning. I get up and shiver to the back of the cart.

There is a movement. A flick of green in the corner of my eye.

I turn, a rush of fear cold in my belly. 'Who's there? Come out!'

My voice sounds high in the snow-muffled silence, afraid.

I move towards the flicker of green but a sound of alarm comes from the mare and I stumble back towards her. Head high, nostrils flared, she is frightened.

'Steady, mare.'

With a hand on her neck, I stare into the dark spaces between the trees. Nothing. Nothing I can see, at any rate.

The sun drops below the skyline and the snow's golden-white fades, all at once, to grey. Beyond the quiet hiss of the fire, everything is silent. Fear stiffens my limbs more than the cold. Somebody is here in the wood but I cannot see them.

Almost afraid to take a breath lest the sound should bring about some change in the air, I turn, slowly, to see what might be behind me.

Nothing.

Keeping my back to the cart, I reach down to the woodpile and grab a solid, wind-broken length. The weight of it reassures me. Darkness is creeping in, a patch here, a shadow there. Is that the shape of a man on the ground, or the dark underside of a snow-covered log?

I stare until my eyes are dry but the shape does not move.

There is a sound behind me. A stagger and an oath, as if a foot has found a hole under the snow. I turn, my eyes screwed tight to see.

Where is he?

The breath pent up in my chest, I look behind me. I cannot see him but I know he is there. I have heard him now. I do not call out again. If he wanted to make himself known, he would have done so. Whoever he is, he means to come upon me unawares.

Two nights and a day I wait for him, in snow and dark and fear.

I have barely slept since the snow started but my craft has trained me to night watches. A charcoal pit must be tended every minute of the five days it takes to char wood into coal. Night and day collyers oversee their stacked and earthed-up pits; night and day the smoke they give off is watched as it changes colour and temper. When a pit of cordwood is first fired and capped off, the smoke that pours out through the thatch of bracken and riddled earth is thick and greyish-brown, the colour of a tabby's underfur. But, as the wood within chars through, the smoke from the top-most vent holes, where the layers of cordwood are lightest, clears and thins to a blue haze, scarcely more substantial than a wavering, high-summer heat. Then those holes must be sealed and new ones made, a foot or so lower.

Only a collyer who knows his craft can be relied on to tend vent-holes at night. What is a commonplace task by daylight becomes an eerie business at night. Plumes of pale smoke rise, swift and silent, in the moonlight. The charring wood shrinks and settles, the earth-banked bracken shows holes and slips as vivid crimson gashes, fiery glimpses of the charring pit inside, like a vision of hell.

Now, as I sit, weary and wakeful through another night, I fancy that God is like a collyer and this monstrous pestilence his charring fire. For, as cordwood is reduced three- or even four-fold by coaling — shrinking and cracking as it smokes and blackens until it is apt for use in the forge — so, perhaps, God is reducing mankind to a third or a fourth part. A destruction of humanity like Noah's flood, where only those useful to God's purposes will be spared.

But, if that is so, then His purposes are strange, for the fire of the pestilence does not take the sinful and leave the virtuous. Those whose sins should condemn them are as frequently spared as the faithful are taken.

Has God fallen asleep, leaving his charring pit to burn and blaze undamped, unchecked? I cannot answer for Him, but, for myself, two nights and days of fitful, wary dozing by the fire have left me stumbling and heavy, longing for sleep.

It is what the watcher has been waiting for.

CHAPTER 7

Sleep nearly kills me. If it were not for the fire-dried sticks I scattered about, my attacker would have been on me before I heard him. He is still a dozen running paces away when I am jerked awake by a single stick-snap.

I grab for the stave at my side. He is almost on me, knife outstretched. I throw myself sideways. His lunge hits the side of the cart with rattling force. He curses and turns. I push myself up again, almost falling backwards as he comes after me. The moonlight shows lips drawn back from teeth, like a fighting dog.

He hurls himself at me. I swing the stave. A glancing blow deflects the knife but fails to disarm him. His snarl turns to a howl as he launches himself again. The blade comes at my belly. Without thought, I throw myself backwards on to the snow and bend my legs in self-defence. He takes a boot in the stomach but keeps his feet.

I scrabble backwards, trying to get away, to stand up. My kick only slowed him and now he is almost on me, knife-arm high, blade ready to stab down. I fall on to my back and kick my legs up again to fend him off.

His full weight comes down on me. My legs buckle, smashing a knee into my nose. As I tense for his knife, footsteps thud. He checks, half-turns and, as he does so, a hammer of a blow lands on his back. He arches backwards with a yell of pain and rage. Before I can move, whatever hit him is swung again, this time at his head.

Freed, I scrabble backwards, desperate to get my feet under me before this new attacker comes for me. The cudgel comes down a third time, though the man on the ground is not moving. The sound of wood hitting bone brings me to myself and, as the cudgel is raised again, I make a grab for it.

'Stop!' I wrench the cudgel from its wielder's grasp and he turns to me, but the moon is behind him and I cannot see his face. It comes to me that I should have run. Too late. 'Enough!'

'He was going to kill you.'

The voice is lower than mine but still has something of the lightness of boyhood. A lad like me, not an older man. I try to speak but, instead of words, my mouth fills with old pottage and bile. I turn away and throw my guts up on to the snow. Again and again, my stomach heaves. My throat stings and the muscles of my belly clench as my terror is cast out. Finally, weak and trembling, I wipe my mouth on the back of my hand and turn to my rescuer. He speaks before I can.

'I'm sorry. I should have stopped him.'

'You did.' My voice is clotted. I put my hand to my throbbing nose. Pain blossoms. I feel his eyes on me as I hang my head and watch nose-blood dripping, black, on to the snow.

'No. I mean, I should have stopped him coming here. I've been trying to keep him away from you. But I fell asleep. I'm sorry.'

I hear his words and open my mouth to reply but my throat is stopped up, thick with relief and rage. As I straighten up, he steps back a pace or two, holds up his palms as if to calm me or fend me off. I shuffle past him and stand, looking down at the man who came to kill me. He is lying on the snow like a shrugged-off cloak. His knife is lying next to him. I bend to pick it up but find my hand hesitating over it, as if the knife itself could wish me ill.

I hear a sound behind me. I spin around but the cudgel-wielder simply stoops to roll the crumpled man on to his back.

'Is he dead?' I ask.

He reaches out and lays a hand on my attacker's chest. 'Can't tell.'

I squat next to him. Careful of my broken nose, I lick the back of my hand and thrust it at the fallen man's face. I count heartbeats. One, two. Nothing. Three, four. A faint coolness spreads over my spit-wet skin. Breath.

'He's alive.' I stand. 'What are we going to do with him?'

'That's up to you.'

'What?'

He shrugs. 'You're the one who shouted stop.'

'He's your friend.'

'No friend to me. We just fell into company.' He nudges the senseless body with the toe of his boot. 'Should've let me finish him. He came at you like a mad dog.'

I remember the bared teeth, the scream, and a finger from the grave runs down my backbone. I am sweating and cold at the same time.

'You couldn't just kill him.'

'Why not? He was going to kill you.'

I feel myself begin to shiver. Legs unsteady, I move towards the cart and sit against the wheel. My hands are shaking as I lean over and put more wood on the fire.

He squats a few paces away. Then, when I say nothing, he pulls a few staves from my woodpile, puts them neatly on the ground to keep him off the snow and sits. A sudden rage rises in me. How can he just sit there, as if nothing has happened? 'Bring him over here. He'll die in the snow.'

'You want to keep him alive?'

I stare at him, feeling my limbs tremble with cold and fear and the effort of fighting for my life. He makes it sound so easy — as if it is nothing to decide whether a man shall live or die. As if this life is mine to decide.

My mind is fogged but I know that leaving him to die would be a sin. 'Bring him over here,' I say again.

He drags the senseless man over to the fire then straightens up. 'I need to go back to our camp to fetch some things.'

'No!'

'He's not going to wake up this side of tomorrow — if he ever does. And I won't be long.' He holds a hand out, palm up, to catch the soft rain that has begun to fall. 'If this keeps up, the snow'll be gone by dawn.' Suddenly, he grins. 'Look at us. We've done everything arse-about-face. We've all but killed a man, between us, without so much as knowing each other's name.' He makes a small bow. 'They call me Hob.'

CHAPTER 8

Hob is proved right. By first light, the snow is all but gone. The trees drip slow, heavy drops, and, in place of frozen silence, the wood is filled with the sound of seeping, trickling water.

Roused from a wary fireside doze by his return, I stretch, stiff and sore from the attack. My face itches. I scoop snow-melt from the canvas and, careful of my nose, scrub the dried blood off.

'Be glad your beard's not come in much yet,' Hob says. 'It's the devil getting blood out.'

I turn around to look at him and a pulse of pure ice runs through my veins when I see that he is standing over the insensible man, knife in hand. 'What are you doing?'

'Just seeing whether he's still alive.' Hob holds the knife up for me to see. 'Whether his breath clouds the blade.' He leans forward over the body. 'Breathing but senseless as ever.' He proffers his blade but the tiny droplets I see might as easily be drizzle as evidence of breath. 'So what do you want to do with him?'

In the sober light of day, I know the answer. 'We should take him to the nearest town. Find the keepers of the peace and hand him over.'

Hob shrugs. 'Sounds like trouble to me. I'd as soon leave him here.'

'What — to be eaten by vermin? Have his eyes pecked out while he's still alive?'

Hob folds his arms over his chest. 'You're very careful of him considering he'd've gutted you and left you for dead.'

'And you're very keen to see him dead, considering you've been living alongside him!'

'I know what he's like. He'd kill you as soon as look at you.'

'You're still alive.'

'Because I'd got nothing he wanted.'

'Well, I'm not leaving him here.' I move to the back of the cart and pull up the canvas.

Hob whistles. 'Are you delivering all that or is it yours?'

I grit my teeth. What he means is, *where did you steal all that?*

'It's all mine.'

I lay the pallet in the empty space between the flour-chest and the press; the cordwood from our charcoal hearth is all gone, consumed by my night-time fires. I turn to Hob, chin point at the still-senseless man. 'What's his name?'

'Edgar.'

'Right. Let's put him in the cart.'

The ground is cold and waterlogged, it sucks at the cart's wheels and Hob is obliged to set shoulder to woodwork as I urge the mare into the pull. Even when we have broken free and the wheels are turning, movement is sluggish, mare and cart both stiff with inactivity.

The clouds hang low and sodden in the sky and, by the time we clear the wood, rain is coming down heavily. Hob ducks around to the back of the cart and I watch, warily, as he pulls something from his pack. A cloak, nothing more deadly. As he shrugs his shoulders into it, I can see from the yellow-gold hang of it that the weave is thick and well-filled.

He grins over the mare's withers at me and runs a hand over the cloth. 'Looks like it cost a pretty penny, doesn't it? Took it from Edgar's bundle.' He shakes the folds out. 'Wouldn't want to say where he got it.'

We set off again in silence. The rain patters, light-fingered, at our hoods and the sound keeps our thoughts inside our heads. The mare plods, muzzle low, rain dripping from her mane and eyelashes.

As I trudge, my boots squelching and my father's overtunic heavy with rain, I fix my thoughts on finding a town and its keepers of the peace. My skin itches with the need to be rid of Edgar.

But my new companion's thoughts are otherwise. As the rain falls steadily, he turns to me, the edge of his hood sodden and dripping. 'Are you set on taking him to the watch?' I meet his gaze over the mare's neck. 'Only, I've been dodging the pestilence the last six months. I reckon I'm alive because I've stayed away from towns and villages.'

'Don't you want to be rid of him?'

'Yes. But I'd just as soon not exchange him for the pestilence. And besides…' He shakes the water from his hood to stop it dripping on to his face. 'Think about it,' he says, looking across at me. 'We get to the town. We take him to the keepers of the peace —'

'Yes?'

'Then what? They're not just going to thank us and wave us off, are they? They'll make us stay until he dies or wakes up. And, if he dies, they'll most likely hang us for killing him.'

'Hang *us*? It was *him* who tried to kill *me*!'

'But they won't know that, will they? Far as they're concerned we're two strangers who've turned up with a next-to-dead body that then goes and dies on them. They'll have to call the coroner. And he'll want to know how this stranger comes to be in their town, dead. He'll think the tidiest idea is to keep us handy.'

I pull the mare up and face him. 'But he attacked me!'

Hob looks at me from beneath his hood. 'I know that. But can you prove it? Come to that, can you prove this is your cart? Who's to say it's not his? That we haven't attacked him to rob *him* of it?'

Cold hackles rise on the back of my head and down my neck as I realise that, far from all who know me, I am at the mercy of any man's false claim.

We slog on. The rain seeps from the hem of my overtunic on to my hose and they begin to cling to my shins. I envy Hob his long cloak.

I do not know what to do. I cannot forget the moment when Hob's thudding blow landed on Edgar's back, when I knew that his knife would not find my flesh. Hob saved my life. But I was reared on forest stories of strange meetings, of men and beasts who are not what they seem. Stories that tell us not to trust too easily those we do not know.

When you meet a man on the road, count his fingers.

Still, Hob's warning words have taken root and I see that, even without Edgar, a welcome is scarcely to be expected. Cricklade may have shut its gates. Cities have. Gloucester kept out every last foreigner from the time the pestilence took Bristol; for all the good it did them.

I shake the heaviness of the downpour from my hood as I turn to look at Hob. 'Have you really been wandering all these months?'

He glances at me, head bowed against the rain. 'Not wandering. Just keeping out of the way.'

'Did many leave your manor?'

'Not with me.'

I wait as he stretches his long legs over a rain-filled hole. 'Where were you going — before the woods?'

'Nowhere. Staying away from where people were, waiting till the plague was done with us.'

He seems so firm of purpose: has the saint sent him to me? Since I left the forest, I have prayed for guidance, for protection.

Is Hob the answer?

The rain thins to a drenching drizzle, the air so thick and grey that it is hard to see where land ends and sky begins. It is strange country, this, without stream or cattle-pond. Is all the water hidden in folds of the land where it cannot be seen from the road?

Then, around noon as far as I can make out, the low cloud begins to lift and I catch a glimpse of something in the distance.

Half a mile or so shows it to be a huge stone building. As we draw level, I reckon it at three, maybe four times as long as our house in Lysington. Its roof is a towering pitch of reed-thatch and its gable-ends are broken by shutters the size of doors. From inside comes the sound of bleating, loud and strong.

I have heard of these sheepcotes. The wool-merchants build them so that the flocks can be brought in during bitter winter nights to stop their wool growing coarse.

I pull the mare up at the side of one of the stone-walled pens in front of the building and tie her reins to a hurdle.

'You're going in?'

I turn back. 'Why not?'

Hob shakes his head as if he can scarcely credit my question. I would feel the same in his position but I am not going to tell him why I have no fear of the pestilence. Not yet. It is too soon to speak of the saint until I know him better.

I walk up to the door and give a shout. 'Anyone here?'

The sheep answer with an even greater outcry but I hear no human voice.

I try again, banging on the door's planks. 'Anyone here?'

No one, it seems, but the clamouring flock.

I slip a finger through the latch-hole and the door swings open. Inside, it is dark and warm and the air is bitter with the piss and shit of scores of sheep; a sharp, high smell, unlike the sweet, rich smell of cattle. Every ewe turns her bony face toward me and bleats her tuneless plea. I have never heard such a noise — it makes the inside of my head hum.

Opposite the doorway, a stout ladder leans against the loft-timbers. I glance behind me. Hob is standing outside the door, watching. I climb the ladder. As my head rises above the loft floor, I see hay lying in winter's-end drifts, a rake and fork stand ready to pitch the fodder into the long cradles beneath, but nobody to do the work.

Feeling for the rungs, I back down and gaze at the scene beneath me. The sheep are divided into hurdle-pens, five down one side of the long building, five down the other. I count the bumping, jostling animals in the pen beneath me: forty sheep in a space not more than twenty feet on a side. No wonder they are eager to be out, their hay is all gone and they have no water. Once, I would have wondered where the shepherd was; now, I only wonder how long he has been dead.

I start opening the pens and the sheep swarm out in a bumping, woolly mass, heading towards their watering-place.

Hob stares after them as the last one chases the rest, hobbling on old feet.

'I'm going to see if I can find anybody,' I tell him.

'I thought we were keeping away from people?'

No, that was you. 'I need to know I'm on the right road.' I am not going to tell him that I lost my way when I had barely begun. That, now, I need to find Cricklade and a good road east.

'You're making for somewhere? A town?'

I hesitate.

'Don't tell me then.'

He says it lightly but something makes me think twice about my reluctance. 'East. I'm going east. To Salster.'

He stares at me as if he thinks I am making it up. 'That's the other side of the country. Beyond London, even.'

'I know.'

He is waiting for an explanation but I have said all I want to for now. I take the mare's reins and turn her towards the path which leads away from the sheepcote and towards the village which is just visible in the grey, wet distance.

There is not a soul to be seen as we head down a slope towards the houses and tofts. Not a boy keeps birds off the winter wheat, not a ploughman stamps the cold ground and sucks his teeth over when he will be able to break the sod. Has everybody fled?

I look back at Hob, following at a wary distance, then turn to the village once more. Perhaps they are all gone north. The Death is travelling up from the south coast, from the ports. If the folk here heard that it was nearby, they might have decided to flee with their goods rather than die on their land. In Lysington, I know, it would have taken only one respected family to up sticks and half the village would have been stacking their handcarts and packing their panniers.

As we pass alongside the churchyard, the mare snuffs the air, her ears back. Does she know that smell for the sweet rottenness of death? I breathe through my mouth to avoid the stench but it is so thick I can taste it on my tongue. The graves have been too shallow, the dead too many. There is scarcely a square foot of grass unturned. Scores must have been buried here since the Death came.

I glance over towards the church's south door, wondering whether corpses lie untended and unburied on their biers in the nave. Or perhaps the parson has suspended nave-vigils to guard against contagion. Master William did in Lysington.

Hob quickens his pace until he is back at the mare's other shoulder. 'If everybody's gone, there might be rich pickings for us.'

'You think people will've left anything useful?'

'Depends how quickly they left.'

Past the church and on into the village, I feel a shiver creep over my skin that has nothing to do with the sly breeze sneaking up on us between the garden-plots. I know this feeling of cold abandonment, of life having moved elsewhere. It is like a deserted charcoal hearth.

When you walk on to an empty hearth there's a lonely chill to the place. Without the collyer and his smoking, earth-banked pit, it lacks life and purpose. This place is the same: silent fields where no man calls to his neighbour or offers news. Houses without toddling children. Gardens tofts empty of busy women.

As we round a corner past a sizeable house, the mare shies at a flapping scramble of wings. A magpie beats at the air, rising over our heads with a baleful look, a scrap of something dangling from its scaly claws.

One for sorrow.

As another shiver chills me, I look around at Hob.

'It's like that story, isn't it?' he says. 'The one where every soul in the village is bewitched and goes through a tree-hole into the fairies' kingdom and sleeps a thousand years.'

'Except, these people haven't been gone long.' I nod towards two cattle that have wandered into a garden plot and are browsing happily on spread-leaved cabbages. I catch myself thinking that it will taint their milk before I remember that there is nobody here to taste it. Besides, they are dry, their udders hanging slack and empty, spring calves swelling their bellies.

We walk on.

There is a scrabble and a loud, clamorous squawking. Chickens cooped up with a cock. I stop the mare and open a gate, glancing back at Hob who looks on in silence. Well-tended rows of leeks and a swept, part-cobbled path speak of a house-proud wife. She must be dead or dying to leave her chickens roosting.

As I lift the latch that holds door to jamb and peer in to the coop, the clucking stops as if a hand has grabbed each feathery neck. Ten pairs of eyes look beadily at me, ten heads turn this way and that.

The cock stalks up to me — all green and gold and scarlet — much as to say, 'about time,' and struts past, to be followed at the scamper by all his mottled-brown hens.

'Martin —' Hob's voice sounds a warning.

I turn to go back down the garden but my way is barred by an old woman. Hastily, I shove my hood back off my head. 'God keep you, mistress.'

She stands in my path. 'Have you come for them?'

Her voice reaches me but not her gaze. Is she blind? Her eyes look clear enough, bright even. And they are stretched wide, their rims red, as if she cannot leave off a horrified staring. I take a step back.

'Come for who, mistress?'

'My William, my Tom. Annie and little Will. Have you come to take them to church?'

The cart. Though it looks nothing like any funeral cart I have ever seen, these are dreadful times; why should a stranger not come to take her dead to burial in a canvas-covered charcoal cart?

'Mistress —' I approach her but, as I come within touching distance, her hand fastens on my arm.

'You must!'

She almost looks at me. Her hand is hot, as if she has been warming herself at the fire though the roof is bare of smoke. I throw a glance at Hob, hiding behind the mare, and let the old woman draw me into the house.

Four corpses are lined up on the floor, each shrouded in worn, patched sheeting, each wrapped crosswise with bands cut from the same cloth. It looks odd to me — this binding of shrouds about the dead — but I know it is only because I am used to stitching.

William, Tom, Annie and little Will: two men of middle height, a woman, a small child. A charcoal cross marks each shroud, its upright running down the body, the arms extending wide across the shoulders. There will be no doubting, on the Last Day, that these are Christian souls. I think of the cross I put on my father — a handspan of red forest earth over his heart.

Breathing through my mouth, I ask the old woman how long her family has been lying here. She has no answer for me. Long enough, I suppose from their head-filling stink, for her to lose her wits in worrying that their souls will be snatched away before they can be laid safely to rest.

I do not want to bury them. Truth be told, I have no wish even to touch them. But I know that, if I want the saint to bless my journey and keep me safe, if I want to prove myself worthy of this second life she has granted me, I have to do it.

Once, I would have asked whether they had been shriven, whether they have the right to lie in hallowed ground. The pestilence has changed all that.

Hob meets me at the gate. 'Well?'

'Four bodies. We're burying them.'

'*What?*'

'You heard.'

'What have these people got to do with you? You don't owe them anything!'

'We're burying them, Hob.'

'No. *You're* burying them. You can shake hands with Death if you like but you're not dragging me into it!'

His face is set, resolute with fear. So be it. I have the saint's protection, he does not.

'At least help me empty the cart so I can put them in.'

'What about Edgar?'

I look over my shoulder. 'She's not going to care. I don't think she'll even see him. She barely sees me.'

So we make the cart ready for the bodies, laying Edgar and all my goods in the old woman's garden.

Hob stares as I take the blanket-wrapped saint from the cart and place her carefully on top of the press.

'What's that?'

'My business.'

He raises an eyebrow but holds his peace.

'You don't need to touch the bodies but I want you to come and help me dig the graves.' I want him as far away from the saint as I can keep him. 'I've got a spade, I'll see if she's got a pick to break the earth with.'

With the old woman lending a hand and Hob standing well away, I get the two men into the cart, one beside the other. The heft of them — no longer stiff, but not slack like a body in sleep either — makes my skin crawl as I lift them in their damp shrouds. The woman and child I manage for myself, before taking a pick from the old woman and turning the mare in the lane.

I look around for Hob. 'Come on then.'

'You go on. I'll be behind.'

When I look back, he is matching me, pace for pace, ten yards or so behind the cart. What is a safe distance from the plague-dead? Nobody knows. I sniff at the sleeve of my tunic to see whether the stench of death has transferred itself to me but I cannot tell — it has soaked into my snot, now.

As I coax the unwilling mare back along the path, I think how gratified Master William would be at my turning gravedigger to strangers. How often did he preach the works of mercy to us? I can hear him now, catechising us on our duties at Easter.

What must we do, in charity, for our neighbours' sake, as Christian folk have been taught since the time of our Lord and the apostles?

We must feed the hungry, would come the mumbled, toneless response, *give water to the thirsty, clothe the naked, tend the sick* — a collective, indrawn breath — *offer hospitality to the wanderer, visit those in prison and bury the dead.*

Yes, we are required to bury the dead. Words that the pestilence has turned from rote-mutter to curse.

I cannot take the mare and cart between the close-set mounds in the churchyard, so I find a strip hard up against the boundary wall where there will just be space for three graves, as long as they are dug end to end. They will not face east but at least they will be in holy ground; if it can be called holy with such a stink of death and decay.

Hefting the old woman's pick, I look down at the ground. Why dig separate graves? Why not dig one deep grave and put them all in? When the Angel of Resurrection comes on the Last Day and calls the dead out, will he really bother himself with tallying bodies and graves?

But I cannot do it — it is too much like the Bristolians' common pits.

'Come on,' I call over the wall to Hob. 'We'll dig three graves — the child can share his mother's.'

And thus, I hope, Annie and Little Will shall go hand-in-hand to Purgatory.

Hours later, we traipse back through the village to the old woman. Her life has been spared but, with her whole family taken, it seems no great cause for celebration. Now that her dead are safely in the ground, how will she live, what will sustain her?

The question is answered as soon as I walk in to the house. She is lying on the bed, her hands folded on her breast.

I do not mistake death for sleep. Not anymore.

She held Death off, stared him down and defied him, until she had seen her loved ones safe. Then, once I turned the mare's head to the churchyard, she had simply lain down on the bed, closed her eyes and let him take her.

'She's dead,' I call out to Hob.

He comes halfway up the path. I can see him from where I stand.

'No surprise there.' He cranes his neck to see. 'She was nine-tenths dead before.'

I cannot bring myself to bury her while she is still warm, so, while her soul goes about the business of taking its leave, we go in search of water.

The village is no great size and we soon find the well. I draw a bucket to slake the mare's thirst, then fill my small barrel.

The silence at the well is unnerving. Is this what is waiting for me from here to Salster — village after abandoned village? Empty houses? Wells with nobody pushing in front because they live here and strangers must wait?

No, I must not take one village so much to heart. Lysington was not abandoned. Half our people died but those who survived stayed. There will be peopled villages. England cannot be dead from coast to coast.

I turn to Hob. 'How many died on your manor?'

He shrugs. 'I left while they were still dying.'

'And you didn't hear any more of it?'

'Didn't look back, didn't go back.' He watches as I tie down the lid of the barrel and begin to lead the mare around. 'Where are you going?'

'Back to the house. To bury her.'

'She's in no hurry. And there's food and goods waiting for us here.' When I don't reply, he makes an impatient gesture. 'Come on, Martin, it's not stealing! There's nobody here to steal it *from*. It's like finding a penny on the road.'

I follow him but my ears are pricked for shouts of outrage as we pull cabbages and leeks from winter gardens, take away half a dozen strings of onions from a store in the corner of a barn and fill bags with beans and peas and the contents of dead housewives' crocks. In one house Hob noses out a half-full jar of honey and a ripe cheese. At the bottom of a cracked pot in another, I find six of last summer's apples, wizened in a mess of straw.

As we reach the old woman's toft, Hob watches me go up the path. 'Do what you have to,' he says, 'I'm going to see what's in the church.'

He is already walking off before I understand.

'You're going to *steal the church's goods?*'

He stops and looks over his shoulder. 'Who is there to care? D'you see a parson, here, keeping vigil with the old dame? No, he's fled with the rest.'

'Or dead.'

Hob shrugs as if it makes no odds. 'Either way, the village is deserted and the church belongs to no-one anymore.'

'The church belongs to the church!'

He makes an impatient noise. 'What's the church done to keep the Death away? Nothing. It doesn't deserve its riches.'

'But it's a sin!'

He begins walking again. 'I'd rather be sinner than beggar. I'll see you at the church.'

Staring after him, I offer a desperate prayer that the parson took all his silver with him. I cannot travel with Hob if he is carrying stolen church goods.

Even without the shrouded corpses, the house still stinks of death. I gaze down at the old woman. Her body is knotted and dry and faded like her old brown kirtle, her headcloth slightly askew, showing one shrunken ear. She did not care enough to straighten it before giving up her soul.

I do not want to put her beneath the earth — she spoke to me, asked my help, carried her man and her son with me to the cart; she seems not yet fully gone. But I cannot sit in vigil for her and, if I do not bury her now, nobody will.

Quickly, I wrap her in the blanket on which she died and find a half-burned stick in the ashes to mark it with the cross. Then, ashamed of my haste to have done with a Christian soul,

I say the words of the *Placebo*. The same psalm I said over my father's grave.

She is barely heavier than little Will as I lay her in the cart. I force myself to find another prayer for her but, as I say the words, my gaze is drawn to Edgar, lying in the lee of the fence. As I stare down at him, there is a strange kind of fascination in the knowledge that he would have killed me if he could. He lies, unknowing and unmoving, as if he was just another victim of the pestilence, waiting to die.

I search his features for marks of evil but, in truth, his face is ordinary. It could sell you nails or dig you a ditch; even — though I do not like to think of it — sing mass at your church.

He is so unmoving that I lick my hand and bend to see if there is breath still in him. Only when the back of my hand cools do I realise I had been hoping he would be dead. I stand, quickly, dragging my hand over my tunic as if I can wipe away the sin with the drying spittle. This is what the pestilence has done to us. With death all around, the passing of a man can easily turn into nothing more than the timely solution to a problem.

But at least my conscience is to be troubled by no further sins today. I find Hob waiting at the lychgate, sullen-faced and empty handed.

CHAPTER 9

Hob and I do not have to wait long for our work of mercy to be rewarded. Within the space of a mile, we come across a roadway and a pair of monks who tell us that this is the road from Malmesbury to Cricklade.

'Where will the road take us after Cricklade?' I ask.

One shakes his head. 'Best ask once you get there.'

'Is the pestilence there?' Hob wants to know.

The answer is simple. 'It's everywhere.'

We stop for the night. As I lift the canvas to take out the ember basket I feel Hob behind me. When I turn he is looking at Edgar.

'He's trouble, that one,' he says.

'I don't think he's going to bother us much, state he's in.'

'He's trouble if he wakes up and trouble if he dies, damn him.' Hob reaches behind his back. 'Let's see what the knife says.'

Though I know what he is about, this time, my stomach still contracts as Hob leans over Edgar's face, knife in hand. With his blade held to catch the lightest breath, he turns to me. 'Defenceless as a new-born kitten. Be easy to just slit his throat, eh?'

'You can't!'

'Didn't say I was going to.' He withdraws the blade, shows me the misted surface. 'Said it'd be easy.'

I set about making the fire but Hob won't let the subject go. 'Even if he does wake up, his wits could be addled. Like this man I knew before — fell from the roof-timbers of a new tithe barn, right? Knocked witless — just the same. Lay on his bed for two days — not a move, not a moan. Priest called, all that. Then, damn me if he didn't open his eyes on the third day and start talking the worst kind of nonsense you've ever heard in your life!'

He is watching me, wanting a response.

'Ranted and raved,' he goes on. 'Kept shouting that he'd been pushed off the roof, that the man who pushed him wanted his wife, that everybody knew what'd happened but they wouldn't say because they were taking sides with this other fellow. You've never heard such a going-on in your life!'

He clearly expects me to say something.

'So, what happened?' I ask. 'Did he come to his senses in the end?'

'No. Kept up his nonsense till the day the pestilence killed him. Led his wife a merry dance of black and blue — I reckon she wished he'd died when he hit the ground.'

I meet his eye. 'And you wish you'd finished Edgar in the wood?'

'He'd have stabbed you and left you for dead. Left you for the carrion-eaters to finish.'

I turn away from him. 'If you deal evil for evil it'll catch up with you in the end.' Or so Master William was fond of saying.

'You can live by that if you like but I'll deal with men as they deal with me. What're you going to do at this town — Cricklade?'

I am confused by this sudden veering off. 'What?'

'Are you still set on taking him —' he jerks his head back at the cart — 'to the watch? Because, I'm telling you, if you go down that road, you're going by yourself. I'm not accounting for him.'

'I have to find somebody who can tell me which way to go.'

'So if we find somebody on the road who can tell us, we won't have to go into the town?'

I hesitate. I need directions but Hob's talk of suspicion falling on us if we take Edgar to the town's authorities has rattled me. 'No. Not if we can find somebody.'

Hob is not what a man would call easy company but I do not want to lose him. Collyers are raised to be always two together — two men to a hearth, one to watch the banked-up pit, the other to sleep. Since I left the forest, I have been trying to sleep and watch at the same time and it has left me half-dead with weariness and worry.

We will have to deal with Edgar ourselves.

CHAPTER 10

The land about us today is different. Yesterday's dry wolds are gone and the last mile or two has become wet and marshy. The road is raised, shored up here and there at its edges with posts and large stones to stop it being sucked into the marsh. A harrier quarters the air overhead and I am reminded of the country on the banks of the Severn, where she floods one year in three.

As the town that must be Cricklade appears in the distance, I begin to fear that we will have no choice but to venture in and ask the way. There is not a soul on the road, nor on the land on either side. I do not want to broach the subject with Hob for we have argued already this morning.

While Hob was a little way off about his necessary business, I tried to give water to Edgar. It was a laborious task and most of what I poured into his mouth trickled down his beard so, as I tried again, I failed to notice Hob striding back towards the cart.

'Martin! What are you doing?'

'Giving him water.'

'Do you *want* to live in fear of him coming after you again?'

'I can't let him die for lack of water!'

'If he was meant to live, he'd have come to his senses by now. He hasn't. You should just leave him.'

I wanted to tell Hob that I am not his servant, that he has no right to tell me what to do, but I did not want to get into a fight with him.

We find ourselves at a fork in the road and Hob turns to me. 'Now what?'

I look past him, putting off the moment when I must reply. Two score yards away, over a causeway on the right-hand prong of the fork, stands Cricklade's town bridge, the wharf on the town side of the river as deserted as the road on our side. We are going to have to cross that bridge. I must know the way. But, before I can open my mouth to speak, a figure comes running towards us along the causeway.

'Hey! You there!'

The shouter is a lad about my own age, but much better dressed.

'God give you good day, sir.'

He waves a dismissive hand. 'God give us all grace. Where've you come from? What's the news? Have you seen others on the road, travelling?'

I am taken aback, do not know which question to answer first.

Hob steps forward. 'We've come from the west. There's been nobody else on the road but two monks making for Malmesbury.' His voice holds no deference and the town's name trips off his tongue as if he has known Malmesbury all his life.

'You've come from the west?'

'From Gloucester, sir,' I tell him. 'Bristol and Gloucester have both fallen to the pestilence.'

'Everyone knows about Bristol. What about Cheltenham — do you know anything of the country there?'

I shake my head. I know Cheltenham — the town is an easy day's travel from Gloucester — but I know nothing of its fate.

He sighs. 'No news but bad news. Perhaps the monks are right and everybody'll die.' His eyes flick to the cart. 'You're not bringing dead?'

Hob is there first. 'No.'

'Just as well. They've got no room for any more —' he inclines his head towards the gatehouse — 'either living or dead. It's the prior's house but the hospital's so full they've had to fill up his hall now.'

I look over his shoulder. If the hospital is as sturdily stone-built as this prior's house, the town must have a rich lord; or perhaps a nearby abbey has set a daughter-house here.

'We're on our way east,' Hob says.

'You're travelling? Not staying here?' The young man's questions take on a sudden edge. 'Where are you going?'

'To Salster.'

He stares at me. 'You're on *pilgrimage*?'

I shrug, nettled by his lofty disbelief.

He looks from me to Hob and back again. 'Wait here while I fetch my master. He'll want to speak to you.'

'Why?' Hob asks.

'Because he needs a messenger.'

Hob's eyes follow him as he runs back towards the prior's house. 'We should go,' he says, turning to me. 'Quickly, before he comes back.'

'No!' The thought of defying a man who employs liveried servants makes my stomach turn over. 'We can't!'

'Martin, there's no can and can't anymore! The pestilence kills lords just as quick as it kills villeins! We don't have to do what young master whats-your-news wants.'

But, before I can answer, a tall man is making his way towards us. His cloak reaches his spurs; a man of influence. He does not wait to come level with us before he speaks. Neither does he feel the need to greet us. 'Miles tells me you're going east.' The liveried young man is at his heels.

'Yes, master, to Salster.'

I can feel Hob's silent growl.

'Then you would do well to go south first. If you go south to Avebury, and then to Marlborough on the Kennet, you will have easy travelling for a good way east.' Though the English names roll off his tongue easily enough, his manner of speech is odd and I wonder if he is more used to speaking French.

'You're a well-travelled man, yourself, sir?' Hob asks. To my relief, his tone is pleasant.

'My lord serves Prince Edward and, where my lord goes, I go. I know the road to Dover, and Dover is but a Sunday ride from Salster.'

'There was talk of a message,' I manage, nodding towards Miles.

'Yes. I am here on my lord's business. A meeting. Which has not taken place. I need to communicate this to my lord.'

'Why don't you send Miles?' Hob asks. He has not taken his eyes from the tall man.

'I cannot trust such an important message to one person alone,' he replies, mildly, 'not with the times as they are.'

'The times hold just as much danger for us,' Hob's chin is high. 'Why should we take your message?'

The cloaked man raises an eyebrow instead of his fist and my heart slows a little.

'I will pay you the carrier's rate.'

'Then find a carrier.'

'Hob —'

But both Hob and the lord's man ignore me.

'Very well. I will pay you twice the carrier's rate.'

Hob shakes his head. 'We'll have to go out of our way — put ourselves at risk of harm, perhaps. Our aim is to keep away from folk. If we go to your lord's manor we'll encounter any number of people.' He holds the man's eye until I can scarcely bear it. 'The pestilence is running all over England.'

'I am well aware of that. And I know that my lord will demonstrate his gratitude.'

'Without meaning any offence, sir, your lord could be dead tomorrow — could be dead already for all you or I know. The gratitude of a dead man's of no use to me.'

I find myself stepping backwards, putting space between myself and Hob before the cloaked man steps up and knocks him to the ground. But he does not move; he responds not to Hob's insolence but to his argument.

'Very well. You shall have a second message to take to my lord's bailiff asking him — or his successor, should *he* have died — to reward you as we agree.'

'Ten shillings,' Hob says.

'*Ten shillings* to go hardly any distance out of your way?'

'Ten shillings to risk our lives on your lord's manor where we're not known and where the pestilence may be waiting for us.'

A look of displeasure draws the man's features together. 'What manor do you hail from, lad?'

'I'm no lad. I'm a freeborn man bound for a new fortune.'

'Then what is your name?'

'Hob.'

'Do you have no other?'

'Cleve.' Hob says, his eyes unflinching.

The man makes a mocking half-bow. Very well, Hob Cleve, I trust that my lord's ten shillings will be sufficient draw to take you to him.'

'It will. And so will the ten shillings you're going to give me now, in case there's nobody left alive on your manor when we get there.'

With a great thunderclap of a laugh, the man bends over and strikes his own thigh with a gloved hand. 'Hob Cleve, tell me why I should not whip you for your impudence?'

'Because then you'd have no messenger.'

The man shakes his head and slaps his leg once more as he turns away. 'Fetch them some ale and some bread while they wait,' he instructs Miles.

With both of them gone, I climb up on the cartwheel and lift the canvas over the clothes press.

'What are you doing?' Hob hisses.

'Getting a bag to stow his letters in — he wouldn't be happy to see either of us putting them in our tunic and we can't lift the canvas in front of him, can we?' I shoot a glance at Edgar who lies, still as death, in the bed of the cart.

Hob grunts and glances in the direction of the Prior's house lest Miles should come back before the cart is safely covered again.

'Are you one of those madmen who thinks all lordship is corruption?' I ask, my voice louder than I intended. 'All that insolence! I don't know why he didn't beat you to your knees.'

Hob leans against the cart and watches me tie the canvas down again. 'The pestilence is changing the world, Martin. It's not master and man, any more. It's who's got something the other wants.'

'Go over the bridge,' the lord's man begins once I have stowed both letters, 'and keep to the main street through the town. At the south gate keep walking onwards a few minutes until you come to the river. Follow it until you get to another bridge then cross there.'

His instructions go on and on — woods, flat land, Chepying Swindon, east, road, Marlborough, river, south, forest — until I have to beg him to stop and start again.

'No,' Hob holds up a hand. 'I've got it.' He looks the tall man in the eye. 'Once we're clear of this Savernake Forest, what then?'

Our instructions complete to the very door of his lord's house in a village called Slievesdon, the man takes a soft leather purse from Miles and counts out ten shillings. These he hands, twelvepence at a time, to Hob. Throughout the whole transaction neither of them so much as glances at me.

Hob gives a nod that does duty for a bow and tips the last of the money into the purse which hangs from his belt. I must get him to put it in the cart, or at least to tie it to the drawstring of his braies and keep it under his tunic; it's not wise to be showing off such a heavy purse.

The tall man raises a hand. 'God speed.'

It is dismissal as much as blessing but Hob has something to say.

'We weren't going through the town and now we are, on your business. I don't want watchmen on the gate pawing through our belongings, laying their hands on us.'

The man turns to his servant. 'Miles, go with them and tell the gatekeepers to let them through unmolested.'

Clouds are racing low across the sky in the stiff breeze as we leave Cricklade's southern edge. Rooks are circling and calling in the rising wind and, at the sight of them, I catch myself looking about for magpies.

I feel Hob's gaze on me.

'You're a strange one, Martin. You were pissing yourself like a girl when I wouldn't bow and scrape to that lordsman, and then you went and ate the bread and drank the ale from that pest-house of as if it was the body and blood!'

The mare suddenly stumbles and pecks at the ground, pulling the rein through my slack fingers. 'Hold up, girl. Hold up.' I rein her in, stroking her neck. I run my hands down her legs and look at her hooves. She's standing squarely and her shoes look tight. I stroke her nose and tell her to be more careful.

'So how come you're so milksop on one hand and so fearless on the other? Aren't you afraid of eating food that's been handled by the sick?'

I glance sideways at him. He refused to touch what we were offered, despite the looks it got him. 'You saw me bury five plague-dead yesterday. I'm not afraid of it.'

'Then you're a fool.'

I face him across the mare's back. 'A fool is one who doesn't show fear where he should — like you with that lordsman! I'm not afraid of the pestilence because it's been and gone in me.'

A scowl makes his eyes small. 'Been and gone?'

'Yes. I was sick, like the rest of my family. But they died and I lived.'

'No one outlives the pestilence.'

I grit my teeth. Years of living with resentful half-brothers have accustomed me to hearing that I'm a liar. 'I did.'

He shakes his head. 'Perhaps you caught a cold while they were ill —'

'I coughed blood. I was fevered and senseless. The parson gave me the last eucharist, said the rites over me. I was as sick as anybody the pestilence has killed.'

'So how are you standing here?'

How carefully did he and his murderous companion watch me in the woods before Edgar's attack? Did they catch a

glimpse of what lies, blanket-wrapped, at the front of the cart?
I shrug.

'Is that why you're on pilgrimage? To give thanks?'

'In part.'

He waits for more.

'A miracle, then?'

I cluck to the mare. 'Who's to say? I know I was all but dead
and now I'm as well as you.'

'Aren't you afraid it'll strike a second time?'

'No.'

'How can you be so sure?'

I keep my eyes away from the cart and give him no reply.

CHAPTER 11

Dusk falls and we stop for the night. As Hob goes for firewood and I start a fire with the few sticks left in the cart, I feel that I might have lived half a lifetime since Edgar's attack in the woods. So quickly have I become accustomed to Hob's presence that the loneliness I have felt since leaving the Dene has already begun to fade.

Had I not already known it, my enforced solitude would have shown me that I am not built for a life removed from other folk. Not like my father.

It always seemed to me that, practical considerations aside, my father would have been just as happy in the forest without my mother and me. For, if our company gave him pleasure, he never showed it.

My poor mother. She must have found the hut in the Dene a sorry substitute for our good village house with its two big rooms and well-ordered garden plot. Though she sang at her work like a woman wholly content with her lot, it was not fair of my father to bring her to the forest and deprive her of the company of other women. Men and women speak differently to each other and my father, though not a harsh husband, was a silent one.

And now he is enfolded with his silence; alone, in the forest.

'Martin?'

I jump, startled.

'Easy, man! You're twitchy as a blackbird.'

I breathe out.

'Where's the hobble? I'll see to the mare.'

I watch Hob out of the corner of my eye. He is bigger than me, probably a year or two older — maybe eighteen summers. Wide in the shoulder and narrow in the hip, he is the kind of youth the girls in our village always gave the glad eye to, the kind never short of a willing mate at maying. His thick, light-coloured hair matches his beard and I know I must present a contrast to anybody who sees us. My mother was fond of telling me how much I look like my father and, even when not covered in charcoal dust, he was dark-featured and black-haired, with the melancholy temper that often goes with those looks. My mother was dark, too, but not so much as him; her hair was the deep brown of a blackbird's wing, her eyes a bright hazel.

The mare hobbled and watered, Hob sits opposite me at the fire.

'How have you been living, Hob?' I ask. Winter is a poor time to forage and his frame bears none of the marks of hunger.

'How have I been living?' He stretches his hands towards the flames. 'Badly, compared to you, my friend. I wasn't half so well-equipped.' He glances at me, mocking. 'You're like a snail, Martin. You're slow but sure and you carry your house with you — everything, even your fire!'

I do not like the comparison but I let it go. 'Packing embers in a basket is a collyer's trick,' I tell him. 'When you leave your house, you take the embers from the fire packed in moss and turf and you light your cooking fire at the hearth when you get there.'

Hob takes a stick from the pile and pokes at the fire with it. 'Well, unlike you, I didn't have a horse so I couldn't bring much with me. I bundled everything I could and made the most of it.' He pauses. 'I'm a handy bowman. I didn't have to eat pease pottage every day.' He grunts at some memory. 'I don't mind drawing and roasting a rabbit or a pigeon but stirring pottage is women's work and they're welcome to it for I haven't the knack.' Our eyes meet over the fire and I know what he is thinking. He thinks I do have the knack.

With the trestle-board keeping me off the damp ground, I lie between the fire and the cart, protected and tolerably warm, but, unlike last night when both of us were half-asleep over our supper, I am unable shake off wakefulness.

Hob is on first watch against the likes of Edgar and I study him through my eyelashes as I feign sleep.

Eyes on the fire, elbows on his thighs, he's all russet and darkly gold in the firelight. If he feels my gaze on him, he never looks at me.

After a while, he takes his knife from his belt and begins polishing the blade with breath and thumb. I have seen that knife at close quarters, moist with Edgar's failing breath. The blade is long and slim with neither pitting nor rust-marks and looks as sharp as the devil. The handle — made of some pale, grainless wood — is separated from the blade by a metal cross-piece, something I have only seen before on the long daggers the Dene's archers carried home from the war. It was whispered that they went about the battlefields with them, finishing injured Frenchmen and looting their corpses.

When he leaves off polishing it, Hob takes to balancing the knife on the flat of one finger and flipping it into the air to catch it as it falls. It is clearly a favourite game — his finger finds the balancing point every time and his catch is always clean.

I wake to find him slumped on the stool, dozing, and the full moon high in the sky. The clouds have cleared and the whole dark vault of heaven is lit with stars. Hob looks up as I stir, rubs drool from the corner of his mouth and tips his head back in a huge yawn.

'If you're awake, can we change places?' He stands and rubs his arse. 'I can barely hold my eyes open, even squatting on this damned stool.' He reaches down for the blanket which has slipped from his shoulders and makes his way around the fire.

'Aren't you going to see...?' I incline my head towards the back of the cart.

'If he's dead, he's dead. If he's alive, he's alive. Nothing we can do till morning.'

He takes my place on the board beside the fire and wraps himself in his cloak and blanket. I look down at him. He trusts me to keep him safe; with his arms bound tight to his body, he could not hope to free himself and find his feet quickly enough to fend off an attack.

I make up the fire and settle myself on my one-legged collyer's stool, blanket about my shoulders. Sitting there, watching the night while another man sleeps, my mind slips back on itself and, after a little while, I find myself rising to my feet, ready to take a turn about the charcoal pit. As soon as I am on my feet, I come to myself and shake my head at my own forgetfulness, but, loath just to sit down again, I tread softly around to the back of the cart and stand, staring at the canvas. Lying beneath it must be like lying in your own coffin — how will he feel, Edgar, if he wakes to that dense, hard weave above him? As if he has been shroud-wrapped for the grave.

But I do not think he will wake. The blows Hob landed on him — the swing that stopped his murderous stab, the crack to the head that knocked him senseless and that second skull-crunching blow — they were enough to have killed a man outright. I do not believe he can live much longer.

I lift the canvas aside, its folds stiff and cold. He lies still, utterly silent beneath the blankets I have heaped on him. On one side of his face, the skin above his beard is bone-white in the moonlight. On the other, it is dark with crusted blood from his head wound. Leaning on the side of the cart, I reach out to his unblemished side. The flesh is cold, colder than the hazel-weave of the cart's side beneath my other hand.

I unsheathe my knife and hold it beneath his nose. The moonlight is too dim to see clouding but, if he is breathing, I will feel wetness on the blade. I count a dozen heartbeats, then pull the knife away and draw my forefinger along the blade. Dry and cold. I reach over to feel one of his hands. Cold, stiff — I cannot easily move the fingers.

Hob looked under the canvas after we had eaten our supper and said that all was well, yet I have seen enough folk die in this last month to know when death-stiffness begins; Edgar must already have been dead when Hob put that last knife beneath his nose. Why did he lie to me? Was it because he thought I would insist on digging a grave there and then?

I begin to pray. *Pater noster, qui es in coelis, sanctificatur nomen tuum.* Our Father who is in heaven, holy be your name.

Master William taught me the meaning of our prayers even before he taught me to read the words. He taught me that there is no magic in Latin and that a priest must be able to explain to supplicant souls what he is saying on their behalf. I made him go over and over the prayers until my mind knew their meaning as well as my tongue knew their rhythm.

Remit us our debts just as we remit those debts owed to us.
Do not lead us into temptation but free us from evil. Amen.

Temptation. I cannot deny that I am as guilty of that as Edgar. Though I called it vocation when I pleaded with my father to release me from the collyer's life, I know in my heart that what Master William's teaching woke in me was ambition. And what is ambition but a temptation to put our own desires before God's will?

But my father saw neither vocation nor ambition. To him, my desire to be a priest was simply disobedience. Defiance of him. *You shall be a collyer with me, and there's an end to it.*

But it had not been the end. Not by a long way.

I open my eyes to make the sign of the cross over Edgar and, as I lean over, the light of the moon shows up a mark on his nose. I cock my head and peer more closely. Yes, there is a shadow on his nostril. More than a shadow — a stain. A small amount of blood crusts the opening of his nostril.

Did he come to his senses before he died — did he flail about and injure himself? Or have Hob's blows to his head somehow caused this blood to leak from his nose?

I bend my head towards his in the moonlight. Is it moonshadow or is his nose a little bent to one side? I move around to see him more clearly. Yes, his nose is definitely skewed to one side at the tip.

I cast my mind back to the fight. I know that I landed no blows on Edgar's face but, perhaps, when Hob's cudgel felled him, he fell on his nose. Could I have failed to notice an injury until now? I have gazed at his face enough, willingly or unwillingly, as I have moved him, dripped water into his mouth, tested for breath.

No. I would have noticed it. Edgar must have woken, been overtaken with terror as he supposed himself to have been shrouded and dashed himself unknowingly against the press.

I pull the blanket over his face and begin the words of the *Placebo*.

When Hob finds me in the morning, the sun has risen into a watery sky and I am already a yard down.

He juts his chin at the half-dug grave. 'Deep enough, don't you think?'

'No.' I thrust the spade into the pick-loosened soil. 'If we bury him as shallow as this, the vermin'll dig him up and scatter his bones.' I haul myself out and hand him the spade. 'You dig for a while. I've got something else to do.'

I use two decent firewood staves, binding them together with a yard of rope cut from the skein in the cart. The makeshift cross's resemblance to the one I placed at the head of my father's grave makes me uncomfortable but there is only so much that can be done with roundwood. I did, at least, strip the bark from the one that marks my father's resting place and cut clefts in both upright and crosspiece so that they were properly jointed.

I lie the cross on the ground next to the pile of earth and stones. Hob stops and rests his weight on the pick's handle. 'Why're you wasting good firewood on him?'

I survey the deepening grave and avoid his eye. Edgar might have wished me dead but I would not have him damned for all eternity. If I do not mark his grave, how will the angel find him at the Last Judgment?

The mare hitched, I turn to Hob. Though his company has lightened my load these last two days, I will not have him think I have come to depend on him.

'With Edgar gone, we are not bound together anymore. If you want to go back to shunning folk and waiting out the pestilence, I'll take the letter to Sir John at Slievesdon.'

He looks at me, eyes narrowed. He thinks I am trying to get one over on him.

'You can keep the ten shillings,' I tell him. 'I'd have taken the letter anyway.'

He grins. 'You would, wouldn't you? Master's boy!' He swings his cloak around his shoulders. 'No, you're all right, Martin. Let's keep company together for a while and see if we suit. As long as you're not making for any towns.'

'Only as markers along the road,' I tell him, relief settling in me like a warmth, 'not as places to stop.'

'Right then. We're agreed.'

I nod, a grin taking control of my face. I am to be one of a pair again, as I have always been accustomed to. Stranger as Hob is to me, it feels as if life has found its balance once more.

'Well then, are we off, or what?'

'Just a minute.' My fingers suddenly trembling, I untie the front of the canvas and lift out the blanket-wrapped bundle. In the corner of my eye, Hob folds his arms. Then, as he catches sight of the saint, he whistles. 'And you were shitting your braies about *me* taking church goods!'

I stand the little figure at the front of the cart.

'I didn't steal her —'

'No, no! No need to play the innocent with me, I'd've done the same.' He moves to get a better look. 'She's a beauty. But who'll you sell her to? Who'll buy church property?'

'I *didn't* steal her. And I'm not selling her. She's mine.'

'Course she's yours. If you found her in a village where everybody was dead, who's to say she's not?'

'I didn't *find her*! She's mine.'

He stares at me like a man forced, by courtesy, to nod at the tall tale of a traveller. 'You must be richer than you look, then. I've never seen such a beautiful statue of the Virgin.'

'It's not Our Lady.'

'No?'

'When did you ever see Our Lady in white, Hob? When did you ever see her with calfskin boots and a yellow braid on her kirtle?'

Hob shrugs. 'Who is she then?'

I draw in a breath. 'Saint Cynryth. The White Maiden of the Well. She's our family's patron saint.'

'Never heard of her.'

Neither had I, until one day in the Dene. 'I'll tell you the story while we walk.'

'We were in the forest, collyering —' I begin.

'What forest?'

'The King's Dene Forest, to the west of the Severn.'

'Were you there in the winter slack, or is that your trade?'

Hob does not understand my sudden bark of laughter, and why should he? Nobody but me knows how deep that question cuts; how it lies at the root of all the strife between my father and me.

'We started out like most — just coaling three or four pits in the winter to bring in a bit extra but my father took to the craft more than he ever did to husbandry.'

In truth, my father found in himself an affinity for the making of coal. In his ability to judge a cord of wood, to screen just so against the wind and burn an even pit, to bank down different ways for green wood and seasoned, he had no equal and his pits yielded more and better coal than those of any other collyer we knew. By the time I was ten years old he had given up our acres to Young Adam, my eldest brother, and spent the months from October to June back and forth to the forest. Where other landholding collyers bought licences for a week here, a fortnight there in the slack winter months, by the time my father passed the tenancy to my brother, the licences he bought were for forty weeks. By and by, folk in Lysington stopped thinking of him as Adam Hillfield and gave that name to my brother. My father became Adam Collyer and my future was decided.

During the months before the pestilence shrank the future to tomorrow's survival, as I grew to match my father in height, if not yet in strength, he had begun to speak of the two of us working as collyers for the king. My mind brings our argument to life once more as my mouth continues to describe our life to Hob.

Wouldn' have to go down Flaxley, then, to sell the coal, he said. *King's men'd come up here, to us.*

The need to take our coal to market always irked my father. Every time we made the day's round trip to Flaxley with a cart full of coal, it would be the same; as the forest thinned and we neared the valley of the Westbury brook where people came with their carts and barrows to mill and trade, my father would fall silent and I would find my tongue.

Greeting the smiths who bought our charcoal, watching them haggle with my father over the price as they hefted the sacks, listening to the different speechways of merchants passing through to buy iron from the forest — everything was exciting to me.

I looked forward to the trips to Flaxley as much as my father hated them. I craved the greetings, the gossip, the everyday talk of neighbours and regular visitors. I longed to be amongst people, to live cheek-by-jowl with them; my father's notion of becoming a king's collyer, of cutting our ties with the village and living like wild men in the forest, caused my soul to shrink like skin in a cold wind. For, once we put ourselves at the king's command and worked to keep his forges stoked, I knew there would be no letting me go back to Lysington for holy days and festivals. My father had set his face against my ambitions.

Church is rotten and corrupt. No son of mine shall have a part in it.

The more my father had planned and looked forward to a life away from Lysington, the more I hated him. I could not help it; in the innermost, most sinful chambers of my heart, I had wished him and his ambitions to be a king's collyer dead.

And now, dead he was. Dead and lying in red forest earth.

'So there you were in your forest,' Hob is tired of hearing about my father. 'Then what?'

'A peddler wandered on to our hearth.'

Did he wander, half-lost in the hills and valleys of the Dene, or was he guided to us by the saint? She has been so much part of our family lore ever since that it is hard not to think that she had a hand in her own arrival that day.

'I don't know what brought him to us,' I tell Hob, 'but he soon had my father by the ears with his stories and the one that took his fancy most was of Saint Cynryth. The peddler had a little carving of her in his pack —'

Hob nods. 'Course he did. And I'd lay money on her having a different name altogether if your father'd been taken with a different story.'

His words bring me up short. 'No — she was like the saint in the story in every way — speedwell eyes, yellow braid, chestnut-coloured hair —'

Hob's face tells me he thinks the peddler knew his job. But Hob judges everybody by his own standards. He took it for granted that I had stolen the saint from a church, now he will not believe that the peddler did not pass off a nameless image as the true likeness of Saint Cynryth.

On most days of the year, my father would likely have agreed with Hob; he was given to suspicion, saw deceit and self-serving where, often, there was none. But the little white-painted figure that was held up for our inspection seemed to melt something hard and cold in him. Admittedly, she was cleverly made, her features delicately painted, fingers outlined on each tiny hand, but it was not that which held him captive.

'Don't tell me your father bought her,' Hob scoffs.

'No.' He did not buy her, he simply held her in his hands throughout the peddler's telling of her life. 'He carved his own image, later.'

'Not that one?' he jerks his head towards the saint.

I shake my head. 'No. A smaller one. Buried with him.'

As soon as the words are out of my mouth, I regret them but, thankfully, Hob shows no interest in my father's burial. 'What was her name, again? ' he asks. 'Cynryth?'

'Saint Cynryth, yes.'

'She must be a saint from your parts, then, because I've never heard of her.'

I find myself defending the saint in the peddler's own words. 'She was a high-born lady betrayed — daughter of a fond father but a jealous king. Her story is from the time before the coming of King William and his Normans, before the harrying of the Danes — from the time of the Seven Kingdoms.'

He stares at me. 'You know her life?'

Yes, I know her life. I am as well-versed in the tale of Saint Cynryth as any devoted anchorite; I could be catechised on any point of it and be found word-perfect. My father was no teller of tales and, when visitors to house or hut asked who the little saint in the shrine might be, his answer was always the same. 'Ask our Martin. He's got the way of it.'

'Yes,' I tell Hob, 'I know her life.'

'Then tell me.'

I shake my head. 'Another time.'

Why do I find myself so loath to share Saint Cynryth's story? Perhaps because she is no longer simply the object of my father's wayward devotion but has become my own saint now, by her saving of me.

CHAPTER 12

The next day dawns bright and blue and windless. The ground has opened out into hills and hummocks and I am reminded of the Cotswold country where I lost my way. But chaseland or woods, marsh or manor, one thing is common to every yard of ground we cover: neglect. Crops that should have been harvested last autumn are rotting where they stand, the wheat mould-furred with grey in the damp air. Fallow land is tall with thistles. Winter acreage lies unplanted. Anybody who survives the pestilence seems likely to die of famine at this rate and I wonder whether peas and beans will be sown in spring. The ground is chill and unwelcoming as yet but, soon, the air will warm in the longer days and the sod will consent to give way to the plough. Or should do, as long as there are men to lean their weight behind the share and boys to lead the teams.

Halfway through the morning, we come to a stream that stands in our way. In summer, when the water is low, I can see that it would be a simple matter to pick a way across from stone to stone dryshod. Now, though the stream is running clear, it is well up its banks. One of us is going to have to doff his boots and hose and lead the mare through.

'Why can't we just sit in the cart and drive through?' Hob wants to know.

'It's the mare. She's always needed leading through water.'

He stares at me. 'Well I'm not walking through that and freezing my bones.'

I bend down and pluck two stems of seeded grass. 'We'll draw straws.' Nipping one off halfway along its length, I roll them to and fro between my palms so that neither of us can see which is which, then hold my joined hands out to him. 'Pick.'

'No. I'm not doing it.'

'Pick. Knowing you, you have the luck of Old Nick and you'll win anyway.'

He makes me wait a few breaths then draws the short straw. He holds it between us. 'I'm not taking my boots and hose off, I'm telling you.'

'And I'm telling you the mare won't go through without somebody leading her.'

'You're too soft,' he tells me. 'I'll get her through.'

He climbs astride and, as I sit safe in the back of the cart, he starts trying to urge the mare through the water, his heels thudding at her ribs, the reins laid on as a makeshift whip.

I do not turn around but I know the mare, I know what she will be doing. Her front feet planted on the pebbly verge of the ford, she will be leaning her weight back on her hocks. She will not go through, however much Hob belabours her.

'She won't go,' I tell him, finally. 'She's always needed leading through water. You won't persuade her otherwise.'

He does not know it, but his treatment of her has made an implacable enemy of the mare. Now, she will take any opportunity to nip at him, to whip her haunches round and knock him off his feet. She was the same with my father and none of his kicks and cuffs could dissuade her from stretching her neck to him whenever his flesh presented itself.

Hob does not like being bested and he swears and curses as he throws his boots and hose into the cart and stands in his braies. His long, sturdy legs show evidence of the sun and I wonder how often he's worked, stripped to his linen, in the heat of the day. It suggests that he had to turn his hand to the most menial tasks — was he a youngest son, too? Or a landless servant?

'Come on then, you bitch of a mare.' He grabs the reins and tries to drag her into the stream but she tosses her head and pulls the reins back. Hob aims a kick at her belly but, being bootless, is not inclined to kick very hard. 'Come on, damn you!'

Two punches and a kick later, I begin taking my boots off.

'Leave off, Hob. I'll lead her through.'

He takes my place as I strip my hose off and sits there, letting his wet feet dry in the air.

'Only you could have such a contrary animal, Martin.'

'She's not contrary. It's the only thing she won't do.'

'There shouldn't be anything she won't do. If you want her to go through water unled, that's what she should do.'

'Every creature has its limits, Hob. That's hers.'

Dusk is settling when the mare throws a shoe on a stony ford. I can see straight away what has happened, she favours the shoeless foot as she comes out of the water.

I splash back in, stubbing a toe as I go, and retrieve the shoe from the icy water. It is thin and very worn; likely the other three are in the same condition.

'We need a smith.'

Hob scowls at the thought of finding a village but he knows it must be done. If she is not re-shod the mare will be lame before we know it.

The thrown shoe causes her to peck in her stride and it seems a long time before Hob spies a village in the distance.

'We should take the saint down,' he says. 'Before I knew better, I thought you'd stolen her. Others might think the same thing.'

It seems the sensible course and I lie the saint, blanket-wrapped, beneath the canvas. I cannot risk having her taken from me by some suspicious parson.

'And we need to get rid of this too,' I tell him. 'It's Lent.'

His eyes flick down to the hare he shot earlier. 'They'll feed us porridge, like you cook.'

'Yes. Because it's *Lent.*'

'You know what Lent is, don't you? It's a penance dreamed up by priests to make other men as piss-weak at they are. To make sure they've got no lust for women or wrestling.'

His words are like a mirror and I see myself through his eyes — kneeling by the fire each evening, stirring pottage like a girl.

I turn away from him and cluck the mare into a dispirited onward limp.

At a meeting of tracks between the village's fields, a fellow with an ox-cart hails us. It is clear, from the approaching smell and the remains in his cart, that he has been carting cow shit to spread on his land.

'God be with you, friend,' I call when we're still a dozen paces away.

He responds in kind, then asks the question that has become a second form of greeting, now, in England. 'Are you sick?'

'No. We're well. And we've seen nobody sick for days. Your village?'

'Pestilence has taken a good number of us. But it's three weeks since the last died. Everyone who's left is healthy enough.'

I hear Hob release a held breath.

The village we are led into — 'This here's Tredgham, under the lordship of Sir Henry Falk' — is bigger by far than Lysington and organised in a very different way. Where

Lysington's tofts are placed higgledy-piggledy, with paths winding between them, Tredgham is laid out almost like a market town, with houses presenting their fronts to the cart-tracks that run, each at right angles, through the midst of them.

Our guide nods along one of these tracks. 'Along there's Appledore. If our smith won't oblige, you could try there.'

I nod and look along the track towards Appledore. A woodland loud with rooks lies between this village and that. I look for smoke but, if there are collyers within, there is no sign of them.

'Better fetch the Reeve before you go near the forge, let him have sight of you.'

Tredgham's Reeve — Geoffrey Levett — is a brisk man of about my father's age. He greets our arrival, and our errand, with a swift regret.

'Our forge is cold until we can find collyers to feed it. And Appledore's too. The pestilence took all our coaling men and there's not a lump of coal to be had in the village.'

Hob speaks up before I can utter a word.

'Your luck's turned, then!' He puts an arm about my shoulders. 'My friend here is Martin Collyer — he's been charring coal since he learned to walk!'

Hob and Geoffrey Levett quickly reach an agreement. There is cordwood already stacked at the hearth in the wood, so I will burn a pit with the help of men he will choose to be the village's new collyers. Then, once the first pit is successfully quenched and broken open, I am to watch my apprentices build theirs and stay with them through the week it will take to char and harvest. In return, we'll be fed and re-provisioned for our journey and the mare will be given four new shoes.

I know I should protest that two weeks is too long, that I can only remain here as long as it takes to burn one pit of coal. I need not confess my fears for my father's soul, I could simply say that we are honour-bound to deliver a letter to Slievesdon.

But I say nothing. I tell myself that a fortnight's rest will be good for the mare. That, with things as they are, we cannot be sure of finding a smith elsewhere before she goes lame. I tell myself that my agreement with Geoffrey Levett is sound sense and has nothing to do with the comfort of being amongst my fellow-men once more, of sleeping without fear of attack, of eating fresh bread and drinking ale.

But unease sits on my shoulder, still, and I fear what our time in Tredgham may bring.

CHAPTER 13

Although being hearthmaster to a pair of apprentices is a novelty for me at first, I soon discover that the men I have been given to teach are neither apt nor avid to learn. Collyering demands care above all things and men whose heart is not on the hearth will never make good coal. Their neglect will lead to the fire consuming the wood instead of charring it and the result will be not fuel but ash.

The pair chosen by Levett are not careful. Of course, they are diligent enough at the outset, with the reeve at hand; they arrive with their stools and their bread and their ale and they show every indication of paying close attention. But, as soon as the reeve's eye is no longer on them, their unwillingness becomes clear, along with their perfect ignorance of the craft.

'Why does the door of the hut face away from the pit when that's where we'll be working?'

'Because that's where all the smoke will come from. If the door faced towards the hearth the hut'd be full of smoke all the time.'

'What's that stack of willow-hurdles there for?'

'To screen the pit from the wind — it makes it burn lopsided if there's a steady wind coming from one direction.'

'Why do we need so many barrels of water?'

'Because when the fire's done its work, then water's poured in to stop the charring.'

'Doesn't it make the coal wet and hard to burn?'

'No, the water turns to steam — you'll see when we break the pit open, the coal will be as dry as dust.'

I give them simple instructions for building the stack's central chimney. They start well but then, instead of stopping when they've reached a sensible height to begin the bulking of the pit, they build and build as high as they can reach.

I show them how to place the staves around the chimney, thickest first; they nod as if they understand but then proceed to use only ells three inches in the round, leaving gaps I could put my hand in.

They pay no attention to what I have said about the slope of the stack, and soon the staves are falling outwards and all is chaos.

Hob pipes up which surprises me; until now, he has been as silent as the so-called apprentices. 'Tom, Will — this is thirsty work!' Trust him to know their names already.

The Tredgham men shuffle and drop their shoulders and nod. 'Aye, Hob, it is.'

Hob. Despite the fact that I am set over them, they have been calling me 'lad' all morning.

We break to drink some ale and I watch Hob's camaraderie with the two apprentices. I may have been put in charge, I may be the only one on the hearth who knows what he is doing, but it is Hob these men will heed, that much is clear.

By the afternoon of the second day, Hob thinks himself a master of the craft.

'This collyering,' he says, 'it's the easiest work I've ever done! Once the pit's built, all you have to do is watch, poke holes, seal them up, and watch some more!'

I throw some riddled earth on to a patch where the bracken thatch has shifted, making the covering dangerously thin. 'Yes, and what is growing corn, once the seed is sown, but months of watching it sprout and grow tall and ripen?'

But, easy though he claims to find the work, Hob has not taken to pit-watching, cannot master the attention needed. Once we run out of needful tasks around the hearth — mending the hut, repairing the hurdles, fetching quenching-water - he becomes bored and restless.

'Let's wrestle,' he suggests. 'Will, Tom — you'll wrestle won't you?'

Tom — the quieter of the two apprentices — whistles through his teeth. 'You might find you've bitten off more than you can chew, there, Hob. Will's a champion in Tredgham. There's nobody can beat him.'

'Is that so?'

Will folds his arms across his chest with a self-satisfied smile.

'Well,' Hob apes his stance, 'I'm not afraid to wrestle with the best. What about you, Martin?'

'I'm hearthmaster, I can't be playing games.'

I know Hob will be the better wrestler. I know it before he and Will strip to their hose. I know it in the same way I know girls will always make sure Hob notices them before they give the eye to any other man.

At first, their bouts are entertaining and there are no underhand moves that would get a crowd hissing or cat-calling. When Will and Tom's womenfolk arrive with food and more ale they are persuaded to watch.

'You'll have to teach Will how to do that, Hob,' his sister, Maud, calls when Hob throws Will neatly on to his back. 'He thought he knew every wrestling throw there was — didn't you Will?'

From the look her brother gives her, I hope she has a husband or a father at home to defend her from his vengeful fists when he leaves the hearth.

While Tom is as good-humoured as ever when he is thrown and pinned, Will is clearly determined to best Hob. He soon abandons fair play and hooks fingers at Hob's eyes, aims punches at his throat. Despite the fact that this last trick could kill him, Hob seems unconcerned; he sidesteps and ducks, grapples and bests, clearly used to fighting men with more lust to win than skill to do it.

In the end, though, he tires of Will's cheap tricks.

'Enough,' he says when the Tredgham champion squares up and declares himself ready for another bout. 'We've fought ourselves out.'

'One last bout,' Will insists. 'And this time, right to the end. No stays, no waiting for the other to get up. The bout ends when one of us admits the other is the better man.'

That kind of contest bears more resemblance to a fight to the death than a bout of wrestling. Hob could end up with broken bones or a blind eye; our stay in Tredgham is already set to delay us by a fortnight without any further hindrances.

'Leave it, Will,' I say.

But Will ignores me utterly. His eyes are fastened on Hob. 'You don't want your pretty face marked,' he scoffs. 'I saw you talking to my sister. You're afraid she won't look at you twice when I've finished with you.'

'For pity's sake, Will,' Tom is losing patience, 'sit down and stop being a fool. Accept it — Hob has bested both of us.'

'That's because he hasn't seen what I can do when I'm not being polite to a guest.' Will waits, but Hob does not stir. 'So you're a coward, Hob Cleve?'

I turn around to see Hob rising from the cordwood stack. 'You'd better ask my pardon for saying that.'

'No! It's true. You won't fight me because you've seen that, in a free fight, man to man, I'll beat you. If you still say you won't fight me, I'll say it again. You — are — a — coward.'

Seeing as he has taunted him into it, Will is ready for Hob's rush and they meet head-on, weight thrown forward, in a grappling clinch. Hob throws Will but is kicked as he tries to make good on the fall and Will springs up to rush at Hob again.

He begins throwing punches like a man possessed by a fit of rage. Or of stupidity. Hob ducks and dodges and Will's fists mostly swing through empty air, but he lands one or two heavy blows that cause Hob to shake his head.

Wriggling free of a leg-hold, Will loses a boot. In a friendly bout, Hob would laugh and catch his breath while his opponent put it on again. Now, he charges forward at Will's uneven stance and knocks him off balance. But, going down, Will's booted foot catches Hob on the kneecap and fells him, buying him time to get his boot back on.

Punch for punch, kick for kick; their throws become heavier, their holds on each other accompanied by vicious grunts as they grip tighter and tighter. Both are breathing hard, neither looking anywhere but at the other. Good humour has gone. Now the aim is to hurt. To fell.

Will — one eye blacked now and an ear swelling from a headlock — breaks from a taut circling to charge at Hob. As his shoulder hits Hob's chest, his hand drops to grab Hob's balls but Hob brings up a swift knee to prevent him. Feeling his opponent off-balance, Will pulls Hob's other leg from under him and tries to get a knee in his stomach to make him yield but Hob rolls, taking Will with him and ending up on top, lying over Will's head and chest.

Will bucks to try and dislodge Hob. Once, twice, three times. But Hob lies fast across him. Again he bucks, this time Hob gets his arms under Will's head and clasps him to his chest. Will wriggles in a frenzy, trying to throw him off. Now, there is a desperation to his movements that I do not like.

'Hob!' I yell. 'What are you doing?'

'Do you yield?' Hob shouts.

More bucking from Will.

'If you yield stamp one foot!'

For the space of four or five heartbeats nothing happens, then one of Will's feet jerks. At the same time, a wet stain spreads over the front of his hose; in his fear he's pissing himself.

'Do you yield?' Hob roars.

This time there is no response. Will has gone still.

I dart forward and grab one of Hob's legs. Tom, catching my intention, takes hold of the other and we pull Hob away from Will, upending him and separating them. As Hob is forced to release his grip, I see Will's face — his eyes wide and staring, his mouth wide open in a fruitless attempt to draw breath while pinned to the muscles of Hob's belly.

We dump Hob and turn to Will.

He is not moving. Before I can do anything, Tom is at his side.

'Will!' He grabs him by the shoulders and shakes him. 'Will! *Will!*

I kneel down next to him as he shakes and shakes. Will's head lolls like a broken-necked rabbit's. As I stare at his senseless face, I see that his nose is lined with white wrinkles where it was flattened against Hob and his lips are a faint blue.

Abruptly, a rattling sound comes from Will's throat. He gives a strange kind of cough and Tom quickly pushes him onto his side as he begins to spew up the contents of his stomach.

I watch as he lies there, spewing and gasping and retching, his beard thick with vomit.

Unwilling to watch, now I know that he will live, I turn away, only to see Hob gazing at Will, his face without expression.

CHAPTER 14

Will went back to the village yesterday without a word to me or Hob and, this morning, his cousin Stephen came out to the woods to take his place. Since Stephen has made no mention of the wrestling bout and shows neither fear of Hob nor particular deference to him, it seems reasonable to suppose that Will has made some excuse for leaving the hearth.

Tom has not spoken about what happened. Is he turning it over and over in his mind as I am? Is he asking himself what would have happened if he and I had not pulled Hob off?

Will's face haunts me. The blueness of his lips, the whiteness around his nose, the wrinkle-lines where his nose had been turned back on itself as Hob gripped his head.

Those wrinkle-lines bother me. They remind me of how Edgar's nose was bent to one side.

Though Will may have said nothing about his wrestling bout with Hob, it soon becomes clear that he has been talkative on other subjects. Subjects he should know nothing about. After explaining to Stephen the bare bones of what we are about on the hearth, I ask him if there is anything he wants to know.

'Yes.' He thrusts his chin in the direction of the hut. 'Is it true you've got a saint hidden in there?'

I glance at across the hearth. Whatever Will has told his family can only have come from Hob — I put them on night-watches together.

Hob comes over.

'You're a bit previous there, friend,' he tells Stephen. 'Get to know the hearth and its ways first and then maybe Martin will tell you about the saint tonight when we're all sitting by the fire.'

'I won't have time for tales — I need to be looking to the pit. One mistake now and everything could be ruined.'

But Hob is not to be fobbed off. 'I can take my turn. You said yourself that night-time is better for seeing holes and slips.'

'Yes, but judgement goes with the light. It takes an experienced man to keep his head and do the right thing in the dark.'

'But you'll be there, Martin. I can call on you the moment anything happens if I need to.'

Stephen takes Hob's advice and, all day, he is as busy about the hearth as I could wish. And he asks sensible questions. I wonder why Geoffrey Levett did not send him in the first place instead of his braggart cousin. Perhaps he owed Will a favour.

But Stephen's doggedness at the tasks I give him makes me increasingly uneasy as the day goes on, for I know that behind all his keenness is a desire to shame me into satisfying his curiosity about the saint.

If I could simply tell the story of her life, all would be well. But that would be to deny her miracle — the one she wrought in healing me of the pestilence. And, if I tell that story, the questions will come. If not from Hob, then from Stephen and Tom. *So where does the statue come from? If you put the one your father made in his grave, where does this one come from?*

I may guess at a commission from a Gloucester carver but I do not know it for sure. What if the appearance of the White Maiden's image at our well is another miracle and not a work of man? Without certain knowledge I must not presume to explain away her very existence, nor yet her sudden reappearance in the press when I was lost and despairing. For no Gloucester image-maker put her there, did he?

Agonised, I weigh and weigh again which explanation might make me more guilty of the sin of pride and vain-glory — claiming a mortal origin for the saint's image or a miraculous one? The decision is no trivial one for I must not offend Saint Cynryth. Both my safety on the road to Salster and the safety of my father's eternal soul are in her hands.

That evening, I can barely swallow the food put before me and I decide that the best course is simply to tell the story of Saint Cynryth's life and let the saint guide my words thereafter.

'Cynryth was the daughter of Halstan,' I begin, 'a king of the south.'

My heart slows its galloping as I take up the familiar words and I could swear I feel the saint smiling at me. She is with me, guarding me, guiding me.

'Born with flame-red hair and eyes the colour of speedwells, Cynryth grew from summer child to tall and fearless maiden. Her voice was as pure and clear as a blackbird's song and her heart was full of courage.'

How well I know this tale; how easily and sweetly my tongue settles to its rhythms. For the first time since the pestilence came, I feel that perhaps not everything from my old life is lost.

'Cynryth was as wilful as she was beautiful and, growing up without a mother, she coveted the freedom her brothers enjoyed. She was her father's darling and, because it made her happy, he let her ride and hunt, carry a sword and shoot with a bow. "She will be married soon enough," he told himself, "and that will end her wild ways".'

They have settled now, as I have, and they relax into my sureness with the tale.

'One midsummer's day, when Cynryth was out hunting in the greenwood with her brothers and the young men of the household, they came upon a strange youth. He wore outlandish dress of shimmering silver, his hair was as white as the moon and his eyes were the colour of dawn. The silken mane of his silver horse cloaked him as it galloped and its hooves were as big as bucklers.

'At first, Cynryth and her friends could not understand the stranger's speech but, as he continued speaking, it seemed to them that his words fell more easily on their ears and they began to understand that he had been falsely accused of killing a man and sent into exile.

'"And now," he said, "I wander the land looking for a new king to swear fealty to."

'Cynryth, knowing that her father could refuse her nothing, said, "Ride home with us, and speak with my father who is king of this country."

'So they returned to Halstan's court and the king welcomed the stranger as courtesy bade him. But, from their first meeting, he mistrusted the youth's strange ways. The young man would tell nobody his name, shrugging his shoulders like one who could not understand human speech. Even when several weeks had passed, when people asked him his name, he said simply, "I am the Exile."

'Despite her father's mistrust, Cynryth fell ever more under the young man's spell. They would spend whole days together, hunting, making music and playing at merrills and, while they kept company, Cynryth tried in every way she could to trick the young man into telling her his name.

'And every time she did so, he would smile and say, "No, no, my lady, you don't trick *me* so easily."

'Eventually, when she had wept and raged and threatened to see him no more, the Exile told Cynryth that, if he was to stay at her father's court, she must do two things. Firstly, she must agree to marry him and, secondly, she must promise never again to ask him his name.

'"For in my country," he said, "a name has great power and, if I give you mine, that power will be gone and I will no longer be able to stay here."

'Afraid that he would leave if she did not agree, Cynryth said that she would marry him if her father would give his consent. Accordingly, she went to Halstan and begged to be allowed to marry the white-haired Exile.

'But the king was full of fury when he realised that his daughter had given her heart to this stranger. "Disobedient girl," he thundered, "you must marry a man of my choosing, a man with vassals to command who can keep us safe against our enemies! If you marry this foreigner, this stranger with no name and no allegiances, our allies will be insulted and our people imperilled!"

'Then, knowing his daughter's wilfulness, Halstan put the matter beyond doubt. He called the young man to him and told him that he must leave at once. "If you are still under my roof when day breaks," the king told him, "your life will be forfeit."

'Guards marched the Exile to the guest chamber and stood outside as he went in to gather his few possessions. But, after a short while, all sounds from the chamber ceased. The guards looked at each other in alarm. One called out, "What are you doing?" and, when there was no reply, they pushed the door open, their swords already drawn.

'The chamber was empty.

'The guards rushed to Halstan's hall but, as they approached the door, the king's priest ran past them, burst through the door, and threw himself before his lord. "Lord Halstan — while I was in my bed, dreaming, an angel appeared to me in a vision. He revealed to me that the stranger who calls himself the Exile is not a mortal man but a fairy! Your daughter is in deadly danger," the priest panted. "For if she goes with him willingly, her soul will be his to command."

'Halstan made all haste to Cynryth's chamber. "Daughter!" he bellowed at the barred door, "Open for the sake of your eternal soul!"

'When nothing but silence came from beyond the door, the king ordered his guards to break it down. With great blows of their axes, the door splintered in time for them to see the Exile's hand reaching through the window to pull Cynryth after him. In three strides the king was at the window, his sword in his fist. Without a word or a look to his daughter he raised his blade and hacked off the Exile's arm. Blood poured out, blood as black as night, and a sound came from the mouth of the fairy, a sound that no human mouth has ever uttered. As the king and his daughter watched in horror, the young man with moon-white hair and eyes the colour of dawn vanished and there stood before them a figure who shone like starlight, wrapped in spun cloud. With a hiss, the figure jumped into the air, uttered a last cry and was gone.'

I look around. They are silent, waiting. They know this is not the end, that Cynryth has simply been delivered from the first of the evils that will threaten her. I take a swallow of ale and continue.

'Cynryth withdrew to her chamber for forty days and forty nights. She ate only bread and drank only water which her servant carried from a well in the woods nearby.

'Then, when the forty days were done, she went to the king.

'"Father," she told him, "God has been gracious to me. For he granted a vision to your chaplain that saved me from a most unholy fate. But it has been revealed to me, during the days of my fast, that I have been saved for a greater cause than marriage."

'At this, Cynryth flung herself on the floor before her father and begged his permission to withdraw from his court to the woods; she would live next to the well which had provided her fasting-water and she would devote herself to God.

'Halstan, believing that she would tire of such a lonely life after a month or two, agreed and ordered that a little dwelling be built there for his daughter's comfort and protection.

'When the day came and her sanctuary was ready, Cynryth said goodbye to her servants and her friends, her brothers and her father. Then, dressed in a simple kirtle and cloak, she went to take up her new life.

'As the months went by and people brought food and other offerings to her in return for her prayers, they began to see their prayers answered. Babies were born to the barren and sick children made well. Wounds did not fester and those on pilgrimage came safely home. By and by, her fame spread and there was talk, far beyond her own realm, of the king's daughter who had given up her royal life for prayer and the common people's good.

'And so, though Cynryth's life was one of holiness and not of disobedient marriage, still, that which Halstan had feared came to pass. A prince, who had thought to ally himself to Halstan by marrying Cynryth and raising sons who would unite their two kingdoms, heard of her life in the woods and was enraged that the whim of a spoiled girl should thwart his ambitions.

'This prince — Aethenoth by name — rode to Halstan's court with his most trusted nobles and demanded the right to marry the king's daughter.

'Halstan, thinking that he had been understanding enough, agreed with Aethenoth that it was time Cynryth returned to court, so he sent his sons, Cynryth's brothers, into the woods to bring her back.

'But Cynryth would not come. She told her brothers that she would rather throw herself in the well and drown than break the vows she had made. She told them that God's curse would be on any man who tried to force her to give up her celibate life. And, sick at heart for their sister, they went back to Halstan with her answer.

'When Aethenoth heard of her refusal to marry him he was enraged, for the story of Cynryth and the fairy Exile who had stolen her heart had reached his ears.

'"Your daughter insults me!" he shouted at Halstan. "She would willingly have married a man without family or name, without land or honour, but she will not marry me!"

'And he determined to ride to the woods himself to marry Cynryth by force.

'But, as Aethenoth was riding hard from her father's court, an angel came to Cynryth and warned her of the prince's plan. Calmly, she put off her clothes, dressed herself in a clean white shift and knelt on the floor beside her virgin's bed to confess her sins and to pray for courage.

'When she heard the battering hooves of Aethenoth's horse Cynryth opened the door and stepped outside. Quickly, before

Aethenoth could reach her, she ran and climbed up on to the well.

'Aethenoth rode into the clearing and saw her there. She was pure and beautiful in her white shift, with her hair unbound and her feet bare.

'"I will not marry you or any man," Cynryth told him, her voice steady. "And if you try to take me I will throw myself in this well. It is deep and dark and I will drown before you can pull me out."

'Aethenoth smiled. He dismounted and walked towards her. "You will not, lady. For you are but a woman, and weak. Better to be married to me — to bear my sons and rule with me — than to cast yourself down into hell in mortal sin."

'"It is no mortal sin," Cynryth told him, "for I am pledged to God and have vowed to marry no man, being married to Christ."

'"And I say that you shall be married to me!"

'Aethenoth lunged towards her and would have caught her hand but Cynryth's angel turned him aside as she slipped over the side of the well and down, down into the cold, dark water.

'And Aethenoth — cursed for his evil deed — ran mad in the woods and threw himself to his death from a high rock.

'When the prince did not return to Halstan's court, Cynryth's brothers went to the woods and, finding their sister's little dwelling empty, knew that she had been true to her word.

'With great sadness, they brought up her body — as white and as pure as if she had lain down to sleep — and bore her back to their father's court to be buried.

'Hearing of her martyr's death, the people brought flowers and offerings and laid them around her well. And they mourned her greatly.

'Soon, miracles were granted to those who prayed at the well where she had been martyred; the dead were raised, crops grew in drought, herds dying of the murrain were healed.

'And then, one day — many years after her death, when Cynryth's name no longer came quick to people's minds and tongues — a barren mother had a vision at the well. She saw a maiden, all in white, carrying a new-born child. And, that very night, the woman conceived a son.'

The fire has burned low by now and I lean forward to put more wood on to the bed of embers.

'And ever thereafter,' I tell them, 'Saint Cynryth was known as the White Maiden and her well as the White Maiden's Well. It lies in woods on a hill outside the city of Salster and there are miracles done there to this very day.'

'Is that where you're going?' Stephen asks. 'Salster?'

I hesitate, flick a glance at Hob whose eyes are fixed on the fire. 'Yes.'

And, in the discussion of routes and likely dangers that follows, the saint, wrapped in blankets in the hut, is forgotten.

CHAPTER 15

Thus far, though I know that Tredgham's parson survived the pestilence's coming, I have not sought him out. But thoughts of my father's unhallowed grave in the forest plagued me all through my watch with Stephen and I barely slept thereafter. I must go and find the priest today, ask him to say a mass for my father's unshriven soul. I need not mention the saint, nor my father's stubborn faith in her which took us both to the forest, away from the protection of the church.

'Go now!' Hob says when I raise the subject. 'The three of us can oversee the pit for an hour. There's no wind, so the pit should burn quietly.'

He is echoing my own words so I can hardly find fault with his encouragement but, still, I hesitate, my eyes on the steady streams of smoke coming from the vent-holes. Can I leave Hob in charge? What if something happens while I am gone and the pit collapses? All our work will be wasted and we will be forced to start again.

I glance in the direction of the hut. I have not left the saint in Hob's hands before. What if she disappears? After all, it would not be the first time. And perhaps, this time, she might not come back.

'Go on, Martin! For a man crossing England in defence of his father's soul you're chary of walking half a mile to church.'

I look about me. All is as it should be. There is nothing for it but to go.

I do not know what makes me look back at the wood as I approach the church over the glebelands, but, even as I turn, I hear the startled crake of a pheasant beating frantically at the air to escape the men who have frightened it.

Tom and Stephen, walking towards the village. Has Hob given them leave to go? Or has he sent them away? They would not have left without his encouragement, I know that. But, freed from the hearth, they are keen to get to the village, that much is clear.

Why has Hob let both of them go? How many times have I told him that collyers should always be two together? He should have let one of the men go back to the village while the other stayed with him.

Perhaps he has sent them to the barn, to see what the cart holds.

I try to close my ears to the demon's words but he knows my fears and picks at them.

Or perhaps he already knows, perhaps he lifted the canvas, in the wood before Cricklade, while Edgar was still prowling for your life.

A sudden alarm chills me. The thought of my father's money-bag, sitting beneath the clothes in our press, has nagged at me ever since we left the cart in the reeve's barn. I should have brought it with me. It contains all the money I have in the world. And the letters. The letters we are to deliver at Slievesdon — what if somebody takes it into his head to steal them?

I turn. The church is a furlong away, at most. I look for Tom and Stephen, on the path towards the village. Though they are a good way off, it seems to me that they are still hurrying. Did Hob tell them to go quickly, be back before me?

A blackbird swoops past, its warning call trailing behind. I turn but can see nobody coming after me.

You have to find the parson and ask him to say a mass. For your father's sake.

My angel's words turn me towards the church again and I stumble on. At the edge of the churchyard, I follow the wall around to the lych gate. With a last look in the direction of the wood, I cross myself and pass through. The gate is recently built, its thatch new and yellow. A wide slab for the body stands on one side and a narrower perch where the bearers can rest on the other. It speaks of a parson who cares for his people and a lord who's dutiful in his dealings with them.

Beyond the gate stand scores of earth mounds, raw against the winter grass, the absence of a single weed-shoot proving their newness. I walk between them to the south door and, lifting the heavy latch, enter the church. The smell of old incense and snuffed candles is so familiar that, for a moment, I am back in Lysington. My hand rises to cross myself, my knee bends before the font and my fingers touch its rim of their own accord.

'Is anyone here?' I am ready to explain myself, the words waiting on my lips. Does the parson know about the saint? Has the whole village heard of her from Will?

Again I call out. My voice rings in the dimness but no answer comes.

I walk in to the body of the nave. Despite the familiar smells, this church is quite different from the Church of Our Lady. Where the panels that separated chancel from nave in Lysington's church rose only to chest-height, here, the rood screen stands higher than a man. And, where ours was of wood, with a curtain above which was drawn back during the mass, here the screen is of stone, carved into window-like tracery. I wonder what it must be like, peering through this lattice of stone to see the parson raising the host, instead of having him in full view.

Hoc est corpus meum. This is my body.

The words of the holy mass; the words I longed to speak, myself, from the first time I put on the white robe as a boy of eight, trailing Master William to the altar where the host and the blood stood in shining silver.

Hoc est corpus meum.

The words of eternal life.

Before the pestilence, hearing those words sent a thrill through me, and the prospect — however dim — of standing in the sanctuary one day, facing east, saying the mass before my people, was what drove me to study, to hope, to defy my father.

But everything has changed, now. The church has failed us. Not prayers nor processions nor masses nor observances have stayed the march of the pestilence one inch. Worse, the church has overseen unholy burials — excused and sanctioned them — and crossed itself whilst doing so. And the miracle that saved me from death came not from a stone-canopied saint but from a girl who chose to make her home in the woods. Like my father.

As I turn away from the rood screen, I realise that I have never been alone in a church before. In Lysington, William was always with us. He never sent us boys on ahead to make preparations while he idled elsewhere; always, if we were in the chancel, he would be there too, explaining, guiding, admonishing, encouraging.

Parson's pups: that's what the people of Lysington called us, William's assistants. But I outgrew puppyhood in his service, walking tall behind him while the raggle-taggle of little white-robed boys scurried after the two of us, casting their eyes aside at the cat-calls and jeers that the manor's youths threw at me.

I have not passed beyond the rood screen with candle and cross since Candlemas. Since my family were taken. All the time my father kept us in the Dene, I tallied each service missed and held their loss against him but, since leaving Lysington, I have not ventured near a church.

I should not have come. I should not have left the saint. There is nothing for me, here.

I throw the door open, crossing myself as I pass over the threshold and duck through the lychgate at a trot. Though it seemed no great distance when I was walking over, now, the grazing common that separates me from the hearth seems to have grown so wide that I will never cross it, never reach the wood. I run and run, head down, eyes on the treacherous ground.

As I come within a bow's shot of the wood, a sharp cry of displeasure jerks my head back up. Black and white. Wings, feathers, beak, claws. A single magpie, coming for me. I feel myself falling, my hands going up to protect my face. As I fall, the bird seems to rear back, its wings chopping at the air, its tail-feathers splaying like rigid fingers stretching for the ground.

Devil's bird, it lands on both feet despite its tussle with the air. It watches as I scramble up, tips its head to one side then hops back to whatever my stumbling run chased it from. It tears and comes away with a full beak. A scrap of bloody fur and bone.

Without thinking, I run at it, clapping and shouting, waving my arms, wanting to drive it off, to banish the threat of sorrow. The magpie throws itself into the air and half a dozen powerful wing-beats see it up and away.

I kick at the pathetic scraps it has left behind, sending shards of flesh-tattered bone in one direction, a bloody strip of fur and sinew in the other.

'Martin!'

I look up. Hob is coming towards me from the edge of the wood.

'Martin!' He closes the distance between us and takes me by the shoulders. 'What's happened? I heard you shouting —'

I shake him off, break into a lumbering run, wanting to get back to the saint.

'Martin?'

'Where are the others?' I do not stop, do not turn my head.

He catches up with me, seizes an arm to turn me. 'What's happened?'

'Why did you send them away?'

He lets go of my arm. 'I didn't send them anywhere! They wanted to go into the village. We were all sitting idle so I let them go.' He stops. I can feel his eyes on me. 'Why did you think I would send them away?'

I turn and start running through the trees, not looking back despite Hob's shouts.

Back on the hearth, I fling aside the covering that hangs at the hut's door. The saint is not there. I left her standing against the wall behind one of the pallet-beds, the blanket wrapped around her shoulders, her head free. And now she is gone.

My heart begins a panicked gallop. *Why did I leave her?*

I spin around to find Hob watching me, his breath coming as quickly as mine.

'Where is she? The saint?'

Wordlessly, he turns and points. A blanket-wrapped bundle is leaning against the cordwood stacked for the next pit.

My hands shaking, I go to her. I kneel, unwrap the blanket. Unmarked and unharmed, the saint gazes at me, her outstretched hand reaching towards me. The linseed-and-summer-hay smell of her calms me.

'Why did you bring her out here?'

Hob squats on his haunches in front of me. Next to the delicate features of the saint his face seems coarse and high-coloured. 'Tom and Stephen wanted to see her. It's too dark in the hut to see properly.'

'She's my saint. You had no right showing her to them.'

'There's no harm in it! Will had already seen her — he sneaked into the hut one morning when you'd gone for a piss — and he'd told Stephen.'

'That's still no reason to bring her out so they can gawp at her.'

Hob shakes his head. 'It wasn't like that. There's something you're not telling them and they want to know.'

'Know what?'

'Well, for a start, why you're hiding the saint away in the dark. Shouldn't she be where everybody can see her?'

'That's for me to decide. She's my saint.'

My father was right. This is what he feared would happen if he told the story of the saint's coming to him. *Folks'd come traipsing through the woods wanting to see her. They'd come pawing at her and touching her. I won't have it.*

'The point is, she's the work of a master.'

'So?'

'So how exactly d'you come to have such a thing?'

I look at him. He came running when he heard me shouting at the magpie. While I was stumbling back to the hearth full of suspicion, convinced that he wanted to rob me, that he might do harm to the saint, Hob was minding the pit and looking out for me. Whatever his actions against Will, against Edgar, he has offered me nothing but friendship.

I lower myself on to the nearest stool. 'If truth be told, Hob, I'm not sure. I thought I knew but…'

Hob pulls the other stool up and sits nearby. 'But what?'

'I found her after my father died.' I swallow. 'I thought my father must've commissioned her, that she'd arrived while I was sick. But— but then she disappeared again.' Hob stares at me, waiting. 'And she came back to me,' I mumble, 'when I was on my journey. When I needed her.'

'A miracle?'

I look away from him. Am I really going to tell him this? For, once he knows, everyone will know.

'A second miracle, perhaps.'

'What do you mean?'

I turn my eyes to the saint, offer her a quick and silent prayer. *Lady, protect me.* 'I told you I survived the pestilence — that I was sick but didn't die?'

He nods. I can see he is still reserving judgement as far as my healing is concerned.

'While I was sick — after our parson had anointed me, given me the rites — my father put me in the cart and took me from our village to our hearth in the forest.'

'To your charcoal hearth?'

'Yes.'

'Why?'

'Because that's where the saint's shrine was. That's where she first appeared to my father.'

'Appeared?'

'In a vision. He had a vision of the saint a week or two after the peddler came and told us her story.'

Hob nods, slowly.

'The vision of her made the hearth holy to him.' I swallow. 'So he took me there. Placed me under the saint's protection.'

'And then what?'

'I woke up, in our hut. And he was lying there. Dead.'

'He was dead when you woke up?'

'Yes. He must have known he was dying.' I hesitate, not sure how much to tell him. 'When I woke up,' I watch Hob's face, 'he'd sewn himself into his shroud.'

He frowns. 'Sewn himself into it? What d'you mean?'

I remember the old woman's kin lying, shrouded and band-wrapped. Not everybody sews up their dead.

'In the Dene we lie our dead on their shroud, gather it in the middle and sew it from toes to crown.'

'So you lay there, asleep, while he sewed himself into his shroud and moaned and cried out and died?'

I hear Richard's suspicion again. *Just upped and died, did he?*

'I don't think there was much moaning.'

'How so?' There it is again. Hob likes this unexplained death as little as my brother did.

My father's still, composed face appears in my eye. 'When I woke, there was blood on my tunic where I'd coughed and coughed. His shroud didn't have a drop of blood on it. Nor his clothes either.' I see again that sad, neat little pile of garments that I found on the stool at the foot of his bed.

'So. How did he die? Quickly and quietly doesn't sound like the pestilence.'

'I think —'

'What?'

I glance over my shoulder at the figure of the saint. 'I think my father struck a bargain with the saint. My life for his. All the prayers he'd made to her should have saved him. Instead, he spent them on me. And Saint Cynryth healed me.'

CHAPTER 16

Our apprentices have brought out the village. Or what the pestilence has left of it.

'Well met friends!' Hob's call makes me jump.

The reeve, Geoffrey Levett, strides forward. 'Well met, indeed, Hob Cleve! I hear you have a saint on the hearth?' His eyes are on Hob, not me. Hob does not turn a hair.

'Yes. Martin's patron saint. And not just a saint but a miracle-worker too.'

'And what miracles has she done?'

This question comes from a small, slight man in modest, clerkly garb. He steps forward as he speaks and Geoffrey Levett turns to him.

'This is our parson, Thomas Hassell.'

We bow to each other but, before I can answer him, Hob is speaking.

'She healed Martin of the pestilence.'

Thomas Hassell looks troubled, as if he might have preferred less miraculous news. 'May I see her?'

Hob turns to Tom. 'She's over there —'

'No!' All heads turn to me. 'I'll do it.'

I cross to the blanket-wrapped saint and take her in my arms. As I unwrap the covering I say a silent prayer. *This is not my doing, lady, do not hold it against me or against my father…*

Then, turning around, I hold the saint up so that her reaching hand stretches out to the parson and his people. There is a collective intake of breath and hands rise in the sign of the cross.

Thomas Hassell steps forward, eyes on the saint. 'May I?' he says again, glancing at me.

I lower the White Maiden's figure so that the length of her is cradled against me and watch him as he stares at her. The expression on his deep-lined face is as unreadable as it is unchanging. He reaches out, reverently, and touches her cloak, her head covering.

'Well?' Levett is impatient. 'Is it this unknown saint? Or have they stolen a church's patron?'

'I don't know her. She's like no saint I've ever seen. But I would dearly love to meet the craftsman who made her —'

'Hold hard!' Hob says. 'We don't know that a craftsman made her.'

Hassell's eyes flick to me, not to Hob.

'Martin doesn't know where she came from, do you Martin?'

The parson pays him no attention; his gaze is still pinned to me. 'Your friend says you were healed. Will you tell us about it, yourself?'

I shift my grip on the saint. She is heavy in my arms, unwieldy.

'The plague came to our manor while my father and I were off coaling. When we got back to the village my eldest brother and his family were all dead and my mother and my new sister took ill soon after the babe was born. So many were dying that they couldn't all be buried in the churchyard.' I falter, remembering Newman's Field. 'And then I fell ill.'

'The lumps or coughing blood?'

'Coughing blood. Everybody in our village was the same. Nobody had the putrid lumps.'

Thomas Hassell nods for me to continue.

'The next day, my father could see I was dying and he called our parson. He gave me the rites.'

I stop. I am not going to tell him that my father took me, dying, to the forest.

'And then?' the parson urges, softly. Not a sound comes from the crowd behind him.

'And then ... I didn't die. I woke up in this world. Healed, like Hob said. With my father's little image of Saint Cynryth in my hands.'

'Not this figure?'

'No, a small one that my father carved himself.' Awkwardly, with the saint propped against me, I hold my hands apart to show the smallness of the whittled saint.

'And this?' The parson inclines his head at the saint in my arms. 'Is it true that you don't know where she came from?' Still, he gives not so much as a glance at Hob.

I crane my head, awkwardly, to the White Maiden's delicate profile. 'I found her. Standing on our family's shrine.'

I know the word will bring to everybody's mind a little household shrine, not a rock-hewn shelf beside a spring in the forest. But I cannot help that. My father's oddness is my business, not theirs.

'And nobody knew how she had come to be there?'

I hesitate. Alone in the forest, there was nobody to ask. 'No.'

'Has she healed anybody else?'

I look past Thomas Hassell to the reeve and answer the question he has asked. 'No. At least, not that I know of.'

'But,' Hob cuts in, 'on our way here, we buried five plague-dead. And we walked through the middle of a town where people were dying on every side.'

I call to mind the old woman and her stinking kin; the grim silence of Cricklade with its empty streets, its shuttered shop-fronts, its deserted marketplace.

'So the saint offers protection from sickness as well as healing?' Levett speaks to clarify not to wonder.

'Yes.' Hob's voice carries not a trace of doubt.

The saint's elbow is bruising my ribs; I pass her across my body to hold her in my left arm. Heads follow the movement.

Healing and protection from sickness. Is it true? And, if it is, are there other folk — in Salster, elsewhere — also wearing out their knees before shrines dedicated to Cynryth, the White Maiden of the Well?

All of a sudden, a vision rises before me, a vision of simple shrines placed next to wells and springs the length and breadth of England. In each, an image of Saint Cynryth in her white kirtle and cloak; before each, a kneeling army of the healed and whole. And the saint shines with a radiant white light, like the pale otherworldliness of the moon

The vision fades as swiftly as it came and I become aware that people are edging closer, that all eyes are on the figure cradled against my chest.

Hob has moved towards the crowd. 'Friends! You know we came here looking for help and that we've proved an equal help to you.'

Nods and murmurs break the rapt silence; such a happy coincidence of need must be a sign of the saint's favour.

'The saint brought us here so that you'd be the first to be blessed by her.' He shoots a glance at me and grins. 'Sorry, Martin — I should say the first apart from Martin. So come and put yourselves under the protection of the saint. Come and receive her blessing.'

His words take me utterly by surprise. I open my mouth to protest but shut it again. What has been said cannot be unsaid. Despite the collective stare of the crowd, I feel the heat of one gaze in particular and half-turn to see its source. Thomas Hassell's deep-set eyes are fixed on me.

'What do we have to do?' a voice calls out.

Hob throws up his hands. 'You don't have to do anything, my friend! Only come and feel the blessing of her outstretched hand.'

It only takes one soul more venturesome than the rest to come forward and, soon, the whole crowd is jostling to touch the White Maiden's fingers with their own; I almost lose my footing as people fight to be the next to touch the saint.

Lift her up to them. I hear the voice in my inner ear and cannot but obey. As bodies press in all around me, I raise the saint aloft, holding her hand above the waiting heads. The crowd quietens, eyes uplifted, and I lower her, gently, until her hand rests on the head of a woman with a child in her arms.

'May Saint Cynryth bless you.' I had not thought to say anything but, as the saint's hand touches the woman's head, the words seem to come from me, unbidden.

Hearing the words, the crowd begins to jostle once more, pushing forward for the saint's blessing.

Again and again and again as men and women and children stand before me, I raise the saint and lower her so that her hand rests, gently, upon each bowed head.

'May Saint Cynryth bless you,' I say, as my arms begin to burn and shake. 'May Saint Cynryth bless you.'

And so they come to our hearth. Some come as gawpers, some come as pilgrims. But, over the next two days, all the villagers of Tredgham and Appledore come out to see her.

Sometimes they come in threes and fours, sometimes in larger parties, but all come quietly, hardly a word passing between them to tell us that visitors are on their way.

I have seen this silence before, in Lysington, in the folk who lived through the pestilence; as if those who survive dare not make too great a noise lest they call attention to themselves, lest the pestilence turn back from its onward march and catch them, too, in an indifferent sweep of its scythe. Laughter is rare, gossiping half-hearted, mothers speak softly to their wary-eyed children.

But, whatever its source, there is something reverential about their silence and, as they kneel for the saint's blessing, again and again I recall my vision. Shrines to Saint Cynryth springing up before wells all over England. Hundreds — even thousands — of people coming to be healed of the pestilence. More and more, I am convinced that the vision was a true one. For towns and cities are spoken of everywhere as the source of the Great Sin that has brought the pestilence down on us whilst the White Maiden, with her particular care for the wells and springs that rise in woods, is untouched by such foulness.

Prayers offered, heads bowed to outstretched fingers and blessings received, Tredgham's pilgrims sit with us awhile by the fire, out of courtesy.

Of course, the talk is mostly of the saint and, more than once, I am asked whether it would not be better for her to take up a place of honour in the church while we are occupied with our collyering. Coming out to the woods is hard for people, they say, and besides, they would feel easier in their minds if she was in the church.

As it happens, Thomas Hassell has not offered the saint a place in his church but, even had he done so, I would have declined it and kept her on the hearth with me. As a mortal woman, Cynryth attached herself not to a church or an abbey but to a spring in the woods. If people want her blessing, it seems only right that they should come to the woods to find it.

That being said, I am more than a little surprised that Master Hassell has not been back to the hearth. He must, by now, have heard the story of the saint's miraculous appearance in the press for Hob prevailed upon me to tell it to the apprentices and I know they will have sent it all around the village.

CHAPTER 17

We quenched the pit last night and broke it open to begin the harvest at first light. When I sent Stephen to the village for sacks, I told him to spread the word that we would be busy about the hearth today, sacking-up the coal but, clearly, some people think their wish to see the saint is more important than our work for a largeish party arrives when we are but a little way into the harvest.

'Well met friends,' Hob calls from his customary distance. 'Are you here to pray for healing from the pestilence?' Some pilgrims come to ask the saint to intercede for sick relatives and everyone but me stands off from them while they kneel before the saint, touch her hand, ask her blessing.

A well-set-up man in middle age steps forward to answer. 'No. But we've heard great things about your saint.'

Coal is black stuff and those who break a pit open very soon become black themselves but the newcomer makes no remark at the state of Hob.

I listen with half an ear as he idles with the pilgrims and I keep Tom and Stephen at our task. We cannot all afford to down tools — I want the coal harvested and the new pit stacked up by this evening.

The family, it seems, are from the manor's other village, Appledore, and everybody from babes in arms to the grandmother of the clan is here. One or two of the party have been on our hearth before — I recognise a girl about my own age simpering at Hob and wonder, sourly, whether she has persuaded the rest of her family to come and see the saint so that she can see him again. Certainly, she wanders to his side whilst the rest of her family are ushering the old dame to the saint's makeshift shrine, a rude affair that we have knocked together from cordwood.

Most of the party, having received what they came for, drift towards the cooking fire and a few minutes gossip with Hob before they make their way home, so that when the calf-eyed girl kneels in her turn, nobody pays her much attention.

'Oh, oh!'

When I hear her cry, my first concern is for the saint. Thinking the little figure must have fallen from the shrine, I turn towards her but stop when I see that she is standing, as before, poised in the act of blessing. The girl's family rush past me, mother first, followed by the other womenfolk and her father. They gather so close about her that it is impossible to hear what is being said. I motion Tom and Stephen back to work, but then a cry goes up.

'A miracle! The saint has done another miracle!'

Thomas Hassell is swiftly sent for. Meanwhile, the girl — whose name is Beatrice — is brought forward to tell her tale from the beginning.

Though demure enough, Beatrice keeps darting glances out from under her eyelashes in Hob's direction. But, when I look over at him to see how greets this piece of flirtation, he seems unmoved by it, his coal-streaked face showing exactly the same half-disbelieving wonder as the rest of the crowd.

Beatrice knelt down, she says, to ask a blessing. Not for just for herself, but for all the people in their little village who are unable to make the journey out to the woods.

Here, looks are shot at me and I see that people believe I have stubbornly refused attempts by their parson to have the saint brought to the church.

As she knelt in prayer, Beatrice says, she heard the saint telling her that she had a great heart — 'That's what she said, when I asked for her blessings on everybody who couldn't come — "You have a great heart, Beatrice."'

With these words still in her ears, the dazed girl had lifted her head to the saint's hand for her blessing.

'And I felt her hand o-o-n my head,' Beatrice stammers prettily. 'Not her wooden hand, I mean, a real hand. I felt the saint's real, warm hand on my head as she blessed me.'

The boy sent to fetch Thomas Hassell comes dashing back with the news that the parson is on his way.

'He says he wants to talk to everybody who was here when the miracle happened,' the boy pants, more than rewarded for his run by the power that this instruction has given him over his relatives. 'So nobody's allowed to go home until he comes.'

The parson arrives shortly afterwards and crosses the hearth to where Beatrice sits. Holding out a hand to the girl, he raises her up before turning to the crowd that has followed him.

'Leave us, please. I would speak to Beatrice alone.'

Everybody shuffles away, darting backward glances at the pair of them as Thomas Hassell begins to speak, his head lowered, close to the girl's.

'You must feel thankful that you came to Tredgham,' Beatrice's father tells me, settling himself at the fire once more. 'You came with a saint who'd done one miracle and you'll leave with one who's done two.'

I stare at him, at a loss as to how I should answer.

'More than two!'

Hob's voice comes from behind me and I watch the man's eyes turn from me to him.

'She'd done at least three miracles before we got here, by my reckoning.' Hob holds up a finger. 'She healed Martin from death.' A second finger. 'Her image appeared on the family shrine, a gift from the saint herself in heaven.' A third finger. 'And she disappeared, only to come back to Martin again when he needed her.'

Beatrice's father shrugs, his eyes on me again. His clothes are probably the ones his wife keeps for high days and holy days; does he feel himself to be above me because I'm black from my craft? 'Still — it's strange, isn't it,' he says, 'how your saint saved this blessing for my Beatrice instead of giving it to you?'

I feel Hob's hand on my shoulder.

'It's not strange at all. Why would the saint want to give Martin such a little, everyday blessing when she's already done a miracle almost as great as bringing Lazarus from the tomb?'

'An *everyday* miracle?'

Hob steps forward until he is standing over Beatrice's spluttering father. 'Yes. Consider: if her child comes running to her for comfort, what mother doesn't put an arm around his shoulders and a hand on his head? The saint loves those who come to her more than any mother loves her child — she's in the courts of Heaven, her love is perfect, and not even the most loving mother's is that. What should she do for people who come to her but put a loving hand on their head to bless them? But in Martin's case —' he turns to me, puts his hand back on my shoulder — 'things were very different. To bring life from death is not an everyday matter.'

Bested, the man rises from the stool and goes over to the parson, still listening to Beatrice's tale.

I do not take Thomas Hassell for a man who will look kindly on being interrupted so, loath to be caught watching, I join my apprentices in riddling the last small coals from the baked earth beneath the pit. Will looks up, expectant, but I am still pondering Hob's words.

A miracle almost as great as bringing Lazarus from the tomb.

Much that seemed uncertain before now seems clear. My healing was the saint's first miracle and she sent the beautiful, lifelike statue to confirm her blessing on me and on my pilgrimage. Saint Cynryth wanted me to make the journey to Salster before Richard ever came to the hearth, bent on sending me away.

'Martin.'

Master Thomas is coming towards me.

'I have heard John Longfellow's daughter's account. Now I want you to tell me exactly how your family came to know this saint.'

Though a few villagers remain on the hearth, reluctant to leave while there might still be something to see, Beatrice and her family are long gone by the time I have told the parson everything he wants to know.

'And you are certain that *you* didn't take the saint from the shrine? That you didn't put her in your press for safe-keeping?'

'Yes, I am.' Does he think I am an idiot? Or a liar, perhaps?

'The pestilence does disorder a man's wits — I've seen it again and again —'

'No. I was healed. I was weak but in my right mind. I know I didn't take the saint down.'

He nods, his eyes on mine. Then, seeming to weigh his words, he asks, 'Is Saint Cynryth a common patron where you come from?'

I shake my head. 'No.'

He waits. Then, when I say nothing more, he asks, 'Had you heard her story before the peddler came?'

Is there doubt in his tone? But she has done miracles now, in his own parish. Surely he cannot still be uncertain of her?

'No,' I admit.

He seems to consider what to say next. 'Well … it's our duty to ensure that her miracles are acknowledged. They must be recorded in the diocese's annals.'

He pauses. Is he waiting for me to say something?

'I'll go to the abbey at Malmesbury, myself,' he concludes when I find nothing to say, 'and make sure it's properly done.'

'But what about the pestilence?' Hob asks.

I turn. How long has he been standing there?

'From the tales we've heard these last few days,' he tells the parson, 'it seems the Death has no mercy on abbeys and priories. If anything, it kills monks for preference.'

It is true. People are beginning to say that if the plague has been sent to cleanse the earth of corruption then the church is as sinful — if not more so — than the rest of us.

'I've been spared thus far,' the parson says. 'If it's God's will, I'll be spared no matter what I find at Malmesbury.'

'But what'll you do if there's nobody left there?' I ask.

Two men who are hovering nearby, pretending not to listen, cross themselves at this vision of an abbey where all are dead and no-one remains to do the work of God. But the parson seems unaware that our conversation is being overheard. 'If there's no-one to help me, I'll find the annals and write it myself.' He takes a breath. 'And, while I'm there, I'll look to see what other records there are of her.'

'Why?'

'Because —' Hassell flicks a glance at Hob as he answers his question — 'I want to see whether other miracles of hers have been attested to.'

'Why?' Hob repeats. 'Isn't it enough to record the miracles that she's doing now?'

The parson turns his shoulder, directing his answer to me. 'From the story of her life — though, I admit, I've only heard it at second-hand — it seems that all the saint's previous miracles were in response to particular prayer. Prayers for healing, prayers for barren women to be made with child...?'

I nod.

'But now, it seems that the character of her miracles has changed. She comes and goes. She brings back those who are all but dead. Her wooden hand becomes like living flesh.'

'So?'

The parson gives Hob the most fleeting of looks. 'I want to see whether there are records of her doing other miracles like the one she did with Beatrice. Whether there are other stories of her image appearing in response to devotion.' Neither of us speaks and he continues. 'The doctors of the church teach us that God made matter *ex nihilo* — out of nothing — only once, when he made the heavens and the earth. Therefore, it stands to reason that he did not make this image out of nothing but that she must have been removed from one place to appear in another. In other words, for her to appear on your family's shrine, she must have disappeared from somewhere else. And, if that has happened before, there will be a record of it.'

Hob is shaking his head. 'That's all very well but don't you think those records might be somewhere else and not in Malmesbury? Perhaps all the records of her miracles are in Salster.'

The parson's expression does not change. 'The abbey at Malmesbury possesses one of the great libraries of Christendom. The life of any saint known to the church will be recorded there.'

Hob sidesteps so that he's facing the parson. 'And what if it isn't? What if Saint Cynryth's life isn't there?'

Thomas Hassell is not cowed. 'If her life is not recorded there, then she's no saint.'

'If she's not *written down* she's not a saint?'

'If she is not *recognised by the church*, she's not a saint.'

'Perhaps only the people know her,' I suggest, trying to keep my voice even, so that the eavesdroppers will not know how much his words, reminiscent as they are of Master William's, have disturbed me. 'The people who lived where she lived, who received miracles at her shrine?'

As the parson meets my eye, it seems — just for a moment — that he will relent but, when he speaks, it is simply to repeat himself. 'I'm sorry Martin, but if she isn't recognised by the church, she's not a saint. And if she's not a saint —' he holds me with his deep-set gaze — 'then she's done no miracles.'

'So if her life isn't written at this library in Malmesbury, then Beatrice is lying? Martin is lying?'

'Or mistaken.' The parson is as composed as Hob is outraged. 'Or taken for a fool by Satan to do his work.' Again, he turns his back on Hob and addresses only me. 'Martin, I think perhaps the time has come to do as people been asking and give the saint a place in the church —'

I see the listening ears strain to hear my response to this but Hob speaks first.

'What? So that you and your church can have all the glory of any future miracles she does — so that people come to you with their gifts instead of to us?'

Hassell looks to me with his answer. 'So that until we know she *is* a saint, people will be protected from deceit.'

'No.' It's out of my mouth before I can control myself. 'She belongs here, with me. She's my saint. You can doubt her but I know what she's done. What she's done for me!'

He holds my eye for an uncomfortably long time. 'Very well. Then I bid you good day.' He bows. 'Tomorrow is the Sabbath. I shall set out for Malmesbury in two days' time and be back as soon as I'm able.'

Hob watches him go. 'I hope he has a slow horse.'

'Why?'

Hob unfixes his eyes from the retreating priest's back and turns them on me. 'If he finds she's no saint then —'

'She *is* a saint!'

'Let me finish. If the church's *records* don't know her for a saint then he'll have been proved right to doubt her and he'll say she's done no miracles. But if he *does* find her life written down in these *annals*, then he'll try and claim her because the miracle was done here, in his parish.'

I stare at him.

'Either way, Master Thomas will bring trouble. We'd do well to be gone before he gets back.'

CHAPTER 18

News of Beatrice's miracle flies from hearth to village to the surrounding country and, within a day, the trickle of pilgrims has become a flood. By the following afternoon there are so many people on the hearth that I have to use the screening hurdles to keep them away from the newly fired stack.

All the talk is of a wooden hand become flesh and, again and again, I am told that the miracle demonstrates the saint's wish to remain here, in Tredgham. And, each time, I rein in my resentment and remind folk that this is not her first miracle, that she saved me from death so that I could make my pilgrimage to Salster.

'But you don't need the saint with you,' one says. 'You could still make the pilgrimage.'

'You see?' Hob says. 'The parson's sown the seed amongst his people — if he finds her to be a true saint of the church he'll try and keep her here. And they'll stand with him.'

I meet his eye. 'I won't leave her here, whatever the parson says. He has no claim on her.'

And besides, the parson's own words about the saint being transported from elsewhere to our shrine in the Dene have shown me that my pilgrimage has a double purpose. For the saint has surely set my face towards her shrine not simply to pray for my father's soul but to restore her to her rightful home.

That night I wake to the sound of my own shouting.

'No. No!'

I am not in the hut. I am standing on the hearth, the saint clasped to my chest in a desperate embrace.

Tom, sitting by the fire, stares at me, eyes stretched wide. Hob stands an arm's length away, his palms upraised towards me.

'Steady, Martin.'

I take a step back, the saint still fast in my arms.

'Is he awake?' I hear Tom ask. 'Or is it like the other times?'

Hob's eyes do not leave mine. 'Course he's awake. And he's here — saint and all — to start the day, eh, Martin?'

I stare at him, his words forming up slowly in my mind. Eventually I understand that a question has been asked and I unstick my tongue from the roof of my mouth. 'Yes.' My voice is a croak.

Hob turns to Tom. 'It's a while off daybreak yet. You may as well sleep for a while. Martin'll keep watch with me.'

For a long while, Hob and I sit, unspeaking. As the fire burns down, I fetch more wood from the pile dragged in by Tredgham's children. The glow of the embers dims beneath the new fuel and I feel a sudden chill.

In the corner of my eye, Hob reaches behind him to pull out his knife.

'What other times have I walked like that?'

He looks up, a frown on his face.

'Tom said, "Is he awake, or is it like the other times?" What other times?'

Hob smooths a finger and thumb along the blade of his knife. 'Martin —'

'Tell me! If a demon is making me walk, making me do its bidding, I need to know.'

He looks at me, wordless. I drop my gaze and stare at the knife. He is weaving the handle to and fro between his fingers.

'It seems to me,' he says, at length, 'that your demon is a biddable one. When this has happened before, I've been able to speak to you, persuade you to go back to your bed.'

'And I've gone?'

'Every time.'

'How many times?'

'That doesn't m—'

'I can ask Tom if you won't tell me! *How many times?*'

He stabs the knife into the soft ground at his feet. 'Three times before tonight.'

'Alone, or with the saint?'

Does he hesitate, or am I simply too impatient for his reply? 'With the saint.'

'You're telling me that I've been made to walk in my sleep four times and, each time, I've brought the saint on to the hearth?'

'Yes.'

'And you've bid me — bid the demon — back to bed?'

He nods. 'Until tonight. Tonight you woke before I could speak.' He pulls up his knife, draws the blade between thumb and forefinger to wipe away the soil.

'Why didn't you tell me?'

'If the demon had tried to harm you, I would have. If it'd tried to take you off into the wood or throw you in the fire. But you just held the saint tight — as if you were trying to keep her safe. That didn't seem a cause for alarm.'

Why would the demon want me to keep the saint safe? Does he mean to use the saint to do me harm?

'Perhaps, in your sleep, you feel the evil spirit's desires and you thwart them,' Hob says quietly, his eyes aglow in the new flames.

I stare at him. If he is right, I have fought the demon successfully thus far. But who is to say how long I will prevail?

The following day I cannot but brood on the demon who commands my sleeping self. The hearth is busy with folk but, instead of answering questions about the saint, I find myself helping Tom and Stephen patch holes in the pit's earthen blanket and cursing myself for not having insisted that they rebuild a section that I could see was unstable.

Is this the demon's doing, too? Is he trying to frustrate our plans, to force us to stay another week while we burn a third pit and my father's soul hovers about the mouth of hell?

Why did Hob say nothing to me about this spirit that possesses me at night? Again and again, he has watched it bend my sleeping wits to its will and chosen not to tell me. How long has this spirit been twined about me? Was it him I felt stalking me, before I sheltered in the wood where Edgar attacked me?

I see, now, how things stand. As the saint came to me in a miracle to protect and guide me on my pilgrimage, so Satan has sent a demon to frustrate and torment me. He is jealous of Saint Cynryth's power and will try and make me doubt her. Or force me to harm her.

Is that the demon's task — to take my hands and use them to destroy the saint?

No. Hob says I have done nothing but walk about the hearth with her. Then again, perhaps he is right, perhaps I feel the spirit's designs and have the strength to withstand them. But Hob also said that the spirit was biddable, that he was able to send me — send *it* — back to bed. Why should a demon be obedient to Hob Cleve's will?

I glance over at him, standing with a group of pilgrims at our makeshift shrine. There is something about Hob — people listen to him. And they want him to notice them.

I hear the sound of thudding feet. Before my wits can catch up, my body remembers Edgar's murderous attack and I find myself backing swiftly away.

A half-grown lad pulls up on the hearth and stands, panting.

Hob comes forward. 'What's the hurry?'

'News,' the lad pants.

'What news?' A man steps up, takes him by the shoulder.

'It's Master Thomas, father. He's dead.'

'Master Thomas —' my voice is strained in my own ears. 'The parson?'

He nods.

Hob turns to the father. 'I thought nobody'd died for weeks here?'

The older man faces him. 'They haven't.'

Dusk is swooping in as the apprentices return from the village. We sit down to eat the food they have brought and they tell us about Thomas Hassell.

'If he'd kept a horse of his own, he wouldn't've been found for a week,' Stephen declares.

It seems that, yesterday evening, the parson told his servant that she could go home to her family for a few days while he visited the library at Malmesbury. She prepared food for his journey then did as she was bidden. But Thomas Hassell had no horse and the man whose mare he had arranged to hire became worried when he failed to come for her.

'Or, more likely,' Stephen says, 'Jed Sparrow wanted to make sure of his money.'

'He left it a good while,' Hob points out. 'You say the parson was supposed to pick the horse up at first light, but this Jed didn't bother going to his house till nearly halfway through the morning.'

Tom shrugs, his expression saying that Hob is a foreigner and cannot be expected to know the character of those involved.

'Whatever the way of it,' Stephen says, 'Jed went to the parson's house and found him lying in his bed, dead as a herring.'

'The pestilence?' I can hardly bring myself to ask the question.

'Nobody knows,' Tom butts in, 'but there were no marks of it on him.'

'And his eyes were open,' Stephen adds, 'all bloodshot and staring as if he'd seen something horrible.'

'Like what?'

Stephen shrugs. 'A ghost? An evil spirit?'

Hob throws aside the heel of bread he has been gnawing at. 'Never mind ghosts — it was most likely a seizure.'

I turn to him, glad of the certainty in his voice. 'Do you think so?'

'Yes.' He looks over the fire at Stephen. 'Your parson didn't strike me as the kind of man who'd be afraid of a ghost or a spirit. He'd've been sending them back to hell two ticks after they appeared. They wouldn't've known what'd happened to them.'

I nod. 'So, if it's a natural death, the coroner won't be called?'

Tom looks at me curiously.

'I don't want to get held up,' I say. 'If we're going to have to wait for the coroner he could be days.'

'That's if he'd even come,' Stephen says. 'I heard coroners've stopped going out to corpses unless it's plain what's killed them.'

And who could blame them? No man would want to examine a corpse knowing that the contagious stink of the pestilence might lurk beneath its clothes.

'Well, it'll be up to the bailiff,' Tom slaps his palms on his knees. 'The reeve's gone to see him.'

I cannot sleep. Thomas Hassell was going to Malmesbury to look for the life of Saint Cynryth, to look for some evidence that she had a claim to be one of the church's own. And now he is dead.

Over and over I hear that exchange between Hob and the parson.

If she isn't recognised by the church, she's not a saint. And if she's not a saint, then she's done no miracles.

So if her life isn't written in this library at Malmesbury, then Beatrice is lying? Martin is lying?

Or mistaken. Or taken for a fool by Satan to do his work.

Have I been taken for a fool? Am I doing Satan's bidding and not Saint Cynryth's?

On the very night that Hassell died — possibly even as he was dying — the demon made me walk on to the hearth with the saint. Why did I wake up that time when I had not woken as I walked before?

And why did I shout, 'No, no'?

Who was I shouting at?

CHAPTER 19

I drag myself about the hearth in the chilly grey air of dawn, weary and grit-eyed. While Hob and Tom sat watching the pit, I tossed and turned, both craving sleep and fighting it, afraid of what I might do once I was no longer in control of my limbs. Now that daylight is safely here, my body wants nothing more than to lie down and close my eyes.

My watch-mate, Stephen, scarcely more lively than me, has taken himself off amongst the damp and sullen trees to piss away the ale he has been drinking since Hob roused us. Satisfied that the pit is quiet, I rest my backside on my collyer's stool, watching the fitful wind smearing smoke from the vent-holes.

Will the bailiff send for the coroner as soon as he hears what the reeve has to say, or will he wait and see the body for himself? These are strange times, when the customary writ cannot always run.

I send Stephen into the village to see what is happening.

A bout of rain has come and gone by the time Stephen gets back.

'Took your time, didn't you?' Tom scowls.

His cousin ignores him and turns to me. 'There's rumours flying all over the place.'

My stomach clenches. 'What rumours?'

He looks at me. 'The hundred bailiff and the coroner are both here. The bailiff's man's gone to call up a jury from Lynd and Chirwell and the reeve's doing the same from here and Appledore.' He gives a twisted smile. 'I've got to be on the jury

— Geoffrey says he wants somebody who was on the hearth while the parson was visiting.'

I catch Hob's eye. He said Thomas Hassell would be trouble but even he cannot have foreseen this.

Stephen sees the look. 'It's because you're strangers here,' he says. 'Coroners always look askance at strangers.'

'Does Geoffrey want *me* on the jury as well?' Tom asks. 'He should have men who know Hob and Martin — they're not strangers to me.'

His words increase my feeling of unease — does Tom think Hob and I need defending?

Stephen shakes his head. 'No. He's got Will — he can speak for what's been going on here.'

Tom is outraged. 'Will was hardly here three days! And he wasn't here when the miracle happened.'

And he has a grudge against us. Against Hob, at any rate.

'So have you done the viewing of the body yet?' Hob asks.

'No, not until the full jury's gathered.' Stephen looks round at us all. 'But I know what he looked like.' The look on his face tells me he is enjoying the fact that he can make us wait. But it also tells me that Stephen had no love for Thomas Hassell. Was the priest not well liked in his parish? Perhaps I was not alone in finding his soul-searching gaze troubling.

'Well?' Hob wants to know. 'What did he look like?'

'Terrible sight, so I heard. Bloodshot eyes. And his face was blue.'

'Hob was right then,' I say, 'it was a seizure. That's how my grandfather died and his face went blue.'

I remember my Gransher sitting down, complaining of a tightness in his chest. Then the pain began and he fell to the ground. He was dead before the parson arrived.

But Stephen is shaking his head. 'According to what I heard, the coroner said, "last time I saw a corpse with a face that colour, it'd been dragged out of a cesspit".'

Tom frowns. 'What'd he mean by that?'

'Don't think he meant anything by it. I think he was just saying.'

'Odd thing to say.'

'Must *be* odd — going round seeing dead bodies every week of the year,' Stephen replies. He is annoyed by Tom's questions, wanted everybody just to be agog.

'What else did he say,' I ask. 'Anything?'

Stephen looks away from Tom. 'Yes. Asked about the saint. Said he'd be coming out to talk to you, see what all the fuss was about. And why the parson was going to Malmesbury.'

As the day heads towards dusk, I begin to think that the coroner has lost interest in us, that he has found more pressing things to do with his time than come and see the saint. Perhaps, even now, he is with the jury at the view of the body.

What would a jury have made of my father's body, I wonder, lying there in his shroud? His eyes were closed, not staring. He did not die of a seizure.

I cast my mind back to his dead face. The jutting nose, the cold skin. He looked like the old woman in the dead village. Calm, composed.

She held on to life until it was safe to die; then, from what I could see, she just lay down and stopped. Is that what my father did — left me safe in the saint's care and gave up his life to fulfil his half of the bargain?

And Edgar? The question forces itself into my mind. *Was Edgar blue about the face?*

Perhaps he was; but I wrapped him for the grave while it was still dark. All I know is that his nose was bent and bleeding.

'Good day to all!'

A lean, heavy-cloaked man is being shown on to the hearth, followed by a fellow with a writing-board. We all gather to greet them and the man I take to be the coroner accepts the offer of a stool and a mug of ale. He is dressed well but not fussily and I notice that he takes pains to ensure a stool and a mug for his young note-taker, too.

'I am Edmund Abarrow, officer to his majesty's coroner for the county. I'm here to conduct an inquest into the death of the clerk, Thomas Hassell.'

We all nod, falling in with his practical manner. His way of speaking is not that of Tredgham but his speech is still easy to understand and not Frenchified, for which I am grateful. But though he might be more one of us than his master, he still wields the power of the coroner's office.

'You two —' he gathers in Hob and me with his look — 'have been here, or so I gather, about twelve days. Is that right?'

We nod.

'And you're on pilgrimage to Salster? The reeve tells me he has your mare and cart in his barn.'

'Yes, master, I'm making a pilgrimage to Salster to pray for my father's soul.'

He crosses himself. 'Not a good death?'

'No. He died unshriven and, by force of circumstances, could not be buried in holy ground. When the saint appeared to me, I knew I had to make for Salster straight away.'

'Ah yes. The saint.' He nods. 'Tell me about her.'

149

Some men are good listeners, others cannot keep quiet for the need to hear their own voice. Edmund Abarrow is a silent listener. Every now and again he asks a question but, for the most part, he simply listens. When I have come to the end of my story with the saint's appearance in the press he draws a long breath.

'But that wasn't the end of her miracles, was it?' he asks. 'Every soul I've spoken to in the village has been at pains to make sure I know the story of Beatrice's miracle. The hand made flesh…'

'Yes, master. It happened here, on the hearth.'

'And it was that which brought the parson, Thomas Hassell, here on the day before he died?'

'Not the day before he died, master,' I tell him, 'the day before that. Saturday.'

'You're taking it for granted that he died on the same day that his death was discovered,' he says. 'But, according to the first finder of the body —' he stops and turns to the secretary.

'Jedediah Sparrow.'

'Yes, according to the man, Sparrow, when he went in to see what had become of the parson, he found him to be not only dead but quite stiff.'

I imagined the unknown Jed Sparrow going towards the bed and, confused by the parson's open eyes, trying to speak to him. Though none of us is as discomfited by the sight of death as we were a year ago, he must still have been taken unawares by what he found when he touched Master Thomas.

'A corpse does not stiffen until several hours after death,' the coroner's officer goes on. 'Therefore, since the parson was found dead at about the mid-point between sunrise and noon, we can suppose that he died during the early part of the night.'

'Died in his bed,' Tom said, 'as we all hope to.'

'Yes,' Edmund Abarrow agrees, 'though most of us hope to have our family about us and a priest to hand.'

'But he *was* a priest,' I protest, the example of Master William in my mind. 'Surely he confessed his sins every night before he slept? He will have died in a state of grace?'

Master Abarrow's eyes narrow as they stare at me. 'Only God knows that.' He crosses himself. 'So, he was here the day before he died. I've heard about the miracle from young Beatrice and her father. Why don't you tell me about the conversation you had with Master Thomas after he'd spoken to the girl?'

I find myself glancing at Hob and am vexed with myself. I do not need his permission to answer.

'He wanted me to explain to him, again, how my family came to be associated with Saint Cynryth.'

He nods. 'Yes, he'd been here on a previous occasion, I gather, to satisfy himself and the reeve that the saint wasn't stolen?'

Though I have no call to feel guilty, I feel the blood rising in my face. 'Yes, and he saw that it was just as I had said — she is my family's patron saint.'

The coroner's eyes flick to the cordwood shrine where the saint has been standing since the rain stopped. This momentary glance tells me that Master Abarrow took swift note of everything on the hearth as he arrived, that his affable manner hides a keen mind.

'And what was his reaction to what every soul in the village is calling the miracle of Beatrice's hand?'

I feel Hob's eyes on me as I reply. 'He was keen to write it in the annals of the abbey at Malmesbury. Said it should be in the diocese's records.'

'So he believed it to be a genuine miracle and not some fancy of the girl's?'

'Yes,' Hob answers before I can even hesitate.

Master Abarrow turns to him. 'You were party to this conversation, too, I believe?'

'I was.'

Unease begins to creep over me. Who has been telling the coroner about our discussion with the parson?

'So perhaps you can shed light on the argument I've heard about.'

'Argument?' Hob cocks his head as if he does not wholly understand the word.

'Yes. The argument between you and Master Thomas about whether or not your White Maiden of the Well really is a saint.'

I watch Hob's face as, first a frown and then a smile reflect his thoughts. 'I think whoever overheard our conversation misunderstood,' he says. 'There was no argument as to whether St Cynryth is a saint, only about the importance of the library at Malmesbury. I did not know its significance and questioned whether the life of a saint from elsewhere would be recorded there but Master Thomas was quite forceful. "Her life will unquestionably be at Malmesbury,' he said. 'It's one of the most important libraries in Christendom."'

'So he didn't question either her sainthood, or the miracles you claim for her?'

'No.'

The coroner fixes him with a long look. 'He didn't say that, if no evidence was found for her sainthood, then folk who claim miracles for her were either mistaken or lying?'

'I believe,' Hob says, looking off and narrowing his eyes as if he is reading the words in the air, 'that what he said was, "Folk are sometimes mistaken about miracles".' He hesitated and brought his gaze back to Master Abarrow's face. 'And sometimes taken for fools by Satan.'

'And are you mistaken?' The officer's eyes move from Hob to me. 'Or taken for fools by Satan?'

'No, sir, we're not,' Hob states firmly as I begin to stammer out some kind of denial. 'And, despite the garbled account you've had handed on to you, I feel sure that the parson didn't think we were either.'

'Is that so?'

'Yes.' I watch Hob meet his eye, open and fearless. 'Master Thomas accepted Beatrice's miracle. What he wanted to see — what he told us *quite specifically* that he wanted to see — was whether it had been recorded that the saint had done this appearing and disappearing miracle elsewhere, as well as on Martin's shrine. And he was keen to know where she came from. Martin believed that she had simply appeared out of the air at his family's shrine, but Master Thomas said she must have come from *somewhere* because God only made something *ex nihilo* once, when he created the Heavens and the Earth.'

Master Abarrow stares at Hob as he waits for the secretary to finish recording his words. I wonder how often the coroner's officer hears phrases like *'ex nihilo'* from those he questions. Hob has a keen ear as well as a quick mind.

'Why did he want to go to the abbey now?' Master Abarrow asks. 'Couldn't it have waited?'

Hob gives him a look which says that the purposes of clerics are as baffling to him as the ways of women. 'I didn't know Master Thomas at all well,' he admits, 'but he struck me as the kind of man who, once he'd made up his mind to do something, didn't wait about for spring.'

Stephen and Tom exchange a glance. If he notices, it will tell the coroner's officer that Hob has accurately taken the parson's measure.

Master Abarrow puts his hands on his thighs as if he is about to push himself to his feet and take his leave. 'Right. Just to be clear. Did any of you see the parson again after he left here on Saturday?'

'I did. At church.' Tom was the only one of us who went to hear mass on Sunday.

'And did the parson seem as usual?'

Tom shrugs. 'Yes.'

'He didn't seem unwell or in pain?'

Tom hesitates. 'The parson was always a difficult book to read.'

'And you three —' the officer's eyes take in Hob, Stephen and me — 'you didn't see Thomas Hassell again after that afternoon?'

We all shake our heads.

'Right.' This time, he does get up. 'I'll just take a turn about.'

He walks around the pit, taking in the steady streams of smoke rising and being whipped away by the gusting breeze. He holds out a hand to the surface of the pit and is surprised that he feels little heat until he touches the banked earth.

'So cool and yet —' he peers down one of the vent-holes — 'all is aglow within?'

'The bracken and earth keep air out and heat in,' I explain.

He nods. 'So much going on beneath the surface,' he muses. 'It's almost like alchemy. You turn wood into coal and that, in its turn, transforms ore into iron.'

I nod. 'Yes.'

Eyes still on the pit he asks, 'You collyers are here all night — awake and alert?'

'Two of us sleep while two are on watch, master,' I tell him.

'And the two asleep — they're in that hut there?'

'Yes.'

Now he looks at me. 'While the attention of the watchers is all on the coaling?'

'Yes. There's nothing else to see at night.'

'No.' He looks around the hearth. 'How far does your cooking fire throw its light?'

'At night? We have it low, just to keep the chill off. We can see each other by it, sitting a yard away, but very little beyond.'

'So the hut is in darkness?' He gazes across at the hut which stands on the village side of the clearing, twenty paces or so away from the smoking pit.

I nod and follow him around the outside of the hut. Then I stand and watch as he gazes from its sack-hung door, through the trees to the glebeland and the parson's house beyond.

At dawn, I emerge from the hut to find Stephen eating before he sets off for the inquest.

He looks bright-eyed for somebody who has had next to no sleep and I tell him so as I slump on to the stool next to him. For myself, I feel heavy, thick-headed, having barely slept until an hour or two ago.

'I've slept well enough,' he says, not looking up from his food.

'How? You didn't come into the hut until I was asleep and here you are up again.'

'I slept here, next to the fire.' He glances up, feeling my stare. 'It's cold in the hut. It keeps me awake.'

'You should be like me and Tom,' Hob says, from the other side of the pit. 'Nothing keeps us awake, does it Tom? Sleep like puppies, the pair of us.'

I grunt at the truth of this. Rousing Hob to take his watch is never easy and I have found Tom to be no better.

Hob leaves off his tour of the pit and sits down next to Stephen. 'A word before you go,' he says, 'just so you're not hoodwinked by your cousin —'

'What cousin — Will?'

Hob nods, reaches for the remains of yesterday's loaf and dips a crust in the mug of ale warming by the fire. 'What did he tell you about why he left the hearth?'

Stephen shrugs and keeps his eyes on his bowl, away from me. 'Said he didn't like the way he got ordered around,' he says. 'Said there were easier ways to make winter money.'

'Want to know the real reason he left?'

Stephen looks up. 'What?'

'You know Will fancies himself as a wrestler?'

A smile breaks out on Stephen's face. 'Don't tell me you beat him?'

'I did as it happens. But that's not what I meant to say.' Hob's eyes are fastened on Stephen. 'Your cousin got a bit above himself. Wanted to fight without stays. Well that's stupid but he rushed me so I had no choice.'

'Sounds like Will. Never would take no for an answer.'

'Then he started fighting dirty. So I had to teach him better manners. I pinned him so tight that he pissed himself.' Hob's look is level and unabashed while he watches Stephen's reaction. 'That's why he left. He couldn't face being on the hearth with me after that.'

I glance at Tom to see if he will put his two penn'orth in, but he seems content to let Hob's version stand.

'So?' Stephen raises his bowl to his lips for the last drops. 'You think he's going to try and get his own back?'

Hob stretches his legs out, folds his arms over his chest. 'He's your cousin so you might know better but he strikes me as the kind of man who'd hold a grudge. If he got the chance to speak ill of me, I think he would. And I'll be honest with you, Stephen, I don't relish the thought of being spoken of badly at an inquest.'

Stephen puts his bowl down and wipes his mouth with the back of his hand.

'I'm not telling you what to do,' Hob says, 'but if Will starts on about me or Martin, you might just want to explain to the coroner that he's not the most even-handed witness.'

As morning passes into afternoon and Stephen has not returned, I try to keep my mind off the inquest and on the work of quenching the stack. Driving off the heat from charred logs is exacting work and demands a man's full attention.

Five barrels we pour into the charred stack, pail by pail, vent hole by vent hole until no more steam comes off and the hissing from within is silenced. Now, we can only wait until tomorrow when the pit will be cool enough to break open and harvest the coal.

A quenched stack is an eerie thing. It settles and cracks at odd moments and, sometimes, if the quenching has not been thorough, it will burn up again if a big slip happens. I once heard a collyer say that it is like watching a man die. Will he rally and burn bright again, live a few more hours or days, or will he just sink slowly and quietly into death?

I stand and watch the pit — no longer smoking and seething in fiery life but just squatting there on the hearth, stray wisps of smoke escaping here and there as the last of the fire dies.

What is taking Stephen so long? Can the inquest still be going on?

If we are misliked as strangers, might the jury be persuaded to suspect that we are, somehow, responsible for Master Hassell's death? Could Will do that, as Hob fears?

If we are accused, where would they take us? With the world as it is, God alone knows when the next assize court will be held.

And what would become of the saint? Would she be impounded with my other goods or would the coroner let her stay here until our fate was decided? In my agitation, I pace the hearth, checking sacks for the dozenth time, moving the hurdles pointlessly from one side to another.

The saint will protect you.

I hope my angel is right but, as the day wears on, fear presses in on me till I scarcely know what to do with myself.

Just as we have given Stephen up, he walks on to the hearth, a bucket of ale swinging from one hand and a full pot of Lenten stew, its hot handle padded with rags, from the other.

'At last!' Hob cries. 'What took you so long? Couldn't you agree?'

Stephen puts his burdens down by the fire and rolls his shoulders. 'Didn't start on time —jurors from Lynd didn't come till after noon.'

'So?' Hob wants to know 'What was the verdict?'

'In the end, we decided that he must've died of a seizure.'

'In the end?'

Stephen glances across at me. 'Let's eat this while it's still hot and I'll tell you.'

'Well, you were wrong about Will,' Stephen says to Hob, as I dole out the stew from the pot. 'Didn't say a word against you. Or Martin.'

A chill, as if a ghost has embraced me. 'Me? What would he say about me? I was the one that pulled Hob off him!'

Stephen darts a glance at Hob and Tom who are sitting on the other side of the fire. Then he shrugs, his eyes on the bowl I pass him. 'I thought he might say something about your walking demon.'

My scalp prickles with fear. 'Who told you?' I stand and point at Tom who is staring up at me from his stool. 'Him?'

Hob also stands. 'Tom didn't tell anybody. I told him to keep what he saw between the two of us.'

'Nobody told me,' Stephen looks uncomfortably at me. 'I'm easily roused — you woke me up with your coming and going.'

I stare at him and understanding rises up like vomit. He slept by the fire last night instead of in the hut with me. He was afraid of what I might do.

Hob folds himself down onto his stool again, leaving me standing, alone. 'If I woke you up with my comings and goings,' I tell Stephen, 'then you know that on the night the parson died I walked on to the hearth and nowhere else! You must have heard me shouting? Hob talking to me?'

He nods.

'Well then! The demon can't have taken me to the parsonage if you heard me on the hearth.'

He doesn't reply.

'Well?'

'Look, Martin, I never said I thought you went anywhere. But I can't say for sure because, that time, I didn't wake up when you left, only when I heard you shouting and Hob calming you down.'

I move back to my stool and sit down.

'So what *did* everybody say?' Hob wants to know.

Stephen moves uncomfortably on the stool. 'Most didn't say much. There were a couple who wanted to know why the coroner said that he'd seen a man dragged out of a cesspit who looked the same.'

'And?'

'He said that if the air's foul enough, a man'll be smothered by it as surely as by a wadded blanket.'

'He's not saying there was foul air in the parson's house?' Tom wants to know.

Stephen shakes his head. 'No. Said he might've been smothered by other means.'

A wadded blanket. A hand held over the nose and mouth. We'd all heard of deformed children smothered at birth like that, or a wounded man likely to die in agony. But a healthy, vigorous person?

'Nobody wanted to argue with him,' Stephen says, 'he's the coroner's officer. But then John Longfellow spoke up.'

'John Longfellow? Beatrice's father?'

Stephen nods at me without meeting my eye.

'What did he say?'

'Said Thomas Hassell should've knelt and been blessed like everybody else, 'stead of asking questions like a man who disbelieved. If he'd asked her blessing, John Longfellow reckons, the parson wouldn't've died.'

Of course, no sooner had this seed been sown in the minds of the jury than there sprang up a desire to bring the proceedings to a close as quickly as possible. Nobody wanted to rouse the saint's displeasure lest they, too, be found dead one morning.

And so it was official. Thomas Hassell had died of a seizure.

CHAPTER 20

Two days later, with the mare newly shod and sprightly from plentiful food and rest, we leave Tredgham make our way south. The clouds that stretched from one skyline to the other when we woke have thinned now, and the grey of the sky is broken through, here and there, to blue.

With the cart re-provisioned, we made our farewells yesterday. As a parting gift, the villagers gave us a pilgrim staff, though they seemed unsure which of us should receive it. It lies in the cart — I am leading the mare and do not need two hands encumbered and Hob is plying his bow, though whether from a desire to eat flesh after the Lenten restrictions of the hearth or to vent his continuing anger at the words the coroner's officer spoke to us before he left Tredgham, I cannot tell.

Master Abarrow came to the hearth yesterday morning. Sir Hugh Etienne, the coroner, had already departed with his secretary but Master Abarrow left his horse at the edge of the wood and came on foot to deliver a brief and pointed message before he followed them.

'You'll have heard that the jury found the parson died a natural death,' he told Hob and me when he had separated us from Tom and Stephen. 'That's the jury's verdict and it stands in the rolls. But I'm telling you this, there's something I don't like about Master Hassell's death on the eve of his departure to Malmesbury. Something I don't like at all. So I shall be keeping an ear out for the progress of your saint. I shall be listening for more miracles. And if miracles there are, all well and good. But if I hear of any more sudden deaths in her path, deaths which ought not to have happened, deaths not from the pestilence, then Sir Hugh and I shall be coming after you and we shall see how a second jury decides.'

As the sun reaches midday, we stop at a ford over a tiny stream to let the mare drink and slake our own thirst. For some while, now, we have been travelling south on a road so well-kept that it must be a king's highway. According to the directions we were given by the lordsman at Cricklade, we are to follow this road until we come to a village that stands on a river.

Tomorrow, or the day after that, if his directions are to be believed, we should reach a town called Hungerford Regis and the road that will take us to our goal.

'In two or three days we'll be at Slievesdon,' I say, wiping my wet hands on my tunic, 'and we can give up these letters and earn our other ten shillings.'

'Maybe,' Hob says. 'If that lanky lordsman's to be trusted.'

I have been trying to forget the harshness of the coroner's words by imagining our welcome at Slievesdon as men worthy of a lord's trust so Hob's churlishness makes me snap.

'Why *wouldn't* we trust him? What possible reason have we got to doubt his word?'

'What possible reason have we got to trust him? I know you were impressed by his servant and his rabbit cloak but all we know about him is that he's good at getting what he wants. He bends and sways with the wind but he'll always be standing at the end.'

I remember the man's forbearance in the face of Hob's insolence, the loyalty which put his master's needs above the inclination he surely had to teach Hob some manners.

'He does what he needs to do to for his master.'

'That's what I'm telling you! He says whatever he needs to, to get what he wants and then he can deny it later.'

'You think he'd *forswear* himself?'

Hob's face says he thinks it as likely as worms in an arse-dragging dog.

'What I *think*,' he says, swaying out of the mare's way as she stretches her neck to nip at him, 'is this. We'll go to Slievesdon — risking the pestilence and other people's interference along the way — and we'll ask for the bailiff and give this oh-so-important letter to him for his master. Then we'll present him with the other letter — the one that's supposed to guarantee our second ten shillings — and we'll find that it says, "this is an impudent fellow who's had ten shillings off me and means to have another ten. Take the ten shillings back, whip him and send him on his way".'

'Well that's easily proved, one way or the other.'

'How?'

'By reading the letter.'

'You can *read*?'

I nod. 'The parson in my village taught me.' No need to tell him just how much William Orford taught me.

'Well, go on then. Fetch the damned thing.'

I do not suggest he holds the mare's head, I simply stop her and climb up on to the cart wheel to lift the canvas and open the press. As I take the folded sheets out of their bag, I see that our soldier took seriously Hob's suggestion that the man who had been bailiff at his departure might, by now, be dead and buried. On the outside of one letter is the inscription, 'For the private attention of Sir John de Loselei', and, on the other, 'For the attention of the present bailiff to Sir John de Loselei'.

I put the letter addressed to Sir John back in the bag and hold the other in both hands. It is sealed with a shoeleather's thickness of wax.

As I stand there, hesitating, Hob reaches over, takes the letter from me and breaks the seal with a quick snap. I catch the merest curl of his lip as he hands it back to me. *Coward*, it says.

The hand is large and surprisingly neat. And, to my relief, it is in English. I had been suddenly afraid that it might be in French. Latin I know, but not French.

'To my friend and the bailiff of my master, Nicholas Alleyne,' I read aloud, 'or, if he is gone to his maker since my departure, to whomsoever has taken up his office, Richard Longe sends hearty greetings from Cricklade where you know the business I am sent to oversee.'

'That's another thing,' Hob cuts in. 'We don't know the business of that meeting he was supposed to have.'

'Does it matter?'

'How do we know? It might. Messengers have suffered for the message before now.'

I hold up the letter. 'Shall I carry on?'

He waves a hand and I turn back to Richard Longe's letter.

'May it please you to know the fellow who carries this letter is Hob Cleve, a self-proclaimed freeborn man.' I feel Hob stiffening at my side but continue reading. 'I have paid him ten shillings, him and his companion, and have promised ten more for bringing the letter I am sending to my lord. If he has delivered Sir John's letter with the seal unbroken, then he is worthy of his ten shillings. If I have read him aright, he will have broken the seal on this and found someone to tell him its contents before now.'

I grin at the sharpness of Richard Longe's perception as I carry on reading.

'If you can persuade him to take up a tenancy on my lord's manor, do so. For I believe he will be reeve within five years and the richest man in the village within ten.'

I look up, expecting to see my own grin on Hob's face. Instead, I find anger.

'Thinks he knows my mind, does he?'

'It's not a slur, Hob. He says you'll be rich.'

He turns on me. 'And I *will* be rich! Make no mistake, Martin Collyer — I'll be a rich man in ten years' time. But not in a village. I'm done with being a manor-boy. When the pestilence is finished with us, if there are still cities standing, that's where I shall make my fortune.' His fists are clenched and his face has a fighting flush. 'And if this man —' he plucks the letter from my hands — 'thinks he can call me bondsman and runaway, then he's —'

I see what he intends and snatch the letter from him before he can tear it. Backing away, I put the letter inside my tunic. 'He doesn't! Where does he say that?'

'*Self-proclaimed freeborn man?*' Hob grinds the words out, his eyes as narrow as his mouth. 'He's as good as accusing me!'

'He's telling this Nicholas Alleyne what *you* told *him*, that's all!'

'But he didn't need to say anything about me beyond my name! He's telling the bailiff I may be taken and kept on the manor!'

'Hob —'

He raises a finger in warning. 'We're not going. Don't think we are.'

I learned long ago that speech only serves to provoke a man in such a mood. The time for argument will come when we stand at the crossroads that will take us to Sir John de Loselei's manor. Hob can turn his back on ten shillings and his given word if he wants to but I will not. I must be blameless if I want the saint's continued blessing.

Why did I snatch the letter from him? I did it without thought, just plucked it from his fingers and back into my keeping. But, now I have it again, perhaps I should destroy it quietly. Because there is more to the letter than I read to Hob. More than I am able to read.

After the dating-line, Richard Longe appended a final sentence in a language I do not recognise, but which I take to be French.

Is it a private greeting between friends or instructions as to how Hob and I should be dealt with?

For an hour and more after opening the letter, Hob does not speak and I become increasingly anxious. Finally, I cannot remain silent. Though the thought of parting from him, of being alone once more, dismays me, I must know what he is thinking. I must prepare myself if he is truly set on breaking his word to Richard Longe.

'If I remember the instructions we were given,' I glance at him warily over the mare's neck, 'we should reach Marlborough soon. And then we have to look for the village where we cross the river.'

'Mildenhall,' Hob says. 'The village with the bridge is called Mildenhall.'

I nod. 'Then we follow the river to Hungerford Regis —'

'And then take the road that leads south to Salisbury and on to Slievesdon. I know, Martin. I was the one who *didn't* get the instructions muddled.'

His eyes are fixed on the way ahead. Does his rhyming off the route mean that he has been thinking about it? Has he changed his mind?

'What are you going to do once we get to Salster?' he asks, suddenly. 'After you've been to the shrine in the woods — when we're in the city itself?'

I shrug; my eyes are set on the shrine and I have thought no further. 'I must restore the Maiden to her rightful place and beg her prayers for my father's soul. Whatever comes after that is God's providence.'

'I'm going to be a rich man.' He is matter-of-fact about it, this wealth a decided thing. 'But I'll need money to start with.' He looks straight at me, his blue eyes clear and open. 'Pounds. So far, I've got ten shillings.'

'Five shillings. The other five is mine.'

He turns away.

Does he know how much money there is in my father's bag? The first thing I did when we went back to the reeve's barn yesterday was to check that it was still there and to look inside. There has been no chance to count it but it's clear that there are several shillings' worth of coins. Perhaps as much as a pound.

'If we go to Slievesdon,' I say, my heart beating faster at the prospect of his anger, 'we'll have ten each.'

Hob does not reply.

'How much do you need?' I ask him.

'I told you. Pounds. Two at least. More if I'm not going to live like a churl while I get started.'

'You're old to be an apprentice.'

He looks over at me. 'I'm not going to *be* an apprentice. I've told you, I'm done with masters and lords. I'm going to be my own master.'

I stare at him. How does he expect to learn a trade if he is not prepared to apprentice himself? 'How do you know how much money you need?'

'Our manor had its share of runaways who got to a town and managed to stay there.' He looks into the distance as if he is watching the scene played out: the flight by night, the reeve's awareness — perhaps days later — that he is a man short, the questioning of friends and family, recompense exacted from the runaway's kin.

'One or two came back when they were rich enough.' His mouth pulls into what should be a smile but misses the mark. 'The old man must've been as sick as a scabby sheep when they rode into the village — his own bondsmen, his own property as they'd been — and he couldn't touch them.'

There is a bitter satisfaction in his voice that draws the question out of me.

'Why do you hate him so much — the man who was your lord?'

I wait for him to tell me to mind my own business. Instead, as if it were a thing of little importance, he says, 'Because I was his heir's son and he wouldn't acknowledge me.'

As we walk into the afternoon, I watch Hob. I watch him walk, I watch him shoot, I watch how he throws that long cloak of his over his shoulders and strides out as if he owns the ground he walks on. Everything about him — his long, straight limbs, his golden hair and beard, his clear blue eyes, those open, wide-flung gestures of his — everything backs up his claim to be a lord's bastard.

I cast one glance too many at him and he catches it.

'What? Have I grown another head?'

'Will you tell me?' I ask. 'About your father?'

'Maybe.'

By the time a bell rings out across the ploughland for the third of the little hours of afternoon we are walking through well-kept acres. Wheat sown in the autumn is already a thick green pelt on the lower slopes and, further up, I can see the tiny patches of dirty white that are grazing sheep.

Ploughmen are out and the sight of them raises my spirits. They are too far away to hail but they see us and one raises a hand.

'Lay brothers,' Hob says, his eyes on the men.

I look about but there are no buildings to be seen. 'Shall we find the house — see if they'll give us shelter for the night?'

Hob looks over the mare's withers at me. 'Hah! You've got soft, Martin, with all that sleeping in the collyers' hut. You don't want to go back to sleeping under the cart, do you?'

I make no reply. It's not the hut that I've become accustomed to but the company of our apprentices. Alone with Hob, I wonder how well I'll sleep. But at least, now, I'll be protected from the walking-demon. I took the mare's worn shoes from Tredgham's smith and, with begged nails, have fixed one to each corner of the cart. If the Devil's promise to Saint Dunstan holds true, his minions cannot reach under the cart for me while horseshoes protect every corner.

'No,' Hob says, 'I can do without the company of monks — especially a nosey abbot or prior wanting to know all about the saint and how we came by her.' He glances over at me and I know he is thinking of the coroner's parting words.

As we make our way south, the hillside on our left steadily closes in on our side of the river, reducing the wide meadow to a thin strip of land beneath the slope. The path becomes ever more clagged with clay, rutted and filled with water and, once or twice, we are forced to put our shoulders to the back of the cart to shift the wheels out of a slough.

Slowly, as we close the distance between us and Marlborough, the stream ribbons and vanishes in the murk of the marshy valley bottom and rooks flap back to their roost in a stand of trees on the slope above us.

'We should stop, make camp,' I say. 'Soon we won't be able to see where we're going.'

Hob turns towards me. 'I don't like the lie of the land here. We're vulnerable from that hill behind.'

'You think we might be attacked?'

'I just think we should keep on until we're past Marlborough.'

I look back the way we have come. In the gloom, I can see nothing but the hills, huge against the darkening sky.

'What if we lose our way?'

'We won't. We only have to stick to the river.'

I am about to argue with him when I hear it.

Ha-ha-ha-ha, ha-ha-ha-ha!

My guts clench and I spin around in the direction of the cruel laughter. The magpie is sitting in a tree a little way off. It stares at me, then gives its mocking cry again. My guts clench as I search the bare branches in vain for a second magpie. One for sorrow. Is Hob right — will we be attacked, will I be left alone again?

I look behind us, catch Hob watching me.

'Let's carry on then,' I say, 'while we've still got some light.'

We plod on and, as the sky drains from blue to black, our world shrinks to the ground beneath our feet. We three might be the only living things left in England.

Then, abruptly, a bell calls us back to the world of men.

'Curfew — must be Marlborough.' I wait but Hob says nothing. 'It's late,' I push, 'the embers'll be fading. We need to stop and light a fire before they're gone.'

He looks back the way we have come, though it will do him no good; there is no moon and we would scarcely see an attacker until they were upon us. While he havers, I decide. Fear has driven us further than sense dictates and I will take my cart and my mare no further tonight. With every rut and hole and crooked stone we risk a broken leg, a twisted axle. I pull the mare up and make sure the cart is level and will not roll.

After lighting the fire, I leave Hob skinning a rabbit he shot earlier and take the mare to the river.

I keep my back to the mare and my eyes trained into the darkness around me as she drinks. How I long to eat meat with Hob tonight and not to have to make yet more pottage from oats and onions. Far from everything I know, I crave comfort. What does it matter if I break the Lenten fast? What does such a venal sin matter, when I have left my father, unshriven and alone, in the red earth of the Dene? And yet, I know I must not. If the saint is to bless my journey, even venal sins must be avoided.

As I return to the fire, I see that Hob has just discarded the rabbit's skin, head and guts on the ground. I reach down and put them on to the fire. Best not to attract foxes or badgers in the night; nor carrion birds in the dawn light to throw a curse over the rest of the day. The magpie from earlier has left me jittery.

The fire spits and hisses like a cat at the blood and wet skin and the smell of burning fur fills my nose. If we were in Lysington, I would wrap Hob's rabbit in straw and clay and bake it in the embers so that the meat falls off the bone when the clay is cracked open. But the fire isn't well-on enough and we've neither straw nor clay to hand, so I watch as he spits the carcass over the thin bed of embers and turn aside to make my own thin supper.

Our meal done, I gather the rabbit bones and set them in a pot to simmer on the fire for broth.

Hob watches me work. I know what he is thinking. *Woman's business.*

'So, are you going to tell me?' I feel his eyes on me from the other side of the fire but he gives no reply. 'Richard Longe was right, wasn't he? You may be a lord's bastard, but you're a runaway, too.'

I risk a glance and see that this is not the question he was expecting. Still, he rallies quickly in his own defence.

'What does it matter what kind of house I was born in? I'm free by right of birth.'

It may be different where Hob is from but, where I was born, a bastard son has no claim on his father's rights.

He stretches out a finger, pokes the end of a stick into the fire. 'What about your father?'

My heart clenches. 'What about him?'

'Free or unfree?'

The cold fist releases. 'Free.'

'And your mother?'

'Unfree till they married.' Not that it's any of his business. 'She was a servant in our house.'

'He married a servant? A woman unfree *and* poor?' It might be Richard speaking; my flesh crawls with chill bumps despite the fire. 'So...' He pauses. I can feel his eyes on me but I will not look up. 'When did he marry her — before or after he got you on her?'

If your mother hadn't been such a slut, Dadda would've kept his cock to himself and you wouldn't be here, Martin!

Does Hob see my hand shake as I stir the broth? I think not — it would surely goad him to more taunts. My rage always roused Richard and Adam to greater cruelty.

'I'm no bastard, Hob.'

'Well *I am*.' He leans forward, hitting his own chest with a closed fist. 'But at least I'm a knight's bastard, a soldier's spawn!'

He glares at me, as if he has issued some kind of challenge. Or as if I had.

'The knight — he was your lord's son?'

He nodded. 'Robert. My father's name was Robert.'

I get the whole story, then; the reason for all the pride and ambition and rage and hatred of lordship that seethes within Hob Cleve. I wonder that he has kept it to himself so long for, once he has started, he cannot stop. Not that it is a long story, or even an unusual one; it might be the oldest story in the world.

His father in blood — this Robert — was esquire to a knight who fought with the king in Scotland and France and, in the year when he was seventeen years old, he came home at Maytime to see his ailing mother. And, as noble young men of high spirits will, he went a-maying with the villagers on his father's demesne lands.

'If it hadn't been warm, that May-eve in the woods,' Hob says, 'I doubt I'd be here. No man likes to bare his arse to the rain and the cold, not even for a pretty face and a maidenhead.'

Did Robert single her out, I wonder, or did the maid with the pretty face have her eye on him? I have been out in the moonlit woods to bring in the may-boughs with sunrise, I have

173

seen how girls put themselves in the way of the young men they fancy.

I meet Hob's eye.

'You've a disapproving look about you, Martin. But you needn't think he forced her. I'm living proof of that, I think!'

Somehow, he reads my ignorance in my expression and gives a thin half-smile.

'Don't you know? If the act gives a woman no pleasure, her womb won't open, there'll be no child.'

I feel a heat rise within me as I picture Hob with the simpering girls who came to see the saint, see the practised way he spoke to them, touched them. No doubt he has experience of pleasuring girls, of taking his pleasure with them. And, no doubt, he can smell the ignorance coming off me. It scarcely mattered in Lysington where I was half-priested already; I find it matters now.

'And then?' I ask. 'Did your father ride up on his destrier and claim you?' It is a cruel question; he has already told me that his grandfather failed to acknowledge him and the apple never falls far from the bough that bore it.

But Hob does not waver. 'Yes! He was proud of fathering a son.'

'So, he provided for you and your mother, then?'

'He would have, if he'd been there. But he was with his lord.'

A man among men, Hob's tone says, a warrior who lacked the time to settle matters of women and their children.

'He asked the old man to make sure we were provided for. Which he saw fit to do —' Hob spits into the fire — 'by telling his bailiff to find a husband for my mother.'

His mother was unfree too, then. On many manors, I know, the distinction between free and bond has become one that no-one cares about overmuch; but if a lord is jealous of his rights and privileges, no unfree man — or woman — can stand against his will.

'So, who was she married to — a man with no choice in the matter?'

'Of course — who else would dare?'

'Was he unwilling?'

Hob spits again, as if his mouth has filled with bile. 'Unwilling? He grabbed his chance with both hands — thought that having the future lord's son under his roof would see him go up in the world. And so it should have —' his voice is tight with fury — '*would* have, if Robert hadn't died.'

I take my knife out and tease some shards of meat off the bones in the pot as I wait for him to go on.

'Every time he came to see us, my father promised he'd persuade the old man. That we'd be freed and provided for.' He stops and sucks in a breath. 'But the old bastard wasn't going to give us our freedom for nothing. He wanted something from my father first. There was a widow he had his eye on — a rich widow with land and no heirs. That was the bargain — if my father married her, he'd get what he wanted for us.'

'Isn't that what lords do?' I ask. 'Marry for fortune?'

'My father didn't want an *old woman*, however rich she was!'

'He could have kept a young woman as well, for his pleasure.'

'My father was an esquire, soon to be knight! He wanted a beautiful woman at his table as well as in his bed. He didn't want to sit and eat with a woman twice his age and look at her wrinkles and her barren belly!'

I wipe my knife-blade on the grass and put it away. 'He didn't marry her then?'

'No.' The word is fraught with pride and resentment.

'So you never got your freedom?'

His glare is ugly in the firelight's dark shadows. 'My father would've freed us. And given us land. He promised my mother. As soon as the old man was dead and he came into his lordship, he'd free us. We'd be the best provided for in the village. A new house — land, sheep...'

'He told your mother? He visited her — you?'

'Every year he'd come back for the maying. If his lord could spare him. Every year. And he always brought something for me. He gave me this.' He pulls his knife from his belt, smoothing the length of its blade with his fingers. 'Taught me how to flick it up and catch it, how to throw it to kill a rabbit.'

A knight's esquire killing rabbits with a knife instead of his hawk? No wonder he and his father had not seen eye to eye; Robert obviously had too much of a taste for the pursuits of common men.

'Every time my father came, he'd say — look after my boy, one day he'll be a free man, he'll be somebody on this manor.' He looks over the fire at me to make sure my listening is rapt enough. 'Every time, he'd tell him, my mother's cur of a husband — look after my boy.'

I wait for him to go on but Hob seems unable to finish his story.

'He died,' I say, finally. 'Robert — your father — he died.' Hob nods. 'How?'

He jabs his knife into the ground at his feet and pulls it back towards him, slicing the turf into a wound. 'He was with his lord. And the king. At the siege of some town in Flanders — I don't know its name.'

It was sieges that had called the Dene's miners to the king's wars. Did our men undermine the walls of the Flemish town where Hob's father died? Did they die there, too, leaving their own children fatherless, their wives widowed?

'What happened? After he died?'

Hob breathes in and out through flared nostrils. 'Nothing,' he says, finally. 'For months. Nothing. My father died in August. We didn't know anything about it until Christmas. The bailiff announced it before the feast — we had to hear it at the same time as everybody else. Damn him to hell!'

Is his curse directed at his father for dying or the lord's bailiff for failing to grant him the privileges of an acknowledged son? I cannot tell and I let him fall into silence.

'The bloody flux,' he says, after a long while. 'That's what he died of.'

The bloody flux — a sickness of the campaigns. According to the foresters back from France, it brought a writhing, gut-twisting pain that made a man fear he would shit his bowels from his body.

'My mother's stupid bastard of a husband didn't know when to give up. Thought we'd still get our freedom. Went to see the reeve.'

I do not need to hear the rest. Hob's face tells a sufficient story.

'Came back dragging a stick. That was the beginning of it. Kept shouting that my father'd never meant to free us, that he'd only said that to get a free fuck out of my mother every time he came home.'

Hob, his chin low, stares at nothing.

I wonder what the reeve said to Hob's stepfather. It seems to me that their neighbours might well have thought that Hob's mother and her husband had made too much of their future expectations, of the golden boy beneath their roof who was going to make them wealthy and free. A man like the reeve, who had earned his position, won people's respect by hard work and honesty, might well take the opportunity to have a small revenge on that kind of crowing presumption.

'Got him back in the end, though, don't think I didn't.' Hob's words come creeping towards me over the fire, low and full of malice.

My stomach clenches and I sit very still as his eyes clamp on to mine. 'Watched him die, didn't I? Watched him die like a dog.'

Hob stabs the ground at his feet, tearing at the turf.

'My mother'd never've died if it wasn't for him. He brought death into our house. The pestilence started at the other end of the village, a mile away from us. Died quickly, families did, one after another. Lay in the church, stinking, unburied. Gravediggers wouldn't touch them. Said the families had to do it. If there was nobody left, the corpse rotted where it lay.'

Again and again, as he speaks, Hob stabs the knife into the ground and pulls it out. Stab — pull. Stab — pull.

'He went to the parson. Said he'd bury the bodies if he was paid. So he did — day after day, he dug pits and threw them in.'

Stab — pull.

'And he brought their death and their stink to our house and she died.'

Stab, pull; stab, pull.

'She died and he didn't care. Said she'd always been weak. She died and *he* lived. He buried her and he buried our neighbours and still *he didn't die!*'

Stab, stab, stab.

'Still, he sat there, in the house, denying me my freedom!'

He stops then and I stare at him. 'But he died in the end?' I ask, finally. 'The plague took him in the end?'

Hob looks up. Slowly he shakes his head, eyes holding mine. 'Not every corpse put in a pit has died of the plague.'

The look in his eyes, dead and cold, almost stops my heart.

He looks down and pushes his knife slowly, deliberately, into the ground.

'You killed him?'

'Does it matter?'

'Yes!'

Now he looks up. 'Does it? Do you know how many people died in my village? Hundreds. When I went to the priest and told him he was dead, do you know what he said?'

I shake my head.

'"Who'll bury them now?" Not "why didn't you come for me?" not "God have mercy on his soul". *Who'll bury them now?* He didn't care that the bastard was dead, or how he'd died. He was just another corpse.' He stares at me. 'Tell me something, Martin — if God and his priests care so little that the folk of England are dying like flies in autumn, *why should I?'*

I take first watch while Hob settles under the cart.

I stare into the fire.

I watched him die like a dog.

Did Hob kill his mother's husband? He certainly wished him dead.

As you wished your father dead.

I thrust the demon's words aside and fasten my thoughts on Hob. Did he kill Edgar? He would have, if I had not stopped him — killed him like a rabid dog. I ask myself Hob's question — *does it matter?* When churchyards are like ploughed fields and blameless acres are sown not with crops but with corpses, does one more death matter?

I believe, in my heart, that it does. But not, I have to admit, as much as it would have mattered before the pestilence came. Perhaps nothing matters as much, now, as it did before.

I look up and see Hob curled at the side of the fire. What if he decides that his life would be easier if I were dead? He needs money for his new, masterless life in Salster and I have money.

But no. He needs me. If he wants use of the cart and everything in it then he must have me too, for the mare will not go anywhere for him. Her unyielding refusal to budge for him has meant that I have had to lead her through every stream on our journey, take her to every drinking-place, bring her back from her hobbled grazing each morning.

No. If Hob wants to arrive in Salster with the appearance of a man of substance, he will have to keep company with me. The question is — now that I have seen how little a man's life might mean to him — do I want his company? And, if not, how can I escape him?

CHAPTER 21

The following day, as dusk draws near and the darkening skies threaten snow once more, we come upon Hungerford Regis. We round a headland and there is the town, spread out before us. Another river joins the Kennet here from the west and, on the spit of land where the two rivers join — an island, more or less — there is a cluster of white, slate-roofed buildings that is joined to the land on either side of the rivers by sturdy wooden bridges.

'That's our way.' I point down at the island. 'Dark's not far off. If snow comes, we'll need shelter.' I look around at him, pulling aside the blanket that covers my head so that I can see him properly.

'You think we should stay there tonight?'

I turn and gaze down at the island's sturdy buildings, screwing up my eyes in the fading light. 'Most likely that's a little priory or a hospital,' I say, the wind almost whipping my words away. 'They'd give us shelter.'

'What if the plague's there?'

I glance over at him. 'We don't need to sleep in the guest-hall. I just want to be out of the wind if snow comes.'

Hob looks up at the swirling sky. 'If we're going to stay amongst clerics, we should put the saint away.'

I nod and move to unfasten the canvas. The knots are stiff to my frozen fingers and I am soon berating myself for not just taking the saint and lying her on the pallet in the back of the cart instead of wanting to hide her at the front, away from casual curiosity.

Finally, I succeed in loosing the knots on one corner and pull the canvas up, resisting the temptation to put my chilled fingers in my mouth so that I can suck the sting and ache from them.

I lift the saint, wrap her in the blanket from my shoulders and lie her gently behind the cart's head-board. To be sure that she lies flat and will not be joggled about as we make our way down to the island, I run a hand beneath her; and there, where there should be nothing but wooden slat, I feel something soft and loose. I wrap my fingers around it and pull it up far enough to see.

The money-bag. What is it doing out of the press?

Hefting it, it seems less full than it was, but I cannot be sure.

I glance swiftly at Hob but he is staring down at the priory, apparently unaware of my find. Did he take the money-bag from the press and put it here, where he could more easily get at it?

Or was it you — I hear my demon's voice — *you that took it from the press as you slept and did my bidding?*

Did I nod off on my watch, despite the one-legged stool? Did the demon take command of my limbs the moment sleep claimed me, did he prevent the stool from tipping me onto the ground and steer my limbs to the cart? If so, I took the bag from the press without the smallest stirring of will or sense.

But why would an imp of Satan's want me to move the money-bag? Unless, the thought chills me, he did not want me to move it but to throw it away, pauperise myself. Is that it? Did the demon try to force me, last night, to fling every penny I possess into the darkness as Hob slept?

The very thought makes the wind seem colder.

The guest hall and dormitories being full of the sick and dying, Hob and I find a place near the priory's kitchen wall, where the heat of the bread ovens warms the stone. With our fire built and the trestle-board butted up between cart and wall to keep the swirling wind off us, we put the pallet on the ground, pull the bundle of blankets from the cart and prepare to sleep in turns, the waking one feeding the fire lest both of us freeze to our deaths in the night.

Snowflakes are hurled around the courtyard by the bitter, scouring wind but they are few and do not settle.

'Snow or not, I'd rather be out here than in there,' Hob says, shuffling the pallet another inch towards the fire and pulling his blankets over him. He refused a place in the stables with the mare, saying he would rather sleep with the cart than with servants who had dealings with the sick. Unwilling to leave him alone with the cart and the money-bag, I opted to stay with him.

As I wrap my blankets around me and make myself as comfortable as I can, I glance up at the infirmary on the other side of the yard where, even now, souls are barely clinging to bodies and others lie in mortal fear of their end. I mutter a prayer for them and commence staring at the fire. I dare not close my eyes or I shall be asleep.

'God keep you, my son.'

The words startle me like a kick. Above me stands a figure in a heavy, hooded cloak and the habit of a monk, a pair of thick but aged boots just visible beneath the hem. He must have come straight from compline instead of going to his bed.

I make to rise but a hand is laid gently on the blanket that covers my head. 'No. Don't get up. It's too cold to be standing about.'

Taking his own advice, he swings a long-legged stool to the fireside and lowers himself carefully on to it, its long shanks sparing his old bones the need to bend too far.

'So,' he smiles, 'this is a strange time to be travelling.'

I mutter agreement. When he says nothing more, I feel compelled to justify my presence. 'All my family's dead but one brother.'

He nods, like a man weary of hearing the same story.

'I'm travelling to Salster to pray for their souls.'

'A long journey.'

I look into what I can see of his firelit face. I would put him older than my dead grandfather but his face has a well-fed, fleshy look that Gransher's never did. Nevertheless, his is a kind and patient countenance and — for once — my courage does not fail me.

'There's a shrine outside the city —' I hesitate and his silence gives me leave to stop if I wish. 'On the site of a woodland cave. The home of a saint.'

He does not remind me that Salster is known only for Saint Dernstan, does not ask me about this forest saint. He says nothing; and it is a quiet, accepting nothing.

'Her name is Saint Cynryth and my father was devoted to her.'

As I speak the words, the spittle dries in my mouth and I feel my heart swell and beat. I wait for his frown to match Thomas Hassell's, for the words which will tell me that there never was such a saint, that the church recognises no Cynryth, knows of no miracles wrought by her. But there is no frown, no words of doubt.

'Her story's a moving one,' I tell him.

'I'm sure it is, son. But it's too cold for stories. I came to see whether you might be in need of a confessor. None of us knows when we might be struck down, these days, and those on a long journey might find themselves in particular need.'

Guilt and failure and cowardice and suspicion and mistrust rise within me and fill my throat so swiftly that I cannot swallow, can barely breathe. I long for release, for the relief of absolution and the knowledge that my soul is clean and pure; for the certainty that, if I am struck down by man's hand or nature's accident, my soul will not be imperilled. Until this moment, I did not know how weighted with sin I had become.

'Are you a priest?'

He shakes his head. 'No. There are no priests left here, nor many of us professed brothers, either. But I may hear your confession, nonetheless.'

'How?' Only a priest, ordained by a bishop consecrated by the Pope himself, can offer absolution to the confessed.

He draws in a deep breath. 'Out of compassion for these mortal times, a decree has been issued that, if there is no priest present, *in extremis*, a man may make his confession to a lay person and be absolved.'

'To a *layman*?' No. Such a thing is impossible. No layman can wipe away another's sins.

'Yes.' His eyes meet mine. 'It has been decreed. The decree *also* says that if men resolve not to leave repentance until they're sick, if they seek out a priest in good time, while they're still well, they are to be given an indulgence of forty days remission from Purgatory.'

He is urging me to confess, now, while I have the opportunity.

I glance across at Hob, a motionless mound beneath his blanket. Is he awake, his ears pricked? I can hardly confess my suspicions of him within his hearing.

The monk seems to read my thoughts. 'We could go into the nave. It's out of the wind, even if it doesn't have the warmth of your fire.'

I rise, stiff with cold, keeping the blanket about me.

'And your companion?'

'I'll ask him in the morning,' I say. 'For now, let's leave him to sleep.'

Hob does not stir when I get back to our fireside, so I make myself comfortable for the rest of my watch; comfortable, at least, in body, for my confession — and the knowledge that I was making it to somebody who could not give me penance — has left me feeling uncleansed.

'Don't be troubled,' the monk said when I gave voice to my unease. 'Have faith in the sacrament. It's the sacrament — and the Lord who gave it — that saves, not the hand that administers it.'

But if no more than faith in the sacrament is needed, then what in God's holy name is to become of the church? If the church and its clerics are not set apart to do God's work amongst men on earth, if any man can hear confession, then why should men, ever again, revere priestly ordination and submit to penance? Why should we pay tithes to a church if it offers nothing we cannot find amongst ourselves?

My teeth chatter and I pull my blanket closer. Perhaps the murmurings we heard at Tredgham were right. Perhaps the pestilence is here to cleanse the church as well as the world.

God has abandoned you all my demon whispers. *You've proved unworthy of Heaven, He's given all of you over to Satan. And when this generation is all gone, He'll create a new race of men who will please him more.*

If that is true then there is no comfort in pilgrimage or in prayer for our dead, and all my hopes are without foundation; I am nothing more than a plaything of Satan, my pilgrimage a hellish amusement.

In the wind-blown silence, I stumble, terrified to Hob's side. Shaking him, I feel the solidity of his shoulder beneath the blanket, feel the force of him, even in sleep. His grumbled complaints about the hour and the cold soothe me like honey on a burn and, as he stands and pisses a little way off, I let his bawdy speculations about what the monks get up to in their dormitories drown out my terrors.

CHAPTER 22

We are ready to go well before prime. The wind dropped some time before dawn, but the day is raw and cold, as if the night's raging has flayed everything in its path.

As we leave the town behind us, common gives way to heathland and heathland to wood. Little hawthorn trees grow on the poorly-cleared margin of the track, along with bracken and broom. A hawthorn twig brushes my tunic and I catch it in my fingers; beneath the soft new bark the knobs of leaf-buds are swelling. It's the first sign I have seen that spring will come, that we will not be prisoners of winter as we are of the pestilence.

I break off the twig and stick it in my belt as a sign of hope.

Hob is staring at me. 'Do you feel it?'

'What — the spring?'

'No. Eyes. Watching.'

I look around, beyond the bushes into the standards and coppiced wood a hundred yards or so away. With the trees naked and the undergrowth winter-low, there is precious little cover for watchers.

I turn back to him. 'Have you seen somebody?'

'No. But I can feel them. Somebody's there.'

I look over my shoulder, back down the track. No figures dart away out of sight, no bracken stirs.

I gather the mare's reins and walk on. Hob is not used to woodland, does not know that the trees have eyes and the wind both voice and ears.

'Thieving gangs trouble your King's Forest of Dene much?' he asks.

'No. Collyers and miners don't take kindly to being robbed.'

'Well, this is a perfect hunting-ground for gangs.' Hob's head moves as he looks this way and that. 'Travellers with money and goods. No villagers wandering past. Plenty of cover.'

Robber gangs. Everyone who has occasion to travel fears them. And I fear them more than most, for I have already encountered a robber. Encountered him, seen him felled, watched him havering between life and death, and buried him.

By the time we break out into open ground, Hob's twitchiness has even the mare jumpy and wild-eyed.

The sky is more blue than grey now, and, in the growing breeze, the high clouds send shadows flowing like pools of day-faded darkness across the heath. Gulls ride the streaming air on their stiff wings, searching for the rich pickings of ploughland. They need to move south and east. Like us.

We soon discover that this heathland is treacherous, that our road dips into sloughs and hollows invisible from a distance. What seemed open and knowable suddenly becomes untrustworthy. I walk warily at the mare's side, watching for what might come at us from the next hidden dip.

Six feet away, Hob's vigilance possesses him, his head moving constantly this way and that as he scours the country for anything that might threaten us.

A rook shrieks at its fellows overhead, making Hob duck. As he straightens up, he reaches out to pull the canvas aside and I watch him take out his bow.

'Are you mad?'

He turns to me. 'What?'

'A man with a weapon is dangerous! Any robber'll know he has to kill you before he can hope to get near the cart.'

A burst of movement ahead turns both our heads but it is no more than a flock of goldfinches whirring up all at once, like a handful of pebbles thrown into the air. I watch them fly away, each bird dipping and rising in time with all its fellows as if they quickly tire then rally. A hundred yards or so off, they descend, all together. And, as my eyes follow them to the ground, I see a movement which is not birdlike.

'Hob!' As I pull the mare up, he turns and I point.

His eyes follow my finger. 'Dogs. Worrying something.'

I strain my eyes towards the darting, circling shapes and, as I watch them, I hear a sound as if my gaze has drawn it to us over the heath; a banging, clanging sound like a cracked bell.

I reach into the cart for a stout stick.

'What are you doing?'

'Going to see who's making that noise.'

Hob shakes his head. 'Leave well alone, Martin. If you get bitten it'll be the end of you.'

I heft the cudgel. 'I won't get bitten.'

'Have you ever *seen* a mad dog?'

'Yes. And killed one, too.'

As I walk away from him, he makes a great deal of taking the mare's reins and preventing her from wandering but I am happy to leave him to it. Better to do this on my own than to be hindered by his fear; the dogs would smell it on him and be driven to a frenzy.

Again I hear the same clanging, tuneless sound, accompanied this time by a shout borne on the wind. I break into a run.

As I come within a stone's throw of the pack, I see that there are only three dogs. They are snarling and rushing at two people in a shallow dip: a woman lying on the ground and a man on his knees next to her. He is beating at a pan and yelling his voice hoarse.

The dogs are bewildered by the noise and they prance back with each blow of wood on copper. If they had hands, they would cover their ears.

I run at them, laying about me. They leap out of my way, one yelping as I catch his haunch a glancing blow.

'I'll try and kill one,' I shout to the kneeling man. 'The others'll run off then.'

I pick out the biggest dog and throw myself at him but he is too fast for me and takes to his heels in the direction of the cart, the other two following. As I stumble after them, my feet catching in clumps of low growth, I see Hob climb on to the cart's off-side wheel and string his bow.

As best I can, I herd the dogs towards him.

An arrow flies and the lead dog is pinned to the ground by a shaft which pierces its chest. The other dogs pull up, looking about for the source of this swift death, but the second dog does not see the arrow that takes it through the head. The last dog turns tail and flees. Hob looses off an arrow but misses his aim, the animal shies but does not stop.

Certain that we have seen the last of it, I leave Hob to retrieve his arrows and turn back to the man on the ground. He is dressed in clothes better than any but our lord had in Lysington. A townsman, for sure.

He looks up, silently, at my coming. Now that I am not distracted by the dogs, I see that the woman he has been protecting is dead. The wind is blowing away from me, else I would be able to smell her. She has died of the pustules and I can see one, burst and oozing, on her neck.

I stretch a hand towards the man's shoulder.

'No! Don't touch me! I'm sick.'

I do not need his words to tell me that. His face is shining with sweat despite the wind and there are sores around his mouth and nose. The desperation that allowed him to beat the dogs off has gone and I can almost see the life seeping out of him.

'Coughing blood?' I ask.

He shakes his head. 'Fever and pain.'

'How long?'

He shakes his head, as if his health is of no consequence. 'I was trying to look after Agnes.'

I look across at his dead wife. She lies in the lee of a hefty handcart piled with cord-fastened bundles. Though she has two blankets and a cloak over her, I doubt that they or the cart would have provided much protection — not in the wind we had last night. A pitiful pile of scorched sticks and tinder that should be a fire is lying on the ground nearby. The man catches my gaze.

'I've never lit a fire before. I couldn't make it go.' He puts his head in his hands and begins to weep.

I sit on my haunches beside him and wait. After a little while, he smears the tears from his face with the heels of his palms.

'Where've you come from?' I ask.

'Andover — south.' He swallows, takes a breath to steady himself. 'Thought going north would keep us safe. But it's stalked us.'

No need to ask why he and his wife are here, where nothing lives but hares and goldfinches and dogs running wild. No village would have taken them in, even had they asked it.

Hob walks towards us, bloody arrows in his fist. 'What news?' he asks from a little way off.

'They've come from Andover. His wife died in the night.'

'What's to do, then?'

I put my hand on the man's shoulder. This time he does not pull away. 'We must bury your wife, friend.'

He turns his bright, red-ringed eyes on me and I notice a dark patch on his cheek. 'No! Not unless you bury me too! I won't leave her.'

'The church has said —'

'No! I promised her! I promised I wouldn't leave her. That we'd be together.' He drags himself over to his dead wife and pulls her stiffening, stinking body to him.

I look over my shoulder at Hob. When he says nothing, I stand and go over to him. 'We can't leave him here to die alone.' I keep my voice low and my head turned away from the man on the ground.

'What, you want to take him with us?'

I shake my head.

'Oh no!' Now it's Hob's turn to shake his head. 'We're not staying here to watch him die! No, Martin.'

'Perhaps he won't die.'

'Don't be stupid!' Hob's voice is a hiss. 'I can see the marks of pestilence on him from here. He'll be dead by this time tomorrow.'

'Then we *should* stay with him —'

'No!' He grabs my arm with his free hand. 'If we do that, he's not the only one who'll be dead. We're sitting targets here.'

I shake him off and look at the dying man as he holds his dead wife in a last, wretched embrace. He is willing his soul to Purgatory after her, that much is clear. There will be no long fight for life.

I look around the frozen heath; despite Hob's twitchiness, it seems an unlikely place to lie in wait.

'If there *were* robbers here, don't you think they'd've had that handcart by now?' When Hob does not answer I turn away. 'I'm going to hear his confession before he falls senseless and can't speak.'

'What do you mean, hear his confession?'

I explain, in as few words as I can, what the monk at Hungerford Regis told me. Hob takes it in without comment. 'And then?'

'Then we'll see.'

'Martin —'

I look over my shoulder.

'Hobble the mare and let her graze, Hob. You've got your bow — you can keep watch over us.'

The man barely has the strength to confess before his eyes close and he falls silent.

When I make shift to move, his eyes half-open once more. 'Swear to me … swear … you won't separate us. Swear it.'

I put my hand on his shoulder. 'I swear it. You'll be together.'

Pulling the cloak and blankets from his wife, I lay them over him. Then, clear in my mind, I make my way back to Hob.

'What have you said to him?'

'I've promised I won't separate him from his wife. I'll stay with him until he dies.'

'No!' He jumps down. 'Martin, they're nothing to us! It was only by chance that we saw them. If it hadn't been for the dogs, we'd've passed them by and been none the wiser.'

'But we *didn't* pass them by. We were guided to them —'

He seizes my forearm. 'But what if it was your demon that guided us? He'd like to frustrate a saint, wouldn't he? And what'll happen to your father's soul if you fall sick, if you don't get to Salster?'

I shrug him off. 'I will.'

'Not if you stay here when you don't have to!'

'I *do* have to. We *both* have to. Or didn't your parson teach you the acts of mercy? Tend the sick! Bury the dead!'

'You don't have to do those things if they're going to kill you! They're for ordinary times not for now!'

I stare at him. That cannot be right.

Can't it? the demon whispers. *The church has changed its mind on where the dead must be buried and who can hear confession. The pestilence has changed everything.*

I feel like Noah, stranded on a hill in a new land — everything I have ever known has been washed away and I am at a loss as to how a man must live in this new world. I shake my head, draw in a steadying breath. 'I'm under the saint's protection. I'll be safe.'

It takes all my courage to turn my back on him and his bow. He could kill me here, bury me and take my goods. That handcart would carry everything he needs.

I have taken no more than half a dozen steps when he shouts after me. 'If you truly believed in the saint, you'd've asked her to heal him.'

As the force of his words hits me, I falter. After Tredgham and her blessing of so many folk there, why has it not entered my head to offer her blessing to this man?

Hob. His hectic eagerness to be out of Savernake Forest has kept me from seeing clearly.

The afternoon wears away. Hob returns from foraging for firewood to find me trying to give water to the dying man.

'God's teeth, Martin, let the poor bastard die! You're doing nothing but giving his suffering length as well as depth.'

I cannot look at him. 'Leave me be. If you want to speed things, get to it and dig a grave.'

Two hours later we have a serviceable grave but still only one corpse.

'Are you going to shroud them?'

I look up and Hob gestures at the couple's handcart. 'Bound to be something on there we can use. She looks like the sort of woman who wouldn't want to be parted from her good sheets.'

He is proved right. Most of the bundles on the cart contain clothing and linen, the quality suggesting that they brought what they could carry rather than everything they possessed.

I wonder at a rich woman's sense of what is needful in fleeing the pestilence. No pans, no precious herbs and spices, only clothes and linens, pewter candleholders and silver spoons, embroidery silks and needles. And a book.

I have seen no great number of books. In fact, up close, I have seen only one before — Master William's rough-bound volume of offices and psalms and canticles.

In that book, the quickly copied text occupied the whole page for economy's sake but, in Agnes's missal, the script forms a small island of black ink in the middle of each page while the remainder of the vellum's smooth, fine-grained surface is taken up with intricate embellishments. Scenes from the life of Our Lady are drawn in painstaking detail and painted in colours that make the real world seem drab; little animals and flowers scatter the page edges; braid-like borders in red and blue and green run across the top of the page, above the written words, and down the edge, alongside the words.

'What's that?'

I hold it out. 'A missal — prayer book.'

'Looks expensive.'

'Yes.'

'Found any money? People with a book like that aren't going to be paupers. There must be money hidden somewhere.'

But we find none. Perhaps they have been robbed, after all.

There is, however, a great quantity of sheeting. I turn to tell Hob that we have shrouds aplenty and see him crouched next to the dying man, both hands outstretched towards him.

'What are you doing?' My voice is sharp. I hear the accusation and so will Hob.

His head snaps round and he drops his hands. Then he shrugs. 'I was going to unfasten his cloak — see if his money-bag was on his belt.'

I stare at him. 'Shouldn't we wait to see whether he'll live?' I ask, eventually.

He shrugs again and lets it drop. But his outstretched hands disturb me. They were headed, not towards the man's waist where his heavy cloak is bound, but towards his face.

Dusk. We have lit our fire and sit before it, backs to the cartwheel. Hob's bow is at his side, an arrow ready.

'You're never going to leave it strung all night?'

'I am. A stretched string's easier to deal with than a knife in the ribs.'

'Why are you so afraid we'll be attacked here?'

He pulls his knife forward on his belt and takes it out. 'You don't know this place.'

I look sideways at him, seeing how the firelight deepens the dark hollows of his eye-sockets. 'Do you?'

He does not reply. His eyes are fixed on the knife, finger and thumb stroking the blade. I look away. Has he been here before? Was he set upon, beaten? But then Edgar comes to mind and, before I can thrust the thought away, I see the two of them hiding in the wood, waylaying travellers, Hob with his bow, Edgar with his knife. A robber gang.

Hob wears a cloak that no villein would ever lawfully possess and I have only his word that he took it from Edgar's pack.

Was Hob attacked, or was he the one doing the attacking?

Sometime after full dark we rise from our places by the fire, me to look at Agnes's husband, Hob to peer into the darkness beyond our fire's glow. Neither of us finds anything worth reporting and Hob fetches the pallet while I take the stool to keep first watch.

As he wraps the blankets around him, he asks, 'You ever heard of a man so keen to be with his wife, even though she was dead?'

'Only in stories.'

He grunts. 'It's not manly.'

I do not reply but Hob has another question for me. 'How do you like a woman?'

Taken unawares, my mouth falls open but no words emerge.

'Buxom and mischievous?' he prompts. 'Quiet and biddable?'

Still I do not answer and he pounces on my hesitation like a dog on a cornered rat. 'Martin Collyer — I do believe you're still chaste!'

'There aren't throngs of women in the forest and I was there nine months of the year.'

I do not believe Hob hears me; his mind is on the act itself. 'Never buried your cock in a tight little cunny... Never felt it squeezing the seed out of you.' He moans and I see him fumbling beneath the blanket. 'There were some ripe young wives with limp-cocked husbands in our village.'

I picture Hob sneaking into a cottage or a barn with a young woman, see him thrusting into her, her arms twined around him as she makes the noises my brothers imitated so often in lewd talk with other lads. My own cock grows hard.

Hob turns away from me and shrugs deeper into the blankets.

I fail at my watch and Hob's snores wake me in the half-light of dawn to a cold fire. I poke through the ash and clods and blackened sticks but find not a single ember.

Hob, roused by my cry of frustration, scowls at the lifeless ashes on the hearth-ring. 'If I didn't know you better, Martin, I'd say you'd let it go out so we'd have to go to Slievesdon to get embers.'

My mouth is open to tell him that I did no such thing, that we can get embers anywhere along the way but I catch myself in time. If the fire's coldness gives him the excuse he needs to change his mind about going to Slievesdon, let him say what he wants.

Still, my guts clench at the thought of finally taking Longe's letters to his lord. I see the writing on the outside of each in my mind. *'For the private attention of Sir John de Loselei', 'The present Bailiff to Sir John de Loselei'*.

I should have let Hob destroy the second one. I fear that nothing good can come of the bailiff reading it. My plan is to simply deliver Longe's letter and rely on Sir John's generosity. And yet I cannot quite bring myself to destroy the letter to the bailiff.

Hob yawns. 'I hope burying your friend isn't going to delay us too long.'

I look over to where Agnes's husband is lying. His face is covered.

Hob watches me stagger to my feet. 'He died not long after you fell asleep.'

I fall on my knees at the dead man's side and bend over him, lifting the sheet that Hob has folded over his face. No bruises, no blue to his lips, no bending of his nose, no sign that anything but a plague-fever killed him.

Since there is nothing else to do once the trestle is loaded into the cart and the blankets bundled on top, we put the dead man into the grave with his wife. This is what the pestilence has brought us to: a death unseen, unmourned by friend or neighbour; a burial unconsecrated by the church. Agnes and her husband were obviously wealthy townsfolk and yet, here they are, committed to unhallowed ground by strangers, their burial watched only by magpies and crows. No almsgiving for prayers, no week mind, month-mind nor anniversary of their deaths to pray them from Purgatory.

I did not even know his name.

Nothing is as it was.

CHAPTER 23

Before long, the heathland is behind us and we are and back into cultivated acres. Some of the slopes are steep and, here and there, Hob is forced to put his shoulder to the back of the cart.

'Why d'you think the saint didn't heal him?'

I look around, surprised. I would have laid bets on Hob putting aside any thought of Agnes and her man as soon as we walked away from their grave.

I shrug, not daring to tell him what I truly think, for fear of another outburst against excessive married love. My belief is that the dead man's promise to his wife weighed against him when the saint petitioned God for his life. He swore that he would not leave her and God has honoured his oath.

'Perhaps her intercession was too weak,' Hob suggests. 'Perhaps all the blessing she did at Tredgham drained her.'

'She's not a water butt that needs refilling! Her power's already given to her, from the holiness of her life on earth.'

Hob puts his head on one side. 'I don't know if that's right, though. Think about the miracle at Tredgham. It didn't happen when people first came on to the hearth to pray to the saint, did it? No — it happened after a week and more, when the store of prayers had built up.' His eyes hold mine. 'We need the saint to be strong, don't we, to see us safe to Salster and to intercede for your father?'

I nod, wary. 'Yes.'

'So we must get more prayers for her.'

Until now, Hob has shown little interest in the saint beyond whether I stole her and I find his sudden wish to discuss how she comes by her power puzzling. I shake my head. 'Even if you're right, how would we do that?'

He smiles 'Don't worry. I'll think of a way.'

We find ourselves in the village of Slievesdon without seeing a soul on our approach. The deserted fields and silent houses do not bode well, though I do not say as much to Hob. His eyes are darting everywhere. Is he expecting an attack or does he have it in mind to start plundering dead men's houses in lieu of our ten shillings?

We walk past recently built dwellings with gardens as yet unfenced and on, into the village proper. A cat surveys our progress from its perch atop a roof. Its solitude disturbed, it stretches out a skinny leg and begins to wash itself.

Hob whistles. 'There's some money here. Look at these places.'

True enough, the houses and tofts look unusually prosperous and well-cared for. From the size of some of the outbuildings, there are families here who keep considerably more than a pair of cows and a pig — half the byres are big enough for a dozen head of cattle. From within one, a sudden bellowing is set up; the beasts have heard the mare's hooves and know it means people — they want feeding.

Everywhere, doors are closed. There is no one fetching water, no one bringing home firewood, no one sitting in the chilly sunshine mending tools. A few chickens are scratching here and there but they pay us little attention.

Then, further along the street, we hear raised voices coming from one of the houses ahead. We quicken our pace and, as we draw near the next house on our right, I see that the door is open. A man's voice — loud and reproachful — carries on the still air.

'Your waywardness was all very well when your father was alive, Christiana, but now he's not here to indulge you and pay the fines, you'd better mend your ways. A court's been summoned and, if you don't come, you'll be the poorer for it.'

'So be it. The tenancy's mine, now, so I'll do as I like, thank you. I shall find a husband.' We cannot see her yet, this Christiana, but she sounds very sure of herself. 'Twenty acres isn't to be sniffed at. Plenty of men in this village'd be pleased with me and twenty acres.'

We have stopped now. It is as if both the mare and I are enchanted by hearing human voices arguing as if the pestilence had never come. We could not go on if we wanted to.

'You *and* your bastard child, I suppose? I'm not going to argue with you, Christiana. I promised your father I'd try and keep you on the right side of the reeve but I'm not going to be found wanting myself. I'm going to the court. If you take my advice, you'll come with me.'

'You go! I'm not going to watch Piers Alleyne and that little queenling demand death dues before the dead are cold in the ground — not even *in* the ground some of them. It's beyond all decency and sense.'

'Very well. But on your own head be it.'

And he comes striding out of the house, dragging a stiff leg with the aid of a stout staff. He sees us and stops in his tracks.

'God give you good day, master,' I greet him.

'What do you want?' He stands his ground. 'Don't you know the Death is here? The pestilence?'

'We have a letter for Sir John de Loselei,' Hob says. '*If* this is Slievesdon?'

'It is. But you're too late with your letter. Sir John's been dead these two weeks. His daughter's lord now. Lady Matilda.'

'We've got a letter for the bailiff too —'

'Bailiff's dead as well.'

Hob takes a step towards him. 'Don't tell me there's *no* bailiff. Somebody must've taken over, if the old one's dead. Who's convened this court you're going to?'

The lame man looks as if he has sucked on a sloe; we have clearly heard more than he hoped. 'The old bailiff's son, Piers Alleyne, has taken charge. You can come and try your luck with him, if you like.'

'Hah!' The woman he called Christiana appears at the door, an infant on her hip. 'That's if the reeve manages to keep folk from tearing the weasel's limbs off! Dragging people in to answer for dues and death duties while their families are dying!'

Ignoring her, the man comes down the garden.

'You can come if you like,' he says again, to us.

Hob turns to me. 'We're in luck here.' His is voice low. 'The bailiff can't refuse us in front of the whole place. We need to go to this court.'

He moves to follow the limping man but I stand, uncertain, held by the gaze of the wayward Christiana. She does not look like the slut the old man has painted her. Her green kirtle looks neat and freshly brushed and her hair is caught up modestly beneath her headcover. I wonder what manner of man fathered the child on her hip. If Slievesdon folk are anything like Lysington's it will likely be a lusty young husband straying from a widow married for her acres.

Her would-be guardian turns. 'Are you coming, Christiana?'

She shifts the child to her other hip and laces her hands beneath him. 'No, I'm not, Harry Crookshank. I'm going to do as I promised her and lay Amice out. You can tell Piers Alleyne that if he wants anything from me, he knows where to find me!' Glancing at me, she lowers her voice, though she appears to be speaking to herself. 'Someone has to be a friend to the dead.'

I watch as Hob moves to join the lame man. Ten shillings or not, is he really going to go into a crowd of people in a village where folk are still dying?

Without touching him, Hob puts out a hand to stay the older man and asks where the court is to be held.

'Under the Saxon oak outside Sir John's — Lady Matilda's gatehouse.'

Hob looks around at me. 'You're spared, Martin,' he calls.

'How's that?'

'Since you've no fear of the pestilence, I was going to send you to the court. But if we're standing in the open, we can both go.' He grins. 'Bring the letters,' he says, as he turns and sets off again.

I make no move to follow him. Who does he think he is to give me orders as if he was my father or my master?

The woman speaks up. 'If you're going to the court, you'd better leave your cart here. Piers Alleyne'll find a way to have it, otherwise. And your mare too.'

Though I am too far away to see the colour of her eyes, I can tell that they are fastened on me.

'You can bring her into the barn. The cart as well, so it's out of the way.'

She is the first person, since I left Lysington, who has spoken to me as if I were an ordinary man about ordinary business. She does not want to know whether I am sick, or where I have come from or where I am going or anything else that reminds me of the chancy times we live in.

I make my mind up in a heartbeat. 'Hob!' I shout after him. 'I'm going to leave the mare and cart in the barn, here. I'll catch you up.'

A hand goes up to signal that he has heard but he does not look around. It does not occur to him that I might do anything but trot after him as he bids. He will do the talking, of course, when we find this Piers Alleyne, and the man will understand — as he is meant to — that Hob is the one who has moved everything in his path to be here, to deliver the letter.

I stand, watching him match his pace to that of the hobbling old man, his golden cloak billowing behind him as the wind catches it, and I am filled with the need to thwart him.

There is no room to turn, so I back the mare up, ignoring her jerking head and bared teeth, then lead her towards the track at the side of the toft.

'Some people do love to give orders,' Christiana muses, her eyes on the two men walking away from us. Then she turns and gives me a dimpled smile. 'Doesn't mean they have to be obeyed, though, does it?'

I pull the mare up and gaze at her, standing there with her child. 'You're not going to the court?' I know this perfectly well. I heard her tell the scolding old man that she has her dead friend to lay out, but I can think of nothing else to say.

'No.' She meets my eye. 'I have better things to do.'

A notion comes into my head with the look she gives me. Or to be truthful, it comes into my cock. Then I picture her friend, waiting to be laid out, and drop my head in shame.

'Will you?' she asks.

I am befuddled by my own sudden lust. 'Will I what?'

'Go to the court? Run after your friend, Hob, with the letter he's so keen to deliver.' She looks at me, that smile dimpling again. 'Or might you have better things to do, as well?'

Suddenly, Hob is the one dancing to the soldier's tune and I am the one cocking a snook at lordship. Sir John is dead, what good will it do to deliver his letter now?

I return her bold gaze. 'I'll have to see what else there might be to do.' Is it *my voice* saying these words?

A roaring sets up in my ears and there is a numb feeling about my lips as I cluck the mare on again. My cock has grown so upright that it's lifting my tunic and I'm glad the mare is between me and Christiana.

She watches me walk towards her, then turns on her heel and disappears into the house. Before dismay can unman me, she is back, holding a crust of bread which the child on her hip is avid to have, reaching for it and making little whimpers of wanting.

His cries answer my case exactly, though it is not my empty stomach crying out for satisfaction.

Once unbarred, the barn doors swing wide open and, with the smell of hay in her nostrils, the mare needs no encouragement to enter.

Christiana puts the child down in a patch of sun before the open shutter and gives him his bread. While he works at the crust with his tooth-pegged gums, she pulls an armful of hay from a tidy stack against one wall and dumps it in the corner furthest away from him.

'Tie the mare here.'

I do as I am bid, though my fingers are so unhandy with confusion that I can hardly fasten the knot. She stands beside me and pushes my hands away so that she can tie the rope.

'What's your name?' she asks as if we were doing no more than stabling a horse.

I am struck with remorse. I have entirely mistaken her purpose. How did I dare think so lowly of her — or so highly of myself?

'Martin,' I tell her, feeling the heat of shame rise in my face at the thoughts I have been having, feeling my cock shrink in mortification. 'They call me Martin.'

She drops the end of the rope and turns towards me, a half-smile on her face. 'Well, Martin, you've caught my fancy.' She tilts her chin up at me and her mouth quirks as if she is holding back a laugh. 'Have I caught yours?'

I seem to have grown another heart in my braies; it swells and thunders along with the one in my chest.

'Yes.' It is better than a croak, but not much.

She stands in front of me, bold and smiling, and comes slowly forward, backing me against the wall of the barn, freeing her bright, auburn hair from her coif as she comes.

The world has shrunk to this dusty corner, I can think of nothing but the teasing smile in front of me and the hot, insistent beating in my cock.

She raises her face and puts a hand behind my neck, pulling my mouth down to hers. Her lips part as they meet mine and I taste her tongue. A sudden, sharp-edged burst of heat shoots down through my belly and into the very tip of my cock and it is all I can do to keep my mouth on hers and meet tongue with tongue. She reaches down and lifts my hand from her waist to her breast. I feel its soft givingness through the wool of her kirtle and stroke it gently, feeling the nipple rise against my fingertips beneath the fabric of kirtle and shift.

She pulls away slightly and I drop my hand but she looks into my face and smiles her crooked smile. 'No, don't stop.'

I begin stroking again and she tilts her head back, her eyes half-closed, her hair tumbling down her back, curling and winding itself up into ringlets.

'For a beginner, you show promise.'

I do not bother asking how she knows. Women have ways of knowing things.

'Now, let's see what you've got for me.'

She catches the hem of my tunic with one hand and pulls it up; with the other, she finds the drawstring of my braies and pulls it loose. My cock free, she puts her fingers around it.

A sound gasps out of me and she laughs, softly, in her throat. 'Good?'

I swallow, nod, keep my eyes closed. I doubt my ability to remain standing, my knees are shaking so much.

Still holding my cock with one hand, she uses the other to pull her kirtle up. This done, she moves closer.

'Lift me up.'

I put my arms around her and lift her off the ground. She has contrived to keep her kirtle out of the way and I feel my cock pushing between her legs.

'Not quite,' she says. 'He has no aim. Lift me a little more.'

I obey and she pushes her hips up, towards me. When she lowers them again, I feel my cock sliding into a hot, close embrace.

'Mother of God!'

I feel her shake. She is laughing, quietly. After a moment or two she asks, 'Better than going to Piers Alleyne's stupid court?'

The court. Dimly, I am aware that Hob is there, waiting for me, waiting for the letter. It seems none of my concern.

I nod.

Another small quake of laughter. 'You are allowed to move, Martin.'

I open my eyes and look into hers. I manage three thrusts before a groan is torn from me.

She pulls me close while I shudder.

'Dear God.' My voice sounds foreign in my ears.

I open my eyes again to find her smiling at me. 'Now that has happened,' she says, 'you can do something for me, and then we will try again.' She lifts herself off my rapidly-softening cock and takes my hand. 'Your wife will thank me for this,' she says, 'when you have one.'

Later, our clothing restored to its proper state, she looks at me, a self-satisfied smile on her face.

'Why?' I ask, my legs still trembling slightly.

She shrugs. 'Because I fancied you. Because my friend Amice, who was well two days ago, lies dead today.' She looks at me, steadily. 'Because we may all be dead tomorrow and I'm sick of waiting for it.' She brushes her hands down the front of her kirtle as if putting an end to the memory of what we had done together. 'Besides, they say there's no marriage in heaven and, if there's no fucking there either, then we'd better enjoy it while we can.'

What she calls fucking, the church calls fornication. A sin. But, as soon as it enters my head, the thought seems unimportant. Doubtless, priests would tut and impose penance but, in truth, who is hurt by what we have done together? Nobody's rights have been taken, nobody's wife coveted. And it was so pleasurable.

She crosses to her child who, bread consumed, is now bored with his own toes and has started grizzling. As she moves away from me, I realise how long we have been in the barn.

'Christiana, I must go to the court.' I stand on the cartwheel and pull up the canvas to find the linen bag.

'Got the letter in there, have you?'

I nod.

'Come on then.' The child on her hip, she is a mother once more.

As we walk down the street, I ask her who Piers Alleyne is.

'Son of the old bailiff, Nicholas Alleyne — he's set to take over from his father but I reckon he fancies himself better than a bailiff. From what I hear, he's constantly at young Matilda's side, she can barely take herself to the privy without him hovering.'

'How old is she?'

'Sixteen.'

'And he?'

'Twenty-five or thereabouts.'

'Ah.'

'*Ah*, is it? Just because that's what's on *your* mind — and other parts — doesn't mean that's what's on his.'

'No?'

She casts a sidelong look at me.

'Is she pretty?' I ask.

Christiana raises an arch eyebrow. 'Why are we talking about a girl you've never met? What about me? Aren't I pretty?'

I shake my head, full of new-found confidence. 'No.' She punches my arm. 'You're beautiful.'

She laughs then. 'Silly boy.'

But still, she moves closer to me, her shoulder touching my arm as we walk.

'Does the court always meet under the Saxon oak?'

'Only in summer, generally. That'll be Piers Alleyne. Now he thinks he's bailiff, he won't want us in the hall. He'll defend his territory like a dog.'

At the far edge of the village, a stone-built grange comes into sight a hundred yards or so ahead of us.

'That's the manor hall,' Christiana says. 'The gatehouse is on the other side. The Saxon oak's there.'

I do not know how to take my leave of her but she solves the problem for me.

'I'll see you when you come for the mare and the cart. I'll give her water when I get back.'

'Thank you.'

'If I'm not in the house, look for me next door.' She gives me her dimpled smile and, swinging her child to her other hip, she walks away.

As I trot in the direction of the Manor Hall, I picture her quick, capable hands laying out her dead neighbour. Hands that —

No. Time to think of other things. First, I need to find Hob.

A jolt runs through me at the thought of Hob guessing what has kept me but I shrug it off. Why should he? To him, I am chaste Martin.

I round the curve of the house's dry moat and there, ahead of me, is the gathered court. Joining the stragglers at the edge, I feel their angry, hostile mood — the air is thick with scowls and grumbling.

I look about, made uneasy by the stares directed at me. Where is Hob?

Having no wish to elbow my way through a pack of surly strangers, I stand to one side, a few yards behind a small group of older men, and watch for him. His golden cloak will stand out amongst the surrounding, workaday russet and I scan the crowd, waiting for a glimpse of it.

This Piers Alleyne may have convened the manor court at an uncharitable moment but a great number of the surviving population seems to have turned out for it.

A voice is raised, wearily, as if its owner is tired of trying to be heard '— and if death dues are delayed unreasonably then there'll be further charges levied —'

A great hubbub rises up at these words and the speaker is shouted down.

'What's *reasonable?*'

'Who's to pay if all the family are dead?'

'Heirs elsewhere can't be sent for while the village is plagued!'

The voice — presumably that of the reeve — tries again and I pick its owner out in the crowd. He looks young. Holds his office courtesy of the plague, more than likely.

'Master Alleyne says that if there are no heirs then the tithing man responsible for the household must choose and deliver the death due from the family's animals.'

'And what if *he's* dead? In case you haven't noticed, the plague goes from house to house — all the men in a tithing'll likely be dead together!'

This objection sparks others.

'Piers Alleyne doesn't know what he's about.'

'Why are you speaking for him, Tom Legge?'

'Yes, let him speak to us directly!'

The reeve looks over his shoulder. As if the crowd's anger has summoned them, a couple appears from the manor hall's gatehouse: a young woman and a man dressed in what looks — across the distance of fifty yards or so that separate us — like a fur lined cloak and hat.

Carefully, as if he is unaccustomed to the action, the man steps up on to the raised platform that is built against the grange's outer wall and helps the lady up after him.

This is the signal for the crowd to surge past the reeve and gather around the dais.

Having seen the lady seated on one of the two chairs standing ready there, the cloaked man remains standing, without word or gesture, until the gathering falls silent.

'With Sir John and my father both dead,' he says in a clear, confident voice, 'there is a need to ensure that everything on the manor proceeds as normal.'

There is an outcry against this but Piers Alleyne — for this is surely him — waits it out before speaking again. 'Now, the reeve informs me —'

'He's not our reeve!' a voice shouts. 'We never chose him!'

'Shut up, Will!' The man I identified as the reeve strides forward. 'Where were you when a new reeve was wanted?' he demands. 'Locked in your house shitting your braies.' He glares at the crowd. 'Which one of you went from house to house seeing who was well, who was sick and who was dead?'

Eyes slide away as he looks this way and that.

'If anybody wants to be reeve instead of me, they can speak up now and stop their whining!'

Muttered words and sidelong glances are exchanged but nobody steps forward.

Piers Alleyne looks out from his dais. 'Is there anybody who wishes to put himself forward as reeve?'

'We shouldn't *need* to choose a new reeve until all this is over,' a voice objects.

'Agreed!' another calls out. 'After the plague's gone — that's the time for all that.'

The rumble of agreement is growing louder and more mutinous.

'Silence!' Piers Alleyne shouts. 'It's not for you to decide when and whether this manor needs a reeve! The very fact that this court has had to be called is proof that you can't be relied on to pay your dues and keep order *without* being overseen.

Tomorrow, Thomas Legge will begin the process of collecting the death-dues payable since the last court.' He looks around. 'Make no mistake, I will see to it that Lady Matilda gets everything she's owed. Every farthing, every egg, every day's labour. Moreover,' he raises his voice over the protests his words have provoked, 'there are the church's dues to be considered. Since the parson's death, I gather that no burial-payments have been made, though burials have gone on apace.'

'Why should we pay to dig our own graves and bury our own dead?'

Piers Alleyne locates the questioner before answering her. 'You can bury your own dead for free if you like, as long as you do it on your own land. If you bury them in the churchyard you'll give the church what it's due.'

'But there's no priest to support!' a voice complains. 'The money's not needed!'

'It's *needed* to find a successor.' Alleyne's tone says he's beginning to lose patience with them. 'No priest will serve, now, for last year's stipend — every man knows his worth and priests are no different. I'll put the burial-payments aside until a new parson can be found.'

'What about our dead till then? Who's going to bury them with the proper words? You should be out there finding a new parson.'

During this unwisely long speech, Alleyne seeks out the malcontent and fixes him with a stare.

'I think you'll find,' he says, at last, 'that it's not *my* duty to procure a new parish priest but the bishop's. It's not for me to usurp his lordship's prerogative.'

'Bishop doesn't give a wet fart!'

There is some laughter at this but the mood of the crowd is not to be turned so easily.

'You could find a parson tomorrow if you cared. You're just scared to leave Sir John's house.'

'Coward!'

Alleyne's head snaps round in the direction of the insult but the crowd is emboldened by this audacity.

'Yes, coward!'

'Co-ward.' A chant is set up.

'Co-ward!' More voices join in.

'*Co-ward! Co-ward! Co-ward!*'

I watch the gathering become a mob and feel a shiver of fear. The pestilence might not kill us all, but it is changing us; this open defiance is something I have never seen before. We have been worn thin with worry since news of the pestilence came last year; nearer and nearer the worry has come until it has flayed us to our very bones. Will the Death come to our county, our hundred, our village; will it come to our house, will I die, will there be a world for my children to live in when it has done with us?

This chance to shout, to rage against Master Alleyne, is also the chance to howl against the gnawing fears and terrors of months. For the pestilence is a coward too, creeping where it cannot be seen, striking when it cannot be struck against.

I look about for a glimmer of Hob's cloak in the blur of people. Where is he? Has he seen the temper of the crowd and left?

It is clear that Piers Alleyne is nobody's fool. He sees the danger he is in and turns to the Lady Matilda who rises from her chair. From my poor vantage-point, her whole body looks stiff with fear and she has her hands clasped in front of her. When Alleyne offers her his arm, she seems, for a moment, unable to move.

Finally, she takes a few steps and the bailiff makes to lead her off the dais. But people have come here at his bidding and they are not minded to allow him to simply walk away. A body of men moves towards the gatehouse and stands in front of it, barring the way.

I watch them fold their arms and plant their feet; will they dare to lay hands on him, on their lady?

The crowd surges forward and I am carried with it.

As Master Alleyne tries to bluff it out and lead Lady Matilda from the dais, one of the men barring his way steps forward and puts up a hand. 'We're not finished here.'

Suddenly, I see Hob. He is running around the outside of the crowd towards the platform.

'Master Bailiff, please wait!'

He leaps up on to the dais, causing immediate outrage in the crowd. Who does this stranger think he is, to put himself on a level with Lady Matilda?

The reeve stalks up to Hob, though he does not dare put a foot on the dais. 'Who are you? What's your business at our court?'

Hob holds up both hands. 'I've come all the way from Cricklade with a message from Master Richard Longe.'

The crowd begins babbling at this news, but my eyes are fixed on Lady Matilda and Piers Alleyne. The surge forward has brought me close to the dais and I see a look pass between them at the mention of Longe's name. She looks stricken, he turns away from her to glare at Hob.

'What message?' Alleyne moves back towards the centre of the platform.

'It's written down.' Clearly, Hob saw me arrive, for he looks straight at me and beckons me towards him.

I make the approach slowly, certain that this is a mistake. Sir John is dead. We should not be here.

'The message is for your late father, Lady Matilda,' Hob explains as I stand before the dais.

Alleyne's eyes are on me. 'And how do you come to have it?'

I come to a halt before him. 'We're pilgrims, master,' I tell him. 'We met Master Longe at Cricklade. When he knew we were travelling east, he asked us to bring this letter to your lord.'

I peer into the linen bag and withdraw the letter with Sir John's name on the front. Fixing my eyes on Lady Matilda, I hold it out to her.

She looks down at it, then at Piers Alleyne who steps forward and takes it from my hand. He turns to the reeve. 'I'm not expected to read Lady Matilda's private communications to her out here, am I?'

Before Legge can speak, one of the men barring the gate moves towards the dais. 'You're not our lord, you're the bailiff's son. The Lady Matilda may take the letter into the house —'

Before anybody can lift a finger to prevent him, Alleyne has jumped down from the dais and struck the man, backhanded, across the face with a gloved hand.

'How dare you tell the Lady Matilda what she may and may not do? Kneel and beg forgiveness before I have you flogged!'

The fellow looks around at the crowd but his neighbours hold back. He licks blood from his lip.

Suddenly, Lady Matilda speaks up. 'I don't mind hearing the letter here.' Her voice trembles. 'You're my people. I have nothing to hide from you.'

All eyes turn to her.

'Richard Longe and some of my father's other retainers went to Cricklade,' she says, her thin voice causing the crowd to push further forward as they strain to hear her, 'to meet the escort of a young man — Henry Garville — who was to come here to be married to me.' She casts a glance at Piers Alleyne who gives a small nod, though whether of approval or permission I cannot tell. 'I hope this letter will give us news of Master Longe. And of Henry Garville.'

She and Alleyne look long and hard at each other. Is it because of what I have lately been engaged in with Christiana, or do I see a tenderness, a longing, between them?

Finally, Alleyne breaks the seal on the letter and his lips move as he reads its contents to himself. When he looks up, there is something in his expression that I do not like.

'Richard Longe regrets to inform Sir John,' his voice rings out as he translates the letter's contents, 'that he has waited over a fortnight for the young man to arrive at Cricklade without any sign of him.' He looks up to see their reaction then drops his gaze to Longe's letter once more. 'He asks whether he should go and seek out the young man at his father's house or whether he should conclude — as seems likely — that the young man is dead, and return home.'

His eyes turn to Lady Matilda who gives him a smile of such sweetness that her feelings cannot be mistaken.

As Alleyne faces the crowd once more, he seems to have grown a handspan since reading Longe's letter. He is upright, taut. Suddenly, I am filled with misgiving.

'We did not need such a letter to tell us what Henry Garville's absence had already indicated.' Alleyne stops, eyes on the crowd, and I know that something significant is coming. 'Therefore, on the death of her father, Lady Matilda, feeling the need of protection in these uncertain times, consented to marry me.' He holds out a hand and his new wife steps up and takes it, her eyes fixed on his face. Alleyne turns back to the crowd. 'We were married three days ago. I am your new lord.'

The uproar is slow to grow, but it quickly gathers pace.

I overhear objections, questions, though none so loud as to be directed to Master Alleyne.

I try to catch Hob's eye to signal that we should leave. Now. But Slievesdon's new lord beckons me to him.

'You have another letter in that bag. Give it to me.'

His expression fills me with the conviction that, whatever Richard Longe wrote to the now-dead bailiff about Hob's worthiness or otherwise to receive a further ten shillings, no good can come of hearing this letter read now.

'It was addressed to the former bailiff, my lord,' I tell him, 'it's not important, now.'

'I didn't ask for your opinion on the matter. It's for me to decide what's important and what isn't. That letter was written to my father. Give it to me.'

It occurs to me that I should run. Alleyne sees it in my face and takes a step forward to grip my forearm. 'The letter.'

I have no choice but to give it to him. When he sees that the seal is broken, he holds the two halves out to me, wordlessly.

'We've travelled a long way, my lord. Our goods have been tumbled and manhandled.'

He shakes his head as if to pity the poverty of my invention, but says nothing more.

Quickly, muttering the words to himself under his breath, he reads the letter. After a moment or two, he raises his eyebrows at me. 'Are you Hob Cleve?'

'No, lord.' I gesture. 'That's Hob.'

Alleyne waves the letter in the air. 'It seems that these fellows have not brought us Richard Longe's news out of the goodness of their hearts, as they'd have us believe, but from quite different motives. It seems that this fellow —' he grabs Hob's cloak and drags him forward to face the crowd — 'has used the pretext of the pestilence to extort a large sum of money from Master Longe. What's more, he's come here expecting a reward.'

The crowd stirs, restless and confused by the sudden shift away from Alleyne and on to us.

He holds up the letter. 'I'll read you what Master Longe says about him.'

What will I do if he reads something other than what I know the letter says? How can I admit to reading it?

'To my friend and the bailiff of my master, Nicholas Alleyne — or, if he is gone to God since my departure, to whomsoever has taken up his office — Richard Longe sends hearty greetings from Cricklade where you know the business I am sent to oversee.' Alleyne looks up at the crowd. 'And now you, also, know the business he was sent to oversee. Marriage business that could not be brought to a conclusion because of the pestilence.'

He returns to the letter.

'May it please you to know the fellow who carries this letter as Hob Cleve —' he gives Hob's shoulder a shake as he names him — 'a self-proclaimed freeborn man'.'

There are whoops and cat-calls at his doubting tone and shouts of 'Runaway!'

I begin to tremble; words that appeared good-natured when I read the letter to Hob — and would, I am sure, have seemed good-natured from one friend to another — take on a darker meaning in Piers Alleyne's mouth. His eyes on Hob, he waits until those in the crowd who want to hear the rest of the letter have quelled those who simply want an excuse to shout.

'He has had ten shillings from me already,' he commences reading again, 'he and his companion —' he indicates me with one hand, eyes still on the letter — 'and has been promised ten shillings more for bringing this letter to my lord.'

He looks up once more. 'Ten shillings,' he tells the crowd. 'He's had *ten shillings* already and now he expects to be paid *another* ten!'

Outrage breaks out once more, all the fury the crowd previously felt towards their self-appointed bailiff deftly transferred to us.

I see the angry faces shouting, men pointing, and I fear that Hob's ten shillings may be the death of us.

Piers Alleyne puts up a hand and prepares to read on.

'If he has delivered Sir John's letter with the seal unbroken, then he is worthy of his ten shillings,' he shouts above the hubbub. 'If I have read him aright, he will have broken the seal on this and will have found someone to tell him its contents before now.'

He looks up from the letter. 'Master Longe believes that to break one seal is permissible, but not the other.' He pauses, as if he's considering the case. 'Master Longe is a soldier and sees things in a practical light. I am trained in the law and, in my eyes, the breaking of any seal is a breach of faith.'

He lets his eyes rove over the muttering, staring crowd before addressing himself to the letter again. As he does so, a sly smile breaks out on his face.

'I do believe Master Longe likes this fellow. He says, "If you can persuade him to stay on my lord's manor, do so. For I believe he will be reeve within five years and the richest man in the village within ten".'

He lets the hand holding the letter fall to his side and gazes out at the crowd. 'My friends, who *wouldn't* be the richest man in the village if he could demand ten shillings for doing a simple task? Who *wouldn't* be reeve if he was allowed to lie and break faith and claim to be one thing when, in fact, he's another?'

A prickle runs down my neckbone as Alleyne's tone shifts from admirer to judge.

'I say if he's had ten shillings already —' his voices rises like a huckster's with a hard sell — 'then he doesn't deserve ten more! What do you say?'

'No! No more!'

Fists are waved in our direction. Nobody knows where we have come from, they cannot weigh in the balance how far out of our road we have travelled to be here; they are simply outraged that a man should earn ten shillings for carrying a letter. If we die here, what will become of the saint? What will become of my father's immortal soul? An icy panic starts in my gut and begins to pour along my veins.

Alleyne holds up the letter once more. 'There's a greeting at the end of the letter,' he tells them, 'written by Master Longe in French, for my father alone.'

The ice in my veins reaches my fingertips and I find I am shaking. What did the soldier say to his friend that he did not want Hob and me to know?

Master Alleyne begins to read. 'Forgive me, my friend, for writing to you in English and not as a friend in our own tongue,' Alleyne reads, 'but I fear that, if this fellow cannot find a way to read this letter and see that I have made provision for him to be paid as we agreed, then the letter which he carries for Sir John will end up in his cooking fire.'

Alleyne takes hold of Hob's shoulders and propels him to the front of the dais, where everybody can see him. 'This is a man who would have burned a letter intended for a lord who fights at the side of the king's heir. A letter containing news of his daughter's betrothed husband.' He pauses, watching the crowd work themselves up into a righteous fury. 'And, for the favour of *not* burning it,' he shouts over the babble, 'he wants a further ten shillings!'

I can feel Hob's tautness from where I am standing. I fear that he will turn on Piers Alleyne. If he does, all semblance of control over the crowd will be gone. They will swarm on to the dais and tear us to pieces.

The Lady Matilda is white and shaking. The braided, uncovered hair, with which she's hidden her real status as wife, makes her seem younger than her years.

Swiftly, I slip behind her husband and fall on my knees in front of her. 'Lady, don't let violence mar this announcement of your marriage — don't let what should be a happy day be remembered as a day of bloodshed.'

Her hands are clasped so tight in front of her that it she seems to be holding herself upright by the pressure of palm against palm.

'Please, Lady! If you don't do something, they'll take us and kill us!'

She gives a little cry but then seems to gather herself together. Taking a breath, she bids me rise. As I do so, she moves to her husband's side and speaks, urgently, into his ear.

He makes as if to put her aside but she grips his arm and looks into his face.

I watch and it is as if the two of them are alone on the dais, each looking into the face of the other. Then he nods and draws her to him to kiss her brow.

With her at his side, he turns to the crowd. 'The Lady Matilda,' he smiles down at her, 'my wife — has a tender heart. She cannot bear the thought that this would be a day of anger and accusation. For, today, we have announced our marriage and she would like — we would *both* like — to remember it with happiness.'

'Not going to give him that ten shillings, are you?'

Alleyne looks for the questioner. 'No. We'll give that ten shillings to the people of Slievesdon, instead. We'll share it amongst the widows of the pestilence who are left with infant children.'

An astonished hush falls over the gathering as people struggle with the reversal of fortunes that this entails. They were summoned here to pay fines and now they are being given money by a man whom they detest but who is, by all accounts, their new lord. It is no great wonder that they are lost for an apt response.

The reeve speaks for them. 'That's very generous, Mast— my lord. But what are we going to do with these two?'

Alleyne turns to us. Now that he has deflected the crowd's dangerous anger away from himself, we are of no further use to him. 'Let them go on their way. See that they leave the village within the hour and that no harm comes to them.'

The crowd parts, silently, as he leads his wife down from the dais and through the gatehouse.

'Right!' Thomas Legge bellows as the gate is closed behind them. 'This court is at an end. If you have animals to render as death-dues, bring them to the lord's pound by sunset. Now, be about your business and God keep us all.' He crosses himself and faces us. 'Come on, before he comes back and changes his mind.'

We follow him, watched by a group of men who have not yet dispersed; the same group that defied Alleyne and prevented him from leaving the dais.

'What are you waiting for?' the reeve demands. 'There's nothing more to see.'

'We'll come with you to see them out of the village,' one of them says. 'Make sure they don't steal from people who're tending the sick.'

His lip is split. He is the man Alleyne struck. Edwin.

Legge shrugged. 'If you've got time to waste, I'm not going to stop you.'

He sets off up the village's main street, Hob and I hard on his heels. We do not speak. We both know how close we came to ending our journey here. For myself, I am weak with relief but Hob's back is rigid; if he were a dog, his hackles would be stiff from scruff to tail. The need to use his fists on somebody is coming off him like steam but he is not stupid, he knows his first punch would be his last. The reeve, I think, would offer us no help.

Out of the corner of my eye, I watch our escort staring at Hob. His cloak, swinging thick about his calves, that knife of his, the money-bag which he insists on carrying on his belt instead of leaving it in the cart like a sensible man. It is not hard to see how the sight of him might have goaded people to anger even without Piers Alleyne's twisting of words. It is easy to see that Slievesdon's people think him a runaway in dead men's clothes trying to ape his betters.

And yet, gentlemen's trappings or not *Christiana preferred me*. The thought comes to me with the sight of her house, like a punch of joy, so swift and strong it is all but pain. It was *I* that caught her fancy — me, in my father's overtunic and my old hood. *She preferred me*.

I stop at her toft and, despite our perilous circumstances, my cock twitches with the memory of what she and I did together. 'I have a cart here, in the barn.'

Thomas Legge pulls up, looks at the house, then at me. 'How did that come about?'

'Mistress Christiana was at her door as we were passing. With a man called Harry Crookshank. When he said he'd take us to the court, she said we could leave the mare and cart here.'

'Did she indeed?'

I meet his gaze but say nothing.

'Then let's see if she's in.'

He gets no response from his calling and knocking at the door.

'She said she might be next door laying out a neighbour,' I call to him. 'Amice.'

Legge nods and makes his way to the next house. Hob and I stand in the lane, our sullen escort surrounding us.

'You've got off easy,' one man says, poking Hob's shoulder.

'How d'you make that out? We struck a bargain with the soldier and *we kept* our side of it. Your village hasn't kept *its* part, so how have we got off easy?'

'Hold your tongue, Hob,' I mutter.

'Yeah, Hob. Hold your tongue,' one of the men jeers. 'Take your friend's advice and keep your mouth shut.'

'Unless you want a good hiding.'

I watch Thomas Legge stand well outside the dead woman's house as he speaks through the open door to Christiana. A few moments later, she comes out, wiping her hands on a cloth tied around her waist. She stops when she sees our escort, just as Harry Crookshank stopped when he saw Hob and me.

'What's this?' she asks the reeve.

'It's no concern of yours, Christiana. Come and open your barn, will you, and see to it that only what went in is taken out?'

She comes away as he asks but, on the threshold of the barn, she turns, hands on hips, to face down the men who are half a pace behind Hob and me.

'Do I look so feeble that I need help opening my own barn? I'll thank you all to wait here. The cart's owner will suffice.'

The doors swing open as readily as before but the sun is no longer shining through the shutter; clouds have covered the sky.

'I gave your mare some hay,' Christiana speaks loudly enough to be heard from outside the barn, then, as we pass out of sight of the door, she puts her finger to her lips. 'They'll search the cart,' she whispers, quickly. 'If there's anything in it you don't want them to have, take it out and leave it here. You can come back tonight when it's dark.'

But I have no sooner put my hand to the canvas than one of the men appears in the doorway. Dark and thickset with frowning brows, he looks like a man it would be unwise to cross. He strides in, his companions behind him. Two of them have Hob's arms twisted up behind his back.

'Right,' the dark-haired man says, 'let's have that money-bag of Pretty-Boy's, shall we?'

Hob struggles and is punched in the face. One of the men cuts the purse's strings and takes it from Hob's belt. He looks inside and whistles through his teeth. 'This must be the ten shillings he got off Master Longe.'

Thomas Legge shakes his head at the man who has taken charge. 'You can't take his money, Dickon. That's thieving.'

Dickon meets his eye. 'Oh yes? And who are your witnesses if you're going to accuse me? Besides yourself, *Reeve.*'

Thomas the Reeve assesses the company. Besides Christiana, myself and Hob, there are eight of them.

Christiana breaks the silence. 'I'll stand witness against you, Dickon Miller. And all of you.'

The miller gives a low grunt of a laugh. 'You? Who's going to take the word of a whore against ours?'

'Anybody who knows you?' Christiana suggests.

One of the men steps forward and slaps her, open handed, across the face. She staggers to one side and he moves to fetch her another blow.

The rage bursts out of me and I charge at him, dropping a shoulder into his gut and driving him to the ground.

Before I can land more than half a dozen punches, somebody pulls me off and hits me, hard, on the side of the head. The world goes black for a moment or two. I fall against the wall of the barn and watch, helpless, as one of them comes after me.

'Enough,' Dickon says, his voice flat and hard. 'You can beat shit out of him later, if you want. First I want to know what's in that cart.'

The canvas is already untied where I took the letters from the press. The Miller lifts it up.

'Well, well, well. This is a nice little haul. You two have been busy.'

'It's not stolen,' Hob says, his voice thick with his broken nose. 'Every stick belongs to us.'

I struggle to my feet, pulling myself up against the barn wall. As I stand, my head pounds.

'Is that so?' I hear Dickon Miller say. 'Let's see, shall we?'

I watch him pulling things out of the cart; the pallet, our cooking pot, the press.

'What've you been doing, going into dead folks' houses and stealing their chattels?'

One of the men has opened the press and found Agnes's book. He hands it to Dickon.

'Oh, so all of this is yours, is it? None of it's stolen, is it?' The miller's eyes are dark and deep-set. He looks not unlike my father.

'There's nothing stolen in there.' I swallow bile.

'I suppose you can read this then?' He holds the book awkwardly, unused to handling anything like it.

'Yes.'

He makes a scornful sound.

One of the others puts on a high, effeminate voice. 'Oh *yes*, I can read it, most certainly.' There's laughter at this and more efforts at mimicry.

I ignore them. 'Give it to me.' I push myself away from the wall. 'Open it on any page and I'll read it.'

Dickon narrows his eyes, suspecting a trick. 'Any page I choose?'

'Any page.' I take an unsteady step towards him.

He pulls back the cover of the book and the pages fall open as if through long use. 'There.' He holds the book out to me. 'Read that.'

I take the book from him and look down at the page. Suppressing a bitter smile, I read. *'Placebo Domino. Dilexi quoniam exaudiet Dominus vocem orationis meae. Quia inclinavit aurem suam mi et in diebus meis invocabo.'*

The *Placebo*, the prayer for the dead. Agnes must have been dwelling on it for the book to fall open there.

When I stop reading, the barn is filled with an uneasy silence. Master William always said I spoke the Latin with a better tongue than many priests but I do not think appreciation is keeping our captors silent.

'Are you in orders, then?'

I turn, keeping my eyes from Hob. 'Enough to claim trial in a church court if ever I'm accused.' It is no lie; I would need far less Latin than I am master of to claim benefit of clergy and dodge the king's courts.

The men look at Dickon, cast glances at each other. They are clearly at a loss, now. My reading has rendered me neither fish nor fowl. I am no priest but I can spout Latin which marks me more for church than manor. Not so easy, now, to accuse me of being a thief. Not so easy to beat shit out of me either, thank God.

'Think you're better'n us, I suppose?' one of them sneers.

I look him in the eye. 'No. But this —' I hold up the book of hours — '*is* mine.'

I think of Agnes and her husband, lying beneath the heathland, the handcart with its bundles of finery marking their grave. My claiming her book seems a fair exchange for hearing her husband's confession and ensuring that his promise was kept.

'You going to tell us that this is yours, too?' a voice crows from the other end of the cart.

Ungentle hands pull the Maiden out of her hiding place. 'You can't tell us you're not thieves, now. This has come from a church!'

I take a step towards him, then think better of it and pull up. 'No. She's mine.'

'What?' The question comes from behind me. 'Image-carver, are you? Make her, did you?'

I knew they would not believe me if I told them the truth.

'That's Saint Cynryth. She's my family's saint. I'm taking her image to her shrine in Salster. To ask for prayers for my father's soul.'

Another uncertain silence is broken as Christiana points at the cart and one of the men holding Hob suddenly cries out. 'Hey, Walter, what d'you think you're doing?'

'Searching the cart.'

'I saw you take something out.'

'I did not!'

'You did, I saw you!'

Two or three of the men move towards Walter but, before they can lay hold of him, he breaks away towards the open barn door. So unexpected is his sudden flight that it takes several moments for any of his companions to give chase.

Once one is through the door, they all take up the hue and cry. All but Dickon and the two who still have Hob's arms behind his back.

As I move towards her, Christiana holds up a hand to me but I know better than to make any gestures of affection.

'Are you hurt, mistress?'

'Not much,' she replies. 'But I fear Walter Little has made off with a money-bag of yours.'

At this, one of the men holding Hob lets go of him and runs out of the barn. With a darting glance at Dickon, the other follows.

The miller looks across at the reeve. 'Well?'

Thomas Legge shrugs. 'I saw nothing stolen.'

Dickon nods, turns on his heel and walks out.

The silence left by his going is broken by the reeve. 'You've got off lightly.'

'Lightly?' Hob is enraged at being told this a second time. 'You call being robbed of every penny we have in the world getting off lightly?'

'They followed you here to teach you a lesson. But are your bones broken? Is your blood spilt on the ground?' He shakes his head. 'No. You got off lightly.'

'And that's it and all about it?' Hob asks, his voice harsh. 'We've escaped a beating so you do nothing?'

The reeve stares at him for a long while. 'You're strangers here. You came to Slievesdon of your own free will because you thought there was something here for you. It was a risk.'

'We came in good faith with a message for your lord,' I protest. 'We didn't *take a risk*, we kept our word!'

He turns to me. 'Sadly for you, you brought an unwelcome message. You gave Piers Alleyne the news he needed to lord it over us. And you've paid the price.'

CHAPTER 24

For days Hob and I have not spoken about what happened at Slievesdon. We have scarcely spoken at all.

Our way has brought us south and east; first to the market-town of Basingstoke and thence over terrain so hilly that I feared the mare's heart would burst, even with Hob's muscles to help her.

A bedraggled group of travellers told us that passing through Farnham would provide us with an easier route to the east, so we find ourselves leading the mare down a steep slope past Farnham's block of a castle and on to the river-crossing that links the town to the suburbs on the other side.

Luck, fate, or the good offices of Saint Cynryth are on our side and we soon find ourselves on the high, dry going of an old trackway. The ground beneath us is firm and, for the first time in days, I leave off worrying that the cart will be broken apart by the sheer effort of hauling it along.

Still, despite the better ground, we make slow progress. Though spring is in the air, it is not yet in the grass and, as we have no fodder for the mare, we are obliged to stop and let her graze when we come upon anything like pasturage. Between the need to feed her and to find firewood, I doubt we are making six or seven miles in a day, though we pack the embers soon after first light and do not put tinder to them again until dusk is almost dark. And I am beginning to worry about provisions. Our supplies of beans and peas will not see us to Salster and, now, we have not a single penny to replenish them.

So far, Hob has been lucky with his arrows, but he has only three; a run of bad luck could see him lose them all. What will he do if we run out of food? Will he stay with me or — now I have no money — will he seek out a better prospect? For all my doubts about him, I would rather have him with me than travel alone, prey to any wanderers. And my night-walking demon.

But, while my thoughts are desperate and unprofitable, the country about us seems determined that all will be well. Ploughing and sowing are going on apace and cattle are being driven out onto the common pastures to find what grazing they can as barns are emptied and haystacks shrink to seed-strewn circles. Every day we see sheep, released from their cotes and home pastures, skittering up on to the sweeping slopes to wait for the warmer days when they will drop their lambs.

The folk of the downs put their faces to the sun and it shines on them as if the pestilence had never come to England, as if churchyards the length and breadth of the land are not stinking and heaving with the dead, as if priests were our only confessors still. But it is not so. The pestilence has stopped up the veins of England, slowing her life to a feeble beat and, though March's warming sun is ripening buds and coaxing out shy, soft-petalled primroses, I have no hope that spring will shrug off pestilence as it does winter.

That evening, Hob stands over me as I lay the fire. He says nothing, but I can feel his eyes as I sit between kindling and wind, coaxing the embers into flame.

He drops into a haunch-squat. 'We must do something to earn some money soon or we will not live to see Salster.'

Though I am glad to have the subject broached, now Hob has brought it up, I find I do not want to hear how he intends to come by money with the country as it is. Today, we entered a village to beg water and, though the villagers gave it to us, it was with ill-will. How on earth might we persuade anybody to let us stay long enough to work when they begrudge us the time it takes to draw water?

I do not look at Hob, confine myself to feeding the weak, wind-blown flames with strips of bark and feathered twigs.

'Don't tell me you don't feel it, too,' he pushes.

'Feel what?'

'The lack of money. The want of a single farthing.'

I do. And I have begun to understand what he, most likely, has always known — that, having neither money nor obvious means to get it, nothing stands between you and starvation except the charity of others. That or theft.

'The saint can help us,' he says. 'She has power to make people devoted to her as soon as they lay eyes on her! Think how the people at Tredgham came to her. And when they came, they brought gifts!'

I turn to the fire again. 'Yes, after she'd done a miracle. People are apt to be impressed by miracles.'

'So we must *tell* people about her miracles! Once they've heard what she's done, they'll be falling over themselves to bring gifts.'

But if the saint's blessing turns out not to confer protection on all and sundry, then Tredgham's coroner will hear of it — I know he will — and we will not be safe.

I reach for a length of firewood. 'No.'

'It's not just to get gifts for us. We need people to pray to her to make her strong. So she can rescue your father from Purgatory.' He waits but is impatient, wants to bludgeon me with his words. 'Martin, don't you *believe* in our saint's miracles? Don't you *want* people to know about them?'

My Tredgham vision dances before my eyes. An army of the healed, Saint Cynryth at their head. 'Yes, of course I do —'

He thrusts his head towards me, towards the fire. 'Well then?' His face, lit from beneath by the growing flames, is eerie — a thing of shadows and glinting eyes.

My father's words come back to me. *Folks'd come traipsing through the woods to see her. They'd come pawing at her and touching her. I won't have it.*

'I'm not going to make a whore out of her, Hob,' I said.

He leaps to his feet. 'Don't you come the virtuous man with me, Martin Collyer!' He stands over me, glaring down. 'You were quick enough to pay *your* little whore weren't you?'

'*What?*

'*Christiana.* Wouldn't pull up her kirtle till you'd ferreted around in the cart to find your money-bag, *would she?*

His words wind me like a fist in the gut. He gives a grunt of laughter. 'Did you think I didn't know? You shouldn't have thrown yourself at that churl who slapped her if you wanted to keep it quiet.'

I stand and face him, my heart thudding with rage. 'I don't care whether you know or not. But it's none of your business.'

'It's my business if your cock makes trouble for us!'

'*Trouble?* You're the one who's made *trouble* for us! Panting up to Piers Alleyne for your damned ten shillings!'

'Oh! And I suppose you weren't determined to bend every arse-licking sinew to go to Slievesdon and keep your *precious word?*

I aim for his nose but he pulls back his head and my fist hits chin and teeth instead. I bend double, left hand clutching my damaged fist and Hob's knee smashes into my face.

Staggering back, I right myself quickly, waiting for him to follow with his fists, but he stands off, running his tongue around his teeth.

'How much did she take off you, Martin? However much it was, it was a bloody expensive fuck — because she saw where you took the money from —' a hand on my chest pushes me backwards — '*didn't she?* And she told that weasel Walter —' another push — '*didn't she?* That's how he knew where to find it!' A final push lands me back on my arse.

'*What are you talking about?*' As I open my mouth, pain shoots from chin to brow. I put my hand to my face; I'm bleeding from nose and lip. 'I didn't pay her!'

His boot catches my thigh. 'Liar!'

'It's the truth!' Again the pain blooms. I spit blood as I scramble to my feet, away from his boot. 'She couldn't've told Walter where the money-bag was because she didn't know.'

'I don't believe you.'

'D'you know what, Hob?' I thrust my bleeding face into his, my words spitting blood at him. 'I *don't care*! I'm sick of you lording it over me because you're some squire's bastard.'

He backs off a pace. 'Calm down, Martin. You're squealing like a girl.'

I spit more blood. The taste reminds me of sickness and death.

'A paid fuck or a free one, you and she together still cost us that purse.'

I lick blood from my bottom lip. 'How?'

He closes the gap between us again. 'Because while *you* were busy discovering what your prick's for, *I* couldn't talk to Piers Alleyne because I didn't have the letter! If you'd come with me instead of following the urges of your knob, we'd have spoken to him and been out of the village before Dickon and his cronies ever turned up for the court.' Hob takes hold of the front of my tunic and pulls my bleeding face up to his. 'You *owe* me, collyer boy, and your saint is going to pay me back. When she's earned us back our ten shillings, then you can say your piece. Until then, you keep your mouth shut.'

I wrench myself out of his grasp, furious at being spoken to like a child.

'Or what? Going to kill me, are you, like you killed your stepfather?'

He stares at me, his eyes cold. 'I didn't *kill him*.'

'Yes you did — you told me.'

He shakes his head, eyes fixed on mine. 'No. I didn't.'

'Yes. You *did*. You said that with God taking lives all around, you didn't see why you should be different. You said he deserved to die. So you killed him and you shrouded him and you told the priest he wouldn't be doing any more burials.'

A look comes over Hob's face, then; a look compounded of grudging belief and amazement. 'All this time ... you've been thinking me a murderer?' He shakes his head.

I stare at him. He seems truly taken aback that I would have believed such a thing. Have I been too ready to think ill of him?

'Well, if you didn't kill him, what did you mean when you said that not every corpse put in a plague pit has died of the plague?'

He takes a breath and huffs it out, as if he's expelling an unpleasant memory. 'I didn't kill him, but I let him die.'

'What d'you mean "let him die"? How?'

His eyes are steady on mine. 'Drank a skinful of ale, fell insensible from it, puked in his sleep and choked on it.'

'And you watched?'

'Yes.' No regret, no contrition. 'And, if he were here now, I'd do the same again.'

'You need a priest, Hob. You've sent a man to his death unshriven and you're unrepentant.'

He shakes his head. 'Don't worry about me, Martin. When God watches so many die without stretching out a hand to save them, why should I believe that he wants me to do differently?'

I open my mouth to speak but he forestalls me. 'And before you tell me how black my soul is, shouldn't you be considering the state of your own?'

The hairs on the nape of my neck prickle. 'What?'

'All this talk of me killing *my* father — what about yours?' He pauses, staring at me. 'No man shrouds himself. Don't you think it's more likely your demon put your hands over your father's face — nose gripped here, hand over the mouth there —' he mimes the actions — 'just enough to stop up the breath of a sleeping man?'

A sweat freezes the skin on my back. 'No! You didn't know my father. He was a strong man — I couldn't've held him down.'

'What?' Hob mocks. 'Not, "he was my father, I wouldn't've harmed a hair on his head"? Straight away you're telling me he would have fought you off?'

'I didn't kill my father!'

'Maybe he was weakened — maybe he had the pestilence. But you couldn't risk the saint healing him as well, could you? You wanted your freedom as much as I wanted mine.'

Throughout my watch that night I am tormented. Is it possible that Hob is right — that I killed my own father, that the demon who makes me walk used my hands to do his master's bidding? I fear it is — after all, there was no horseshoe over the roundwood lintel of our forest hut. And there were no plague-marks on him. None that I could see.

If the demon did pinch my father's nose with my fingers and cover his mouth with my palm, did he find the seeds of the act in my own sinful soul? He would have if he had looked there, for I wished my father dead often enough.

For nothing would move the man! Not Master William's appeals, not my mother's soft persuasions and certainly not my own pleadings, could soften my father's resolve. Always, his answer was the same. 'Martin shall be a collyer with me.'

Not that he stopped me learning from William. He was proud that I could read and write, would ask me to read the licences he brought back from the Verderers court.

'Read me the words, Martin. I know what it allows me but I never heard the words before.'

And it was his pride in me that kept my hope alive. Surely he would not continue to deny me a place at the abbey school when he saw how much Latin I knew, how I could recite the prayers and offices from memory?

But his determination proved the equal of mine. Well before the pestilence came, I had begun to wish that I had never sat at William Orford's feet or walked behind him in white, for a desire unfulfilled is a desire made twice as potent.

Finally, when neither his bad temper nor the frequent use of the back of his hand could cure me, my father had beaten my pleadings out of me. Each fall of the rod had been accompanied by a grunted word.

'I — will — not — hear — no — more — of — this — non — sense.'

There had been more, much more, but the burden of it had been conveyed in that first sentence.

My father had never beaten me with such anger before and, stroke after stroke, I had learned to favour his own sullenness over my natural inclination to argue and persuade. It was then that I began to picture in my mind how mishaps might befall him.

A burn that festered. A slip of the coppicing axe. A fall that pushed bone through skin and let poison into his blood...

And then the pestilence came.

And I woke to find him dead.

CHAPTER 25

We stand on the track and gaze up at the village on the slope above us. If I narrow my eyes, I can make out smoke hanging on each roof-line, kept from rising into the air by the drifting rain. There is no pestilence here. Nor has there been for, if the pestilence had been and gone, there would be houses cold and empty.

'Nobody will question us going into the village for water.'

Hob's voice startles me and my gaze is jerked towards him. His face gives the lie to his words; any villager might balk at welcoming such a battered stranger into their midst. To the blackened eye and swollen nose he got at Slievesdon, I added a split and swollen lip last night when my knuckles mashed it to his teeth.

Not that I have any reason to suppose I look better. I am reminded of Hob's knee smashing into my face every time I wipe away the rain.

Since the village came into view, he has insisted that, when we ask for water, we present the saint to the people. But I do not want to do it, I am plagued by a fear that Hob will play the peddler and cry aloud the power and virtues of the saint.

Come and see our miraculous saint!

Pay your penny and receive her blessing!

As we make our careful, zig-zag way up the slope towards the village, I watch him from the corner of my eye. The rain has eased to a fine drizzle but his cloak, like the blanket round my shoulders, is heavy with water. Feeling my gaze, he glances at me, flicking hanging drips from the sodden edge of his hood as his eyes meet mine. 'How are we going to protect the Maiden from this rain?' he asks.

All morning, the saint has been under the canvas, wrapped in a blanket, safe and dry. Now, in my mind's eye, I see cold raindrops gathering on her face, joining to make larger drops, running beneath their own sudden weight down her cheeks. I see the chestnut of her hair trickling down the delicate pink of her brow, the russet mingling with the blue of her eyes and the black of their lashes, running in dark rivulets towards her lips, the mingled colours dripping from her chin on to the smooth white of her kirtle. What will the keeper of her woodland shrine say if I bring her back in such a state?

'You can't Hob! We can't risk it. We'll have to leave it till the rain stops.'

'It may not stop for days.' His voice is tight, flat, like a quelling hand slapped down. 'We've got no money. Our food is running out.'

I wince as the wheels thud and creak over a sheep-track. This journey is pulling the cart apart, joint by joint.

'Well?' Hob is impatient.

I pull the mare up and, as she stands, snorting her hot breath into the drizzle, I untie the canvas and pull myself up on to the wheel to reach into the bed of the cart. As I do so, the spoke beneath my feet groans as if it will snap. I jump back down and bend to see the damage.

There is no break or visible crack but a man does not need to be a wheelwright to fear a noise like that. The wheel is surely weakening.

Hob comes around the cart. 'What was that?'

I straighten up. 'All those rutted paths up and down the hills. The cart wasn't built to withstand them.'

'Is it going to last till Salster?'

I shrug but, in truth, I doubt it.

'How much could the mare carry?' he asks.

'Without a saddle to tie things to or panniers to put them in, not much.'

'We could sell the cart and buy panniers.'

We could. We would travel faster and be able to choose our roads more freely than we can with the cart. But I am unwilling to give it up. It will be more fitting for the saint to arrive at her shrine set up above the herd on the cart than to peer out of a pannier bumping on a horse's flank. And besides, the cart is mine; if I were to sell it, Hob would demand half the money left over from buying pack-horse trappings in repayment of his ten shillings.

'No,' I say, 'it's good for a few miles yet.' I stand on my toes and pull out Hob's bow and the pilgrim-staff from Tredgham. 'We need to lash these together at the top,' I tell him.

He shrugs. 'Let's get to it, then.'

Though the saint stands well back inside the dry, canvas-gabled niche we have fashioned, I take no chances and wrap her in a blanket until we come within sight of any villagers. The rain has eased but drizzle hangs in the air.

We stop at the edge of the village and I feel Hob's eyes on me.

'Go on.' He points at the saint. 'Nobody'll see her in that.'

Testing the spoke with half my weight first, I stand on the wheel and ease the blanket down to reveal the Maiden's face, offering a silent prayer for her forgiveness as I do so.

It is not long before our presence attracts interest. A man in a leather hood appears, a young boy at his side.

'Good day, friends. You're a mite battered!'

Hob grins. 'Some churls disliked our good looks.'

The fellow returns his grin. 'So — what news?'

'Apart from ugly churls, only good news,' Hob says. 'We've seen nobody sick for four days.'

The man rubs the back of his hand over the beard on his chin, relieving an itch on face or hand, and glances aside at the boy who smiles up at him. 'You're not sick, yourselves?' he asks, turning to me.

'No, we're well.'

Hob opens his mouth and I wait for him to start — to tell this fellow that not only are we well but I have been miraculously healed of the pestilence.

'We'd be grateful to fill up our water butt,' he says. 'The mare's thirsty and we've a long way to go.' He hesitates, then adds, 'To Salster.'

'Salster? Don't you fear going so near to London as that will take you?'

Hob smiles. The man has given him a feed-line that a huckster's mate would be proud of.

'No, friend. We have our saint who protects us,' he turns and sweeps a hand around to the Maiden. 'We're taking her to her shrine in Salster. But —' He stops, as if he is weighing whether to continue.

'What?' Leather-hood's curiosity is aroused.

'She's not just *any* saint,' Hob begins. 'She's an English saint — one of our own.'

The man stares at the Maiden with what seems like new interest. 'Well she's a beauty, that's for certain.'

Hob takes a step towards him. 'And not just beautiful but a miracle worker, too.'

The man frowns but, instead of explaining, Hob clears his throat as if he feels he has said too much. 'We need water, friend,' he says, in a different tone. 'Can we walk on?'

In this village, we are allowed to dip the well-bucket ourselves and, as I set about filling the butt, Hob chats with our guide who has introduced himself as Symond.

Rain or not, people need water and those coming to the well spread news of our arrival so that we are quickly surrounded by a curious crowd. I am surprised at their willingness to approach us but their fearlessness is soon explained.

'As long as you don't see a corpse dead of the plague, or breathe the breath of the sick, you're safe,' one woman assures us. 'Our lord has travelled to France and Venice,' she adds, 'so he knows the way of it.'

'You're late,' a man remarks, nodding at the saint.

I turn to him. 'How so?'

'Lady Day's been'n gone.'

Lady Day. The Feast of the Annunciation.

'That's not the Virgin!' Symond corrects him. 'That's a saint. An English saint.' He turns to Hob. 'What did you call her?'

Hob gives a smile of such sweetness that he seems almost touched with saintliness himself. 'Her name,' he looks about at the gathered people, 'is Saint Cynryth and she's from the time before the Conqueror came, from the time of the Seven Kingdoms.'

Nobody wants to listen to a story in the rain so they take us to the church. I bring the Maiden, wrapped in her blanket, while Symond's boy takes the mare and the cart to the tithe barn.

Somebody guides me to an empty niche in the fine, stone-built rood screen and motions for me to put the Maiden there.

'Everybody'll be able to see her, then,' he says, patting my arm and ambling off to sit on the pile of trestle-boards left over from the Lady Day court.

As I watch the crowd listening to Hob, I realise what close attention he must have paid every time I told the saint's story in the woods at Tredgham. The words he uses are my words, from Saint Cynryth's childhood fleetness of foot — 'swift as a breeze in April' — to the gleaming whiteness of the shift she wore to her death.

He observes my own pause for breath after cutting off the Exile's arm and hissing the fairy's departure, before beginning the second part of the Maiden's story.

They listen, without so much as a shuffle or a cough as Cynryth grows from jilted lover to steadfast bedeswoman; they listen as she rejects all husbands but Christ and is pursued by the single-minded Aethenoth; they weep as she is martyred and they smile through their tears as her intercessions seed a babe in a barren womb.

'For ever afterwards,' Hob finishes, casting his eye around, 'St Cynryth was known as the White Maiden and her well as the White Maiden's Well. It lies in woods on a hill outside the city of Salster and there are miracles done there to this very day. And that,' he says, 'is where Martin and I are bound.' He turns to me.

I clear my throat, attempt a smile to match his own. 'We're taking the Maiden to her shrine at Salster.' My glance at the statue is followed by every eye present. 'I'm going to present her to the keeper of the shrine in return for his prayers for my father's soul.'

Hob does not interrupt, says nothing about the saint's miraculous appearance at our well-side shrine or the fact that she might have come, miraculously, from the shrine where we are bound.

A voice is raised, hesitantly. 'You're brave. I wouldn't want to be on pilgrimage now.'

There are murmurs of agreement, a sucking of teeth and an exchanging of glances. Hands rise to make the sign of the cross.

I wait for Hob to speak, to take up the story of my father and his devotion to the saint. But he says nothing. I wait, but the silence seems to grow and grow until it fills the church like the weak grey daylight. I wait for somebody to speak but not a voice is raised and the silence presses in on me, like the weight of red forest earth, until I can barely draw breath.

I seek out Symond's face, waiting for him to ask about the miracle Hob spoke of when we met, but perhaps he thinks that the story of the barren woman is miracle enough.

I turn to look at the Maiden and, as I fix my eyes on her, the white of her garments begins to glow in the gloom of the church and she seems to grow before my eyes until she reaches the stature of a living woman; a living woman reaching out from her niche to the people who stand before her. With my eyes on her reaching hand, it seems to me that the whole company is kneeling before her, like my Tredgham vision.

'My father was devoted to Saint Cynryth,' I hear myself saying. 'She appeared to him in a vision in the woods where we worked as collyers and he made a shrine to her at our well.' I look up. Every soul is watching me, waiting. '"All wells and springs that rise in woods are particularly mine to care for" — that's what she told him — "and your well shall be mine, too".'

Why are none of them are looking at the Maiden? Have they not seen how she glows, how tall she has grown?

'My father made a statue. Not this one — a small, rough statue which he put in the shrine.' I look at them, at their waiting faces. 'That statue carried years of prayers — all my father's devotion.' I hear my voice and it does not sound like my own. 'And he put it on my chest, pressed it into my hands, when I was dying.'

A woman takes a step towards me, puts a hand on my shoulder. I realise that there are tears running down my face.

'I was dying of the pestilence,' I tell them. 'I'd been given the last eucharist, anointed. I was ready.'

The woman's hand in still on my shoulder. She looks into my eyes. 'And yet you're alive.'

'Yes. My father put his saint into my hands and she healed me.'

Dusk is coming on inside the church. We have been here half a day and Hob has yet to ask for a penny. He has asked for nothing but the water we came for. Has he realised that it would be wrong to make money out of the saint?

From the sanctuary of the rood screen, I watch as he beckons people forward to kneel and ask the saint's blessings; I hear him tell a glad-eyeing maid that Cynryth reaches out in tender love, 'as she reached out to the Exile — not seeing his treachery but seeing only a soul in need.'

Did he say those words to Beatrice? Did she ask the saint to reach out a tender hand to her, in love?

He has not mentioned Beatrice's miracle. Not a word has been spoken about soft hands or special blessings.

Symond has been home to fetch his family. His wife, like him, is in the early part of middle life, a stout kind of woman whose straining seams speak of abundant food and prosperity. They have three children with them, two girls about my own age and the boy who was with Symond when we first met.

He introduces his wife. 'This is Margery.' The lady and I bow pleasantly to each other. 'And these are my treasures,' he rests a hand on each blond head in turn, 'Avice, Agatha and Alan.'

Alan grins and dips his head. Avice glances at me with a sly smile and I feel myself blush, remembering Christiana. I am almost glad of Agatha's indifference.

'Your saint,' Margery begins, folding her arms comfortably beneath her ample bosom.

'Yes?' I try to give my attention to her rather than to Avice who is trying to hook my eye.

'Her statue shows no tokens. What do folk know her by — just the whiteness of her gown?'

I think of other English saints — Edmund with the Danish arrows of his martyrdom, Dunstan with the tongs he used to hold the devil by the nose while he shod his cloven hooves.

'Yes,' I tell her, 'her whiteness. She's the White Maiden.'

'So — have you got anything for us to remember her by? Anything that'll keep us mindful of our prayers to her?'

Hob, shaking his head sadly, fixes his eyes on me. 'No, we have nothing.'

Two days later, I wake to a morning of blustery chill. Lying wrapped in blankets, my hood pulled down over my brow, only my face is cold and I am loath to get up. Being buffeted by the wind until your whole body is as cold as your face is an unhappy way to begin the day.

Through half-open eyes I see Hob sitting at the fire, his cloak pulled around him, hood up. Though his back is to me, I can tell that he is working at something.

I slide out from under the cart, pulling the blankets with me and subject my straining cock to the cold damp air, feeling the chill on the sensitive skin, remembering for the ten dozenth time Christiana's hand and the gasp that came from me when she wrapped her fingers around me.

I look up, away from the base of the ash-sapling where I am directing my piss. Off to my right, the sun is rising through heavy clouds. Ahead of us, a steep scarp rises to travel long miles into the distance, into the country between here and Salster.

The strong, steaming arc falls to away a dribble and, as always, my body gives a shiver. As I shake myself off, I wonder whether such a quantity of heat leaving my body draws in an equal quantity of cold. Then another, similar thought slips in on its heels. When Saint Cynryth drove the pestilence out of me, did something else rush in? Can it be that the Devil's demon lives, not in the air about me, whispering in my ears, darting in to seize control of me when I sleep, *but in my very being*? That, as the pestilence which should have killed me was banished from my body, the demon was drawn in?

My cock is shrunken and shrivelled in my hand. I tuck it into my braies and pull down my tunic but I cannot tuck my fear away so easily; suddenly my soul feels as poor and weak as my piss-withered cock. Is that the price I am to pay for my life — that, for the rest of my days, this demon will live, curled like a basking snake *within me*, taking my unconscious limbs at night time and using them to do whatever his master wishes?

Or, if I fulfil the task for which I was healed and restore the saint to her shrine, will the demon be driven out?

I look over my shoulder to see whether Hob has heard me stir. He shows no signs of it, his back still bent over whatever task he is about. I stare at him, at the movements that shiver the surface of his golden cloak.

All day yesterday, after we had left the hospitality of Symond's village, I bit back the questions that were pushing at my lips to be asked.

I thought you were going to ask for money?
Why didn't you tell them about Beatrice?
Why are you content to go so slowly?

The track we followed all day was uneven, canting the cart to one side, and, wary of damaging the wheels, I kept the mare to a pace that would usually have had Hob gnashing his teeth. But not only did he keep a civil tongue in his head, he urged me to let the mare graze at every opportunity.

When I asked him why he was suddenly so careful of her welfare all he would say was, 'You'll see.'

I walk around to the other side of the fire to see what is occupying him. I would not have guessed at his occupation in a hundred years.

He is making braids.

His fingers flip the strands over, pass them under, pull them tight, flatten the braid and start again. Next to him are three braided strands a handspan long; each has a loop in one end, a carefully-worked knot at the other.

'Where did you learn to do that?'

He shows no surprise at the question. 'My mother took finger-braid to market every week. It's not as good as woven but it's quicker and cheaper.' He glances up. 'So it sells.'

I look at the finished braids. They are clearly designed to circle a wrist, knot passing through loop as a fastener.

'Are you planning to take them to market?'

He shakes his head, his eyes on his working fingers. 'These are tokens of the White Maiden,' he looks up. 'You heard that dame in the village — people want tokens to remind them to offer the saint prayers.'

Now I see the care with which he's chosen the colours for his braids — white with a thread of gold for the Maiden's braided kirtle, white with green for the trees of her home.

'Where did you get the silks?'

'Agnes and her husband. You took the book, I took the silks.'

'And you're going to sell them to people?'

'Yes. Prayers we'll give for free. Blessings we'll give for free. But tokens'll have to be bought.'

We have been walking only a short time when we see a solitary monk coming towards us. Unlike every other traveller we have encountered he walks right up to us. Hob moves smartly to one side and the monk grips my arms with strong, blunt fingers.

'Are you headed for Guildford?' he asks. 'Or are you making all haste to Salster with your saint?'

He smiles at my surprise. 'Your fame has gone before you. I've just come from a village this side of the ford. They're waiting for you.'

Once the monk is safely on his way to Farnham, Hob grins. 'That's why we couldn't hurry yesterday,' he says. 'The boys from Symond's village needed time to run all the way to the next manor and tell them about the miracle-working saint who's coming along the road.'

Sure enough, a mile or two further on, the lookouts appear. Children too young to be useful in the fields are sitting like a flock of meadow-pipits on the common grazing of the hillside above us and, as soon as they see us, they spring to their feet and fling themselves up a cow-track towards the village.

'They're here! They're here!'

'They've come with the saint!'

'The saint's here! She's come!'

Hob turns to me and I cannot keep a grudging smile off my face.

'A peddler told me something once,' he says, all easy pride now I have acknowledged his cleverness. 'If you've got uncommon merchandise, make sure news of it goes ahead of you. It's better to arrive when people are already agog to have what you've got than to turn up and set about drumming up business.'

He holds his hand out towards the slope we will have to climb. 'Behold. A village all agog for our Maiden.'

Agog indeed. And well informed by the hares sent running.

Quickly surrounded on all sides, we answer a gabbled question here, confirm a detail there, as we make our way into the village.

At the church, we are treated as long-awaited guests and given fresh bread and good, well-flavoured ale. The wife who brings the bread is full of apologies for not having anything else to bring us — 'But, with it being Lent...'

I wait for Hob to brush aside her objections but he assures her that fresh bread is treat enough for men who have been cooking pottage for themselves every day.

When we have eaten and drunk, Hob stands.

'It seems you all know how Cynryth came to be the White Maiden,' he says, 'but something I haven't heard anybody mention this morning is Beatrice's miracle — can it be that you haven't heard about Beatrice and the saint's hand?'

He knows full well they have not: he said nothing of it in Symond's village and I followed his example. Faces look up at him; a new story is always welcome and, with the pestilence threatening, a story of the miraculous is preferred above all others. I watch the listening faces as Hob speaks. To my surprise, though he tells the story well, he does not gild the lily.

'The truth is, neither of us —' he turns to me, bolstering his story with my wordless evidence — 'saw the miracle taking place. No, we were talking to Beatrice's father and brothers. And then … we heard her give a little cry.' He pauses, his eyes everywhere in the crowd, fastening on each person, tightening the thread by which he is drawing them in. '"Oh, oh!" That's all she said.' He pauses again, then repeats, 'Oh, oh!' more slowly, and, this time, it sounds — even in my ears — like the annunciation of a miracle.

'When Beatrice raised her head beneath the saint's hand for her blessing,' Hob says, 'what she felt on her head was not the dry, hard benediction of a wooden hand,' he thrusts out his arm towards them, fingers stiff, palm up in the reaching manner of the saint, 'but the warm, soft blessing of a woman's living hand.' As he speaks the words, his hand turns over, his fingers lose their rigid hardness and curl downwards, like a mother's hand resting on the head of an infant. 'The saint's wooden hand became flesh.'

He holds his hand there, for a moment or two, and every person watches, rapt, as if each one of them is there, beneath those warm, curled fingers. Then, he drops his hand to his side.

At once, there is a great outbreak of murmured astonishment, neighbour turning to neighbour in scarcely-contained amazement, mouths and eyes equally wide.

'Wood turned to living flesh!'

'What was her name?'

'Beatrice.'

'*Beatrice.*'

Soon, her name is as familiar to them as their own and they begin to wonder whether they, too, might feel the hand made flesh. A line of people eager for the saint's blessing begins to form before the font, some on their knees, some preferring to wait their turn standing. And, as at Tredgham, I stand, the saint in my arms, and lower her hand on each supplicant head.

A yard or two away, Hob has gathered a crowd about him and, out of the corner of my eye, I see one of the young wives put a hand on his arm. 'How did you come to be in that village where the saint did Beatrice's miracle?'

And as I pronounce, again and again, *St Cynryth bless you, today and always*, Hob tells the story of how the mare threw her shoe and we ended up coaling in Tredgham so that it could be replaced.

'And, while you were there, the miracle was done and scores of people blessed,' she says, her hands clasped in wonder.

Hob nods. 'Yes. The saint caused the mare to throw her shoe at the *very place* where the miracle could happen.'

The young wife pulls in a breath, looks around at their companions, then back at Hob. 'So there were two miracles at Tredgham,' she says, 'not one. The miracle of the saint's hand and the miracle of the thrown horseshoe.'

While the older folk discuss this second miracle, the girls are more interested in the braids that Hob has brought out. All the blessings sought having been granted, I watch him lacing a white and gold braid between his fingers while the prettiest maid in the church stands at his side.

'If you do this before you sleep, then the saint'll protect you all night,' he says, weaving the braid under one finger and over the next. 'Having this bound to your fingers will remind you — ' he glances into her eyes — 'of the saint's hand reaching out in tender love.'

'Show me how to do it,' she commands, clearly used to having young men do her bidding.

'Must I bow while I'm at it?' Hob asks, mocking.

The girl blushes but holds her ground.

Hob nods and holds his left hand out, to demonstrate. 'As you lace,' he tells her, 'you say this prayer. White Maiden of the well —' he passes the braid under his second finger — 'daughter of King Halstan —' over the ring finger — 'betrayed lover of the exile —' the girl's blush deepens at these words as Hob passes the braid under his little finger — 'faithful bride of Christ —' the braid comes back — 'protect me now —' under the ring finger — 'and all those dear to me —' over the next finger — 'this night and every night.' He pulls the braid tight and meets her eye.

'And then, during the day —' he slides the laced strand from his fingers and wraps it around her wrist, careful not to touch her, lest anybody see — 'you wear it fastened up, like this.'

As knot passes through loop with the merest resistance, the girl gazes at Hob, her face pink, her lips parted.

Now, after Christiana, I know what that look means.

I look away, at the crowd of people in the church and, again, I am reminded of the vision the Maiden granted me at Tredgham: an army under her protection. And there, in the midst of them, stands Hob.

Hob Cleve. Despite all that I know of him, all I suspect, can it be that the saint has chosen him — just as she has chosen me — to bring that vision to pass?

CHAPTER 26

Guildford behind us, we follow the track along the towering scarp as it runs eastward. The going is slow today and the view that stretches ahead of us seems unchanging, however long we walk.

I believe we must be on the cusp of April, today, for the sun is hot when the clouds part in front of it and the breeze is warm. Soon, if the warmth persists, bees and butterflies will appear and the swallows will bring summer with them.

Around us, leaves are already showing on the smaller saplings — the may and sycamores are the furthest advanced but the hazels are not far behind. Blackthorns are already in bloom and the abundance of their white flowers reminds me of snow.

Is Hob expecting news of the saint to have raced ahead of us again? This is sparser, hillier country than we had before Guildford; if we want to find a village, we shall have to go further down, into the vale. These slopes are good for sheep-grazing but a plough-team would be hard-pushed to turn much of the land for crops.

As the sun sinks and dusk approaches, I think of the bread that we have packed into the flour chest along with a good half-pound of cheese given to us by one of the village's woman. She may have hoped that we would save it until after Easter but she did not require our promise to do so and I am glad of it.

When we stop for the night, Hob takes the mare's hobble from me as I come around the cart. 'There's something I want to do while it's still light enough to see,' he says. 'Can you go and see about firewood this time?'

I have no wish to sour the good humour he has been in since he conceived the notion of the braids, so I do as he asks.

Hob does not look up when I let the unwieldy bundle drop from my shoulders at the side of the cart and untie the cord. He is working away with that knife of his on what I take to be our pilgrim's staff; but when I look more closely, I see that he has helped himself to a coppice pole from somewhere and is notching one end of it, as if it were an outsized arrow.

I look about for some indication of what he is doing and see a horseshoe lying at his side. My first thought is that the mare must have thrown another shoe but, when I peer at her in the half-light she is standing four-square.

I do not need to go many paces toward the cart before I see the empty corner-joint at the front. A fine sweat breaks out on my back. The horseshoes fixed to the cart are all that prevents the demon from forcing me to do his bidding while I sleep under it. Hob knows that.

I stoop and pick up the horseshoe.

'Hey, put that down!'

'You can't take the horseshoes off the cart!' What is he trying to do, drive me to my death at the demon's bidding?

He flares up, leaping to his feet. 'And you're going to stop me, are you?'

I take a step backwards, cradling the horseshoe against my chest. 'No wonder you wanted me out of the way, you knew I'd never let you leave me unprotected.'

'Oh, stop squealing like a girl, Martin!' He throws the staff to the ground and sits again. 'You're not unprotected, are you?

I'm here to stop the demon harming you. And what about the saint? Don't you trust her to keep you safe?'

I stare down at him.

'You don't, do you? You have more fear of the demon than you have faith in the saint. Shame on you, Martin. Shame on you.'

I feel my heart thudding in my chest. Is he right? The fears that plagued me at night before Hob rescued me from Edgar have not entirely left me. They are lodged in me like the demon. But Hob is right — surely the saint will protect me? I walked on the hearth at Tredgham and did no harm to myself or others. And Hob was able to bid the demon in me lie down again.

'You still haven't told me what you're doing.' My voice sounds weak and I cough to clear the hard lump of fear siting in my throat.

'Light the fire before the embers cool too much and then I'll tell you.'

Apprehension makes me cack-handed and it takes me twice as long as usual to get the fire going. With every breath I examine my conscience. Has Saint Cynryth found me wanting in my devotion — has she seen in my inner heart a lack of faith, born of Master William's doubt about her? Has my weakness of faith been allowing the demon to grow strong?

Finally, the fire alight, I take the peas and beans and garlic we were given in the last village and set them to boil for a pottage. 'Now,' I say, trying to sound calm but only succeeding in sounding querulous, 'tell me what you're doing.'

Hob flicks a glance at me, then rises to fetch the horseshoe which I laid on top of the canvas above the empty corner. 'It wasn't my idea, as it happens,' he says, sitting again. 'It was the saint's.'

'What are you talking about? What idea?' My heart is banging my ribs again. How dare he? She is not his saint. He has never even knelt beneath her blessing hand. How dare he declare her the author of his own designs?

'Look, Martin, you've heard what people've been saying — they want the Maiden to have a sign. They want to be able to know her by the miracles she's done.'

'She has a sign — the white braids!'

'But they don't signify a miracle, do they? They just call to mind her kirtle, her name.' He raises the staff he has been working on and taps the top. 'When I walk into a village carrying the very shoe the mare cast on the ford, people will know that a miracle's happened and they'll want to know all about it.'

'But Cynryth's miracles are to do with wells and healing! How will it help to start talking about horseshoes?'

He shakes his head. 'Those were the miracles she did *before*, Martin. She's doing new things, now. You heard them yesterday. The saint did two miracles at Tredgham — one when she caused the mare to throw her shoe on the ford, another when she blessed Beatrice.'

He looks up at me, eyes dark in the gloom. 'This was *her idea*,' he says again. 'I wouldn't have thought of it but she came to me in a dream last night. She stood before me. Like this.' He flicks his fingers into the gap between us, showing how close the saint stood in his dream 'She was a life-size woman. And in her hand —' he mimes the saint's reaching posture — 'she was holding a horseshoe, offering it to me.'

Fear-hackles rise on my neck. Why did she offer the horseshoe to Hob and not to me? Is she punishing me because I have not spoken of my vision, because I have kept it hidden in my heart like a treasure?

Hob eyes my silence and speaks again.

'We've got wristlets for the hand-miracle. But she knew we needed something to show people the miracle of the thrown shoe.'

He sits in front of me, limbs long and straight, head held high, his cloak fastened so that even I, who know he does not possess one, look to his side for a sword.

Has the saint deserted me in favour of a more fitting champion?

For almost two weeks, news of the saint seems to run along before us. As we follow that long, long hill-line, that wave of land that seems to run along England as the great bore runs along the Severn, travelling long distances without ever losing height, we are greeted everywhere as men who have been awaited. And, everywhere, we find hearts ready to welcome Saint Cynryth and give thanks for her miracles. Parents send their children off to tell aunties and uncles, friends and cousins that a saint is coming who may keep the plague from their doors. We see them, sometimes, dawdling back in the sunshine, full of self-importance and with little bundles full of items sent as thanks. They grin at us and show their white wristlets and one or two of the boys carry little staffs topped with a bent nail or a horseshoe-shaped piece of horn.

White braid about the wrist has become the mark of 'the White Maid's children'.

When we stop, I look into the anxious eyes of mothers and I see that, whether they believe in the power of my saint or not, they bring their little ones because any hope of protection, any hand held up against the pestilence, must be grasped.

So they wait for us in villages and at the roadside. They hail us from far off, knowing us as soon as we come into view by the saint who stands proud at the front of the cart, her hand reaching forward to greet them. And they know us by Hob's staff.

Their speechways fall ever stranger on our ears as we travel further and further eastwards and sometimes a word here and there is foreign to us, springing from a different soil. But we are welcome, that much is always clear. For our saint and Hob's staff, we are welcome. Indeed, people have begun to speak of the horseshoe staff as a relic in its own right and tales of its miraculous powers have begun to spread, seemingly of their own accord.

The staff is said to jerk in Hob's fist when there is a village, just out of sight of the track, where we should stop. It is said to dowse springs with uncanny exactness. And it is said that, if a man so much as touches it, he shall be given the knowledge of his own fate under the pestilence.

'I gripped it in my fist —' I hear one fellow say to his companions, 'and I saw, straightaway, that I wouldn't die. Saw myself old and grey I did, with strong grandsons keeping me!'

One day, I even hear it said that the Maiden has given Hob a portion of her own power to reward his faithfulness in bringing her to the shrine in Salster. But, at this, Hob shakes his head. 'No, no!' he says, glancing sideways at me. 'It's Martin who's bid to take her to Salster. I'm just the keeper of the horseshoe.' But I know that, whatever he says, the rumour will persist. And no wonder; as he strides along, the miraculous staff in his hand, he is tall and golden in the spring sunshine, like the hero in a story.

Mile after mile, the track beneath the wheels of the cart is the whitish colour of the chalk these hills are made of and we see quarries and scrapes scattered everywhere.

The going is strenuous and the cart is showing signs of hard usage. My running repairs can be seen in the new lengths of rope which weave in and out, lashing sides to bed and re-securing bed to base. In one of the villages, I ask a wheelwright to re-nail the rims and to cast his eye over spokes and felloes. His opinion is that we will not get to Salster without new wheels.

'Best make your mind up to spending money before you get there. Sooner rather than later, too, if you'll take my advice.'

But Hob is unconvinced that repairs are needed. 'The cart'll be fine. It just creaks — all carts creak.'

So they do. But Hob will say that the cart is just creaking until it falls to firewood in front of our eyes; he wants the money for Salster. The only coin he is happy to spend goes on more silks — and flax which is cheaper — for the braids.

We come across a churchyard, the cross hung with garlands of primroses and stitchwort and violets. Palm Sunday flowers, wilted but not yet brown. It is Holy week.

Invited to lodge in the village for the celebration, we creep to the cross on our knees on Good Friday to confess our sins, we rise at dawn on Sunday for the Easter vigil, we process to church for the great Resurrection Eucharist.

But I am sick at heart.

Every other Easter, when Master William placed the host on my tongue, the knowledge that the bread had become the real body of our Lord, that I had taken his very substance into my own, filled me with wonder and awe.

Now, the taste of the host is the taste of my own death. Only by swallowing and swallowing in a dry throat can I stomach it.

A decision lies a day or two ahead of us. We have been told that, once we cross the river Medway, there are two routes to Salster. One will take us back up on to the slopes of the Down, the other north to the city of Rochester and thence east and south to Salster on a better road.

We have no shortage of advice — everybody has an opinion about the way to take. In other times, it seems, the choice would be easy — the road from Rochester is more direct and better-kept and, as long as pilgrims travel in a group large enough to deter robbers, they are safe.

But the road from Rochester to Salster starts in London. And London is dying.

A day or so before we must look for the river-crossing we find ourselves in a sunlit churchyard waiting for the boy who has been promised a ha'penny to run and find the parson. It has become our habit, when we enter a village, to make straight for the parish church and its priest, drawing villagers to us on the way.

A crowd has already gathered and I can see more figures coming to us along the paths that lead to the church. Yesterday, we stopped in a much bigger village and, no doubt, word of saint Cynryth's power has travelled here ahead of us.

I watch them coming. Saint Cynryth's army.

Soon, I am the only soul in the churchyard not paying Hob any attention and the parish priest has made it known that he will celebrate a mass and ask for the saint's blessing on the parish.

At his request, I take the Maiden from the cart and carry her in to the church and, as his assistants swarm about him and pass through to the sanctuary to make preparation, I place her on the waist-high boarding of the rood screen.

Looking through, I see two boys, already scrambled into their white robes, laying fine linen on the stone surface of the altar. They are slapdash, grinning and gurning as they straighten the heavy cloths, one on top of the other, racing each other out to the vestry in a stiff-armed scurry.

I feel a world away from them. Though scarcely three months have passed since I did the very same office, I have lived another life in those months. If I were to pass through the screen and take the embroidered altar-cloth in my hands, it would not mean to me, now, what it meant then. Before the pestilence, I fulfilled even the smallest part of the eucharistic ritual in the hope that, one day, I would watch my own assistants doing the same.

But, even if my yearning to be a priest had not been stilled by the pestilence and its aftermath, I would no longer be able to convince myself of my vocation. I lack the essential virtue of chastity, Christiana has shown me that. And not just Christiana but all my thoughts of her — my lusts for her — since we left Slievesdon. Despite everything that happened to us there — the loss of our money, the risk to our lives — I know in my heart that I would do no differently if we were given our time there over again. The sensation of my cock sliding into the warm, slippery embrace of her comes to me now and I stifle a groan.

I drop to my knees before the rood screen to ask for forgiveness before the mass begins.

'Do you have a wheelwright in your village?'

The man I have asked the question nods. 'Yes. Thomas Prynk's son Geoffrey's a wheeler, he's at the far end of the village if you want him.'

I thank him and adjust my hold on the saint. I must wrap her safely and lay her in the cart before I do anything else.

Hob strides after me, the linen bag that once held my mother's needles and threads hanging heavy with coins at his waist.

'Martin — I thought we'd agreed? We don't need to waste money on new wheels — chances are, we're less than a week from Salster. The cart'll last, I'm sure of it.'

The saint swaddled in a blanket, I turn to him. 'Well, I'm not. Those wheels are fit to spring their rims and we'll be going nowhere when that happens.'

'They'll last a week, surely? It might be less — four or five days.'

I pull the canvas back, aware of the interest our conversation is causing. 'And then what?' I ask, between my teeth. 'You're set on staying in Salster and making your fortune there, but I'm not. I don't know what I'll do. I may need the cart.'

'Oh, so *I've* got to part with my money so *you'll* have a cart?'

'You've had the benefit of it all this way!'

'Yes, and the pushing and braking of it up and down half the hills in England.'

People are watching us. I should walk away but I am tired of Hob always thinking he can get the better of me. 'You didn't have to come with me.' I keep my voice low. 'You could've stopped in any of the towns along the way.'

'I'll do better in Salster than in any of the little piss-pot towns we've passed through.'

'Fine.' People are pretending not to listen but I know their ears are on stalks and I slide my words out carefully. 'But since it's my cart that's getting you and your goods there, you can pay half for the wheels. How much money have we got?'

We have been selling braids at a steady rate. Despite the outlay on thread we should have a good few shillings put by.

Hob shrugs, the horseshoe staff in its accustomed position against his collarbone. There are still some braids hanging from the upturned shoe, unsold, and I shiver at a resemblance I have not seen before to the fripperies that hang from the nails on a peddler's stick.

'Don't know,' he says. 'I haven't been keeping count.'

'What d'you mean you haven't been keeping count?'

'What I say.'

I stare at him, convinced that he is lying but unable to account for why.

On the other hand, now I stop to consider, I have never seen him counting the money he has taken in. He weighs the bag in his hand at the end of the day before stowing it in the press, but never has he piled pennies and ha'pennies into shillings.

'Let's count it. Then we'll know how much we've got.'

'Suit yourself. But you can count it — I'll be out there making it.'

He stalks off and I turn to the cart.

I take the knotted corners of the old shirt in which we keep our takings and lift it out of the press. Seeing that the remnants of crowd have followed Hob, I settle down where I am, in a corner between the lych-gate and the churchyard wall and begin unpicking the knots.

Before I am halfway through counting, I know something is amiss. There should be more money than this — far more; Hob has been selling braids with the scarce, gold-coloured thread for more than the green-threaded ones and I know we made a good number of them — nearly all our silk and flaxen thread is gone.

Even with today's takings added, what is in the shirt will not buy me one wheel, let alone two.

What has Hob done with the rest of the money?

I knot the shirt again and lay it in the press. By now, he must know that I have discovered his treachery. What lies is he hatching as he stands amidst the little crowd of people by the churchyard cross?

I rest my back against the cart and watch him. Now he smiles, now he laughs, now he speaks earnestly, his head thrust slightly forward as he tries to explain something to one of his would-be customers. I know his patter. The braids are no mere trinkets, he will be assuring them, they are reminders to prayer, solemn oaths that the blessings received by the kneeling supplicant will be acknowledged daily and the saint's intercession sought.

When we started out with the saint, we had nothing but her, he will tell them. *But people were avid for tokens — 'how will we remember her when you're gone?'*

So closely am I watching Hob that I do not notice a fellow approaching me until he speaks.

'I hear you're wanting a wheelwright?'

I turn to the speaker. An older man, maybe thirty-five, he is wearing a tunic that has seen better days and boots whose soles are bound on with strips of rawhide.

'Yes. Are you Geoffrey Wheeler?' I hope not, for if a man's prosperity announces his competence then this man is unhandy at best.

'No. Geoffrey's my brother. That's him —' he turns and points — 'standing over there with your friend. The tall one. Want me to introduce you?'

'No. Thank you. Let him finish his business with Hob, first.'

He gives a mirthless grunt. 'He won't be doing any business. Not Geoffrey. He'll just be watching other fools parted from their money. He's the tightest bastard west of the Medway.'

I wait in the shadow of the lychgate for the wheelwright. If he is mean with his money, he is unlikely to be easy-going in other respects and I am loath to deprive him of whatever entertainment he is getting from watching Hob.

As I wait, I steadily bank down the rage burning in me so that it cannot consume my wits. I need to think what to do.

If I confront Hob, he will deny that he has taken any money from the press. I need to think where he might have hidden it.

Where could he put a quantity of coins so as to be sure I would not happen upon them? Not in the press or in the flour chest with the beans and peas. Not amongst any of my household goods, for I am often in there hunting for something.

No. He must have them somewhere about himself.

I stare across the churchyard. In the sun's warmth, he has doffed his tunic and stands there in his shirt and hose, feet apart, chin up. The tunic will be in the cart somewhere, quickly rolled up and stowed out of the way. His cloak, however, is never hastily wadded; he always folds it with care and puts it where it will come to no harm, well away from ember-basket and butt, near the saint at the front of the cart.

He wraps himself in it at night, preferring it to an over-tunic, and it is the only item of his clothing I have ever seen him take a needle and thread to; he pulled the hem down by standing on it when he was getting up from the fire. Straight away, he asked if I had any thread finer than the stuff we use for the braids and I gave him what remained of my mother's thread — the same stuff my father used to fasten his shroud. And a ridiculous time he took about it, too, thinking about it.

The cloak's hem.

I see, now, what Hob has done. He has taken as many pennies as he can and has sewn them into the hem of his cloak. Made of such a quantity of good-quality weave, it is heavy with its own weight — the addition of a few ounces of silver would make no great difference to the way it hangs and swings.

I turn to the cart. The mare, thinking my sudden movement means that we are on the move, raises her head from her cropping and I rub her withers as I go past. 'No, old girl, you munch on.'

Quickly flipping up the canvas, I reach for the cloak. Hob has folded it inside out, so that the surface everybody sees is kept away from the charcoal dust that still works its way from the willow-weave of the cart's sides. I unroll it and shake it out so that I can get to the bottom hem but, as I do so, a small stain catches my eye. I look at it more closely, bringing the fine woollen weave up to my eyes. It's a darkish brown and is only visible deep into the weave, most of it having been worn away by contact with Hob's tunic.

I touch my tongue to it and, as I work up spit in my mouth and move the taste from the tip to the rest of my tongue, I taste its familiar tang. Blood.

If it was on the outside of the cloak I could believe it had come from Hob's nose when he was beaten in the barn at Tredgham but it is on the inside, protected from spatters. The blood must have got there when the cloak was folded up, folded inside out.

An image of Edgar's dead face springs into my mind: the crust of blood around his nose, the dry trickle into his beard. Is this Edgar's blood, proof that Hob made sure he never woke up? Though it is no more than I have long suspected, it is a shock to see actual evidence that Hob is a murderer.

A murderer? Is he? Edgar was going to die anyway. He couldn't even to swallow the water you trickled between his lips.

Such is the condition of my soul that I cannot tell whether the words come from my angel or the demon.

I straighten up and fling the cloak wide over the canvas in the sunshine. As soon as I put my fingers to the hem, I can feel the coins. Moving the fingers of both hands around the hem, testing as I go, I feel the pennies butting so close against one another in the thickness of the material that, here and there they overlap. How many has Hob sewn in? I do a quick calculation. If the hem is six feet long there could be ten shillings' worth weighing the cloak down. Ten shillings; enough to buy my wheels.

I look across the churchyard to where Hob is standing. He is watching me.

Geoffrey Wheeler and I are halfway across the glebelands when Hob catches up with us.

'Where are you going in such a hurry?' He falls into step at my side and I glance across at him. The horseshoe staff is bare of braids now.

'To Master Wheeler's workshop.'

Hob grabs my arm, tries to draw me aside. 'I've told you,' he says, his voice low, 'we can't afford it.'

I stop and turn to face him, pitching my own voice so that it will carry to the wheelwright's ears. 'I think you know we can.'

Hob glances over the mare's neck, then turns so that his back is to Geoffrey Wheeler. 'Even with the money I've hidden, we still can't afford it — not if we're going to make our way in Salster.'

I scarcely hear the second half of what he says. 'You don't deny hiding it?'

'Don't be stupid!' His voice is a hiss. 'After what happened at Slievesdon? One of us had to make sure it didn't happen again.'

I drop my voice. 'Why didn't you tell me you'd hidden it?'

He looks me in the eye. 'Martin, you're an honest man. Lying doesn't come easily to you. If some cut-throat bastard had put a sword to your neck and said, "is this all the money you've got?" he'd've seen in your face that it wasn't. Easier for you not to know.'

'Well, now I *do* know. And that money is getting us new wheels.'

'Half of it, you mean. Only half that money is yours.'

The warning in his voice enrages me. I turn on him, shoving him back. Taken by surprise he falls on his arse and suddenly I am standing over him.

'If you want to divide that money now,' I tell him, 'then we part here. The cart needs mending and that's what I'm going to do.' He tries to rise but I put a foot on his chest. 'How much do you think people would have believed in the saint if we'd turned up on foot, with me carrying her on my back, or you pushing her in a handcart? Eh?'

Hob takes my boot and makes to pull me over. I yank it out of his grasp and he rolls to his feet.

'And if we do part company here? What'll you do without my bow to protect you?'

His tone makes me want to smash my fist into his face, wipe off that sneer.

'I could get somebody to travel with me and the saint in half an hour if I needed to! I'd have no shortage of takers.'

'Even though the pestilence is coming?'

'*Because* the pestilence is coming! What better protection than a pilgrimage?'

'Keeping away from it.'

His words fall between us with the weight of a dropped stone and sit there, waiting for one of us to stumble over them and carry on.

But the heat of the argument has left me. I turn away. 'I'm going to get new wheels for the cart. You can come, or not, as you please.'

Geoffrey Wheeler examines spokes and felloes, axle and shoes.

'Whoever made these wheels was no friend to you. The elm for the hubs wasn't seasoned properly — it's shrunk so your spokes are loose. That's what all your creaks and cracks have been about. Then there's the felloes — they've taken a right battering, nails or no nails.'

'We know the wheels're worn,' Hob snaps. 'Any fool can see that. What we want to know is how long they'll last?'

The wheeler takes a long look at Hob. 'If any craftsman tells you he knows how long another man's work'll last then he's a liar or a fool. But I'll tell you one thing — only prayer and luck are holding these wheels together.'

'How much,' I ask, 'for two new wheels?'

'It's not just wheels you need, your axle's almost gone too.'

Hob folds his arms. 'How much? And how long?'

'Well, you're fortunate,' Wheeler tells him. 'I've got a pair of wheels that will suit.'

'Never mind our fortune.' Hob is sour. 'How much?'

'Two pounds,' the wheelwright says, folding his arms across his chest. 'For wheels and axle.'

'*Two pounds?* We're not talking about a whole new cart and a horse to go with it!'

'Six shillings is more what I was thinking of,' I said, remembering what my father had paid the wheelwright who made our cart and dropping the price to a bargaining position.

'Maybe before,' Wheeler says. 'But I could be dead next week and who's going to provide for my family then? 'Sides which, from what I hear, you'll be lucky to find a craftsman alive from here to Salster that's got all he needs to ply his trade.' He looks from me to Hob. 'If you want new wheels, you'll be wise to have them now.'

Hob turns to me and shrugs. 'No point debating it. He's made our decision easy. We haven't got two pounds. We'll have to take our chances.'

I ignore Hob and pay attention to Geoffrey Wheeler. I can see he has a proposal to make.

'You mentioned six shillings?' he says.

I nod.

'I'll tell you what I'll do.' He unfolds his arms and puts a hand on one of our failing wheels. 'Give me your six shillings and that staff with the horseshoe on it and you can have your wheels.'

I wait for Hob's response. Over these last weeks, I believe he has come to feel that carrying the staff makes him my equal in the eyes of the saint. Whilst her statue belongs to me, the Maiden revealed the miracle of the cast shoe to Hob.

He stares at Wheeler. 'This staff — this shoe — is a reminder to me and Martin that the saint does miracles when we need them.' He lets the wheelwright take this in. 'So I'm thinking — why shouldn't she do a miracle with these wheels and stop them falling apart before we reach Salster? Why shouldn't I trust her and tell you where you can put your wheels and your new axle?'

Wheeler shrugs. 'If you want my opinion, it's a miracle they've not fallen apart already. By rights, either one of those wheels could've failed weeks ago.' He hooks his thumbs in his belt. 'You don't want to test your saint too far.'

'No. And I don't want to displease her by selling a relic of one of her miracles!'

Wheeler's eyes follow the staff as Hob lifts it slightly off the ground.

'What if you don't sell it?'

Hob's eyes narrow. 'What?'

'Let's say we forget about the six shillings. Then let's say that, out of the goodness of my heart, I *give* you a new pair of wheels. And you — out of gratitude — give me the staff.'

'I thought you needed money to leave to your family in case you died?'

'But I shan't die, shall I? With the staff, I shall have the saint protecting me.'

What Hob says next is so unexpected that Geoffrey Wheeler must see my astonishment.

'Martin and I will have to think about it. We'll take the mare on to the common for an hour or two and then we'll be back.'

'Well?' I ask, once the mare is grazing and we are sitting in the shade of the cart.

'Well what?'

'What are we going to do about the staff?'

He looks at me as if I have grown another nose. 'You don't think I'm going to let him have it?'

'Then why're we sitting here? Why aren't we in his workshop haggling the price down?'

'Because I'm not going to pay him either.'

A cloud crosses the sun bringing up gooseflesh on my arms. 'We've got to have new wheels.'

I might as well not have spoken. 'Listen. The wheelwright doesn't expect me to let him have the staff. And if I did, he'd know it was worthless — why would I exchange such a powerful item for two cart wheels and an axle?'

He plainly wants me to wheedle his plan out of him but I am not going to give him the satisfaction. I turn my back on him and lie down in the sun.

I wake to the sound of voices. My face is hot and my mouth dry as I sit up and look about me. Hob is standing a little way off with a group of villagers.

'I told him I needed to think about it,' I hear him say, 'but I couldn't part with the staff. It's too precious.'

I stand up and my head spins. I need a drink of water.

As I go around to the back of the cart and the butt, Hob's words become clearer, louder.

'— even they're precious.' He tosses a glance over his shoulder. Does he see me? 'They keep off the demons who'd like to do the saint harm in the dark hours. Everything to do with the saint and our pilgrimage is precious. She can use anything to her purposes.'

He's talking about the other horseshoes attached to the corners of the cart.

I dip a mug into the butt but I have barely started drinking when I hear a shout coming from somewhere away to my left, in the direction of the track we followed to the village this morning. Something about the shout makes me turn towards it. Behind me, I hear voices coming closer; Hob and the crowd of folk around him have heard the shout, too.

'It's Oswald,' a voice says, 'from over Little Wrothcliffe —
Alan and Tom Lyche's cousin. What's he want?'

'Hey, Oswald!' another shouts. 'What's to do?'

All of a sudden, a lark goes up — startled by us, perhaps —
and I follow its urgent flight. Soon, it is lost to my eyes and all
I can see is the cloud-chased blue of the April sky. But still I
can hear it. I listen to the song, loud and high in the sky.
Obstinately, I listen to it as the words of Oswald the Lyches'
cousin batter at my ears and I try to push away the weight of
sorrow and dread that is filling my chest.

But I cannot. As the lark trills its love song with its little
handful of strength, I hear the words every soul in England
dreads.

'The pestilence is come.'

CHAPTER 27

Oswald stands a couple of dozen yards downwind of us and tells the story in a voice more suited to calling cattle home. It seems that Dode, a morning's walk from here, fell victim to the pestilence a week or so ago. 'Every living soul there is dead,' Oswald tells the crowd.

Hob and I look at each other in perplexity. 'All dead — *everybody* — in a week?' I shake my head.

'It must have been there longer, friend,' Hob calls. 'We've seen the pestilence in our own villages — it moves slowly from house to house.'

'Not in Dode. Men went into the fields in the morning hale and healthy, came home at midday hot and feverish and were dead by sunset.'

Again we look at each other. That does not sound like the pestilence we know — neither the carbuncles nor the coughing blood.

'Did they cough blood?' Hob calls.

'Some did. Some didn't. Those who lasted longest did.'

'Did they have patches on their skin? Black patches?'

'Some. Not all. Some hadn't a mark on 'em. But when they had skin-patches they were reddish, not black.'

Not a mark on them. Like my father. Is this how he died — hale and well when he packed our cart and left Lysington, dead by sunset? But I have not time to ponder the question for Oswald is telling his tale.

'The last to die was a child,' he calls. 'The story comes from her. No more than seven years old she was and she saw the whole village die. Went to the church when she couldn't find a house with a soul in to give her comfort. That's where our parson found her, dying.'

'Are any sick in your village?' one of the villagers around us calls out.

'Not yet. But Dode is our nearest neighbour. And the parson gave the rites to the dying child. Nobody better come near.'

'And you?'

'Me and mine are bolting our doors as soon as I get back. Tell my cousins in Sibbertswell, will you? That's what I came for.'

By the time I bring the mare back to the cart, most of the Sibbertswell villagers have gone to spread the news. Hob and I look at each other. The pestilence's coming puts thoughts of all else aside.

'What should we do?'

He shrugs, half an eye on the remaining villagers. 'They've had the saint's blessings,' he says, for my ears only. 'There's nothing else for us to do — now she either answers their prayers or she doesn't.'

I try to fill my mind with the vision of saint Cynryth's army beneath her banner, walking through the woods to her shrine. People healed, people saved.

'You think we should just go?' I ask.

'Don't you?'

'No. If the pestilence is so close it may be in front of us, too. The wheeler's right — if we don't get new wheels here, we may never get them.'

I say no more, leaving him to think as I back the mare between the shafts. When she is ready to pull, I look up but, there, instead of Hob, I see the tall, lean figure of the wheelwright. He is panting.

'Is it true? Is the pestilence coming?' Despite the handful of his fellow-villagers who are standing there, he addresses the question to us.

'We don't know any more than you,' I say. 'A fellow called Oswald brought the news.'

'So it's true — it's killed Dode — everybody?'

'So he says.'

'And you?' He leans over, hands resting on his thighs. 'Are you just going to leave us now?'

'You've had the saint's blessing,' I hear myself echoing Hob's words. 'There's nothing more we can give you.'

'You can give us the staff.'

Hob speaks for the first time. 'No. The thrown horseshoe was a miracle for us and for Tredgham. Not for you.'

Wheeler straightens up. 'Then keep the horseshoe and leave us the staff! It'll have power of its own from the horseshoe being fastened to it for so long. Leave us one of the other horseshoes off the cart.'

Hob fastens his eyes on to Wheeler. 'You'll give us our wheels in exchange?'

For the space of half a dozen thudding heartbeats, the wheelwright does not respond. He just stands, his face hiding his thoughts. But I know the dread he feels. The Death is coming. Now it has come to it, he will give anything he has to save himself and his family.

'You'll have to stay in the village a day or two,' he says, finally. 'I've got the wheels but I need to find you a new axle.'

The deal Hob has struck with Wheeler is already known to half the village by the time we walk up the street to his workshop.

People rush towards us, holding out purses full of money.

'I'll give you five shillings for one of those other horseshoes.'

'I'll give you six and a cheese.'

'I'll give you ten!'

I recognise some individuals from the churchyard; one or two are wearing white braids. But their previous keenness to buy tokens seems a poor, weak thing in comparison to the desperate way in which they try to press money on Hob now.

'The pestilence is coming, you must leave us some protection!'

'You've got the saint, you don't need the horseshoes as well!'

'Please!'

'*Please!*'

Hob's eyes flit from one to another. For the first time, he appears unsure of what to do.

'How can I sell the horseshoes to the highest bidder?' he asks. 'Are the richest of you the most virtuous?'

There is an outcry both for and against this proposition. But, before Hob can say anything more, Wilfred appears. 'We're calling everybody to the church,' he tells his parishioners. 'With the pestilence so close, we must decide what's to be done.'

Hob and I watch them go.

The village meeting, feeling the absence of its lord who fled north long ago, is guided to a decision by the reeve and the parson.

'The parson told everybody as how you wouldn't sell the miracle-horseshoe,' Geoffrey's wife, Edith, tells us. 'Said that we were having the staff and one of the other shoes off your cart instead —' She looks at us then, and at her husband, making sure that this is the agreement we have reached, that we have not gone back on it in the meantime. 'So then he said, "That means there are two horseshoes left that the mare was wearing at the time of the miracle." He said he knew that people'd offered money for them, but it wasn't right that they should go to those who can afford to pay.'

I picture the outcry that broke out at those words. What was the point of working hard and saving if your family was not going to benefit from it? Everybody might as well be idle.

But the parson and the reeve, together, prevailed.

'Every family,' Edith tells us, 'is to pay so many pennies for each acre of their holding, so nobody owns the shoes and everybody does.'

'And who'll keep 'em?' her husband asks.

'They'll be in church where everybody can go.'

Now that he will have the same access as the rest of the village to the horseshoes, I half-expect Geoffrey Wheeler to go back on his agreement, but it seems he feels he is getting the better bargain.

'I shan't have to leave my own hearth to be within reach of my horseshoe,' he tells us. 'It'll be here, with me and my own, behind closed doors.'

His words bring unwelcome memories of the tight-fastened shutters and doors that came to Lysington with the pestilence. Never before had people stopped up their houses to keep their neighbours out; but, with the first death, brother began to shun sister and aunt to turn away niece for fear of what might come indoors with them.

Two days later, we leave Sibbertswell, richer by two tight new wheels and twenty-five shillings. Not to mention a set of worn horseshoes which we have hammered into place on each of the four corners of the cart to keep the Devil and his demons away.

'You won't miss your way,' a villager tells us when we ask how we will find the Medway crossing. 'By the time you need to leave the track for the road down into Snodland you can see the town away on your right. Barring accidents, you'll be there before dusk.'

'And there's a bridge there?' Hob asks.

'Not a bridge — a ford, a causeway. Hard, flat rocks that cross the river. With the little rain we've had this last fortnight or so, you should find it easily passable. But do it in daylight — you don't want to miss your way.'

Looking back at Sibbertswell as we climb the slope to the trackway, I shiver. The clouds that came in overnight have brought a chill breeze with them, yesterday's shirt-and-hose weather is gone and Hob and I are back in our tunics again.

But it is not only the chill air that is raising gooseflesh; I am worried about what we will find on the London road. These last weeks, going from village to village and seeing in every one a green, unturned churchyard, I have become accustomed to the mixture of dread and hope felt by people whom the pestilence has yet to touch. Arriving with the promise of the saint's blessing and with the news that we have seen no death for weeks, it had begun to feel as if we were travelling through another England, one that had escaped judgement. But Dode's fate is a reminder of what we will find on the Rochester side of the river.

As the afternoon wears on, clouds gather until they cover the sky from horizon to horizon. Evening will come early.

'There'll be no crossing the river before tomorrow,' I tell Hob.

He makes no reply but I see the set of his jaw. He does not want to be held up.

Daylight is already dwindling to dusk when we see the thatch of Snodland's houses below us, and, beyond their huddle and scatter, the river. The mare puts her muzzle up into the gusting breeze. She can smell rain.

As I turn her head down the road that will take us to the crossing, I see magpies land twenty yards or so away. They stare at us and I urge the mare on to be past them. But Hob stops me. 'Wait.'

I think he must have seen the birds too, that he means to chase them off, but he turns to the cart instead. As he unties the canvas, I count the magpies. I cannot help myself.

Six. Six for hell. What will we find in Snodland? Something that wishes us ill.

Hob pulls out the pilgrim-staff that was given to us at Tredgham and hands it to me. Its thumb-hold has been cut off the top and the end newly notched. When did he do that?

He retrieves the miracle horseshoe from the press and motions for me to give him the staff back. I watch as he fits horseshoe to notch, tapping the bottom of the staff smartly on the ground so the shoe beds more securely in. Once, twice, three times he strikes it, then he tweaks at the shoe to see whether it is secure. Three more taps on the ground. Six taps. Six magpies. Whatever he has planned, it can bring us no good.

Before I can ask him what he is doing, Hob leans the staff against the cart, lays hold of one of the worn horseshoes we nailed on at Sibbertswell, then twists and pulls it free.

He holds it up to me. 'Shall we leave it here or take it with us?' Clearly taking the look on my face for amazement at his strength, he explains. 'Left it loose, didn't I?'

'What are you doing?'

'Miracle still stands, doesn't it? This —' he lifts the staff off the ground — 'is still the shoe she threw on the ford?'

'Yes, but what about that one — why have you taken it off?'

'What horse wears five shoes?'

I do not ask him what he means for I find I do not want to know. When he has tied the canvas down once more, he grasps the staff as if it is a symbol of office and he a man of importance. 'Right, on we go.'

The news is good; the pestilence has not reached Snodland. At an open alehouse door we ask about lodgings.

'There's a bed for you here if you're not looking for luxury,' the alewife tells us. 'And we've stabling for your mare.' An alehouse trying to be an inn, then. Maybe this close to Salster pilgrims are happy to find any kind of bed. The poorer-off, anyway.

'What about the cart?' I ask.

'For threepence, the boy here'll sit in the yard with it all night and raise a cry if anybody comes near.'

Hob looks the boy over; he is no more than eight or nine years old. 'How do we know he won't thieve from the cart himself?'

'Because he's my son and I say so.'

Unabashed, Hob grins. 'Good enough.'

She turns to the child. 'Better go and ask the butcher if we can have his dog for the night.' As he runs off, she turns her attention to us. 'The dog's a good 'un. My lad'll most likely fall asleep halfway through the night but I swear that dog sleeps with one eye at a time.'

'Will the boy be safe with it?' Hob sounds nervous. I remember his fear of the dogs that snarled and lunged at dead Agnes and her husband.

'My Watkyn's the only boy in Snodland that doesn't torment the poor beast. Dog loves him for it. He'll lie down and play dead for my Wat.'

'As long as he doesn't lie down and play dead if robbers come by, he can do what he likes.' Hob follows the woman inside while I unharness the mare and stand, watching her eat the hay and horsebread that comes with the price of stabling. I know I should follow Hob but I am loath to move. For all the places I have seen since leaving the forest, I have never yet paid money for my bed and board. I do not know what's expected. Do you just eat what is put in front of you, or can you ask for something else? Will a bed be provided or should I take in the pallet? Will there be a piss-pot where we sleep or will we have to stumble over anybody else who shares the room to get into the yard?

Troublesome as these questions are, there is a matter that weighs upon me more. The lintels of the inn — both front and back — are bare; no horseshoes to keep the Devil out and, once asleep, I will be at the mercy of the demon who makes me walk.

I am still standing there when Watkyn walks into the yard with a huge dog at his side. The brute stands as tall as the boy's chest and, catching sight of me, sets up a bark that would cause any robber to shit his braies. Watkyn puts a hand on its head. 'Quiet.'

The dog turns its muzzle to look at him and the boy nods.

'Does it have a name?' I ask.

Watkyn turns to me readily, used to strangers. 'The butcher just calls him "dog".'

'But you've got a name for him?'

Watkyn smiles and I see the gaps where his milk teeth have not yet been replaced. He is younger than I thought. 'I call him Growler.'

'Good name.'

He scratches the brute's head. 'Wish I was the butcher's apprentice. Then I could sleep with Growler in the shop.'

'You'll make more money selling beer and stabling horses. And you won't smell of blood all the time.'

'I don't care about smelling of blood. And I don't want to be like him.'

'Him?'

His eyes meet mine then slide away again. 'Scaff. Him my mother's married to.'

I lean against the cart's wheel and fold my arms. 'You don't like him?'

The boy shrugs. I see his point; who knows what I might repeat? 'What've you got in your cart?'

'Food. Clothes. Some tools.' I grin at him. 'And a saint.'

In a moment, he turns from wary would-be butcher to round-eyed child. 'You can't have a saint in a cart!'

'Who says?'

'Saints live in church.'

'What about processions?'

He looks at me as if he suspects me of trying to catch him out. 'No procession today, is there? Easter's past.'

'It is. But I still have a saint in my cart.' I untie the canvas and lift out the blanket-wrapped figure of the Maiden. 'Want to see her?'

He nods, curls bouncing over his brow.

I unwrap the saint and Watkyn comes a step closer. As he sees her reaching towards him, he stretches his hand out and the two hands — one wooden, one flesh — touch, fingertip to fingertip. The boy stares at the Maiden, his eyes almost as blue as hers.

'She's called Saint Cynryth,' I tell him.

He frowns, his eyes still on the saint.

'I'd never heard the name, either, when I was your age. She's from a long time ago.'

Now he looks at me.

'Shall I tell you her story?'

His eyes move towards the door to the alehouse.

'It's all right,' I tell him, 'you're getting paid to watch the cart. So make sure you watch carefully while I tell you the saint's story.'

He fetches a bucket for me to sit on while he perches on a chopping block. Though the stools in the cart would be more comfortable, I have no wish to belittle his hospitable act and I thank him sincerely for his kindness.

'Cynryth,' I begin, 'was the daughter of Halstan — a king of the south.'

I am almost at the end of my tale when a man appears in the yard.

'What d'you think you're doing sitting there like the King of England?'

I stand, ready to account for my presence in the yard, but the man's eyes do not move as I rise and I realise that he is staring past me at Watkyn. This must be Scaff.

'The boy's working for me. This is my cart — he's watching it for me.'

'Looks to me like he's sitting wasting your time and his.'

Unaccustomed to townsfolk, I am at a loss as to how to treat him. His speech is coarse, made worse by the language hereabouts which, in his mouth, has a leering quality which I did not notice in his wife's. If he was a village man, Scaff's clothes would suggest he was somebody of the middling sort, my equal: his boots are sound but not expensive, the shirt which hangs out over his huge belly — he has no tunic on — is of decent quality but old, as are his hose. His manner however, is churlish and since, tonight at least, my money will be keeping the roof over his head, I feel I have the right to speak as I like.

'If I want to pay him to waste his time, then that's my business, isn't it?'

His eyes narrow in his fleshy face. 'How much are you paying him?'

'What his mother asked.' I have learned some quickness from Hob.

'Which is?'

'What would you've asked?'

'Sixpence.'

'Then I'd have laughed in your face.'

The man makes to step around me to the boy but I stand in his way. 'I meant no harm. I was telling him the story of the saint whose shrine we're going to.'

'Pilgrimage? Haven't you heard of the pestilence where you come from? If it catches you it'll kill you. You and the rest of your half-witted family.'

I am close enough to punch him in his fat gut, to bring my knee up into his winded face and smash his nose, to kick him in the balls. And I want to. I want to sink my fists into his fat flesh and hurt him. For my mother, for little Eleanor, for Master William. Even for my father and Adam. They are all dead while this bullying fool stands before me, alive.

'It did catch me. It caught me and half my village. But they're all dead and I'm alive. Thanks to the saint.'

He may be a bully but Scaff is no fool. The news we bring of the pestilence in Dode would be enough to draw the crowds by itself but, since we have the saint and tales of her miracles too, he flings his doors wide and doubles his prices.

Soon, the benches are spilling men off their ends and Hob is into his third telling of the miracles at Tredgham. I would just as soon be out in the yard with Watkyn and the dog but, since we sat down to eat, there has been a steady press of men wanting to know our news.

Scaff, meanwhile, is drawing men to the table where he has a game of dice going. It seems he is determined to have as much of their money as he can separate them from before barring his doors to the pestilence.

'Come on,' he says, 'if we're all to die within a week — if, indeed, we may be dead tomorrow — let's have some sport while we can!'

Later, when there are no new ears wanting to hear from us, we sit and drink our ale, quiet for a few minutes. Hob points with his chin to the dicing table. 'Watch Scaff,' he murmurs. 'He's always ahead of the others. He makes sure to lose a little here and there, but he's always ahead.'

'So?'

'He's cheating.'

'How do you know?'

'Nobody wins that often unless they're palming loaded dice. Besides —' his eyes are on Scaff's companions — 'those others are so drunk they hardly know what they're doing themselves, let alone what he's doing.'

I am not interested in the gamblers. Let them look to their own pockets. I stand up. 'I'm going outside for a piss.'

A pile of horseshit and straw stands next to the stables so I piss in that. With only one, poorly-lit lantern over the back door, the yard is dark but I spot Watkyn lying on top of the cart, the canvas beneath him, two blankets over him.

I walk over and tug on one of the canvas-ties. Straight away the boy sits bolt upright. 'Who's there? Growler!'

The dog, who has been ignoring me, ambles over. By now, the boy has recognised me. 'D'you like my idea of sleeping up here? It means nobody can come and pick me up and put me in a sack.'

I look at him, sitting on the flat top of the press. I could lift him up with one hand. And put him in a sack if I wanted to. But the dog would be a different matter. He knows me, saw me talking to the child earlier on. I suspect he would be less forgiving of anybody else who came near.

'It's a good idea. But you'll get wet if it rains.' And there is rain coming. I can feel it in the air. 'Why don't you lie underneath the canvas? There's a wool-stuffed pallet under there.'

He jumps up, full of enthusiasm for this comfortable idea, but then sags back down again. 'I might not hear them coming, then.'

I see he does not want to be thought a baby, inadequate to the task he has been set.

'Ah,' I say, 'but just think — if anybody tries to lift the canvas to steal my goods, they'll get the shock of their life when they see you!'

He jumps up again. 'They might think I'm a ghost!'

He scrambles down to untie the canvas at the back and looks over his shoulder at me. 'You won't tie the canvas down again will you? Not while I'm inside?'

'No.' I reach down to scratch the head of Growler, who has moved to the boy's side. 'Your friend here'd probably rip my throat out if I tried.'

Back inside, Hob is standing near the dicing table, in conversation with two men. One hand keeps the horseshoe staff protectively against his collarbone.

'Why *should* I sell it to you?' I hear him ask. 'I've already turned down more money for it than you've seen in a month of Sundays.'

'How much did these others offer you? Whatever it was, we'll double it!'

'Don't flatter yourselves, friends, you aren't that rich!'

'How much was it then?'

There is a look of anger on Hob's face now and, if I did not know that he had designs on their money I would swear it was real. 'What's it to you?' he snaps. 'I've told you, the horseshoe's *our* relic — Martin's and mine — and I'm not selling it!'

'How are we supposed to protect ourselves then? Why're you telling us about your saint if you keep all her relics to yourself?'

'You can receive her blessing. Ask for her protection.'

It's my voice that has spoken.

'What, here?'

'She blessed people on the charcoal hearth at Tredgham — that's where the miracle of Beatrice's hand happened.'

The place suddenly falls quiet. Men glance sidelong at each other but say nothing.

I move towards the bench where I left the saint, wrapped and safe but, as I make to pass him, Hob puts a forestalling hand on my arm.

'The cart'll be safe, don't worry.'

'I'm not going to —'

'Watkyn and the dog are there,' he continues as if I have not spoken, 'the other horseshoes'll be safe.'

'What other horseshoes?'

Hob turns to the man who asked the question. 'A horse wears four shoes, my friend. This —' all eyes turn to the staff as he raises it — 'is only the one she threw.'

I follow Hob out into the yard just as a thunderous barking is set up.

Hob backs off so hastily he almost falls on his arse.

'Down Growler!' I call. 'Good dog.'

The canvas is thrown back and Watkyn's head appears. I wave at him. 'It's all right, Watkyn. It's me.' Before the boy can say anything, I face Hob. 'You're not selling those horseshoes, Hob.'

'Oh, Martin, don't be such a girl! We can get some others tomorrow and nail them on — we're staying inside tonight —'

'I'm not talking about the demon.'

Hob ducks his head. 'What then?'

I keep my voice low so that Watkyn will not hear.

'You can't sell them as relics — they're not the ones the mare was wearing.'

He stares at me. 'So? They've been on the cart that's carrying her.'

'For a day!'

He shrugs as the sound of small feet landing on the ground is followed by an anxious question from Watkyn. 'You're not going already are you? It's not dawn yet.'

Hob holds his hand out to me. 'Your knife.'

'What for?'

'I'm not using mine to prise the shoes off.'

'Martin?' Watkyn looks up at me.

'No, we're not going yet.'

'Shall I get back under the canvas then?'

I lift the canvas for him and watch him lie down on the pallet. When I drop the canvas and turn around, Hob is still holding his hand out.

'Knife?'

I slap it into his hand and leave him to do what he wants.

When I rejoin the drinkers, a man is on his knees in front of the saint, while two more stand behind him. Only now do I see what a risk I took in leaving her here. As I move to her side, Hob comes back in.

'Look, boys!' Scaff calls above the hubbub. 'We've got relics in our midst! Let's see 'em then.'

Hob looks as if he'll deny the request and Scaff laughs nastily. 'Or do we have to pay to look?'

'A cat may look at a king,' Hob says. 'Come and look all you like.'

Slowly, as if weighed down by his own flesh, Scaff rises from his place and comes towards us. His face is flushed and beaded with sweat from the heat of the fire and the ale he's consumed.

He takes the horseshoes from Hob, one at a time, and examines each of them. 'They don't *look* very miraculous.'

'I'm not saying they *are*. All I'm saying is that the mare was wearing four shoes when we went into the ford, and only three when we came out.' He lifts the staff off the ground. 'This is just the one that the saint caused to be thrown so that we'd make our way to the smith at Tredgham.'

'How much?' one of the men asks. And then half the drinkers are speaking at once.

'I'll play you at dice for them.'

'Three shillings —'

'How do we know they'll work against the pestilence?'

Hob chooses to answer this last one above all the others. 'You don't. But I can tell you that *not* having them will give you no protection whatsoever!'

'Three shillings.' It's the same voice as before.

Hob turns to him. 'I turned down ten yesterday. Why would I sell for three today?'

'Because nobody's offering ten.'

Chuckles and grins are stifled as Hob shrugs. 'It's not me that wants to sell — it's you that wants to buy.'

A strange sort of haggling follows, as Hob's stubborn insistence that he is not minded to sell drives the would-be buyers to offer larger and larger sums. Only when the offer stands at twelve shillings a shoe does he finally shake three hands and send their owners off to bring him his money.

'Can't you wait till tomorrow?' one grumbles. 'My wife'll have me by the balls for waking the household up.'

'If you can't master your wife, I can't help you.' Hob grins. 'But I want my money now. Martin and I'll be up and gone early — I'm not waiting for you to get your sore heads over here — I could be here half the day, especially if your wife's yet to give you back leave of your own balls.'

With the last of them gone in search of their savings, Scaff bolts the door and leans his weight back against it. Then, to my astonishment, he begins to clap his hands, slowly, mockingly, head nodding and greasy chins wobbling as he gazes at Hob.

'By God it does me good to see a craftsman at his work,' he says. 'You could sell bones to a butcher, lad!'

Hob raises one eyebrow. 'I've sold them nothing they weren't pissing themselves to buy.'

'And that's the trick, isn't it? Make 'em wild for what you've got. Make 'em think it's worth their last farthing and their youngest child's life.'

Hob folds his arms. 'You don't think protection against the pestilence is worth twelve shillings?'

Scaff moves away from the door towards his ale. 'If it was a *proven* protection, that'd be a different thing. That twelve shillings'd be the best money those fools ever spent. But if you're telling me those shoes are proof against the pestilence, then you're a liar.'

Hob does not move. Not a muscle-twitch shows the slightest concern at what Scaff has said. 'You heard every word I spoke,' he says. 'You know full well I never said a word about anything being proven.'

The landlord takes a pull at his ale mug and wipes his mouth with the back of his hand. 'No,' he concedes, 'they talked themselves into that.' His eyes remain on Hob. 'But what they didn't talk themselves into was thinking that the shoes they're buying were the ones the mare was wearing when she threw that one.' The hand not wrapped around his beer mug points a finger.

Hob is not to be stared down. 'I never said they were.'

'No. I listened to you not saying it. You said that the mare was wearing four shoes when she went into the ford, and only three when she came out. Then you shook that bloody staff of yours and said that was the one that *just happened* to be thrown.' A half-smile takes his face over; it makes him look even fatter. A drip of sweat falls from his lowest chin to his shirt.

'I got a good look at those three horseshoes and I know they're from a different set than that one.' He nods towards Hob's staff.

The hairs on the nape of my neck rise and I look over my shoulder, convinced that somebody is sneaking up behind me.

When Hob says nothing, Scaff begins again. 'Want to know how I know? Easy. The tool that punched the nail holes wasn't the same. These ones are squarer — the holes in that one're longer and narrower.'

Hob's gaze has not wavered. My mouth is dry.

'My father was a blacksmith,' Scaff goes on, 'so I know.'

'So why aren't you a blacksmith?' Hob wants to know. 'Why are you serving thin ale and cheating your friends out of their money at dice?'

'I don't cheat, lad.'

'Of course you don't. You're just more canny than them about what you bet on —'

There is a sudden shaking of the shutters, as if somebody has thrown a handful of pebbles; the wind has finally brought the rain and is driving it on, over the houses and streets of Snodland to the river. I shiver and am glad that Watkyn is beneath the canvas.

Scaff leans his elbows on the table. 'I can't help it if the men who come here to play dice are fools.'

Hob moves towards the table where Scaff is sitting. 'So, what do you want?'

Before he can answer, his wife comes in and stands over him. 'All the pot-guzzlers gone home then?' Her face is flushed and her arms bare from hot work in the kitchen. She is the opposite in build of her husband, small and slight.

'Shut up and leave us, woman. There's men's business to do here.'

She remains uncowed. 'You mean dice?' Her hands go to her hips. 'Isn't it enough that those dice have lost you one business already? Do you think I'm going to let you ruin me as well?'

Without rising from his seat he turns with surprising speed and catches her across the face with the back of his hand. 'I said shut up and go.'

Quick as a flash, she leans past him and snatches up his ale-mug. Before he can see what she intends, he is being hit about the head, the hollowness of the mug ringing where the wood of it strikes his skull.

'Don't you tell me what to do, Scaff, or I shall make you regret the day you married me. I shall cut off your balls while you're snoring and put them in the pottage. I shall tie you like a hog and roll you to the fire and leave you there to render your fat down!'

I stand, watching her belabour him until he gets to his feet and grabs the hand that is wielding the mug. 'Shut up woman!' He rips the mug from her grasp and flings her to the floor. Her head cracks a bench as she falls and she lets out a shriek.

Before I can move to help her, there comes a hammering on the door.

'Scaff! Unbolt the door, damn you — it's pissing down out here!'

Scaff, ignoring his wife who is rocking backwards and forwards, one hand to her head, rises and crosses the room to the door. He throws it open and grabs the man standing in the rain, pulling him in bodily.

The returner shakes himself like a dog and holds up a money-bag to Hob. 'Twelve shillings to the very farthing.'

Behind me, Hob speaks as I cross to Scaff's wife. 'Count it out on to the table so I can see it's all there.'

'Do it yourself!'

Hob's tone does not change. 'I want you to do it. It's your money. You account for it.'

I ignore the man's grumbling and bend down. 'Mistress — can you stand up?'

She struggles to her feet. 'Oh, I shall have him one day,' she growls. 'I shall cut his lights out and feed them to the butcher's dog, I swear I shall.'

Despite this threat, I can see that she is unsteady, so I put an arm around her to guide her back to the door through which she entered.

'Get your hands off her before I break your neck!'

Scaff has turned his attention from the money-counting to me and his wife.

'She can't stand,' I tell him, still heading for the door.

'Then let her bloody crawl!' he rises to his feet and kicks the bench away behind him. 'I mean it,' he roars, 'let her go!'

I stop. I can feel the woman at my side gathering her strength. A hand pats my chest. 'Let me go, son. I can manage.'

I step away and watch as she makes her way to the door which leads to the brewery and, beyond that, the kitchen. When she is gone, unwilling to remain in the same room as Scaff, I make for the door to the yard.

'Where d'you think you're bloody going?'

'To see that my horse is well stabled,' I speak at the door rather than turn to face him, '*if* that's all the same to you?'

Scaff says no more and I open the door.

As it turns out, I cannot see the mare for the stables are fastened with a lock and chain so I make my way to the kitchen and rattle the door to be let in. I see an eye put to the finger-hole and drawn back again before the door is opened by a half-grown boy.

Shaking the rain from my tunic, I look for Scaff's wife and see her sitting on a bench in the corner furthest from the door. She seems uninterested in my sudden arrival so I turn to the boy who let me in. 'I wanted to see my mare was all right but the stable's locked up. Does he always do that?'

The boy nods but it is Mistress Scaff who answers. 'Got fined for letting a felon escape by night last year. What he did wasn't our fault but Scaff's not about to let that happen again.'

That explains the expensive lock and chain. Scaff is counting on it to keep him from having to pay out any more fines.

I want to ask about the felony but the smell of meat is making me hungry again. 'Is there any of that stew left?'

Her head back in her hands, his mistress tells the boy to give me a bowlful. 'And some bread, Halkin,' she says, 'if there's any left.'

As I eat, Halkin goes about his pot-scouring and fire-damping and sets the flour and provings to stand for tomorrow's bread. His mistress, meanwhile, mutters threats against her husband. The boy takes no notice of her grumbling so I assume this is something he is accustomed to. Still, my being in the kitchen will only make more trouble for Mistress Scaff if her husband finds me there. My stew finished, I stand.

'I'll go back in through the other door,' I say. She nods but does not look up. I tell Halkin we will need some embers for our basket in the morning, incline my head in thanks to him for the stew and leave.

I am about to pull the back door open when Hob emerges from it and grabs me by the shoulder. 'No. Don't go back in yet. I need to talk to you.'

He pulls me over to the stable, where the thatch overhangs the door, partly sheltering it from the rain.

'So?' I ask.

Hob grinds his teeth. 'Bastard watched each man pay me and go away with a horseshoe,' he says, 'and when the last one's gone, he says —' At this, he breaks off to hit the stable door with the heel of his palm.

'Says what?'

He glares at me. 'That unless I give him the staff, he'll tell them that their relics are fake. And then he'll go to the constable.'

'So?' I say again.

'So I told him I'll give it him in the morning.'

I stare at the pale oval of his face in the dark. 'And will you?'

'Not a chance! We're leaving. Now.'

I shake my head. 'Haven't you seen this?' I lift the chain that fastens the door and drop it, clinking against the sturdy planks.

'Shit!' He sucks in a deep breath. 'I could go on alone — meet you somewhere on the other side of the river.'

'And you'd take the money, I suppose?'

'Well, yes! That'd be the point. If you keep it he'll just have it off you, won't he? In fact, I should probably take our other money as well, so that when he searches the cart there's nothing for him to find.' I feel his eyes on me but cannot see his expression in the dark. 'Where shall we meet?'

I blink. Surely he's not serious? 'Nowhere. I'm not having you go off with every penny we've got.'

'Don't you trust me?'

I take a breath. 'What if I go and you stay to play the innocent with Scaff?'

I see his head move in the dark. 'No. That won't work. You know the mare won't go anywhere for me.'

'Then we both stay.'

'So you *don't* trust me.'

'It doesn't matter whether I trust you or not — anything could happen once we're separated. You might get robbed.

You might fall sick with the pestilence. You might get lost! It's better if we stay together. Simpler.'

I wait for him to argue, to try and persuade me, but he says nothing.

'Is he going to let us keep the money you got for the horseshoes?'

Hob grinds his teeth again. 'Says he wants half.'

'Could be worse. He could have taken all of it.'

'Yes, and I could just break his bloody neck!'

He kicks the door-jamb.

'We're still left with eighteen shillings,' I say.

'Eighteen shillings?'

'Yes. Three lots of twelve makes thirty-six shillings, don't they? If Scaff's taking half, that's eighteen shillings for him and eighteen for us.'

'Right.'

And, in his uncertain saying of that one word, I know why Hob stalked off in the churchyard at Sibbertswell, why he told the first man to come in with the purse tonight to count the money out for him. He cannot count high enough to reckon such large sums.

Hob's stepfather truly must have been a landless pauper, nobody who farms his own acres lacks the ability to reckon. No wonder he has not tried to leave me and make his fortune in any of the towns along the way; he needs me to make sure of our money.

I wake to find myself standing in the darkness with an urgent need to piss. I turn my head this way and that, looking into the grave-deep blackness for the smallest spark of light.

I should not have lain down. I told myself that I could just rest, that I need not sleep, but the demon must have lulled me.

Here, where there is no protection, he has taken control of me again.

Again, the need to piss presses on my bladder, up into my standing cock. I look about me, trying to pierce the dark, to find the thin seams of light that run around shutters. If I can find the window, I can place myself in the room.

As soon as Scaff left us alone, Hob tried those shutters only to find them barred from the outside.

'There's no getting away from it, Hob,' I told him, 'he's having that staff.'

Even now, if he is true to his word, Scaff is guarding the door.

'Don't think you can sneak out in the night,' he told us as he lifted two thin, straw-filled pallets from a pile in the corner of the room. 'I shall be lying on the other side of this door with a knife in my hand, waiting for you.'

Mean though the lodgings are, I'm loath to piss inside. Not without a piss-pot.

Which way is the door?

I crouch down, reach my hands out in front of me, push my fingertips cautiously along the dampness of the floor. Nothing. A quarter turn. Reach out. Still nothing. And again. Nothing. On the final turn, I find what I am looking for. The edge of a pallet. But am I at its side or its end?

Taking care to touch only with my fingertips, I trace the surface. A short seam. The end, then. Is Hob lying on this pallet or is it the one the demon raised me from? I cannot reach out in case I wake Hob. I cock an ear. No sound of breathing.

I call to mind the way the room is laid out. A door halfway along one long wall. A window out on to the yard in the shorter wall to the right. The wall on to the street is blind; Scaff does not want people climbing in and out of his lodgings.

We laid our pallets against the wall with their short ends facing the door, six feet or so between them. I cannot hear Hob's breathing; this must be mine.

The need to piss is becoming almost too great to bear. I head for the door, blind as a mole in its tunnel. At first I can feel only the rough plaster of the wall but, finally, my fingertips find timber planks. Inch by careful inch — I must not hit the latch and make it rattle — I find the bar. With infinite care, lest the wood squeak, I lift it out of its socket.

Will Scaff be there? Is he there now, as he threatened?

I let the door swing towards me, holding it all the while.

The room where we sat eating and drinking is as dark as the one behind me. Carefully, I put my hands out, my heart vying with my bladder for which will burst first. Staring into the thick blackness in front of my eyes, I crouch down, feel inch by inch before me.

Ale-soaked, rotting rushes. I move forward, feeling blindly. Nothing. No sleeping Scaff on the threshold.

With the prospect of escape and release urging me forwards, I begin to make my way towards the back door.

Inching forward, I hold my hands low, looking for wooden edges lest I run into a table or bench, my ears on stalks for sounds of Scaff. If he was a yard away, he would hear my heart for it is knocking my ribs like knuckles.

With every cat-soft footfall, I become more convinced that Scaff is there, that I can hear his breathing, that — at any moment — his ham of a fist will fall on my shoulder and pull me back.

The air stirs — a draft sneaking in from outside, or Scaff coming towards me?

I begin to move more quickly. The door cannot be many feet away.

There is a thud, loud in the darkness. A pain that makes me cry out. I have walked into a bench. I reach down and grasp my shin, trying to rub the pain away.

Now he will know I am here, for certain. Now he will come for me.

The pain throbs along my shinbone as I listen to the dark air. I know there is somebody there, can feel a presence.

Hobbling, crouching with my hands in front of me like a child shooing chicks, I stumble in the direction of the door. As I reach it, my desperation is such that I cannot stop myself flinging the bar up and yanking at the latch, all attempts at silence overcome by the fear of what is behind me. The rain has stopped but the wind is swirling around the yard. Before I have gone more than a few paces, the dog, Growler, is at my side, nosing me. I put a hand out to him and stumble in the direction of the midden. I stand and empty my bursting bladder with my head turned back over my shoulder lest I have been followed out into the yard. But I can hear nothing save the thumping of my heart and the sound of my piss streaming into horseshit and straw.

Was Scaff there, sitting at a table, waiting for me or Hob to run for it? Is he standing in the doorway now?

The fear of finding my way back through the benches and tables to the lodging-room, the fear of being caught by Scaff, almost lures me into staying here, in the yard, till daybreak. I could crawl under the canvas with Watkyn —

No. I must not sleep. I must not put myself at the demon's mercy again. I *must not* sleep until we can get away from here, find a village and another set of horseshoes and nail them on to the cart. It is plain that I cannot keep myself awake through one night, let alone however many there may be until we reach Salster. I must arm myself against the demon. The nearer we get to Saint Cynryth's shrine in the woods, the greater the danger. For neither the demon nor his master will be content to see me put the Maiden in her rightful place. My fear — my greatest fear — is that the devil will use me to destroy the saint, that his demon will grip my knife with my own fingers and cut off her reaching hand; that he will take her up in my arms and set her on the coals of the fire.

Perhaps I should stay in the yard. The cold and the need to walk about will keep me awake.

No. I cannot stay out here while Scaff and the saint are inside. I must keep her safe.

The thought brings an icy shiver of memory. *I must keep her safe.* I catch at the memory, pulling it back, like the last, vivid moments of a dream, before it can fade away. Dark. Night. In our hut on the charcoal hearth. On my knees by the bed my father died in. *Must keep her safe.*

Not so much with my mind's eye as my mind's touch, I recall the heavy solidity of the saint, wrapped and safe in my arms. I feel the awkwardness of pushing her, further, further under the roundwood-framed bed. A blanket-parcel, invisible, tucked against the dry turf of the wall. Out of sight. Safe.

The shiver comes again. But this time there is no memory, just an icy certainty. There was no miracle of re-appearance. Saint Cynryth did not come to our wellside shrine from her own in Salster. Did not hide herself in the press to appear to me when most I needed her.

It was me. All me.

Sleeping, I hid her. I took her image from the well and hid her before Richard came. And again, all unknowing, my limbs moved without my waking will, I put her in the press. Safe.

But was it the saint herself who had guided me, deep in slumber, or the demon who lives within me?

Must keep her safe.

She is leaning, now, unprotected, against the wall by my pallet. Scaff could slip in, take her.

Quickly, I move back to the doorway. The clouded moonlight spills no further than a pace or two into the ale-room and, despite standing to one side and craning my neck around the door-jamb, I can see neither figure nor movement.

Closing the door with as little noise as I am able, I make my way — crouched and reaching out to avoid a second injury — back to the right-hand wall and, after a few heartbeats' searching, the lodging room door. It is open, just as I left it. I stand on the threshold, listening for sounds within. Nothing. No feet shuffling, no breath drawn ready to attack me as I go through.

Careful not to rattle it, I pull the door gently to me, thankful for silent leather hinges. When it is firmly closed again, I let the latch settle quietly into its socket and turn around.

I cock my head into the darkness and strain my ears. If Hob is still sleeping soundly, I will hear his slack-mouthed breathing.

I hold my breath and listen for his. Nothing. Only the squeak of bats as they flit in and out beneath the eaves outside the shutters.

Is he awake, breathing lightly, silently, listening for me?

Hob must not know that the demon has made me walk again. After last night's setback, he needs the saint, more than ever, to make money for him. If he knew that my night-walking might put all his plans at risk I fear what he might do.

Slowly, I move forward and feel for the edge of a pallet. I tug softly. It moves easily towards me, empty. Mine, then.

I lower myself down only to leap up again with a cry that I cannot contain.

I have been stabbed!

I roll off the pallet, hitting my head on the floor and crying out again.

Frantically I reach around my ribs to where I felt the point go in. No blood. My fingers search but I fail to find even a slit in the cloth.

Cautiously, stretching my ears backwards for any sign that I have woken Hob, I reach out in front of me. My fingertips brush against smooth coolness and I stroke my hand along the length of the familiar form, from cloak to head-covering. It was the saint's reaching hand that stuck so painfully into my ribs.

I sit back on my haunches.

What is the saint doing on my bed?

Even as I ask that question, another pushes itself into my mind. Why has Hob not woken up? Despite my crying out and tumbling from bed and clawing at my tunic for a wound, he has not stirred.

I still my breathing and listen. The silence is as deep as the darkness.

On my knees, I shuffle to the edge of Hob's pallet and lean down, close to where his head will be. Breath stilled, I listen.

Nothing.

Hob is not there. There is a gap in the dark air where he should be lying. I put a hand to the pallet. Nothing but straw-stuffed sackcloth.

I pull up the pallet and feel about on the floor beneath. The staff is still there, where Hob put it.

Why has Hob left it here? And where has he gone?

CHAPTER 28

I wake to Mistress Scaff's voice.

'Wake up! Wake up! You've got to go! There's pestilence in the house!'

Hob is already halfway across the room. 'Who's sick?'

'Not sick. Dead. Scaff is dead.'

I stand, muzz-headed. How did I fall asleep? The last thing I recall is lying on my pallet, the saint in my arms, my heart thudding as I wondered where Hob was, whether he would be back.

'Dead — where?' Hob asks.

Mistress Scaff points. Hob moves and I follow him into the main room.

Scaff is slumped over a table.

I rub my eyes, clear the thickness of deep sleep from my throat. 'Did he have a fever last night?' He was sweaty, I remember, but I thought that was the fire and the ale.

'Don't know. He never came to bed.'

And she was glad of it, no doubt, and never came to see what was keeping him.

'He needs to be buried as soon as may be,' I tell her. 'Before anybody else can catch it from him.'

'What'll the parson say? He hasn't had the rites.'

Of course. Scaff is the first. They have no experience of the pestilence here. Until now, Scaff's wife has had no reason to understand that a single priest cannot be in six places at once, that many will die without the comfort of the last eucharist. That lesson is learned swift and hard when the pestilence strikes.

'Dispensation's been made,' I tell her, feeling how strange the word seems on my tongue now, where, three months ago, the language of the church was as everyday as the language of the charcoal hearth. 'The Pope's decreed that God will know his own, whether or not they're shriven, whether or not they're buried in consecrated ground.'

She gapes at me, almost more shocked by this news than by her husband's death.

'But they'll bury him in the churchyard?'

Scaff is lucky — as the first, his body will find no shortage of space in the parish yard. 'Yes,' I say, 'but you must fetch the priest now.'

The door closes behind her and Hob turns to me. 'Think this is how it was at Dode? Well in the evening, dead by morning?'

'Must be. But why didn't he go to bed, lie down? He must've felt himself sickening.' I cross the room which was full of such obstacles last night, and stand over Scaff. He stinks of piss. His bladder emptied itself as he died.

'What're you doing?' Hob wants to know.

'Just looking.'

'What for?'

I do not know. For, if this is the same sickness that took my father and the villagers at Dode, there will be nothing to see.

The priest stands in the doorway, fingering the beads at his belt. 'Should we call for the coroner? Is it certain it's the pestilence?' His fretful eyes do not leave Scaff's slumped body. 'Have you looked for the marks of the pestilence on him — the black patches, the lumps?'

'He'll not have the pustules,' Hob says. 'He was well last night — no fever, no pains. There's been no time for them to come up and corrupt.'

The parson narrows his eyes at him. 'You're quite the expert.' His beads continue to run through his fingers, as if he thinks that will count as prayer and keep the pestilence at bay.

'Knowledge hard earned,' Hob says. 'Half my village died of it.'

The priest takes a cautious step over the threshold, holding his clean robes clear of the matted rushes. 'You're the one everybody's talking about, then — the one who was healed by this saint?'

'No.' Hob jerks his head in my direction. 'That's Martin.'

The cleric's eyes turn to me. 'You'll have no fear of infection then?'

I know what lies behind his words. 'I'll lay him out if that's what you want.'

'No!' the widow protests. 'That's not right!'

The parson takes her arm with a soft white hand. 'Would you rather put yourself at risk? Leave Watkyn orphaned?'

She gives no answer; but neither does she pull away.

'Perhaps it would be as well to do it together?' I suggest. 'If the parson and I lift him on to the table, then you, mistress, can go for water to wash him with and a sheet for shrouding.' Neither of them moves. 'We should get him into the ground as quick as may be.'

'It's true then — the stench of the dead infects the living?'

I shake my head. 'I don't know. Nobody does. But I do know that those who nurse the sick, who lay them out, most often take the sickness themselves.'

He bites at his lip and lets go of the widow's arm. 'Do as he says, Mistress.'

Getting Scaff on to the table is one thing — his corpse is fat and heavy but not unmanageable — but getting his clothes off is another. Though his limbs are not setting into stiffness yet, it's hard to lift his arms and peel his shirt off. Hob stands in the corner, refusing to come any closer and the sweating parson and I are forced to do the job ourselves. Beneath his shirt, Scaff's flesh is covered in such a thickness of hair that it is difficult, in some places, to see the dead white flesh beneath. He looks more bear than man and I feel a brief pity for him — it must have been nigh on impossible to keep this pelt louse-free.

'Is this what the flesh of the plague-dead usually looks like?' the parson wants to know.

I think of my mother, stripped and washed; Scaff's body shows none of the purplish-black marks that were scattered over her chest and upper arms, nor is he thin as she became during the three days she sweated and vomited and coughed blood. Scaff's body does not look diseased — it looks like the corpse of a well-fed, idle man who has just upped and died.

'No,' I say. 'But Dode's folk died more quickly than anybody I've heard of and some of them had no plague marks. Perhaps it has become more deadly now.'

'And yet, also more merciful,' the parson replies, 'so that people do not suffer long in agony.'

Hob sneers. 'I thought the agony was supposed to mean you'd suffer less time in Purgatory. That's what our priest said. Useless article that he was.'

The parson is suddenly halfway across the room. 'You'll not speak ill of God's anointed!'

I watch Hob over Scaff's body. He moves not a muscle to defend himself, just stares at the priest who stops short.

'I'll speak ill of whoever I please,' he says, evenly. 'And I'll tell you this as well — if God anointed our parson for a virtuous man then he's a very poor judge of character.'

The priest stands stranded in the middle of the room, at a loss in the face of Hob's contempt.

'If you come and lift his hips,' I suggest, 'we can get his hose and braies off.'

What does it say about Hob that the priest turns away from him and back to a plague-dead corpse with something like relief?

Mistress Scaff arrives with a ewer and basin while we are removing her husband's hose. Beneath, his braies are wet and sticking to him and neither the priest nor I are eager to touch them.

'Oh, let me!' Exasperated, his widow elbows us out of the way and yanks the undergarments down his legs. I stare at his overhanging belly — could he even see his cock any more or did he have to piss by feel?

The widow has started her washing with his face and head. Abruptly, she looks up at me. 'Did he get in a fight after I left you last night?'

'No, mistress.' Not wanting to shame her in front of the parson, I forbear to point out that she belaboured him about the head herself.

'Well, his lips are bruised and broken inside,' she says. 'Look.'

She pulls Scaff's fleshy lower lip down and I can see that the skin inside has been broken, as if he has bitten at it.

'Perhaps he bit at them in his agony,' the priest suggests, coming cautiously closer. He puts out a hand and then pulls it back. 'What are those bruises —' he points — 'on the forehead, there?'

'There was a disagreement between us,' she tells him, flatly. 'And a give and take of blows.'

I see the parson giving her a sharp look but my eye is drawn back to Scaff's lips. Bruised and cut on the inside, as if something mashed them against his teeth. But on the outside, they are bluish. Just like Thomas Hassell's lips.

Where was Hob when I went out into the yard last night? Was his the presence that I felt with me in the darkness of the aleroom? Was he making sure that Scaff would not take the staff and his eighteen shillings from him?

I look at the dead man's nose but it is not bent, just bulbous and dark red, as it was last night.

The parson looks from me to Hob. 'Did you see this exchange of blows?'

'The whole room saw it,' the widow tells him. 'You know we was never shy of our disagreements, Master John.'

'They weren't hard enough blows to make him senseless,' I say in her defence.

The priest nods and seems satisfied.

'I can manage now,' Mistress Scaff wrings out her cloth. 'If you just wait until I have him washed, then we can lay him on his shroud and wrap him.'

Later, with the dead man ready and waiting for the funeral cart, I fetch the basket and collect embers from the kitchen fire. Out in the yard, I see Hob coming through the back door.

'Scaff'll be buried by sunset — they're digging the grave now.' He comes to stand at my side as I flip up the canvas at the back of the cart. 'We should go.'

'Before other people start dying?' Despite all the fine words he employs in the service of selling braids, Hob clearly does not trust the Maiden to protect him.

'More to the point, before people notice that nobody else *is* dying.'

I start knotting the ties. 'What d'you mean?'

'You're not going to tell *me* Scaff died of the pestilence?'

I glance up. 'What else would he have died of?'

He shrugs. 'Your demon took you walking again last night.'

His words, or rather the meaning I detect in them, causes something to slice into my belly, cold and sharp. 'Only in the lodging-room. When I went out, I was awake — I needed to piss.'

He leans against the cart, shakes his head unhappily. 'No, Martin. You went out twice. The first time you scrabbled around with the saint — I could hear you with her — then you went out into the aleroom. You were out for a few minutes then you came in and shut the door behind you.' He rubs his chin with the side of his hand, his eyes on me. 'A few minutes later you went out again — quietly.'

'What about you?' Filled, as I am, with a cold, sweating panic, I have not forgotten Hob's empty bed. 'You were out last night as well.' My fingers shake on the rope loop. 'When I came back in, you weren't there.'

He moves his head slowly from side to side. 'No, Martin. You're mistaken. I didn't get up all night.'

'What? After all that ale?'

He pushes himself away from the cart. 'You know me. Bladder like a bull.' He stops, then seems to come to a decision. 'Right, while you finish here and sort the mare out, I'm going to see where we can buy more silk.' He moves towards the alleyway and the street.

'You're not wanting to make more braids?' I call after him. 'Haven't we got enough money now?'

He does not look back, just raises a hand. 'I won't be long.'

I stand and watch him stride away down the alley.

Deliberately, I put thoughts of the demon out of my mind. Whatever happened to Scaff, Hob is right; we should go. For, if people believe that we have brought the pestilence here, there could be trouble.

'He was telling lies.'

Watkyn's voice makes me jump. I look down at him. 'Who was?'

'Your friend.'

'Hob? What lies?'

'He *did* come out in the night — he lifted the canvas, woke me up.' The dog, Growler, is no longer at the boy's side. He must just be back from returning him to Harold the butcher. 'Growler doesn't like him.'

'Doesn't like Hob?'

'No. He bares his teeth whenever he comes near. And his hackles go up.'

'Hob's afraid of dogs.'

'That's stupid! I'm not afraid!'

Pride straightens Watkyn's back, sticks his chin out. He — a little lad — is more valiant than a grown man. I grin at him and he grins back.

'He only wanted his cloak, anyway. Told me not to tell anyone he'd been up. Said he didn't want Scaff to know he was lying there shivering.'

His cloak. I think of the bloodstain I found on the inside, where it had been wadded up.

In my mind I see Hob folding the cloak, inside out. I see him standing behind Scaff and holding the cloak over his face. Did he contribute another dint to Scaff's head to subdue him?

'Did he say anything else?' I ask Watkyn.

'He complained that Scaff was mean to only give you one blanket each.' The boy looks at me from under his fringe of curls. 'Called Scaff my father.'

I make a wry face; I can imagine what short shrift he gave Hob for that mistake.

'Told him he was no father of mine, that he could go to the devil for all I cared.' He stops. I assume he is ashamed of his words, given that Scaff may well be gone to the devil, but his next words give the lie to that. 'He said that I mightn't have to worry about Scaff much longer. I asked him what he meant and he said there was a plague coming and Scaff'd most likely get what he deserved.' Watkyn watches my face. 'Is that true? Does the plague kill bad people and let the good ones live?'

I cannot lie to him, he will know the truth of it soon enough.

'No. The good die with the bad. And sometimes the bad live on and prosper.'

I am about to ask him whether he would like the saint's blessing before we go when his mother comes rushing in to the yard. Her eyes fasten not on Watkyn but on me. 'Another man's sick. Tom Gerasse.' She looks at me as if I should know the name.

'Who's he?'

'One of the men you sold a horseshoe relic to last night.'

Not me, I want to tell her, *that was Hob. I had nothing to do with that.*

She holds me with her eyes. 'His wife wants those six shillings back. Says you're welcome to your relic — it's no use to her.'

Six shillings? Tom Gerasse didn't have the courage to tell his wife how much of their money he had spent.

'Mistress.'

I turn at the sound of Hob's voice. The alewife's anger has so taken me aback that I did not see him come back into the yard. He looks her in the eye, the model of an honest man. 'I'm very sorry for this lady but I didn't ask her husband to buy our horseshoes. It was him and his friends who persuaded me to sell. They all but went down on bended knee and begged me to sell them.'

'That's as may be, but knowing she's married to a fool doesn't help Marjorie Gerasse. By sunset, by all accounts, she'll have no husband and precious little money. Having that six shillings back would make a world of difference to her and her little ones.'

'Hob —' I begin. But he is already answering her.

'That's not how the world of buying and selling works — you know it isn't. If you sell a man a jug of ale and he takes it home and drinks it and then comes back and tells you he wants his money back because his children have no bread, do you give it him?' He gives her no chance to answer. 'No, of course you don't.' He shrugs. 'If Tom Gerasse didn't have six shillings to spare then he shouldn't have pressed it on me. I'm not responsible for his fecklessness.'

'It wasn't fecklessness — he bought your relic thinking it would keep his family safe! But it hasn't.'

'Keeping folk safe from the pestilence is the saint's business, not mine.'

She takes a step towards us. Mindful of her readiness to resort to blows, I step back but Hob holds his ground.

'You sold him a relic which has no power.'

'Mistress Scaff. You weren't there, so you don't know what was said. But ask Martin, he's an honest man — honest to a fault, I could say. Ask him whether I ever said that those horseshoes had the power to prevent plague.'

Her eyes cut sideways to me but she keeps her mouth closed. She will not give Hob the satisfaction of obedience.

'Did I, Martin?' he insists. 'Did I say those horseshoes had power?'

We have already been through what Hob did and did not say with Scaff.

'No.' I clamp my lips shut.

The alewife's eyes are cold and I stand, discomfited, beneath her stare. 'My boy likes you. Says you're a good man. Kind. Until today, I've always thought him a good judge of character.'

I cannot look at her. Not while a purse with twenty-five shillings in it lies in my press. Twenty-five shillings collected from the parishioners of Sibbertswell for the purchase of the horseshoes worn by our mare; horseshoes that truly might have been thrown in a miracle, except that only one could be.

There is a moment when I might loose the canvas, throw open the press and snatch up the purse. *Take it to Tom Gerasse's wife*, I might to say to her in that moment. *Give it to her.*

But the moment passes.

She looks from me to Hob and back.

'You're no better than Scaff. Neither of you. You say just what he'd've said. Business is business.'

Her scorn shrivels me, like salt on a slug.

'But your saint is a woman. She'd have compassion on a woman who'll be a widow before the day's out.' She spits, deliberately, on the ground at our feet. 'You shame her.'

As we walk down Snodland's main street, towards the causeway that will take us across the river, I see every countenance we meet turned in anger and enmity against us. Word has obviously gone around about Tom Gerasse and the uselessness of the relic he acquired at such vast expense.

Nobody touches us — forethought for their health overcomes their detestation — but I feel their stares reaching into my flesh. I try fixing my eyes on the ground ahead of me but then the cat-calls begin.

'Good riddance!'

'Yes — take your false relics and go!'

'Damn you for plague carriers!'

'Run! Run!'

This last is from a gang of apprentices who begin picking up stones from the street and throwing them in our direction. Fortunately, all the large stones are well bedded in and there are no stones big enough to break bones but pebbles can hurt when they are flung by a strong arm and we cover our heads with our arms in self-defence.

As one apprentice runs up behind us, apparently thinking to shy his stone at Hob's head from a lesser distance, Hob turns and charges at him, bringing him to the ground. He pins him and begins punching his face, in a fury. I can see the rest of the gang rushing towards us and I pull Hob off.

'Leave him. Or they'll beat us to death.'

Hob stands up, his knuckles bloody. 'Come on then!' he roars at the advancing crowd. 'If you think we've brought the plague, come and take me!'

They skid to a halt at these words, those behind almost flooring those in front. Their dander is up so high that I believe they had forgotten the pestilence.

'Yes! Not so brave now, are you?' Before they can stoop to pick up more stones, Hob charges at them, cloak flying, knife in his hand. He looks deranged, plague-mad, and I do not wonder that the apprentices turn tail and flee.

As I watch them run back up the street, each disappearing up a different alley, I see a small figure coming towards us. I wait, knowing full well that his mother has sent him. He wastes no time.

'Will Gerasse is my friend,' he begins before a woman passing by tries to pull him away by his tunic.

'Come away from him, Watkyn.'

The boy shakes her off and fixes his gaze on me once more. 'He was going to be apprenticed to the cordwainer. If his mother can apprentice him, that's one less mouth to feed. She needs the six shillings for his fee.'

Hob hears his words as he stalks back to the cart. 'In a week's time she'll have no mouths to feed, including her own,' he says, as if he is speaking to a grown man not a boy barely old enough to be put out to work. 'If the father's died of the plague, they'll all be dead of it soon.'

Watkyn ignores Hob and directs his words to me. 'Not everyone dies. You didn't.'

'No.'

'Will needs his apprentice fee.'

I nod and motion him to take the mare's reins. Before I can begin untying the canvas, Hob has me by the arm.

'What're you doing? Their money's no good to them when they're dead!'

'The boy's right. They may live. Not everybody in a household catches the pestilence. You didn't.'

His grip on my arm tightens and I see his jaw clench. 'If you give him that money, the other two'll be out in a flash wanting theirs back as well.'

In that moment I make a decision. And, even as I make it, I know it is one I may quickly come to regret.

'I'm not giving them your money, Hob — you can keep that thirty-six shillings, I don't want a penny of it. I'll keep the rest as my share.' This makes us almost even — the twenty-five shillings from Sibbertswell and the ten shillings or so in the press. 'We can use the money you hid —' I drop my eyes to the hem of his cloak — 'for anything we need before we reach Salster.'

Is there a slight lessening of grimness on Hob's face? He gives a curt nod.

'If you must. But make it quick. We need to be over the river and gone.'

I open the press and hold the knotted shirt out to the boy. 'I'm giving this to *you*, Watkyn. Wait a week and if the widow Gerasse is still alive, give it to her. If she's dead and the children alive, give it to whoever takes them in. If, in a week, they're all dead, it's yours. You can use it to apprentice yourself to the butcher.'

CHAPTER 29

Noon has come and gone and, with it, most of the clouds. Ahead of us we can see the dog-leg in the river where the bridge takes the road to London. Rochester's castle squats above it on a bluff, standing guard.

Hob takes hold of the mare's bridle and pulls her to a stop. She rolls her eyes and bares her teeth at him but plants her feet just the same.

'We're better off not going inside the walls,' he tells me. 'We can skirt through the suburbs and pick up the road to Salster that way.'

'D'you think those outside the walls'll be spared if the pestilence is inside?'

Hob picks at his beard. 'It's not about the pestilence.'

'What then?'

He drops his hand, his eyes still fixed on the buildings that rise above the walls. 'It might just be wiser to keep away from people.'

'Why?'

He glances at me. 'I don't know what happened to Scaff —' he puts up a hand to forestall my protest. 'I know you say you had nothing to do with it — and I don't care, bastard had it coming, either way. But —' he stops till I look him in the eye — 'I think the demon that makes you walk at night is getting stronger.'

Though my stomach clenches, I say nothing, waiting for some kind of explanation.

'At the beginning — when I first saw you walking, on the hearth at Tredgham — I could tell the demon what to do. I'd say, "Go back to bed, Martin, everything's as it should be," and you'd go. Or I'd say, "Put the Maiden back where you found her," and you'd do it.' He stops, his eyes watchful, seeing how I take this. When I give a nod, he continues. 'Well, last night, I heard you get up. Not surprising — you weren't taking much care to be quiet. I called out to you, softly, so as not to wake anybody else — still thought Scaff might've been lying outside the door, bastard that he was. But you didn't answer me. So I knew it was the demon making you walk. I thought I'd better get you back to bed before you stumbled into Scaff.' He stops again.

'So?'

'I said, "Martin — go back to bed," but you took no notice. Then you opened the door and I said, louder, "Don't go out there!" but you just went, and let the door swing open behind you. Even that didn't wake you.'

'Did you follow me?'

He pulls at his beard again. 'No.'

'Why not — weren't you worried about what the demon might make me do?'

'I was a damn sight more worried about what it'd do to me if I tried to stop it! The staff and the Maiden were in the room with me —' He stops.

'And you thought you'd just let the demon do as it liked?' He shrugs. Is he just a little ashamed of himself? If what he says is true, then perhaps it is wise to keep out of the city. But I am in need of protection, myself.

'If we go into the city, we could find a smith, get some more horseshoes for the cart. Keep the demon away.'

He eyes me. Is there a new wariness in his gaze? 'We could. But with you giving in to Scaff's shrew of a widow and dishing out silver like there was no tomorrow, I wouldn't trust those other men not to come after us for their money back. If they start asking after us and they find out we were here, looking for more worn horseshoes...' He puts his forearms on the mare's back. 'We can find a smith elsewhere. We've got food and water enough for today and tomorrow. Let's just find the Salster road and get on it.'

I do not want to concede. I want four horseshoes nailed to the corners of the cart again before night is anywhere near falling. But Hob's argument holds weight — all along the Downs we have been preceded by goodwill and received with open arms; if the people of Salster are to welcome their saint back amongst them, it would be better not to come trailing a reputation for trickery.

'All right. The next lane we come to, we'll take.'

We start off again towards the walls. The road is empty but for us and, to right and left, this place has the feeling of having been deserted, given up for dead. Roofs sprout crows instead of smoke, and starlings hop amongst garden plantings with nobody to shoo them away. I see a cat darting around the side of a house and wonder whether mice and rats move out when the people who have unwillingly fed them are gone.

We come to a church overlooking the river, its small yard spread around two sides. My eyes are drawn to an untidy little row of people and I pull the mare up.

They are standing on the south side of the church, beneath the small, old-fashioned windows of the nave. At their feet, a long trench has been opened up.

I narrow my eyes and see a figure in what must be clerical robes raise his hand to make the sign of the cross. He speaks, bows and turns away. Two of those left at the side of the trench begin shovelling earth into it.

As we watch, the remaining folk leave the edge of the pit and make their way towards the lych-gate on the roadside. A young man has his arm around his wife's shoulders. The other two — an older man and woman — walk as if they know nothing of each other or the couple ahead of them. All keep a distance from each other, though God alone knows what difference that will make. They have lived with the pestilence or they would not be here.

'How many?' Hob asks, inclining his forehead to the common grave.

'Twenty-four,' the older man answers. Then, seeing Hob look over his shoulder at the trench, adds, 'They're laid four deep.'

'At least,' I say, 'you have a priest to see them into the ground.'

'Till he dies, like the rest.'

Then, with no more said at parting than he offered or was given in greeting, he leaves us.

We are scarcely fifty yards further on when we hear a cry behind us. 'Good day to you!'

We turn and see the parson from the burial catching us up. 'It's so rare to see travellers these days. Where've you come from?'

'Today, just over the river from Snodland,' I tell him, 'but we've been travelling for weeks. From the King's Dene Forest in Gloucestershire.'

He smiles. 'Where all the iron comes from.'

I smile back; his pleasure at knowing something about my home is a fragment of courtesy from another time.

'What brings you to Rochester? We're not able to offer much in the way of hospitality any more. If you'd come a year ago, you'd scarcely have been able to drive your mare along this road, but now...' He looks about him. 'So many people used to come and go. Pilgrims to Saint William's shrine.'

I draw him back from his melancholy reflections. 'We're on a pilgrimage ourselves. To Salster and Saint Cynryth's shrine.'

He frowns. 'Salster's shrine is to Saint Dernstan.'

'Yes — at the priory church. But Saint Cynryth's shrine is in the woods to the north of the city.'

'Burdynge Forest? I've never heard of a shrine there. Nor of your saint.'

'Saint Cynryth,' I repeat. 'I don't suppose she is well-known amongst pilgrims. I believe she's mostly worshipped there by local people.'

She shakes his head, eyes anxious. 'I know Salster. But I've never heard anybody speak of a saint called Cynryth whose shrine is in Burdynge Forest.'

We part company with the priest beneath the wall of a vineyard. He assures us that if we follow the road that skirts it, we will find ourselves on the Salster road just below the east gate.

'I hope you find what you're searching for,' he says in parting. 'At least in Salster you'll find a city that's survived the pestilence. Pray God we'll be able to say that, here, soon.'

As we follow the line of the wall, I peer over at the sprouting vines. It seems to me that God cannot have abandoned us utterly if the plants in the ground continue to grow and our beasts still thrive. He has not decreed a laying waste to all life as He did in the flood.

Hob turns to me. 'Don't suppose there'll be enough monks left to harvest those vines, come autumn. I reckon the abbeys are in for a thin time of it.'

'You think so?'

'It's not hard to see.' He raises an eyebrow at my questioning look. 'Who becomes a monk? Men with no land or prospects. Same with lay brothers — they're only there to put food in their bellies. Now there's going to be so much land wanting tenants that anybody who wants it can have it.'

'Not everybody'll be able to afford to buy their way in.'

'They won't have to! Lords aren't stupid. Or, if they are, their bailiffs're paid not to be. Entry fees are all well and good when there's more men after land than there's land to go round. But the bailiffs are going to have to think again, now. Now, they're going to be begging men to take on land just to get it worked and keep their lords provisioned.'

He looks around at my silence.

'I'm telling you, Martin — the lords aren't going to have it all their own way anymore. Not by any manner of means.'

When we find the road to Salster, it is level and well-kept. Despite the lack of recent traffic, little grass has grown up and the stones are well-bedded.

After walking for so long in the shadow of a scarp that was fit for little but pasturage, it feels strange to be walking through good, cultivated acres. Not that half of it has been tilled or sown as it should be by now. Land that ought to be scattered with crow-scaring boys lies fallow, still raggedly stubbled from last autumn's harvest and sprouting early weeds, their new leaves bright amongst the shorn dun stalks. Sheep are still folded here and pretty miserable they look, too — head-down and scrawny. We see more than one dead lamb, crows and magpies perched on the small carcasses, cawing self-satisfied defiance.

'The ewes have no milk,' Hob says. 'Not surprising — look what they're pastured on.'

The feasting birds' calls turn my stomach and I am glad when they are so far behind us that we can neither see nor hear them.

It has been weeks since we slept in the open. All along the Downs, in village after village, we have been lodged in barns and byres in return for the saint's blessings; and, in each, I slept under the cart, doubly safe beneath a roof and the horseshoes' protection. Still, we fall easily enough into our old routine. I put water in the cooking pot so the beans can soak before the fire is lit and Hob takes the cord to go for firewood.

Before he sets off, he stands, watching me work. 'Are you still fretting about what that priest said? About not knowing the saint?'

I shrug. He has been observing me more closely than I knew.

'Don't worry, Martin! We've made her known across half of England, why shouldn't we do the same in Salster?'

As I watch him go, I turn his words over. He is right, we have made Saint Cynryth known across half the country; is it my task to do the same again in Salster?

I call to mind my Tredgham vision: the saint in shining white, standing in front of a well-side shrine, an army of folk kneeling before her.

All this time, I have thought it was a vision given to sustain me, to show me that it was right to share the saint's story amongst those we met on our pilgrimage. But perhaps there is more. Perhaps the vision also shows me what I must do when we reach the woods outside Salster.

Dusk is draining away to night. On one side of the fire, I sit stirring pottage; on the other, Hob is braiding silk. Each drawn away from the other by our own thoughts, we have not exchanged a word since Hob returned with the firewood. So, when he speaks, his voice startles me and my hand jerks the spoon against the side of the pot.

'You know, Martin, if nobody in the city knows our saint — if it turns out that the priest was right and there is no shrine — what we must do is establish her in one of the Salster churches.' He works away, not looking up. 'We'll have no shortage of takers. When the city's priests hear we've got a saint who's done miracles before our own eyes they'll beat a path to our door.'

Has this been his plan all along? To use the saint as his best route to riches? He wants no master, is not prepared to learn a trade, how else is he going to make his fortune?

I keep my eyes on the contents of the pot as I speak. 'If there's no shrine in the woods, then I'll establish one.' I swallow, keep my gaze on the bubbling pottage. 'But not in the city. Not in a church.' I keep my voice level. 'Her shrine must be in the woods.'

Over the rim of the pot, I see Hob's hands stop their braiding. I feel him looking at me.

'In the woods?'

'Yes.' The spoon trembles in my fingers as I stir.

'That's all very well, Martin. But it's not just a wood we're talking about, is it? Not just an arse-end manor's worth of standards and coppice. The parson called it a forest. I can't see foresters welcoming a shrine. Not unless they get a cut of the profits.'

'Then I'll put it on the edge. It'll be easier for people to find, there.'

'It'd be a damn sight easier still if it was in the middle of Salster!'

The pottage is getting too thick. I add water with an unsteady hand.

'How would people find your shrine?' he wants to know. 'Have you thought of that?'

No. I have not thought of such practicalities. I am still clinging to the belief that we will find Saint Cynryth's shrine in the woods, just as it was in the peddler's story. Hob is the one who schemes and plans. But I do not say that.

'If there is no shrine remaining, my task will be to build it.'

'Your task.'

I do not respond. I have learned the danger of that edge to his voice.

'When did building this woodland shrine become *your task*?'

I look up at him. The braid has fallen from his thigh as he leaned towards me. I shrug.

'No, come on, tell me! You said you wanted to give her to the keeper of the shrine, in return for prayers and masses for your father. You never said you were going to *build* a shrine if there wasn't one there already. When did you decide that?'

I can feel him staring at me but I cannot meet his eye. 'I had a vision.'

'When? Today?'

'No. While we were in Tredgham. But I didn't understand what it meant until today.'

A bat flits overhead, flipping away from us, disturbed by the smoke rising from the fire.

'How d'you know this vision was from the saint? How d'you know the demon didn't put it in your head?'

It is on the tip of my tongue to say that the demon only comes to me at night but, as soon as I feel the words forming, I know them to be untrue. The demon has whispered in my ear, night and day, since I woke up in the hut. Since Saint Cynryth healed me.

'Think about it,' Hob says. 'Where would the Devil rather see a miracle-working saint — in the city, where pilgrims flock to see Dernstan's bones, or at the edge of the forest, out of sight, out of mind?'

His knife is in the ground at his feet — stuck there after cutting the silks to the right length. As he waits for me to answer, he tugs it free and wipes the blade clean, drawing it slowly between his thumb and forefinger.

'It wasn't the demon. The vision was from the saint.'

'How do you know?'

'How did you know it was the saint telling you about the horseshoe? That it was a miracle when the mare cast it on the ford?'

He shrugs. 'She was there, in my dream.'

'And she was there in my vision!'

'In a shrine in the woods?'

'Yes. And an army of people was kneeling before her.'

He nods slowly, his eyes on me. 'A powerful vision.'

'Yes.'

'Powerful enough to deceive you, Martin.'

The first watch is mine. Terrified of falling asleep while Hob is not awake to watch for the demon, I am braiding silk as Hob has taught me but the movement of my fingers cannot still my racing thoughts.

I try to put Hob's words about the demon out of my mind. He is wrong. I would know if my thoughts were being twisted. The Maiden will protect me. She has always protected me.

Hob lies on the pallet on the other side of the fire. He looks only partly like the waking Hob. Without the darting watchfulness of those blue eyes, without his tall swagger and his charming smile, he is just another runaway.

Is everybody so reduced in sleep? Is that why the demon finds it so easy to take my limbs and turn them to his own ends?

I rise and tread softly over to the cart. Taking the Maiden from her place, I bring her back to the fireside and stand her before me.

Despite my best efforts, she is suffering. Her cloak and gown, once snow-bright, are dulled now and the white of her head-covering is worn thin from the touch of endless palms. I meet her outstretched hand with my own and find it greasy from heads and fingers. Still, I am loath to rub the dirt away lest flesh-coloured pigment come with it.

Though the memory that returned to me at Scaff's lodging has shown me the truth of her disappearance from the shrine, still it seems to me that her coming to my father while I lay dying was a sign. She did not keep him from swift and sudden plague-death but I know, in my heart, that she stands between him and the gates of Hell, guarding his soul until I can pray at her shrine, have masses said to speed him from Purgatory.

I lay my hands on her shoulders and look into her speedwell eyes. I would pray to her, ask her for another, clearer, truer vision of what my task in Salster is to be once my father's soul is safe. But I dare not close my eyes lest I fall asleep.

It occurs to me not to wake Hob but to stay on watch all night. Then, tomorrow, I could sleep in the bed of the cart. But no. We will go nowhere if I sleep during the day, for the mare will not walk for Hob.

I will see out my watch and sleep while Hob does his. I must trust him to keep me safe.

'Martin! Wake up! *Wake up!*'

My father is calling me. It must be my watch.

There is a heavy blow to my chest, another to my head. '*Martin!*' But they are blows dealt in a dream and I feel no pain.

I feel a great thud as if I have been thrown to the ground and the pain suddenly bursts into life. I cry out.

'Martin — are you awake now?'

'Yes.' The pain in my shoulder tears away the last shreds of sleep.

'Is it you, Martin? Really you?'

Hob's face is pale in the darkness above me. There is a grinding at my right shoulder. His knee.

'It's me.' My head is thick, my tongue too big for my mouth. 'Get off me!'

'Not until I know he's gone.'

I struggle for breath. 'Who?'

'The demon!'

I blink.

'Say the *Paternoster*,' Hob demands.

'What?'

'Say it. Then I'll know it's you speaking not the demon.'

'Can't breathe.'

He lifts himself an inch off my chest. The pain in my shoulder doubles.

I cry out and he sits on my chest once more. 'Say it.'

'*Pater noster qui es in caelis*,' I gasp.

'Good enough.'

He gets off me and stands up. I pant; my chest hurts. I close my eyes, then open them again. The left one does not open properly. I put my hand to my face. Painful. Swollen.

I try to sit up. My head whirls and I let myself fall back again. 'What happened?'

'You came at me with your knife. I'd fallen asleep and the first thing I knew was you knocking me backwards off the stool.'

He lowers himself into a crouch next to me. I turn and see him putting a hand to his left ear. When he brings it away, it's dark in the dying firelight. Blood.

He wipes it on the grass.

I force myself to sit up. My face throbs and I put my hand to the swelling.

'I think my knee did that,' Hob says. 'As we went over together. That's when you did this.' He motions towards his bloodied ear. 'I had to take your knife off you before you did worse.'

I feel sick. I lean forward and rest my forehead on my knees.

I hear Hob move away. Good. No more talking for a minute.

There is the scrape of the lid coming off the butt. Then something being dipped in.

When Hob comes back he puts a wet cloth to my eye. I pull back but he holds the cloth out to me. 'Keep it on your eye. It won't swell so much.'

I put the dripping cloth carefully to my eye. It stings like a slap and cold water runs down my face and neck.

Hob stands up and takes a log of soft, dead wood to the fire. Breaking it into three over his knee, he prods the embers into life and lays the pieces on, one by one. It is so dry and rotten that it catches almost immediately and, in the new, yellow flames, I see something pale lying on the ground a few yards away.

'What's that?'

Hob follows my gaze and rises from his fireside crouch.

'It's a sheet,' he says as I go after him. He squats down next to it and picks something up. He looks at it in the firelight but says nothing.

'What have you got there?'

He does not look at me but keeps his eyes on whatever is in his fingers, turning it this way and that.

'Hob?'

'It's a needle. A threaded needle.'

He puts it back on the sheet; the thread is dark against the linen.

'What's it doing there?'

Hob looks at me, then down at the spread-out sheet, its folds forming shadowy lines in the light from the fire.

'I think,' he says, carefully, 'that, after you'd killed me, you were going to sew me into my shroud.'

My stomach heaves and I turn aside. But the bitterness of bile and curdled pottage cannot blot out his words.

CHAPTER 30

We are on our way before sunrise. The mare snorts complaints into the grey silence and her shoes strike visible sparks from the stones in the road but there are no other sights or sounds in the still mistiness of not-quite-day.

Neither of us speaks. It is possible that we might reach Salster today and I am determined that no tardiness shall delay us.

Can I walk all day? I have to. I cannot spend another night at the mercy of the demon. But I am far from certain that I have the strength to walk from before sunrise to after sunset. I feel as I did when I woke, alive and healed, in our forest hut — shaky in my limbs and befuddled in my mind.

Only one thing is certain. I must get the saint to her place in the woods.

According to the Rochester priest, Burdynge Forest is to the north-west of Salster. 'You'll skirt around the edge of it as you follow the road into the city,' he told us.

But I am determined not to skirt the edge of the forest but to go right into it. If the Maiden's shrine is there, she will guide me to it. And, if it has crumbled to dust since the time of the Seven Kingdoms, she will show me where to re-establish it. Now, more than ever on my pilgrimage, I must put all my faith in her. If the demon sees so much as a chink of doubt, he will slip in and misdirect me.

'Lady protect me, guide me.' I say the words behind my teeth, not wanting Hob to hear me.

He does not trust me anymore.

As the light of day broadens out the land about us becomes clear. Lowish hills to our left, more imposing slopes away to our right. The chanciness of yesterday's weather is gone and today is blue and spring-green. Perfect travelling weather. The saint's hand is over me, she has heard my pleas.

Hob sees a church tower on the edge of a hamlet.

'I think we should find the parson there,' he says, nodding in the direction of the church 'ask him to drive this demon out of you.'

He stops but the mare and I press on. 'No. If we keep going we'll be there by nightfall.'

'What about the demon?'

'He'll leave me when I've brought the saint home.'

Hob stands, planted, but I keep walking, my eyes fixed on the road ahead. I have to keep looking forwards, for if I catch a glimpse of the canvas, its colour reminds me of the sheet on the ground. I see the needle and the thread that trailed from it, dark as his own blood, as Hob held it aloft. And I see another needle, the one that lay beneath my father's dead fingers.

No! He died of the plague. *Quickly and without marks, like the folk at Dode.*

But after last night, however much I repeat the words silently to myself, I only half-believe them.

I keep drifting into something like sleep as I walk. My legs take me along but I feel as if I am floating above the ground, as if my boots barely touch the hard stones of the road. My poor boots. Their soles are more hole than hide now; two days ago I cut the feet from a pair of old hose to patch them and protect me from the road.

Again and again, my head nods, my chin hits my chest, my legs wobble and then, somehow, I am upright again. How long did I sleep before Hob punched me awake? An hour? I slept less than half the night at Scaff's. My body craves sleep as a drowning man craves air.

And Hob sees it. 'Martin, we need to stop. You're dead on your feet.'

'Later. When we eat.'

That wary look is back on his face and he does not argue. Mastery has a sweet taste but I cannot waste time savouring it, I must use all my will to stay awake and keep moving forward.

Noon. A town lies ahead of us, straddling the road.

Hob wants to stop and buy food. 'If we're going to walk all the way to Salster today, I'm eating a pie or two now,' he says.

The thought of food makes water run into my mouth. I swallow and my empty belly growls; last night's supper ended up in the grass.

I glance across at Hob. He has his good ear turned towards me but I know the other is a bloody mess with a gash that has near torn it in half.

I try to feel the knife in my hand, slashing at Hob's neck, slicing his ear. But I cannot. I have never fought a knife-fight. I do not know how it would feel to throw myself at Hob, my mind possessed with the thought that I must kill him.

I rub at my knotted belly, feeling the hard, underfed leanness of my own body. Something hot to eat would do me good.

It is clear that a pilgrim-city is close at hand. This wayside town has more places where ale and food can be bought than its size could possibly justify. Not that all are open today; the shutters are closed beneath many signs and there are few people on the streets.

'Pestilence'll be the death of us one way or the other,' a baker says as he hands over two loaves of bread and some of his wife's cheese. 'Either it'll kill us quick, or lack of folk to sell to'll see us starve to death.'

Before the pestilence came, he tells us, the shops on either side of his bakery would sell dozens of pies in a day. 'And not just them — there's four others making pies in town and then there's the inns as well. Now, we couldn't make pies if we wanted to — no market, see? No animals going to the butcher. Not a pound of fresh meat to be had, not for love nor money.'

But everybody still needs bread and townsfolk hang back from the shopfront while we are there, waiting their turn to take their loaves and retreat to their houses.

One bold fellow asks whether we are on pilgrimage, tells us that Saint Dernstan's bones have not availed to keep the pestilence away from Salster's priory. 'You'd be as well going home now,' is his opinion, 'for if his relics won't keep the pestilence from those who tend his shrine night and day, what will they do for you?'

I say nothing but Hob protests that we have not come for Dernstan but for Salster's other saint.

He shakes his head. 'Salster's got but one shrine.'

'What about Saint Cynryth?'

The man shakes his head. 'Never heard of him.'

'Her,' Hob says.

'Never heard of her, then. Where's her relics s'posed to be?'

'In a shrine in Burdynge Forest.' Hob seems to have turned spokesman for the saint now and I keep silent, clutching our loaves and cheese.

He shakes his head. 'No shrines in Burdynge Forest.' He says it as if he has quartered every inch himself. 'Not since time out of mind.' He scratches his armpit. 'What Burdynge's got is more deer'n a man can shake a stick at. One of the king's favourite places to hunt, so they say. Stays at that palace the bishop's got.'

'Is the bishop in Salster with his people?' In truth, I do not want to prolong this conversation but something in me yearns for proof of a churchman's fidelity.

'Thomas Wardine? Dead. On his way back from seeing the pope.'

The bread is new and still warm in the middle. Hob and I sit at the side of the road and eat a loaf between us, straight off, with half a pound of crumbling white cheese. The mare, unhitched to forage for herself, browses happily, watched by a straggle of cudding cows and their barelegged herd.

'So Burdynge Forest is a favourite with the king,' Hob remarks. 'Not going to be too happy, is he, if you clutter it up with shrines?'

I glance across at him. Whatever he says, I have no choice but to follow the wishes of the saint. It is the only way to be sure that my father's soul — and my own — will be safe. The only way to rid myself of this demon.

I get up and brush bread crumbs from my tunic.

'Let's get on.'

As I approach the mare to hitch her up again, she moves away from me and I can see that she is favouring one of her back legs. I take her by the bridle and walk her forward. Yes, there it is — a definite heck in her stride. I call to Hob to hold her and I pick up her hoof. There, stuck between the shoe and the tender quick is a stone. I straddle the hoof and rest it between my knees before reaching for my knife to lever it out.

My knife isn't in its sheath. I drop my head, close my eyes. Where is it?

I see Hob, his ear bleeding.

I had to take your knife off you before you did worse.

Hob took my knife. He still has it.

I crane my neck around to see him. 'Can I have my knife?'

'As long as you won't come at me with it.' He grins but the barb catches. I watch as he reaches around for his own knife and pulls mine from the sheath where it's nestled behind his long blade. He hands it to me, resisting slightly as I take it. Then he grins and releases it into my grasp.

The stone removed, I return the knife to my own sheath. Something twinges, a memory. I try to force my tired mind to pay attention, to draw the memory up, but, try as I might, nothing comes.

The afternoon wears on and long, slow slopes begin to tire both us and the mare. On steepish downslopes, Hob and I put our backs to the front of the cart to brake it and, on the drawn-out, sweeping rises, he puts his shoulder to the back to help as the mare pants, head down, flanks dark with sweat.

'Martin, it's against all sense to try and get to Salster today — we'll never get there before curfew.'

I blink, feeling the stiffness in my eyelids, the ease with which they close. If we stop, I will have to spend another night under the thumb of the demon.

'Let's walk another mile or two,' I say. 'Then we can decide.'

The shadows from the setting sun are long and I am beginning to stumble in my stride. The second time I fall, Hob pulls me up and stands in front of me.

'Enough, we're stopping here.'

I raise my head and look along the road. 'Is that Burdynge Forest?'

Hob looks over his shoulder at the country spread out below us. 'Must be.' He turns to me. 'An easy morning's walk to Salster. We can stay here and still be in the city before noon tomorrow.'

I lean against the mare and try to think of something to say. But I am so tired the words will not come.

A mile or so back we passed a town on our left hand side. We seem to have walked for a long time since, but I can just see the roofs and towers of its monastery if I look back along the long, slow hill we have just climbed. Following a straight road is hard going, it seems you walk and walk for very little ground gained.

I turn the mare's head and she plods gratefully off the road and on to the sheep-cropped turf.

'How much firewood have we got?'

'Enough,' Hob says. 'We won't need to keep the fire in all night because there'll be no need for embers. Tomorrow, we'll sleep beneath a Salster roof!'

I do not tell him that tomorrow I will be in the forest. No matter. I can make the fire last, make sure that there are embers enough to take with me.

I wake to find Hob shaking my shoulder. 'Martin. Come and have something to eat.'

When did I fall asleep? I remember sitting down for a moment against the wheel of the cart while Hob unhitched the mare... It was still light then but dark has crowded in since.

I work some spittle into my dry mouth and swallow. 'I thought you didn't cook?'

'I do if there's no choice. And you were dead to the world.'

His words send a cold shiver over me. I rise on watery legs and follow him to the fire where both stools stand waiting for us. Hob has been busy.

'Feel better?'

I nod. Though I still feel as if I have wool for wits, the ache for sleep has dimmed. 'Weren't you worried?' I ask. 'About what would happen?'

He shakes his head. 'It was broad daylight when you went to sleep. And I've been keeping a close eye on you. Even with the demon in you, I reckon I could still knock you down. You only got the better of me last night because I was dozing.'

Is that true? Does the demon simply use my strength or does he have his own to add so that he would be able to overpower even the likes of Hob?

Or the likes of your father.

It is all I can do not to cry out. With fear pressing in on me like a fist around my heart, I look over at Hob but he seems to have noticed nothing. We are so close to Salster, all he can think about is the fulfilment of his dreams. Does he believe he has talked me out of my resolve to stay in the forest, establish the Maiden's shrine there?

We eat his pottage in silence; it is edible, if not appetising. How will I manage for food on my own in Burdynge Forest? I shall have to hope that I can buy food from people on the road; if I build the shrine, pilgrims *will* come, we have seen enough proof of that on the road where people have flocked to see the saint on a cart.

His supper finished, Hob stretches his legs out towards the fire and looks over at me.

'So. Tomorrow we'll be in Salster. What d'you think your father would say?'

My father. I see his nose pointing towards the roof of the hut. His bony shape on the bed beneath his blanket. His hand over the needle through the seam in his shroud. Last night I laid out a shroud ready for Hob—

'He would've wanted to come with you — wouldn't he — if he hadn't died?' Hob's voice breaks into my fears. 'After seeing you healed, I don't suppose anything would have stopped him coming on pilgrimage to the saint's shrine.' Hob raises an eyebrow. 'The demon would have been in trouble then — two of you to try and control.'

There is no doubt who would have been the stronger. No doubt at all. There would have been no walking in his sleep for my father. He would have spat in the demon's eye.

That's why you killed him!

'No!'

Hob's eyes are on me immediately. 'What? What's the matter?'

I shake my head. I am not going to tell him that the demon is whispering in my ear.

'Guilty conscience?'

'Don't start, Hob.'

He looks at me, silent for once. There is pity in his gaze, I can feel it, even with my eyes fixed on my supper. A sick prickling chills my skin as I think of myself rising from my bed in the hut and putting a hand over my father's mouth, gripping his nose with my fingers.

I swallow, unable to speak.

Hob shrugs. 'Whatever happened to your father, Martin, you certainly tried to kill me last night.'

'Not *me*, Hob!'

He waves away my objection. 'All right. You know why the demon wants me dead, don't you?'

'Why?'

'To stop me making you see sense about establishing the saint's shrine in the city. He knows that would bring pilgrims to her and he'd far rather you kept her in the forest. Out of sight, out of mind.' He likes that phrase. 'The demon knows people're lazy. They won't go out of their way, even to see a saint. Think how the villagers complained at Tredgham — wanted you to put the Maiden in the church, said you were making it difficult for them to come for a blessing —'

'They still came, though.'

'Yes. But they could see Tredgham woods from their own doors. They might have resented the walk but it wasn't so far. Your shrine could be miles from Salster.'

'If I build it at the edge of the forest, pilgrims will see it, coming and going.'

'Those coming from the north and the west will. But what about those coming from the south, the east — from France?'

'France?'

'Isn't that what you want for her? To be known and worshipped in all of Christendom? Isn't that what she showed you in your vision?'

'Yes, but —'

'Then you're putting her shrine in the wrong place!'

'If that's where the saint wants it, that's where it's right for it to be!'

'But Martin —' he leans towards me, his beard red-gold in the firelight — 'are you sure that you're *listening* to what the saint wants? How can you be sure it's the voice of the saint you're hearing? If actions speak louder than words, you're the demon's servant, not hers!'

I feel as Edgar must have done after Hob's first blow across his shoulders — agonised, winded, terrified of what would come next. How could he *say* that? Being possessed at night is one thing but to say that I am the demon's *servant* —

'The demon knows that taking the saint to the city will make her shrine popular,' Hob presses on. 'The last thing he and his master want is a shrine where thousands of pilgrims come, where miracles are done. So he tried to force you to kill me so that I couldn't make you see sense.' Hob sits back. 'I'm sorry, Martin, truly I am. I know you think that your vision of the saint was telling you her shrine must be in the forest, but —' He stops, shakes his head as if he has thought better of what he was going to say.

'What? But what?'

Hob pulls at his beard as he looks over the fire at me.

'Look, I know you think that the only thing that matters to me is making money but that's not true. I'm not saying it *doesn't* matter — it does, I admit it. You've never known poverty — you come from a family that had money and the means to make more. But I *have* known it, and I'll never willingly be poor again. The saint, God bless her, knows that.'

His eyes flick to the White Maiden and back to me. 'She chose me to be your companion in the full knowledge of who I am. She knows I have dreams. She knows those dreams need money and she hasn't begrudged me that because she knows I'll always protect her — and you.'

He stops, fixes his eyes on me. 'Whatever my faults, the Maiden chose *me*, Martin, as much as she chose you. She drew you to the wood where Edgar and I were staying. She showed me that I must protect you from Edgar. And then, in leading us to our meeting with Richard Longe, she showed me that I had to stay with you, that you'd be the means to my fortune as much as I would be the means to yours. And hers.'

I am lost in Hob's words. What is he saying — that the Maiden has chosen him to protect her, even from me?

I stare at him but he says no more. I look around at the cart, at the Maiden standing against the wheel. And I know what I have to do.

I stand up and walk over to the cart. My legs are unsteady but I feel a strange kind of elation, freed from fear. I sit down next to the Maiden, my back to the wheel, its hub between us.

Hob has not moved but his eyes have followed me.

'I'm not the demon's servant, Hob. What I do when I'm asleep he *forces* me to do. He takes my limbs and he inhabits them. They're his actions, not mine. My will has no part in it.'

He watches me but says nothing, waiting for me to explain.

'I want you to tie me up.'

My words jerk him into life. '*What?*'

'I don't want to do the demon's bidding, willing or unwilling. If you tie me up I can't do you — or the Maiden — any harm.'

He frowns, clearly unhappy with the idea. 'But what about you? You won't be safe.'

'If the demon wanted to do *me* harm he could've done it a long time ago.'

Hob puts his hands to his head, scrubs at his scalp with his fingertips. 'What if we're attacked in the night and I can't get to you in time?'

'We won't be.'

'But what if we *are?*'

I shrug. Why should we be attacked tonight, of all nights? 'Just tie me up, Hob.'

'All right,' he says, finally. 'If that's what you want.'

'It is.'

Unwilling to stand again, lest he think my resolve is wavering, I tell him where to find the rope. He brings it and gooseflesh rises down my backbone as I remember taking the same rope to bind the cross that I put on Edgar's grave.

He holds the skein up to me. 'Sure?'

'Yes. If you tie me to the wheel, I won't be able to move but I'll be able to sleep.' I shuffle myself into a comfortable position. 'There. If you loop it over both my shoulders and tie it behind my back you should be safe.'

He follows my directions and binds me to the wheel. He pulls until the rope is firm but not tight then ties it.

'Pass me your knife, I'm not using mine to cut rope, it'll blunt it.'

I struggle to get my hand behind my back to reach my knife but I manage it and pass it to Hob.

'What about your hands?'

'Tie them in front of me.'

'D'you think you could untie those knots with your teeth?' he asks when my hands are bound.

I try. 'Maybe.'

'Better tie your hands to your feet then.'

He ties my ankles together, loosely, then he takes the long end he has left and loops it between my wrists before tying it off. Now the knots are out of reach of my teeth.

He pulls my knife out of the earth where he stuck it and slides it into his own sheath behind his knife.

'Satisfied?'

I nod and he turns back to the stool.

'Sleep for a while,' he says. 'I'll wake you when it's your watch.'

Relieved of demon-dread, I do sleep for a while but I am woken by aches and soreness. The seemingly comfortable position Hob tied me in has now turned tormenter.

I can see how long I have been asleep by the state of the fire and the woodpile — most of the firewood is gone and the embers are turning ashy.

A small wind blows across my face and I look over at Hob. I am not surprised to see him asleep — often I have woken in the morning to find him drowsing and the fire almost dead. He has always refused to sit on my one-legged collyer's stool, told me I was welcome to have my arse tipped on to the ground for the crime of falling asleep if I liked, but he was damned if he was going to submit to it.

I glance at the fire again. The embers are fading. I should wake Hob and get him to put more wood on. I will need those embers later.

Will you?

I lean my head back against the cart's wheel, remembering all the things Hob said last night.

If actions speak louder than words, you're the demon's servant, not the saint's.

No! I strain against the ropes that bind me, willing the pain in my shoulders to drive out the terrible notion that everything I have done might have served the demon's ends rather than those of Saint Cynryth. Again and again, before my unwilling eyes, I see the sheet that I laid out last night as a shroud for Hob, see myself rolling his dead body on to it, gathering it over him and sewing it from toe to crown.

Would I have stripped him first, taken his good boots and his tunic and his golden cloak? Would I have left him in shirt and braies or stripped him naked?

My father's clothes had been folded small on the hut's stool, all but his braies. An act utterly unlike his usual habit.

Did I strip him, fold his clothes?

No. *Not me.* The demon.

If I had succeeded in killing Hob, the demon would have been guilty of the crime, not me. And, just as I have no memory of attacking him, I would have no memory of killing him. I would simply have woken up in the morning to find him dead in his shroud.

Would his face have been left uncovered, his nose pointing to the sky, his hand on his chest, fingers covering the needle I had left there?

Would his eyes have been bloodshot and staring, like Thomas Hassell's?

Would his lips have been cut and bitten on the inside, like Scaff's?

I groan but I cannot push these thoughts from inside my head. I want to get up, stride about, kneel before the saint and ask her blessing.

The saint. I turn my head to see her beside me.

'Lady, guide my thoughts. Help me!'

I close my eyes in prayer but hear nothing, see nothing, feel nothing. Nothing but discomfort. The bones of my arse are grinding into the ground and pains are shooting into my shoulder blades from my backbone. I badly need to stand and stretch.

But it is best not to think about relief. These bonds protect me.

Instead, I think of the decision that faces me once dawn comes. Should I go to Salster with Hob? Should I trust his vision over my own; his vision of the saint in a parish church, drawing pilgrims with fat purses?

I try to picture the shrine that might be made for her. Carved and painted, it would glitter here and there with a gold which has nothing to do with the sunlight in the forest; the Maiden would stand on a pedestal instead of the lip of a well, covered by a canopy of stone instead of trees.

Is that what she wants? I crick my neck to look at her in the dim light of the night sky. The only shrine she has ever known is a scrubbed-out rock niche behind our forest cistern. No carved stone, no gilding, no pedestal or canopy; just a crack such as a fairy might walk through into our world from his own. A crack my father cleaned and cleared to be worthy of a saint whose particular care are the springs and wells that rise in woods.

When I began this pilgrimage, it was for my father's sake. I promised myself that I would pray for his soul at Cynryth's shrine. And, if I was to discover that there was no shrine in the woods — and it seems that there is not — I was determined that I must go to Salster and offer prayers to Saint Dernstan. I would never have strayed from that intention but for my vision of Saint Cynryth at a well-side shrine, multitudes kneeling before her.

A vision that was slipped into your mind by the demon to mislead you.

I must not let the demon blind me to my father's need. I must go with Hob tomorrow. I must go to the priory church and fall on my knees before the shrine of Saint Dernstan and ask him to intercede for my father's soul. I can decide what to do with the Maiden later.

A sharp pain shoots up between my shoulder blades. I must wake Hob, get him to untie me. If he had left my knife stuck in the grass beside me after he finished tying me up, I might have been able to wriggle close enough to pull it out and free myself. But he put it in his belt-sheath.

The twinge that pulled at me when Hob returned my knife, yesterday, hooks at me again. This time, it snags a memory from the depths and holds it up to me.

My knife.

When Hob borrowed it in Scaff's yard to take the horseshoes from the cart, I did not wait for him to give it back to me but left him to his prising and went inside. He did not return it until earlier today, when I needed it to take the stone out of the mare's hoof.

At the time I thought he had simply kept it after I attacked him; but, now, I realised that I had been mistaken. Hob had never given my knife back to me.

I could not have tried to kill him last night *because I did not have my knife*.

Icy prickles raise every hair on my body.

You came at me with your knife. I hear Hob's voice, full of matter-of-fact courage. *You came at me with your knife*.

But I could not have done that. I did not have my knife. He did.

I did not attack Hob. And yet, his ear was ragged and bloody.

I try to think, but my heart is beating fit to burst my rib-cage. He must have cut his ear himself.

And the shroud? Did I lay that out, or did Hob do that too?

Hob might have been asleep but he was on watch — he claimed I had knocked him off the stool so he could only have been dozing. Surely it was impossible that I had got up, untied the canvas, thrown open the lid of the press, found the sheet and laid it out, all without rousing him?

My head is light, whirling with mingled relief, rage and terror. I lean back against the wheel. The demon has not made me its slave. I did not attack Hob. I did not lay out his shroud.

But if I did not, then Hob did.

I swallow a gulletful of bile, the pain in my shoulders forgotten in the painful beating of my heart.

How did he do it? Did he watch the demon raise me from the pallet then quickly dart past me to take the sheet out of the press? I see him lay it out, looking over his shoulder to make sure that I am still wandering, my limbs not my own, putting the needle and thread on the top. I see him pulling his ear out from his head with his left hand, slashing quickly at it with his right, before he can change his mind; I see him laying hold of me and drawing me backwards towards his upturned stool, beating at my chest and head and shouting fit to wake the dead.

Is that how it was? Or did he tire of waiting for the demon to make me walk and take things into his own hands, drag me sleeping from my bed, rain blows on me, yell till I woke?

Yes. That must be how it happened. Hob would not risk the demon leaving me alone. And, with no horseshoes on the cart, I was sleeping next to the fire where it was easy for him to lay hands on me.

I close my eyes, try to think. How long has he been planning this? Since I told him that my task was to build a shrine for the saint? Or even longer — ever since I told him about finding my father in his shroud?

All the doubts he has been slipping into my mind about how my father died — has each one been carefully planned? Has each suggestion, each fear, each assurance that he did not care what I had done, been preparing me to believe that I might try to kill him in my sleep too?

I did not kill my father. The knowledge makes me almost light-headed with relief. He died like the villagers at Dode, swift and sudden, without plague marks. But it was the Death that killed him, not me. That has been nothing but Hob's lie, all along.

And what about Scaff? Hob was callous — *I don't care, bastard had it coming either way* — but he tried to sow a seed of doubt by telling me that I had left the lodging room not once but twice.

But it was not me who went out to the cart to fetch his cloak and tried to swear Watkyn to secrecy, it was Hob; he stood to lose the pilgrim staff and eighteen shillings. And, whatever he says, I know that he was not in the lodging room when I came back from the yard. Was that what woke me from my demon-dream — the scuffle of Hob setting upon Scaff?

A sick dread coats my body in sweat beneath the blanket Hob tucked so carefully around me. If Hob killed Scaff to keep the staff and the horseshoe money, did he kill Thomas Hassell to keep the saint? Was he so worried about what the parson would find in the library at Malmesbury that he left the hut, the deep-sleeping Tom undisturbed by his going, and murdered the priest?

The coroner's talk of foul air did not persuade the jury to suspect that Master Thomas had been smothered but, if he had seen the blood that I saw on Hob's cloak — blood I took to be Edgar's but which might have belonged to Thomas Hassell — he might have instructed them to bring in a different verdict.

That cloak of Hob's; that heavy, golden, densely woven cloth — is that the last thing Thomas Hassell's bloodshot eyes saw in this world — wadded in Hob's hands and coming down towards his face, blotting out light and life?

Has Hob snuffed the life out of anybody who stands in his way, who threatens him?

I look across the dying fire. His head is lolling on his chest, his breathing noisy. While he thinks me fooled, cowed by what the demon has made me do, I am safe. But how can I do what the saint wants without making myself a threat to Hob, without putting my life in danger?

CHAPTER 31

It is a bitter thing to watch a new day dawn knowing that the world is not, today, as you thought it was yesterday.

I am a fool. I, of all people, should have known that wishing something never makes it so. Wishing did not persuade my father to let me go to the abbey school. It did not keep the pestilence from Lysington. It did not grant my mother joy with a new babe. And wishing to believe it has not made Hob Cleve a trustworthy man.

I see, now, that every word of his, every deed, has been said and done in the service of his own fortune. At every turn — from the moment of our first encounter in that snowy wood — he has seen how events may be managed to his advantage. Quick and ruthless, he has played on my slowness and my trust.

He has lied to me the whole time we have kept company together. No, he has not simply lied, for there is something akin to honesty in simply saying something that is not true; a lie can easily be disproved. What Hob has done is to twist the truth. He has taken words and happenings and thoughts and he has twisted them together to make a new thing: the world as he would like it to be. Like his braids, his world is composed of so many different strands — strands which weave over and under and through and around each other — that it is impossible to see clearly where falsehood ends and truth begins.

But this I do see: his intention has been to make me mistrust my own judgement. To make me mistrust myself so that I would rely on him. So that I would fall in with his plans. His plans to become a rich man in Salster.

He thinks the saint can make him rich. He slipped, in his anger after Slievesdon and the loss of all our money, and told me as much. But she can only make him rich if she is in Salster, amongst those whose money can build her shrine, raise a chapel to house it, form a religious guild devoted to her. The guild of Saint Cynryth, the White Maiden of the Well. It has a ring to it.

Hob will have the barren wives of rich men coming to kneel before her and receive her blessing; he will have them wearing a white braid as a token of their daily prayers for a child, an heir. He will have the parents of sick children offering money for her intercession and the safe delivery of their offspring from the palsy or the falling sickness or a fever. He will have widows making braids for him by rushlight and pilgrim-badge makers carving little horseshoe moulds.

Hob will make an industry out of the saint. Or he would if I let him.

I must not let him.

I look over at the fire. I need embers. I must act now. It must be the saint that guides me, not fear of Hob. I must remember that Saint Cynryth healed me and hold that knowledge to my heart. My father put her into my dying hands *and she healed me.*

I take a breath but it seems to fill scarcely half my lungs. I am stiff with fear. Breathe. And again. My heart is punching at my ribs but I can sit here no longer. I must have those embers.

'Hob!' Another breath. '*Hob!*'

He rouses, wiping the drool from his mouth and sitting up with a grimace. He puts his hand to the side of his neck, kneads at it with his knuckles.

'Can you untie me? I need to move.'

'Is it really you?'

'Of course it's me.' I do not have to pretend irritation.

He nods and stands, stretching and yawning as he does so. 'It's nearly dawn. Why didn't you wake me before?'

'No need.'

'Did you sleep much?'

'Enough, I think.'

'Any trouble…?'

'No.'

He nods.

'Hob! Untie me.'

He moves closer. 'Quicker still, I'll cut you loose.'

He reaches around for his knife.

'No!'

His hand is still behind him. 'What?'

I try to slow my galloping heart. The sight of him reaching for that knife while I am trussed and helpless is too much. 'Rope's expensive. Just untie me.'

He hesitates, then drops his hand.

'All right. Though what we'll need rope for in Salster, I don't know.'

For a moment, as he reaches behind me, I think perhaps I will go with him to the city, despite his treachery. I could go to the priory and pray at Saint Dernstan's shrine and then come away again, back to the forest.

But a moment's reflection shows me that I must not do that. As soon as we were inside the walls, Hob would be twisting the truth into his own shape, charming people into his world, setting alight ideas about the saint and her place in their city. I cannot let that happen.

'D'you think the city gates'll be open?' I ask, aware that I must say something.

'Don't see why not. If that clerk in Rochester's right, the pestilence is gone from Salster. No point shutting the stable door *now*, is there?'

I make a noise that might be taken for agreement and wait for Hob to finish untying me.

Feet finally released, I try to stand but my legs refuse to support me. Hob helps me up and I lean against the cartwheel.

'Are you going to be able to walk?'

I nod. 'I just need to move about.' In truth, I feel like a sapling bent over for so long that it has grown into the curve. How long would a man have to be bound in the same position before he started to grow crooked, too?

'Plenty of time,' Hob says. 'It's not properly light yet.'

While Hob stows the pallet and the cooking pot, I put what embers remain into the basket. The moss is almost dry — I should have found some fresh, yesterday, instead of relying on dampening it.

'Why are you bothering?' Hob asks. 'We'll be in Salster tonight.'

'Forest habit,' I tell him, trying to sound as if it's of no real consequence to me, either way. 'Always have the means to lay a fire, just in case.'

'What, just in case they turn us away from Salster?'

I shrug.

He smiles indulgently and shakes his head. 'With a bit of luck, neither of us'll ever need to lay a fire again.'

As I raise the canvas and stow the basket, I see that my hands are shaking. 'Planning on having servants to do it for you, eh, Hob?'

'All in good time, Master Collyer, all in good time.'

'No.'

He looks around in surprise.

'Not Collyer. I'm not a collyer any more. And I won't be — that life's over. Here —' I swallow. 'In Salster, I'm going to be Martin of Dene.'

He sticks out his bottom lip. 'Suit yourself.'

'Are you sticking with Cleve?'

'Hadn't really thought about it.'

'Is it the name of your manor?'

The look he turns on me is cold. 'No.'

I give him a half shrug. 'Doesn't matter then, does it?'

We have been walking some time now and I have had no sign from the saint that a particular spot is where she wants me to establish her shrine.

The Rochester parson was right — the road skirts the edge of Burdynge Forest and, if there is a track or a path that runs into the woods from this side, I cannot see it. But perhaps I have been too timid — perhaps I should have insisted that we make our way through the woods?

Furlong after furlong, I scan the ground around me, looking for a likely spot.

'Here, lady?' I ask, silently. 'Show me where.'

I watch for birds to give me a sign, as the goldfinches did when we came upon Hugh and Agnes, but see only rooks over the trees. I look for a lark, listen for the song that hovers between earth and heaven, lifting men's eyes up. Surely a lark would be a sign?

'Show me, lady,' I murmur as we crest another hill. 'Show me where you want your shrine.'

But the air is silent. I hear no larks, see not a fluttering wing.

The sun climbs the morning sky and still there is no sign. Am I wrong? Does the saint want me to go to Salster with Hob before finding a place to build her shrine?

No. That cannot be. Once we were in Salster he would never let the Maiden out of his sight. I might even be in greater danger in the city. Given the worn and battered state of us, nobody would question my sudden death, especially as Hob would come ready with stories of the swift deaths at Dode. Salster would bury me as fast as it could, without thinking twice about coroners or foul play.

I glance across. Hob's eyes are set on the city ahead.

The mare will not go anywhere for him so he needs me to get as far as the gates. Once we are within the walls, could I go to one of the priests at the priory and tell him the whole story, get him to witness my giving Hob his share of the money while I take the saint?

No. Hob is more persuasive than me and nobody knows us in Salster; who is to say who the saint belongs to and what has happened on our journey?

There is no help waiting for me. I must find my own path. And soon.

As we close on the city, the uneasy feeling creeps up on me that I must have missed a sign from the saint. It cannot be right to be too close to Salster, lest pilgrims feel that the shrine is hardly worth stopping at. I can almost hear their words. *Oh, we don't want to stop now — we're almost there. Better just to press on and have more time in in the city.*

I look about me. Here, at the top of this rise, the treeline is a stone's throw away to our right but away to our left is more open country, falling away in a gentle slope and rising again to hills in the distance. The crest of a hill is, surely, a good place for a shrine? Pilgrims would be glad of an excuse to stop for a while and catch their breath and they could look about them, see what the weather will do as they cover the last couple of miles to the city.

My heart begins to thud in my chest and my bowels gripe. I glance over my shoulder but the saint is safely stowed beneath the canvas. 'Here, lady?'

There is no reply but, as I stare across at the hornbeam and oak shapes of the forest I see a sudden glint. I narrow my eyes. No, I was not mistaken. The sun is glinting off a thin thread of water. I cannot see whether it comes from a spring that rises in the wood, but it is a sufficient answer to my prayer.

It must be now. Fear rises in me like a flood but I have to believe that the saint will protect me.

I swallow the fear. Take a breath. Pull the mare up.

'Tired?' Hob asks.

'No.' My heart is hammering against my ribs. My breaths are coming hard and sharp. 'I'm stopping here. I'm not coming on to Salster.'

'What?'

With shaking hands, I lift the canvas to get at the press. This is my only plan; if it does not work, I have no other. I know Hob's ruthlessness. My lack of cunning may cost me my life.

'You said, once, that you needed two pounds to get your start in Salster. Well, with what you've got in the cloak, and your thirty-six shillings from Snodland, you've got more than two pounds already.'

I lift out the bag of money we were given for the horseshoes at Sibbertswell. 'I've taken the ten shillings that was mine for carrying Richard Longe's letter to Slievesdon. You can have the rest. That'll mean you've got over three pounds. Plenty to get you started.'

His eyes move from the purse to my face. 'So where are you going?'

'Nowhere. I told you, the White Maiden's shrine has to be in the woods. I'm going to put it over there.'

He turns in the direction of the glint of water, then looks back at me.

I clench my jaw and wait for his anger, for him to duck under the mare's neck and grab me by the tunic. But he does not move. Instead, he begins to laugh.

'Martin, listen to yourself!' He shakes his head again. 'You can't just stop at the side of the road and build a shrine!'

I keep quiet. I am not going to argue with him.

'Come on — don't be a fool.' He hooks his thumbs in his belt. 'Put the money back in the press. Come to Salster, get yourself sorted. It'll be far better to find a place in a church for the saint — then you can come and set up a shrine out here later, when her name is known.'

I stare at him. This is how he twists things; by saying things which appear full of good sense. But good sense and being right are not always the same thing.

'I'm staying here.'

He shakes his head, as much — it seems to me — in confusion as in denial. 'You can't.'

My heart is shaking my chest so hard that I can feel the bile rising up my throat. I swallow. 'I can. I am.'

'No! We've come all this way together. You can't just decide that we part company now.'

'Then stay. Help me build the shrine.'

It is a bluff. The last thing I want is for him to stay.

'Our fortune's waiting for us in Salster, Martin, not here on the side of the road!'

'Your fortune, Hob, not mine.'

'But the saint brought us together — brought us all this way! You can't just tear us apart now. That's not what she wants!'

'Don't presume to tell me what the saint wants, Hob — you've got no right!'

My heart is still racing but now anger is driving out fear.

'Who says I've got no right? Didn't the saint choose me to protect you? Didn't I save your life?'

'If you did it was for your own ends — because you saw better prospects with me and my cart than with Edgar!'

For once, he is not quick enough to disguise the expression on his face; I have shocked him.

'Don't bother denying it Hob. You switched allegiance from Edgar to me because it suited you.'

'Do you blame me? Edgar was a brute. He would've killed you.'

'And are you any different?'

His eyes narrow. 'When have I done *anything* but look after your interests?'

'When you tried to trick me into thinking that I'd attacked you!' I see the spittle flying out of my mouth with my words. 'When you tried to make me believe that I'd killed my father, that the demon had controlled me from the beginning!'

'What?' his face loses all expression.

'Don't try and deny it. I couldn't have attacked you with my knife because I *didn't have it*. You didn't give it back to me after I'd lent it to you in Scaff's yard — not till yesterday when I was seeing to the mare's foot.'

'And this?' He indicates his torn and bloodied ear. 'Did I do this, as well?'

'You know you did! And laid out the sheet to prove that I'd planned to kill you and bury you.'

'Martin, listen to yourself! You're raving, man!'

'No, Hob. My mistake has been in listening to you. But I won't make that mistake again. I'm staying here.'

He comes around the mare. 'No. I've nursemaided you for weeks. The saint belongs to me as much as she does to you, now. I have a say in what happens to her.'

Anger makes me unwise and I take a step towards him. 'No! You don't!' I thrust the money-bag at him. 'Take this and go to Salster. I'm staying here.'

He tosses the bag on to the canvas. 'The saint's coming to Salster with me, Martin, whether you come or not.'

'No.'

'Stop saying no!' He pushes me backwards.

'I'm not coming to Salster!'

'Fine. You can stay here and I'll take the cart.'

Has he forgotten that the mare won't go for him, or is he so convinced of his own power that he thinks he can compel her?

'No.'

His fist moves so fast it has hit me before I am aware of movement. The shock is sickening. I stagger back.

'Come on then —' Hob's fists are ready to hit me again — 'we'll fight for it. Whoever wins will take the cart.'

'No. It's mine.' My mouth feels odd as I speak.

His fist slams into my half-closed eye. I hear the skin split as much as feel it, and I fall to the ground. Before I can think about getting up, his boot has caught me in the ribs.

'Come on. Get up. Let's fight for it.'

I crawl away, retching, holding my side.

He follows me, his fists clenched. 'Come on. Get up!'

I use the cart's wheel to haul myself up. My head throbs and every breath stabs at me. Hob has broken my ribs.

He grabs me by the shoulder. 'I'm taking the cart.'

More by luck than judgement my swinging fist catches him on the nose. He staggers back, hands to his face.

'Take the mare if you think you can,' I manage, my battered jaw filling my face with pain at the slightest movement. 'You can sell her in Salster.'

'Mare's no bloody use to me. I'm taking the saint.'

'No. She's mine.'

He comes at me, his full weight bearing down on me. I know I must not let him get me on my back. Not after what I saw him do to Will in Tredgham woods.

I stagger backwards, towards the rear of the cart. The remainder of last night's firewood is in there. If I can arm myself, I might be able to hold him off. But Hob sees where I am going and runs at me, pushing me aside.

'Going to batter me, are you, Martin?'

My eyes on him, I back off a pace or two.

'That's it, run away!'

I stop. I cannot let him drive me away from the saint.

He lunges at me. I flinch but I stand firm. Hob laughs.

'I'm taking the cart, now, Martin. Don't follow me.'

I step towards him. 'You're not taking it.'

He laughs again and walks towards the mare's head. He lifts the reins and clucks to her. 'Come on.'

The mare does not move. 'Come on, damn you!' He pulls at her bridle but she pulls her head up and plants her feet. 'Move, damn you!' He turns and punches her in the ribs; she whips around, teeth bared, and bites at his shoulder.

I see my chance. Moving as quickly as the pain in my ribs will allow, I snatch a shortish length of sound wood from the cart and rush at Hob. I aim for his head but he fends off my blows with his shoulders.

'Kill me, would you?' he yells.

Is this what it has come to? Must I kill him if I want to stay here?

He throws himself towards me. I get in a blow to his head but it glances off and he comes on. Helpless beneath the blows that thud into my head and ribs, I fall to the ground. A boot stamps down on the hand that is fumbling for the stick. I cry out in agony but, before I can move, he has dropped and has me pinned, his knees on my shoulders, his hands coming towards my face. I squirm and buck in terror, whipping my head from side to side so that he cannot get a grip on my nose, clamp a hand over my mouth.

He punches me, a hard blow just under my eye. It stuns me and his hands are on my face. I cannot breathe. I try to shake my head free but he moves up my body so that his knees are on either side of my head, his feet on my chest.

Legs and body free, I buck and lift, trying to throw him off but he does not let go.

My head feels as if it will burst and my chest heaves with breaths I cannot draw in. Pinpoints of light flash in my eyes and I hear a rushing in my ears.

With the last of my strength I kick my legs up and get one knee around his neck. I pull and he falls backwards.

Air rushes into me and I roll on my side, panting and gasping.

A boot smashes into my side. Something hits my head with a horrible crack —

'Come on, you bloody animal, he's here! It's him!'

I hear a muted jingle. I know that sound. It's the mare's bridle when she tosses her head. She does that when she is being contrary. Where is she?

My eyes are closed. I try to open them. One is stuck shut. Through the other, the world is grey and floating, as if someone has spat in my eye. I let the eyelid fall.

'Come on!'

I am jerked to one side. Pain stabs my ribs, wakes my wits. Hob hauls me up, hefts me like a slipping sack, my left arm over his shoulders.

'Hold that.' He puts something in my right hand but I cannot seem to grasp it.

'Damn you!' I feel him bending down then up again. 'Hold it.' I feel a leather strap being wound around my wrist and hand. The mare's reins. She will not go for Hob. He needs me to lead her.

'Now, come on, stupid animal.'

I am jerked forward again and I feel the reins tightening, pulling my hand up. Pain from fingertip to elbow makes me cry out.

Another step. My hand is pulled backwards, skewing me around painfully. The rein tightens on my mangled hand, pulls my shoulder. Hob is bending beneath me, pulling against the mare. 'Come on, damn you!'

'Stop.' The word is clear in my mind. But what come out of my mouth is something else, something thick and slushy.

Hob straightens up, shrugs me into a half-standing, half-leaning position.

Every move me causes me pain. I try to stand, to make him let go of me. As he ducks out from under my arm, my legs almost buckle. I stagger forward, collide with the mare's shoulder. She shies and tries to sidestep but comes up against the cart's shaft.

I lift a hand to her neck.

'Easy, girl. It's all right.' The words are a mush of baby-sounds.

The mare steadies and looks around at me from the white of her eye.

'Make her walk.'

I try to stand upright.

'Make her walk and I'll let you live.'

I do not want to go to Salster. Not with Hob. Not with Hob and the saint. But I want to live.

Painfully, I gather a small amount of spittle in my mouth. I work my tongue around my loosened teeth and spit. The gobbet is bright red on the ground. I raise my head and right myself, using the mare's withers to pull myself up. As I stand, I feel something running down my face. I wipe it off with the back of my crushed hand. Not blood, some other liquid. It is seeping out of the split beneath my eye.

I feel sick. My head is throbbing. The pain from my jaw is like nothing I have ever felt. It must be broken.

There will be bonesetters in Salster.

The saint is taking pity on me, giving me permission to go to the city.

'Make her move. Now!'

I dread another blow. I manage to get both feet properly under me and stand up as straight as I can. Rib-ends grate and I gasp, doubling over.

'Now!'

I suck in a cautious breath and lift myself up again. Another breath. One foot in front of the other and a cluck for the mare, a wet, sloppy imitation of the sound she is accustomed to but, still, it persuades her forward. I stumble into a shuffling walk at her side, bent over to protect my ribs.

'Good,' Hob says as if we have just agreed some small thing. 'Good.'

I cannot tell how long we walk before Hob stops us. My world has shrunk to the pain in my body and the ground I must drive it to cover. I measure distance not against waymarker trees on the skyline but against the stones beneath my shambling feet. One yard gained, and another, and another. Yard after yard, foot after foot, inch after panting, gasping inch goes by beneath my downcast eyes. In every step there is pain — the mare seems to sense it for she half-turns and whickers every now and again.

I can feel a breeze, warm against my battered face. The morning is wearing on.

We are on a long, long hill. I am bent so far over that I keep losing my balance and falling, only to be hauled up again. The agony in my ribs each time almost deprives me of my wits.

There is the sound of bells. One of the little hours. Terce or sext? I raise my head until I can see the sky; by the sun, sext. I must have lain senseless some time before Hob dragged me to the mare's head.

'There.'

I look up. I see a church with a hospital or leper house next to it. The churchyard is full of the dead, a pestilence-pit. I drop my head again.

'Salster,' Hob says.

I shake my head. I do not want to be in Salster.

'Not here,' he says, taking my shaking head for denial, 'there.'

I look up, my head pounding, my jaw a solid lump of pain, and follow his pointing finger. There, beneath the hill we are standing on, is Salster, its priory huge and white in the midst of it.

'Another mile and we'll be there.'

The thought of another mile of pain reduces me to tears and I fall to the ground, almost at the mare's feet.

'No, Martin, you can't die yet. You've got to get me to Salster first.'

My head hangs between my knees. I shake it slowly. I have not the strength go on.

'Don't start saying no again, Martin. Come on.'

I cannot even raise my head. There is too much pain. I just want to lie down and not move.

'Come on! Get up!'

Broken ribs grind as Hob's boot connects. I cry out and fall to one side. The mare skitters as I fall against her back leg and her iron-shod hoof comes down on the side of my head in a sickening but short-lived pain. Then, no more.

CHAPTER 32

My eyes open. I am in a hospital. There are beds down both sides and a well-swept floor of flagstones.

Two men stand together. One wears a monk's robes.

On the bed in front of them, a body lies, battered, bloody and utterly still.

The monk speaks. 'The brother who let you in said you brought two bodies.'

'No. The second wasn't a body.' The other man moves. A wrapped bundle stands next to the bed on which a corpse lies. 'It was this — the reason for my pilgrimage.' He bends to unwrap the blanket from the figure. 'This is Saint Cynryth, known as the White Maiden. She's a saint from the old times and my father — God rest him — was very devoted to her.'

The monk shakes his head. 'I'm sorry, friend. I don't know your saint.'

'You will.' The man speaks with assurance. 'For she's done miracles. She healed me of the pestilence when I'd been given the last rites, when I'd drawn my last breath. She healed me and I sat up, alive, when all around me were dead.'

The monk nods but he does not seem much moved by this testimony.

'We were collyers, my father and I, in the King's Dene Forest. That's where we first heard of the saint. But she's native to Salster. In the time before the Normans, the time of the Seven Kingdoms. She'll be a great saint again, when people hear of her miracles. As great a saint as your Dernstan.'

'Perhaps.'

'She's guided us here — every step of the way. She's granted visions and done miracles. A young girl knelt beneath her hand for a blessing —' the man lifts the saint and lowers her fractionally — 'and the hand on her head became flesh, not wood.'

At this, finally, the monk does turn. 'The wood became flesh on her head?'

'Yes. And not just for her. For many others afterwards, too.'

The monk's face says he does not know what to think. 'What did you say her name was?'

'Cynryth. She was the daughter of Halstan, a king of the south, in the time before the Normans came.'

I know this story. I wish I was closer to the men, so that I could see their faces.

As if the wish has pushed me, I move, like goosedown on a breeze. I see their faces. And I see the face of the corpse. Dark featured, battered. He looks like somebody. Kin to me, perhaps. Dark, like my father. My father is dead but this corpse is not him. Battered, his face bruised and swollen, one eye closed and weeping; one hand lies on his breast, bloody and misshapen. My hand. *Me.*

I stare down at my own battered, unmoving face and I hear the monk ask a question.

'Where did you say you came from?'

'From the King's Dene Forest, in Gloucestershire.'

'And you are a collyer?'

'Yes, I am Hob Collyer. But, here, I shall be Hob Freeman. For I am free born and as a free man I come to Salster with my saint.'

Hob Cleve. He is twisting a new truth. The truth he wants. He wants to be me. The corpse is me. I am lying there. Am I dead now? This floating in the air, is this Purgatory?

No. This is the world. And Hob Cleve is bending it to a shape that suits him.

The world. And I am in it. Lying there, dead. How, then, am I looking at myself?

The monk is speaking again. 'What will you do, now?'

'I'll go to the priory and pray for my father's soul. And then I'll find a place for our saint in Salster. I promised him, before he died, that I'd bring her back to her city and see her properly honoured.'

'A place for her?'

'In a church, or the priory.'

No! She must be in the woods! She must be where springs rise. She has the care of wells and springs. He must not confine her here for his profit. I will not let him.

'*Martin.*' I turn my eyes — or such miraculous sight as I have, being outside my body — from my corpse on the bed. Next to it stands a man, dressed in good green cloth, as if he is going to a fair with his family. He smiles — an unaccustomed expression from him. My father.

But he is not smiling at the corpse on the bed, he is smiling up at me. Can he truly see me, floating here?

'*Martin.*' It is my father's voice but I hear it in my head, not out there in the world. '*Come with me. I'm safe now. Leave this sad world and come with me.*'

Something in me longs to go with him. My heart? My soul?

I look away from him, fasten my gaze on Hob Cleve. He is holding the smeared and touch-stained statue of our little saint. The saint I have served all these weeks. He is claiming her.

'*Come, Martin. Come and join me.*'

Is that the right thing to do? It would be so easy to float away from the pain. My father is safe, my task accomplished.

'You must go to the priory,' the monk tells Hob, 'speak to the new prior, tell him about your saint. If she has done miracles, he will welcome her, I am sure.'

No! She must be in the woods. Her shrine must be in the woods. I had a vision. I know I did. The saint healed me. And she sent me a vision.

I feel myself drawn away from my father, towards the battered little figure leaning against Hob Cleve's legs. Her hand is reaching out to me. Reaching in that gesture I know so well.

I move towards her, slowly, so slowly. And, as I move, she is transfigured before my eyes until she is no longer a supplicant-worn statue but a living, breathing woman. A woman whose white kirtle and cloak shine and dazzle, like water from a sunlit spring.

She reaches out to me. Not to the poor corpse on the bed but into the air above her. She does not speak but her hand reaches towards me. And, as I am drawn silently down to her, in her eyes I see the Exile, the fairy she reached out to as he fled from King Halstan's wrath.

I turn to my father and he smiles. He knows what I have seen.

Now, I know what I must do. I must be Halstan's priest who woke from his revelation-dream and ran to the king to warn him about the Exile's true nature. I must be Halstan himself, who swung his sword and thwarted the fairy's plan. I must not let him have Cynryth.

'I must pray for this poor dead soul.' The monk turns to the body on the bed but there is no pity on his face. He is sated with death, it cannot move him now. Yet he will do what needs to be done.

I watch his hand rise to the poor, broken brow.

'*Placebo Domino*,' he begins. The prayer for the dead. I hear the meaning of the psalm as well as its Latin words. 'I have loved, and the Lord will hear the voice of my prayer.'

I will my dead mouth to open, give evidence that I am alive. But I am in the air, not in my body. How can I return?

'Because he has inclined his ear unto me,' the prayer continues in the monk's dry, quiet voice, 'while I am alive I will call upon him.'

I try to move, will myself to descend into the body lying there and call on God. Is it too late? Must I go with my father to Purgatory?

I look around for him. But my father is gone.

'The sorrows of death have surrounded me, and the perils of hell have found me.'

I hear the words but my soul cries out. *I am not yet in hell. I am here, still!* God cannot mean to leave the saint in Hob Cleve's hands. Saint Cynryth cannot. I have brought her all this way, she will not abandon me now, nor I her.

I look to one side, away from the body Hob beat and kicked into doing his will, to the saint. She looks upwards no longer, now her gaze rests on the body on the bed. My body. Me.

'I met with trouble and sorrow, and I called upon the name of the Lord.'

The words of the prayer fill my heart. *Lord God*, I call out, *let me live!*

How many times has this monk sat with the dead, intoned the Placebo? He uses no missal, he has it by heart. At the end, he will sign me with the cross and all will be done. If he reaches the end of the prayer, if he says, *Placebo Domino: in regione vivorum*, I will be dead and despatched into the land of eternal life.

I look in desperation to the White Maiden. Still her cloak and kirtle are dazzling in the gloom and, as I watch her gazing at the still and silent husk of me, I feel myself drawn down, as if her gaze will draw me out of the air and restore me to my body.

Down, down.

Am I going to death or life?

Down.

Dark.

'Turn, O my soul, to your rest —'

The monk's voice speaks the prayer which will speed my soul but I cannot see him now. All is dark.

His voice continues. But all is dark.

'For he has delivered my soul from death, my eyes from tears, my feet from falling.'

The penultimate line. I hear the saint's voice and struggle to open my eyes, to speak.

He has delivered my soul from death!

Breath rushes into me as it rushed into Will on the hearth at Tredgham when I dragged Hob from him. Life and pain and hope and light rush in as I open my eyes.

I must be Halstan's priest! I must be Halstan!

'*Placebo Domino*,' I gasp, '*in regione vivorum.*'

I will please the Lord in the land of the living.

EPILOGUE

May 1350

'Today. I want — to go — today.' After all these months, I might be able to speak without pain, but still my words are slow, sentences stiff and sometimes jumbled. Still, I am alive.

'Where do you want to go?'

'Church. See the saint.'

'Which saint?'

Which saint. As if there could be more than one that might concern me. But Brother Biddulph is not to know. Though he has saved my life, tended me through fevers and chills, pain and delirium, though he knows my body and its injuries better than I know it myself, he does not know me, or my history. With my speech stopped up for so long by a mangled jaw and disordered wits, he does not know why I came here. He does not know the vision the saint gave me.

'Saint Cynryth,' I tell him, taking pains to produce the sounds in the right order.

'The White Maiden?'

'Yes.'

He draws in a sudden breath, as if it is he who will walk out of the infirmary, through the physic garden and out of the hospital entrance, not me. 'It's a fair step. The Aldermen's Church is at the other end of the city, almost.'

'I can walk.'

'But you've not walked so far yet.'

He is wrong. I have walked a good distance every day. While he has been at his work in the infirmary or in his workshop, I have walked around and around his garden, rejoicing in the life and abundance of his plants. I have walked up and down the stone steps that climb the outside wall to the infirmary's first floor, joy in my heart at the sight of the beautiful city that is revealed to me as I climb.

I can walk as far as I need to. I know it.

'I can. Today. Now.'

Biddulph looks at me. Does he see what my father used to see when he called me 'mulish'? Or is my face so changed that no expression, now, will ever be the same? I do not know. But, if it is changed, so much the better. For I am not the youth who left the King's Dene a year and a half ago. I am no longer, even, the man I was when Hob dragged me into Salster. A year of pain and slow recovery have seen to that. I am grateful to be alive and, for that, I have not only Biddulph but the saint to thank.

'Very well then. I'll find somebody to take you.'

The lay brother he finds to accompany me is as loose-lipped a fellow as I've ever met. He does not know how to keep his thoughts to himself and, worse, he wants to know mine, too.

'You're the one Hob Dene rescued, aren't you — when he brought the Maiden to Salster?'

When *he* brought the Maiden. Yes, they all think that, now. All these months, while I have, perforce, been silent, Hob has been talking, talking, talking. Claiming the saint for himself. Claiming my name and my life for himself as he claimed my money and my goods. He has told Salster that the saint is his, and his alone. If folk know of me it is only as some poor fool who was set upon within sight of the city and almost killed. A poor fool rescued by Hob.

My guide takes my silence for acquiescence and draws breath to start again, but something in me rebels. I refuse to be 'the man Hob saved'. I will not be his man in perpetuity. I pull at the lay brother's arm, halting him. 'No. I'm not him.' I shake my head, knowing my thick speech sounds less than convincing. 'That was — another man.'

He looks at me, mouth open as if to argue about it, then he seems to change his mind. He shrugs. 'If you say so.'

We set off again, my limp keeping us at an old man's pace, and my companion takes up where he left off. 'Got a nice altar, the White Maiden has. The other parishes must've been spittin' feathers to see such a miracle in Master Edgar's church. But Hob Dene knew his business, didn't he? Went straight to the biggest and best.'

I make no response, the bile rising in my throat at the mere thought of Hob going to this priest, this Edgar, and parleying a place in his church for the saint. *It'll work to both our advantages. We will both come out of this the richer, and you, my friend, will be the man who offered Salster's forgotten saint a home in her own city.*

'Folk come from all over the Weald to see her. From Cranbrook and Tenterden, even.'

My heart swells at his words. People are coming to the saint — her people know her once more! But, of course, Kentish pilgrims will not satisfy Hob, however many there are. He will want them coming from Exeter and Gloucester, London and Norwich. From France, perhaps. And all making their offerings.

'Alderman Hob sends word out with the carriers and the clothiers who come here for cloth. He tells everybody about the saint and her miracles.'

I nod, encouraging him. Galling though his admiration of Hob is, I am grateful to have this fellow's company. After my long sojourn in the safety of the cloistered infirmary, Salster's crowds disturb me. Still partly crippled in speech and body, I am fearful of being jostled and falling, of being asked a question I cannot quickly answer.

And the noise! From the safety of Brother Biddulph's garden, I have only ever heard the cries of street hawkers and the bell of the crier in the distance, carried on the wind. But here, on Salster's main thoroughfare, they batter at me till I could weep.

To calm myself, I conjure a memory of the saint to my mind's eye. Not her little wooden image, much worn by our journey to the city, but the shining, lifelike figure who appeared to me when I lay, battered almost to death, in the infirmary. She saw my soul hovering in the air above my poor, battered body and she reached up to me, gave me her blessing, and drew me back to life once more.

For months, I waited for her to appear again in a vision or a dream. To come and tell me what I must do, how I must rescue her from Hob. For, had she not preserved my life so that I might realise the vision she gave me — an army of the healed and whole flocking to her shrine?

But no new vision came, no dream.

Instead, the months of slow healing, of bone-knitting and word-finding, have taught me humility. Taught me to accept that, perhaps, I am no longer required. That, back in her own city, with her own folk, the saint may have the power to gather her army without me.

But, humility or not, these past few days, I have known that the time has come to make a test of it. Soon, I must leave the infirmary and make my way in the world. So, if the saint will not come to me, then I must go to her. I must know, once and for all, whether I am hers, still. Or whether, weak as I know myself to be, she has no further use for me.

Hope and dread both stir in my breast as I slowly heck and stumble towards the northern end of the city. Hope that, when I stand in front of her image, the saint will come to me as she has before. That she will appear in all her brilliant white, and dispel my fears. Dread that she will not.

The lay brother disturbs my thoughts. 'See that, up there?' He points at a high, white tower. 'That's the Aldermen's church.'

The nearer we get to church, the more my heart hammers at my ribs. The more my guts roil within me. After all this time, I will see her again. I will stand before her and I will know.

As I limp doggedly onwards, my guide continues to prattle. On and on about the splendour of Easter, a month and more ago, now; about the preparations for the plays of Corpus Christi; about the great fires of wood and bone which are, even now according to him, being built outside the city walls for St John's Eve.

It's only May, I want to tell him. Time enough for midsummer revelries. But I cannot say the words, for the battle between hope and dread has rendered me mute.

Finally, standing before the Aldermen's church, I see it is a haunt for pilgrims. Sellers of trinkets are gathered there, shouting their wares and conducting business in noisy little knots.

'Saints' badges!' one cries. 'Brave Saint Dernstan! The White Maiden of the Well! Salster's saints — show your friends in the village!'

Almost against my will, I hobble over to look at the goods he has laid out on his little hand cart. Just as his patter suggests, the cheap and tawdry badges represent two different saints.

But I would not have known Saint Cynryth from her image. Her badges are smaller than those for Dernstan and, instead of a pin to fasten them to cloak or hat in the usual way, they hang on a white ribbon.

I look closer, peering at the blurry pewter image. 'This is not the White Maiden.'

The seller looks at me, his false friendliness falling away. 'What do you know about it?'

'She has her arms out like this,' I say, reaching towards him in imitation of the saint's posture. 'But your image is like this.' I spread my arms wide as if to embrace a long-lost brother.

'You try making a flat badge with hands coming forward. Can't be done. Now, are you buying one or are you pissing off?'

I turn away. This gimcrack is not my saint.

'Get your saints' badges here!' The hawker's voice mocks me as I move towards the church door. 'Brave Saint Dernstan! The White Maiden of the Well!'

Inside, my knee bends of its own accord at the font and my fingers find its pilgrim-worn edge. The smells of incense and candle-smoke, old stone and soot, are so familiar that my eyes fill and a lump forms in my throat. I fight back the tears, I must look to the future and not the past.

Besides, when I look about me, the differences between Lysington's humble little church and this grand one are obvious. Here, there is a wide central nave and, separated from it by sturdy pillars on each side, a north and south aisle. Every wall boasts a number of grand paintings — the Wheel of Fortune and the Acts of Mercy, the Day of Judgement and the Labours of the Seasons. There is fresh paint everywhere — much green and red and yellow on the columns, flashes of precious gold and blue on the rood screen's fluting. Has the church recently been made a gift or do the aldermen always see it new-painted for Easter?

'This way.' The lay brother takes my arm and leads me, like a dotard, to an altar in the south transept. My heart, quieted by the familiarity of so much around me, now begins its thumping once more, beating on my ribs.

And, suddenly, there she is — Saint Cynryth, on her own altar! My heart soars; and yet, I should not rejoice, for this is not where she should be. Her rightful altar is in a woodland shrine, next to the well which saw her martyrdom, not here in a smoky, borrowed corner of some other saint's church.

Slowly, my head spinning, I make my way towards her. Her beloved hands reach towards me and I put mine out to touch hers, fingertip to fingertip. As always, her little figure is strangely warm to the touch.

I wait for something to happen, for my vision to fill with the blinding light of her heavenly form. But the air remains dim, her wooden image lit only by the candles beside her and the light from the smoke-smirched window behind.

I move closer. Perhaps, if I can breathe in the smell of her, that linseed oil and sweet hay fragrance, she might be restored to me. But, as I put my face to hers, all at once, I see how changed she is. Someone has repainted her but the work has been quickly and clumsily done, her features almost as blurred as the pewter of the cheap pilgrim badges outside. And her cloak is the wrong colour. It was always white, like her kirtle, but now it is green. Hob's doing.

I gaze at the little saint's eyes. In the light of day, they were a bright, speedwell blue. Now, in the candle-lit gloom, they are dark and dead. And they no longer meet mine, as they did when she appeared on our well-side shrine, while I carried her the breadth of England. Now they look past me, as if I were not here.

I shut my own eyes tight and fall to my knees before her.

Lady, do not forsake me, now! Show me that I am still your champion, still the one to bring you home!

But no vision comes. Instead, words slide into my mind. Insistent, like a taunt. Like a smirk. *Hob's her champion now, not you. He's the one to do her will. You failed. You're yesterday's man.*

No. *No!* I stay there, my knees cold on the flagstones, the muscles in my feet cramping painfully from the long-unused position, but I do not move to ease them. Bearing the pain proves my devotion to the saint. Shows her what I will endure for her if only she will come back to me.

For minutes I kneel there, making no answer when the lay brother says he must leave me, not moving aside despite the tutting of a family who come to the altar and seek to kiss the saint.

The muscles in my thighs begin to twitch and then to tremble. And still the saint does not reveal herself to me.

Please, Lady! If you still love me, if you wish me to serve you, please show yourself to me as you once did.

At last, I can kneel no longer and I fall sideways, my newly-knit bones crying out at the impact and the hardness, and I lie there.

After a time I cannot measure, kind hands raise me, a tender voice speaks to me, and I am led with gentle firmness away from the Maiden's altar. Leaning against a pillar, I can find no words but my rescuer simply pats my shoulder and I am left to recover as best I may.

When, finally, I am able to open my eyes once more, I turn my head to Saint Cynryth. There she stands, in her new white and green, reaching out to pilgrims who would pray to her. But not to me. Not anymore. My heart, which previously beat so fast and so insistently, now seems leaden within my chest. Though I am alive, though my father's soul is safe, the vision I have cherished all these months is gone.

For the saint has chosen Hob.

If the vision she gave me of a shrine by a well is to be fulfilled, then Hob must do it. She is my saint no longer.

HISTORICAL NOTES

Post-apocalyptic novels are popular at the moment but most of them are based in the near future after some event which has not, in fact, heralded the end of the world. In 1348, when the plague known contemporaneously as the Great Death — and, since, as the Black Death — began to sweep across Europe from Asia, people genuinely thought that this might herald the Apocalypse, the literal end of the world as it had been. Of the four horsemen or harbingers of the Apocalypse, the first was the conqueror of men, seen by churchmen as pestilence. He was to be followed by war, famine and death and, together, the Biblical prophecy was that they would kill 'a fourth of the earth'. In fact, the great pestilence killed more than a fourth of the people of Europe — somewhere between a third and a half depending on what models are used.

So, the England that Martin and Hob travelled through was one that had been devastated both physically and psychologically by the plague. Nobody knew what kind of England might survive such an unprecedented visitation, if anything and anybody at all survived. Nor did they know why this was happening though there was a general agreement at the time that it represented God's judgement on sinful humanity.

It's difficult for us to put ourselves into the mindset of a fourteenth-century person. We no longer live in a world in which the only explanation for what happens is 'God'. Any 'apocalypse' which overtakes us now will be of our own making (war, climate change, nuclear or biological weaponry) or of natural causes (pandemic, meteor strike). The people of the fourteenth-century were not so lucky. They had no idea why this was happening or what to do about it.

As to the specifics of the book, St Cynryth does not exist, I made her up. However, Martin's attitude to her and her statue are, as nearly as I can manage for presentation to a modern audience, the attitudes of a fourteenth-century semi-educated youth.

Hob's attitude towards God and the church is different but also representative of what happened as a result of the plague. People felt that the church — whose priests were supposed to keep the peace with God on the people's behalf — had failed them and, as a consequence, turned away in despair. Clearly, either the church was ineffectual or God did not care. A fatalism overtook many people and England's attitude to the church changed. The Black Death hastened the popular movement towards clerical reform and a move towards what would later become Protestantism — the notion that each man must make his own way with God, unmediated by the church.

The peasantry's attitude towards the rigid medieval social hierarchy also changed with the Black Death. The rich and powerful were not given preferential treatment by God in the matter of who lived and died so people drew their own conclusions. Their overlords were no more worthy than they were. Perhaps the notion that each man was born into the station he was fitted for and could not change lest he anger God was wrong. Hob takes this attitude to its logical conclusion.

A NOTE TO THE READER

Dear Reader,

Thank you so much for taking the time to read *The Black And The White*.

This book changed my life in quite a significant way. As background research, I went to the Forest of Dean to take part in a charcoal burn done the medieval way — known as an earth burn and carried out as described in the book. Though I'd only intended it as research, my partner and I became hooked on the three-day long process which takes place every year at the Dean Heritage Centre and, even though we then lived in Kent, we started coming to Gloucestershire as volunteers on 'the burn'.

Eventually, wanting to relocate closer to my family in Wales, we settled in the Forest of Dean. Now, following the sad death of the organiser, Peter Ralph, to whom this book is dedicated, my partner Edwina and I have taken over the running of the earth burn ourselves.

If you'd like to know more about the background to *The Black and The White*, you can read my historical note below. If you'd like to know even more, the two books that I found most interesting and helpful were: *The Black Death: An Intimate History* by John Hatcher — a history of the plague as it affected one village in Suffolk, Walsham, and is compelling reading — and *The Scourging Angel: The Black Death in the British Isles* by Benedict Gummer — a more academic study covering the progress of the plague over the whole of Great Britain.

As you will probably know, reviews make a huge difference to authors and enable us to reach more readers so, if you have enjoyed *The Black and the White* enough to write a review on **Amazon** or **Goodreads** I would be very grateful.

Meanwhile, if you'd like to know more about me and other books I've written, I'd be delighted if you visited **my website**. You can also follow me on my **Facebook page, AlisHawkinsAuthor** or **Twitter** where I post regular updates about my work and links to other authors I admire.

Meanwhile, if you'd like to know more about the background to *The Black and The White*, read on.

Alis Hawkins

www.alishawkins.co.uk

Sapere Books is an exciting new publisher of brilliant fiction and popular history.

To find out more about our latest releases and our monthly bargain books visit our website: **saperebooks.com**